BLACK

AS

SNOW

BLACK

AS

SNOW

NICK NOLAN

PUBLISHED BY

amazon encore

Published by AmazonEncore
P.O. Box 400818
Las Vegas, NV 89140

ISBN-13: 9781612180052
ISBN-10: 1612180051

For Jaime

An Excerpt from *The Book of Holocene*

The mouth of the cave amplified, like a megaphone, the new-born's cry so loudly that a pack of wolves atop a mountaintop twisted their heads in unison, straining their ears. They were accustomed to the sounds of man, but this cry was different. So while snowflakes accumulated on the wolves' backs, many pairs of yellow eyes stared through the darkness toward where the sound originated. Would they hear it again? Eventually the hackles on the lead wolf's neck settled, he dipped his head, and the pack resumed its silent passage atop the moonlit snowdrifts.

The boy's birth had been difficult, so his mother was attended to by the other women, the eldest of whom registered neither concern nor relief on her timeworn face as she prepared her remedies. She had helped other mothers come through worse childbirths than this to give life again; she had also seen others bleed to death, leaving their babies motherless. Milkless. Cursed. The old woman dabbed the new mother's face with water as she whimpered, too weak to have her cries speak of her agony.

Outside, the men stood in a circle under a sparkling ceiling of stars. Most waited for the sky to lighten so the hunt could resume, the younger ones waited for their women to return to their beds, and a single hunter waited for the birth to be over so he could see his son. Finally, he was beckoned inside.

With relief, he saw that his woman was sitting up. He smiled, showing her his pride and delight. But she did not return his joyful expression. Instead, she clutched the writhing child close to her breast while covering his face.

And as the man drew nearer, fear washed over his woman's features. He glanced at the others, and they looked away. What could be wrong?

He squatted to see the baby, but she only held him closer. He became forceful, and she began to wail. He pulled the covering from the baby's face and fell back, startled. *Something is wrong with my child!* he thought. He peered closer.

The infant's skin was red and smooth, and the eyes—they were also wrong: too far apart, just like the forehead was too flat and high. And the nose was hardly a nose at all. But the strangest feature was the shape of the head. Could that have been why the birth was so difficult? The head was too large, and the child's limbs were unusually thin. This would be no strong warrior or hunter!

He tried to pull the changeling from her arms, but she wrenched her body toward the wall of the cave, using her back as a shield. The old midwife pushed herself between him and his woman. She put a hand on his shoulder and smiled in spite of her own fears. He stepped back and turned. He began to make his way out of the cave. The infant yowled.

He has a strong will, thought the man upon hearing his son's cry. *Maybe he will look more like me as he grows. It is still too soon.* And he began to hope. But the man did not have a wolf's hearing, so he could not discern the difference.

Years passed and the child approached manhood. He was distant. Curious. Aloof. Quick of mind and body. But he was never of the tribe; he always seemed the foreigner, the outsider, but a leader of his young peers at the same time. He seemed made of what they all were, yet in possession of some unknown quality.

The others were suspicious of him, and they whispered behind his back.

There was a hunting accident, and the father was killed. And without his father, the youth was shunned. The young man packed his belongings and left his mother, left his few friends. Then he found happiness at last with one like himself: they found each other, as if the gods had arranged their union. She too had been shunned. But together, they had a baby, and another after her—and these children met others like them and spread to the corners of the earth.

Thus, a new species of Man began populating the earth.

Friday Night in January

The lights cut suddenly, and most everyone in the entire stadium began a steady pulse of clapping. Then a chant began: "*S'bas-chun! S'bas-chun!*"

Eddie glanced around in sudden panic, momentarily disoriented by the expansive darkness and the deafening chorus of shouting fans. Because he was at the very top of the stadium, behind the highest rows of empty seats, the darkness nearly made him swoon.

He grasped the railing to steady himself.

"*S'bas-chun! S'bas-chun! S'bas-chun!*"

The clapping and chanting became a roar, and the floor shook.

"*S'bas-chun! S'bas-chun! S'bas-chun! S'bas-chun!*"

Through the darkness Eddie saw a point of white light down on the round stage; at first it was barely noticeable, but then as it expanded people began quieting. By the time it illuminated the entire stage, most of the crowd had fallen silent. Then, just as slowly as the circle of white had grown, it began to close in upon itself: smaller, smaller, smaller, until almost nothing remained—like the full moon leaving the earth's orbit and disappearing into deep space.

Once again, the stadium and everything within was completely black.

Black.

Moments passed.

Then Sebastian himself appeared on the stage, lit by a blinding light that might have brightened the jagged pits of hell—his arms outstretched and head thrown back, his magnificently sculpted torso provocatively bared except for the deeply cut white robe hanging on him. At once he threw his hands up and shouted to the crowd: "*Change...the world...with...me!*"

The crowd gasped and cheered so loudly that Eddie covered his ears: "*S'bas-chun! S'bas-chun! S'bas-chun! S'bas-chun! S'bas-chun!*"

Sebastian began waving at his ecstatic fans as the turntable beneath him rotated—as if he were the figure inside some magical music box—while the overhead lights illuminated him dazzlingly. His spiked, honey-colored hair shone like a crown of gold atop his head, while his heroic young features emanated *the eternal glow of love.*

Women—and men—screamed in adoration.

"Together, we *will* change the world!" Sebastian sang to the crowd in a voice suggesting the low notes of a string bass, expertly bowed. "Together, we *will* help those who cannot help themselves!"

The turntable stopped rotating and began pushing him up into the air. As the fabric that had been puddled around his feet straightened and fell into a white tube, it gave the impression of the young man being eight feet...then ten feet...then nearly two stories tall. The crowd gasped and applauded, and Sebastian began gyrating atop his perch as some thumpy dance music cued. "You've come to alleviate misery!" he shouted. "You've come to spread happiness to each other and to love one another! *You've come because you dream of a better life for all creatures!*"

The stadium lights pulsed, music blared, and people leapt from their seats clapping, stomping, cheering, and crying. Moments later the lights dimmed, the music faded, and the pedestal sank halfway toward the floor and stopped. Sebastian dropped his hands to his sides, and a soft glow sparked beneath his robe that pulsed *bright-dim...bright-dim...bright-dim*, as if emanating from his own heart, while providing in tantalizing silhouette his spectacular physique shadowed against the inside of his robe.

"I *love you all* for being here with me. I cannot thank you—" he began, but the crowd's cheering rose like a tsunami. Sebastian held out his hands, and quiet returned.

As Eddie watched this young false prophet launch into his sickening soliloquy, he began to refocus on his own task at hand: *that which God has asked me to do.*

The crowd roared in response to more of Sebastian's long-winded presentation about some journey he took and all the *amazing* people he supposedly met on his way.

Why do people care about this false prophet and his lies?

Why do they give him their money?

As Sebastian continued spewing his propaganda, Eddie drew in a deep breath, slipped on a pair of gloves, bent down, and slid the case from beneath the seats.

He fingered the twin combination locks, and the latches sprang open.

Atop his platform, Sebastian continued: "Here's a man who donates medical equipment to disabled kids in the war-torn Middle East. All he wants to do is to alleviate the suffering of these kids who've been maimed and have lost arms and legs."

Eddie drew out the segments of the rifle, then fitted and twisted each piece carefully into the other until he had a weapon complete with stock, barrel, scope, trigger, and flash suppressor.

"There was a time," Sebastian continued, "when I, the leader of a religious organization, convinced you to give me money so I could spread the message of Evo-love. I am now ashamed to admit it, but a lot of that money was spent on luxuries for myself and my mother. But tonight I am *not* asking for your money for myself; in fact, I'm begging you to give it to someone else."

With his heart beating madly in his chest, Eddie pushed the bullets into the chamber and then, as quietly as he could, cocked the gun. The metallic snap was terrifically loud to his ears, but no one below him seemed to notice. *So far so good.* He wiped the sweat from his forehead with his arm, raised the gun, and steadied it on the railing in front of him. It took him a moment or two to find his target, but once Sebastian was in his crosshairs it was evident that only one shot would be needed.

Something moved at the bottom edge of his vision, and he lowered the rifle. *Shit!* A guard was strolling by just ten or so rows down, so he carefully withdrew the gun from its rail-top position and laid it on the floor. Then he listened impatiently as Sebastian, rising again on his pedestal, babbled about some clinic in Chicago and some guy in Alabama and a teacher and kids in Asia and so on.

What a convincing thief! He almost sounds like he believes what he's saying!

Eddie saw that Sebastian's rotating pedestal had once again reached its highest level, and the crowd, including the guard who'd stalled out ten rows below him, began cheering mightily as the music boomed and the lights dimmed and red and green and orange and purple and blue laser beams flashed and sliced through the stadium's darkness. Eddie once again picked up the rifle, rested it on the railing, closed his left eye, and fitted his right eye against the scope.

The lasers were distracting, but Eddie's years of experience hunting in all kinds of conditions had trained him well.

His steady crosshairs followed the ascension of the revolving, white-robed figure.

Then carefully...*so very carefully*...he squeezed the trigger.

CHAPTER 1

Four Months Earlier
Tuesday Evening in September

❧

"Promise me you won't laugh," Reed whispered into her phone, "but I think...I *think* Brandon's going to ask me something big tonight. *Really* big." She examined her features in the mirror and wished for the thousandth time that the end of her nose were just a bit smaller. *Maybe I should get it fixed.*

"Are you sure?" Ellie asked, her electronic voice wary. "Why do you think so?"

"Why do you think he won't?"

"You know how I feel about him."

"Look," Reed began, "Brandon and I've been *very happy* together for over two years. I'm in my last year of college, and he just got that great job at Google in Seattle. This morning he said he needs to talk to me about something important, so he's coming by at seven and I'm making him dinner.

"Ellie, I think he wants me to come with him to Seattle when he moves...and he knows how I feel about just living together. I might've been pushing it last week, but after a couple of glasses of wine I told him that at twenty-two, my parents would kill me if I moved in with a guy without a ring on my finger. They're *actually* starting to talk about grandkids."

"Great way to scare a guy off," Ellie told her flatly. "You should've also announced that you have herpes just to make sure he never comes back."

"*Actually*, he said he understood completely and that his parents are just as old-fashioned as mine are—Ellie, why aren't you happy for me?"

Ellie hesitated. "Look, sweetie, if you think Brandon's the guy for you, then go for it. It's just that…there's something about him I don't like—maybe it's because he won't make eye contact with me. It's creepy talking to someone who's looking over your shoulder all the time."

"I think you scare him—just like you scare *all* men," Reed laughed. "But Brandon's everything I could want: he's smart, he's straight, he's hard working, he's good looking—"

"But can you trust him?"

"He's never given me any reason to doubt him. Why do you ask?" Reed hesitated. "*Do you know something?*"

"Before you commit to anything, I'd check his phone when he runs off to the bathroom—slip him a few of those old laxatives you probably have stashed away somewhere so you'll have more time to investigate. Then check his address book and everything—and be sure to check his 'sent' texts, because most guys are smart enough to delete the ones they get from other girls, but they forget about the ones they've replied with."

"You're paranoid."

"*No*, I'm worried about you relapsing—which you've done each time you found yourself single. Remember what happened after you and Jeremy broke up?"

"I was *only* seventeen," Reed snapped. "That was ages ago. And you're forgetting one thing."

"What?"

"Brandon and I are happy together. We have a *great* relationship. He's *not* Jeremy."

Ellie sighed. "You're right. I'm just an angry bitch because Coby won't commit to me. Anyhow, will you let me know what happens? I gotta run."

"I'll call you later."

—

By a quarter to seven—with her casserole dish of homemade lasagna bubbling fragrantly in the oven—Reed had showered, dried her hair, touched up her face, and changed dresses three times before deciding on her favorite linen sundress—it was short, white, and strapless, and it flaunted her smooth, cocoa shoulders and long, graceful legs. Then she slid her feet into a new pair of Aldo sandals and scrutinized her reflection in the bedroom's mirrored closet doors.

OK, I guess.

Reed hurriedly set the table: her tomato red Pottery Barn dishes and crystal wineglasses, white napkins atop bamboo place mats, and tall red tapers set into her grandmother's silver candlesticks. Then she switched out the white napkins for black linen upon realizing that the lasagna's tomato sauce would register inelegant stains. Finally, she lit the candles around the living and dining areas and then cued up a jazz mix on her iPod: Sarah Vaughn, Stacey Kent, Madeleine Peyroux, with a little Astrud Gilberto thrown in for off-key flavor.

At just before seven Reed sat down in the club chair by the window in view of the street, but she decided this position would make her seem too eager. So she switched her perch to the sofa and adjusted the folds of her dress after noticing the parchment-hued linen was already showing creases. She glanced at her watch.

Did she have enough time to change? Brandon would be here any second. She performed a quick mental inventory of her closet and recalled that most of her lightweight dresses were either in the laundry or at the dry cleaners.

She tapped her fingers on the sofa's arm. *Hmmmm.*

Maybe that black silk cocktail dress she'd had on earlier *would* look better—at least as the evening wore on. And she wouldn't have to worry about tomato stains on it, either.

She got up from the sofa and trotted into her bedroom, shucked the linen dress, slipped the black number up over her head, and contorted her arms to zip up the back. She tugged at the hem, glanced in the mirror, and looked at her watch: it was almost a quarter after the hour now, and still no Brandon.

She went to find her phone, snatched it off the kitchen counter, and checked it.

No messages.

He must be on his way.

She checked on the lasagna and saw it had browned perfectly, so she shut off the oven. Then while examining her makeup in the mirror a final time, Reed considered what sort of wedding she'd like. She definitely wanted something at a church, maybe even at her family's old Baptist church in Van Nuys, for old time's sake. Or maybe she could convince the ancient Reverend Johnson to perform the service at some place nicer…like the country club in Ballena Beach overlooking the rocky coastline.

Will that be too expensive?

He hasn't told me yet how much he'll be making at Google.

Of course Brandon would have some opinions about the service and the reception, and she'd consider his ideas—just nothing in Las Vegas, that was for sure. *Absolutely no Vegas.* As long as the service was Christian and was held somewhere nice, here in Los Angeles, that's all she really cared about.

With an excited smile on her face, Reed ambled over to the iPod and adjusted the volume down. *How did Astrud Gilberto ever get a singing career?* She sat back down on the sofa, with her phone placed on the coffee table before her.

She strained her ears for the sound of tires crunching leaves in the gutter out front, but she heard nothing but the traffic blowing by in gusts.

Where the hell is he?

She reread the earlier text message from her phone's tiny screen: *Something important we need 2 talk about. B there at 7?*

A wave of panic shot through her.

Everything's fine. Maybe he meant 7:30...

At 7:40 she got up to check her e-mail.

Her breath caught as she saw a message from Brandon. It had been sent at 7:18.

She blinked at her laptop screen. *God, please no...*

Her unmoving index finger hovered over the mouse. *Do I really want to read this?*

Finally, she slid the tip of her finger across the metal pad and tapped the unread mail icon:

Dear Reed,

I'm so sorry to do this to you this way...

CHAPTER 2

After rechecking the address on the tilting street-side mailbox, Dyson piloted his Honda carefully down the steep, serpentine entrance road to its end where the old chateau loomed above the flat, placid sea.

But the place looked abandoned.

Twin rusted wrought iron gates stood chained and padlocked, the darkened windows seemed to suck any remaining light from the dusky sky, vines stretched upward from the base of the building to its mansard roof, and even the bronze dolphin fountain at the hub of the circular, cobblestone driveway was filled with trash and leaves.

So Dyson notched his transmission into reverse and backed his way carefully up the driveway, and then he parked his car on the Pacific Coast Highway.

In case someone comes looking for me.

Then he hiked back down the little road, his hands jammed deep inside his pockets against the early autumn seaside chill and mumbling the Lord's Prayer for protection as he went. At the bottom, he located the bell on the side entrance gate and depressed the button.

Moments later, the door handle buzzed. And as he began making his way across the uneven cobblestone toward the chateau, the massive front door creaked open and a heroically built man wearing snug jeans and a torso-hugging black polo shirt emerged.

As they approached each other, Dyson found himself so taken aback by the young man's exceptional looks that he almost tripped on the uneven cobbles; his olive skin, chiseled features, and spiky black hair reminded Dyson of some European playboy soccer player.

It's OK, he told himself. *I can do this.*

"I am Olivier." He extended his large hand. "You are Dyson?"

His voice carried an elegant accent and seemed far too deep for such a young man.

He probably smokes.

"Hey," Dyson replied while grasping his hand. *Warm.*

"Thank you for coming." Olivier put a comforting hand on Dyson's shoulder. "Please join me inside."

Dyson scanned the living room. With its high, gabled ceiling and generous length, it looked big enough to drive a semitruck inside, and the magnificently carved marble fireplace on the west wall looked castle-worthy. But the once grand room now stood nearly empty except for an incongruously cheap, green sofa sectional flanked by a pair of garage sale–looking end tables, a beige La-Z-Boy recliner with stained headrest and arms, and a mammoth, grotesquely carved wooden buffet that might have been transferred to the chateau from the set of *Dracula*.

"Will you please have a seat?" Olivier motioned to the sectional. "I would like you to watch something before we talk."

As Dyson eased himself down onto one end of the cold vinyl, the alabaster sconces on the walls dimmed, and the scant furnishings lost their dimensions and faded to silhouettes. Then the monstrous flat-screen television—it was almost the size of a king bed—on the far wall turned on, and Dyson began watching a clip from one of Sebastian's gatherings.

After a few minutes Olivier, standing *contrapposto* next to Dyson with one thumb hooked into his jeans, aimed the remote at the television with his other hand and muted the sound. "What are your thoughts?"

"He's a fake." Dyson fixed his stare upon the flickering monitor while trying to ignore Olivier's intoxicating scent. "And what he's doing is evil." He turned from the screen to face the younger man. "Sebastian Black is a lying thief, and he's got to be stopped."

Olivier's dark eyes flashed. "You and I, we think alike. This *religion* of his is nothing more than an elaborate deception to build his wealth and celebrity." He reached over and laid a hand on Dyson's shoulder. "But I did have a revelation about him during prayer recently, which is why I asked you here; I have reason to believe that his emergence and popularity, at this point in time, is part of God's plan."

"How so?" Dyson asked indifferently.

Olivier withdrew his hand and began pacing the room in a slow saunter, hands on hips and shoulders back. "It could be the beginning of the end," he replied. "Lucifer. Jezebel. The seven prophetic churches. *Armageddon.*"

Dyson laughed. "For the last thousand years every time there's a big earthquake or a flock of birds fall out of the sky, some people think it's the End of Days."

"No one knows these indicators better than I." Olivier looked at him, onyx eyes glinting. "But of Sebastian Black's role in God's plan, I am completely serious."

"How so?"

"As Sebastian himself points out during his performances"— Olivier began pacing and gesticulating—"too many in the world are suffering: bankrupt countries, earthquakes, oil spills, and other disasters of nature; there is threat of nuclear war from Iran and North Korea, those endless African famines, and so on. Then when you think there can be no adding to these human tragedies, Sebastian Black appears, displaying Satan's mind-reading trickery while building his 'Kingdom of New Man.'"

As Olivier continued his walking soliloquy, Dyson became transfixed not only by the athletic grace of his body, but also by the sublime mechanics of his facial expressions as he spoke. He watched the young man's solid, yet perfectly drawn eyebrows tilt up innocently at the center while relaying a hopeful message, his heavily lidded dark eyes penetrating and intense. His white, even teeth looked almost too large for his mouth—a mouth with full lips frequently moistened by a sensuous flick of his pink tongue. But any suggestion of femininity was offset by his strong, aristocratic nose and the beard stubble. He was an Adonis, his features and physique hand-selected and carefully assembled by God.

"I'm…I'm sorry," Dyson cut in. "You lost me there."

Olivier winked at him. "As I was saying, Sebastian's intention is to take the place of Our Lord in a world that's forgotten who God is." He stopped in front of a bank of tall, mullioned windows and looked out to the twilight-tinted ocean. "Revelation predicts the arrival of such false prophets," he said to the glass, "and his coming could begin the End of Days."

Dyson chuckled. "I think you're giving this guy *waaaay* too much credit, but I'm interested in your point of view. So…what about the Jezebel you mentioned before?"

Olivier turned to him. "Kitty Black." He enunciated each syllable of her name. "This woman, Sebastian's mother, could not more closely resemble the whore Jezebel, whom Revelation describes as the hidden power behind the dark throne."

"Maybe so," Dyson said. "I can see that. But you haven't told me what your plan is, or what it is you want from me."

"Actually, it's both you *and* your wife I want," Olivier explained. "Her blog posts exposing Sebastian are especially articulate and passionate. But I understand that she will not personally communicate with anyone without her husband's prior approval."

"That is true." Dyson half smiled. "Amber does only what I tell her to. And she's not interested in working with anyone but me."

"She might, after she learns of my motivation."

Dyson thought for a moment. "What do you actually know about my wife?"

"Only that she was close to Sebastian once. They had a brief relationship."

"So did lots of women. *And men.*" Dyson grimaced.

Olivier smiled. "But what is different about your wife is her strong faith in God and His one true church. And not only does she maintain an especially fierce anger toward Sebastian, but she also knows sensitive information about him."

"But why should we get involved with you?"

"My family has a glorious history," Olivier proudly replied. "We are keepers of a long tradition."

Dyson shot him a skeptical glance. "Like?"

"We are a very, *very* old family. From a place called Thyatira, in what is now Turkey."

"I've heard of that before." Dyson squinted at Olivier. "Isn't Thyatira one of the seven prophetic churches of Revelation?"

"You are an intelligent man and a capable Bible scholar." Olivier grinned. "I like you."

"Thanks." Dyson felt his cheeks flame.

Olivier crossed the room to where a trio of elaborate crystal decanters was displayed atop the massive, gothic buffet. "Do you know the passage from Revelation, 1:18–28?" he asked, his sonorous voice echoing off the bare walls and floors.

"I…used to, but it's been a while."

Olivier pulled off one of the decanter's crystal stoppers and half filled a pair of highball glasses with viscous, yellow-green liquid. He turned and presented one glass to Dyson, clinked both their glasses together, and sipped from his own.

"What's this?" Dyson asked, looking suspiciously at the contents of the glass.

"A family tradition."

Dyson sniffed the substance and placed the glass on the table beside him. "I don't drink."

"Our Savior drank," Olivier said. "The gift of the vine is one of life's great pleasures." He raised his glass to Dyson. "Please. Enjoy this with me."

Dyson held the Chartreuse up to his mouth, knowing he was about to throw away three weeks of sobriety. Then he sipped it. "Jesus, this stuff tastes like tree sap." But he took another sip. "So what were you saying about Thyatira?"

"My family began watching and waiting in Thyatira nearly two millennia ago…watching and waiting for moments in time exactly like this one." He sipped the Chartreuse again and then began swirling the glass in his hand.

"For what?"

"There is a passage I have recited every morning almost since I could first speak; it was taught to me by my father, just as his father taught it to him. Perhaps it will help you to understand."

"Can you just—you know—get to the point?" Dyson tossed more of the liqueur into his mouth and swallowed. It felt like sunshine streaking down his gullet.

"*Notwithstanding,*" Olivier began, "*I have a few things against thee, because thou sufferest that woman Jezebel, which calleth herself a prophetess, to teach and to seduce my servants to commit fornication, and to eat things sacrificed unto idols. And I gave her space to repent of her fornication; and she repented not. Behold, I will cast her into a bed, and cast those who commit adultery with her into great tribulation, unless they repent of their deeds. And I will kill her children with death—*"

"That's cheery," Dyson cut in.

"*And all the churches shall know,*" Olivier continued, "*that I am he who searches the reins and hearts, and I will give unto you according to your works. But unto you I say, and unto the rest in Thyatira, and those who do not know the depths of Satan; I will put upon you none other burden.*"

Olivier paused, and Dyson looked at him. "Is that all?"

Olivier caught his gaze and nodded. "Yes," he lied.

"I still don't understand why I'm here. That passage could mean just about anything."

Olivier slid the remaining Chartreuse down his throat. "Although my family dates back to Alexander the Great's general Seleucus I, now we are almost gone. Thyatira, now known as Akhisar in Turkey, has become little more than a forgotten city."

"And?"

"Although Thyatira was one of the cities where Christianity once flourished, during one of the Muslim invasions my family fled to France, where we have lived for centuries. It is in Paris, and Alicante in Spain, and Madrid that I was raised and educated, although we still own vast estates in Akhisar. But most of this land is almost worthless now, of which I am the sole heir, just as I was heir to my family's once magnificent chateau here in Ballena Beach." He raised his glass in salute and waved it in the air.

"So you're broke. Join the club." Dyson snickered. "What does all of this have to do with Sebastian and Kitty—or better yet, with me and Amber?"

Olivier put his glass down and folded his arms over his chest. "Even though Thyatira was considered by some to be the least important of the seven churches of Revelation, John's letter to my family at Thyatira was the longest written; this was because our church was closest to his heart. Thus my family was anointed with an especially holy task: we became 'watchers,' who look and listen for signals of an impending Apocalypse. As you know, Revelation states that the false prophet and the Antichrist will work in concert with Satan to destroy the world. There is no doubt that Sebastian Black is either a false prophet or the Antichrist himself. It is my reasoning that if he is eliminated, we can prevent Armageddon from coming to pass."

Dyson laughed. "Did you just say *'prevent Armageddon'*?"

"Yes, my friend. You heard me correctly."

"But we *want* Armageddon to begin," he argued, leaning forward on the sofa. "All Christians want Christ's kingdom on earth to be here, now."

"But my family—"

"Aren't you disgusted," Dyson interrupted, "with all of the godlessness and evil that's invaded every corner of our society? Don't you believe that the sooner He comes back, the better it'll be for everyone?"

"Listen to me," Olivier commanded. "Listen before you close your mind to the truth."

Dyson sat back, his arms crossed defiantly. "You're losing me here."

"My friend, I *agree* with you," Olivier explained, his face illuminated by a disarming smile. "However, I am also a spiritual humanitarian. There is so much suffering in the world right now; there are too many who have been tortured and traumatized and starved and abused. I cannot sit idle and imagine them going through the trials of Armageddon without first knowing Christ."

"And?"

"If we don't stop Sebastian Black, many more souls will be lost forever. It would be like"—he glanced up at the vaulted ceiling, and then his stare drifted down to meet Dyson's—"like a *holocaust* for souls. There are millions who might never find redemption because Christ's message has been so tragically eclipsed by Islam and Buddhism and by every other false religion, including this ridiculously named 'Evo-love.' It has always been my family's mission to restore and to expand the worldwide church of Christ, to influence the direction of as many souls as possible, and *only then* to allow Armageddon to take place."

Dyson mulled this over. "So your family's mission for the past two thousand years has been to prevent the Apocalypse...*until the right time?*"

"Now you understand!" Olivier grinned, and his spectacular white smile shone out from the semidarkness. "And we have done an amazing job, haven't we?"

"You mean that your family has actually run into this situation *before now?*"

"Several times," Olivier boasted. "For example, the surrender of Joan of Arc at Compiègne was one of my family's more noteworthy successes."

"You're joking."

"My friend, God expects us to use our free will *and* our resources to push forward His plan. What do you suppose the Inquisition was based upon? Why did you think so many false prophets were killed? We cannot risk starting the Apocalypse until the time is right."

"But how do you know that *right now* isn't the *right time*—especially with how the Internet is destroying more and more lives every day?" Dyson asked.

Olivier looked surprised. "How do you mean?"

"Pornography"—Dyson cringed as he spoke—"and people committing adultery, and the most disgusting sexual practices are at everyone's fingertips now. With the Internet, the hand of Satan has reached up from hell, and his pull on people has never been stronger. I also think"—he sipped the last drops of Chartreuse from the glass in his hand—"that the longer we wait for Armageddon, the more people will be lost."

"So you are saying that Christ's church is a sinking ship," Olivier suggested, "and better to...*escape* on God's holy life rafts now than to wait until we are underwater completely?"

"Yeah." Dyson stared at him in awe. "That's exactly what I mean."

"And...avoiding temptation." Olivier hesitated. "This is something you know about?"

Dyson looked away nervously. Then he returned Olivier's gaze. "Um, yeah."

Olivier paused. "I believe we men are more susceptible to temptation than women. This is why Satan made Eve tempt Adam and not the other way around; a woman's flesh is not as... *hungry* as ours."

Dyson laughed. "Now there I agree with you."

"But of your concerns about the Internet," Olivier continued, "I believe this technology can also be a tool of Christ." He went to Dyson and took the empty glass from his hand. "After all, pornographic books are printed on the same paper as the Bible, my friend. It is the message in the words that matters." He made his way back to the buffet and refilled their glasses. "For example, over the past few weeks I've been warning Sebastian Black and the Jezebel with e-mails sent from computers using anonymous proxies. These messages are reminders about God's wrath and are very specific about our plans for him should he choose not to abandon his blasphemous ministry." He handed Dyson his freshened glass. "Then, after last night's performance, I sent him a message demanding an end to his actions. And if he ignores our deadline, I will summon God's Furious Angels to descend upon him."

"Oh come on," Dyson giggled, and he threw back more of the Chartreuse. "You can summon *God's furious angels?* Do they carry machine guns instead of harps? Wear helmets instead of halos?"

"In a manner of speaking, they will," Olivier replied.

"I don't get it."

"I am seeking Christians with military, law enforcement, and legal backgrounds, and people like you and Amber who have discovered the Truth through their own tribulations. God's Furious Angels will be technologically equipped and well armed, but unlike other militant groups who are trying to ignite the Apocalypse, we will be doing our best to prevent it—for now." He smiled. "And I am hoping that you will agree to be my right hand in stopping Sebastian, just as Jesus sits at God's right hand helping him to conquer Satan."

"No." Dyson shook his head emphatically, eyes wide. "After those Christian militants were arrested for plotting to kill those cops and then set explosives along the funeral route, the FBI and Homeland Security are watching for groups like yours." He looked nervously around the room. "If I'd known you wanted to involve me and Amber in something like that, I would've *never* come here." He stood up abruptly. "Great! Now I'm probably on some crazy watch list!"

Olivier raised his hand in a *stop* gesture. "No one knows about us, my friend. I have only recently begun gathering people, and I have taken great measures to ensure anonymity."

"I *don't* want to be part of your group." Dyson gulped the rest of his liqueur. "I've already been in jail once."

"You disappoint me," Olivier blandly told him. "You pretend as if you love Our Lord and hate Sebastian Black, yet here you are presented with the opportunity to do God's will and you refuse it."

Dyson's eyes scanned the expansive room as his ears trained toward a police siren wailing by on the highway beyond. "Of course I love Our Lord. But this other thing is mostly between Amber and Sebastian. She's the one that's got revenge on her mind. And don't get me wrong, I hate the guy for lying to people and for what he did to Amber, but I figure that just like everyone else who denies the truth, he'll eventually suffer the wrath of God."

"You mention Amber's revenge. What does she plan to do?"

"I'm not saying."

Olivier dropped his head and kneaded the back of his neck. Then he raised his eyes to Dyson's. "You and she know he has very tight security at his events."

"Amber and I blend in with average people. They won't notice us—and his gatherings aren't the only places he can be found."

Olivier nodded. "Agreed. But you know that by pursuing God's justice alone, you'll be taking an unnecessary risk. Being soldiers of God means joining an army, not becoming suicide bombers."

"I'm always careful." A slow smile opened Dyson's face. "And Amber's determined; she's already gotten close to him once."

Olivier paused. "You know, he might foresee that you and she are coming for him; I would imagine that her emotions are still raw, and she may not be able to adequately shield her thoughts from his telepathy—especially after having been so *intimate* with him." Suddenly his expression displayed regret. "I didn't mean to say that. And I am sorry for bringing up such a sensitive topic with you, her husband."

"Do you actually believe that magician's trick of his?" Dyson laughed, ignoring Olivier's insinuation. "He can't read minds! But if he could, I'll bet he could smell your avenging angels faster than he could sense one or two old friends."

Olivier shook his head. "Sebastian would never see us coming because the only one who sees the intentions of our hearts is God."

"And Satan," Dyson reminded him.

"Satan can be fooled." Olivier glanced down at his watch, then crossed the room to the foyer, turned up the lights, and pulled open the chateau's door. "I'm so sorry, but I must make a phone call to Europe." He turned to Dyson. "Are you with me?"

"No." Dyson got up from the sofa and made his way—wobbling a bit—toward the foyer. "But I'll let you know if I change my mind."

"I'm afraid you are losing a great opportunity," Olivier said as he moved in close to Dyson. "But you are a very smart man, and I believe you will soon realize that we are simply two sides of the same coin." He flashed Dyson a seductive smile.

Dyson backed away. "Look. The guy's a fake and an asshole. But I don't think he's anything more than that. And if I really thought otherwise, maybe I'd let Amber join you in this—but only because we think Armageddon needs to happen now. *Today.*"

"But you will let me know should you change your mind? I should *very* much like to work with you. And your wife."

"Yeah, sure." Dyson caught the intimacy in Olivier's stare, and he looked away.

Dyson marched off into the night while Olivier stood on the door's threshold watching him begin his resolute ascent up the driveway.

Finally alone, Olivier began reciting the final verse to the passage he'd learned as a boy—the crucial lines he'd chosen not to share with Dyson: "*And he that overcometh evil and keepeth my works unto the end, to him will I give power over the nations…and he shall rule them with a rod of iron; as the vessels of a potter shall sinners be broken to slivers.*" Olivier closed and bolted the heavy wooden door. "*And I will give he that overcometh evil the morning star,*" he said while climbing the steps to his office. "*The morning star shall be his.*"

CHAPTER 3

Wednesday Morning

"I can't do this anymore," Sebastian announced to his mother.

"But you were magnificent at the gathering last night," Kitty argued. "The returns were unsurpassed."

"I'm not talking about *that*. That's the easy part." Sebastian glared at her. "I know you just got the same e-mails I got. I'm sick of these people, Kitty! Sick of them!"

"Those people are as stupid as they are crazy. They'll never follow through on those threats—if you could call them threats. I don't understand why you're so upset about a bunch of jumbled Bible quotes."

"I've got a *really* bad feeling about these people," Sebastian said, his voice low and ominous. "They're up to something beyond those e-mails. I can sure feel it, but I don't know what it is yet."

Kitty fluttered her hands dismissively. "You need to learn to let these things go. You've always been such a nervous child."

"I am *not* a child, Kitty. I'm almost twenty years old. And are you forgetting that Christian militants have murdered doctors and blown up abortion clinics? If they think I'm some false prophet or Antichrist, can you imagine what they're going to do to me?"

"Why, are you performing abortions now?" Kitty asked with a chuckle. "Or is it that you're causing too many?"

"That's not funny. You know I'm always careful now."

"I'm just trying to bring a little levity to the situation." Kitty fumbled for her cigarettes, pinched one from the pack, placed it between her lips, and lit it. "Look, just forward those new e-mails to Agent Singer," she said, her syllables blown out in smoky puffs. "I'm sure he'll tell you to disregard this one, just like the rest."

"The FBI laughs at me." Sebastian crossed his arms over his chest and began walking a line in front of the penthouse's long bank of glass walls. "They think I'm a liar, or I'm crazy."

"Well, I know you're not crazy, and I also know that these people are toying with you." Kitty sucked in a heavy drag. "You're famous, and fame shakes nuts from the trees. Believe me, I completely understand why you're nervous about this, but I wish you'd just move past it."

Sebastian halted and turned to face her. "You know that's not all."

"Are you still upset about that little boy and his family?"

"Of course I am! They're dead because of me!" He turned back to look beyond the expanse of glass, oblivious now to the grid of buildings and streets below the penthouse that had once transfixed his gaze.

Kitty drew in a sharp breath to protest, but then thought better of it. Instead she smiled sympathetically at her son. "Little Luke would've died with or without you," she said, settling back into the white leather Barcelona chair. "But I understand how you feel. Really I do."

"You can't possibly," he laughed, shaking his head. "You don't understand what this is like for me—the half lies, the manipulation, the constant scrutiny—and now with these psychos

21

harassing me and with what's happened to Luke, I'm ready to throw myself out those windows." He pointed to the walls of glass and then trained his finger over at her. "People are onto us, Kitty. It's only a matter of time."

Kitty sighed. "I understand more than you realize. But if you're really considering walking away from this, you know it'll be the end of this penthouse, the desert home, the vacations, the cars. And most probably, it'll also be the end of all those pretty girls and boys—and I know what *that* means to you."

Sebastian shrugged and resumed his pacing. "I'm over that."

"Really?" Kitty laughed. "I've come to learn that men never get *over that.*" She tried to think of a way she could assuage his fears and stop him from leaving. "But how will you, after all you've said and done, explain your exit from your ministry? People will demand answers. You can't just disappear."

"And why can't I?"

Kitty shifted in her chair and swiped the long cascade of black hair from her face. "Have you considered yet how it'll look for you to leave our mission at this point? We're just now getting some-where. That *Vanity Fair* feature last month was big, but the *Today Show* next week—that'll be huge." She glared at him, but he only glanced away. "Sebastian, look," she said while getting up from the chair, "we'll get a couple of bodyguards and move somewhere more private. But we can't stop now, we're just beginning to reap the benefits of everything we've worked so long and hard for, and there's no way I'm giving it up." She began stepping lightly toward him, but stopped when she caught the coldness in his eyes.

"You mean what *I've* worked for," Sebastian snapped. "If it wasn't for me, you'd be nothing."

"I could say the same to you."

"You've used me, Mother. You've *used* me."

Kitty laughed. "You're reducing what I've done for you to that? That's hardly fair."

"But it's the truth!"

"If you only knew."

"You lie, Mother. All my life, you've lied to me."

"Sebastian, I've always only had your best interest at heart, and whatever personal benefit I've reaped has been secondary." She made her way tentatively to him and began circling him, with her Christian Louboutin pumps clicking atop the travertine floor like a metronome. "If I've fabricated all of this, then how might you explain your remarkable IQ or your exceptional beauty? And do you think everyone has your natural athletic stamina, both on the field and, from what I've heard, in the bedroom? God knows you didn't get those attributes from me." She chuckled. "And what about those voices and visions—"

"That's enough," Sebastian warned.

"I'm just reminding you that few people on this earth have these gifts."

"That doesn't mean I have to be a part of this circus."

"But you're a performer, Sebastian, an entertainer! You give people what they need, and they pay for it. You're no better or worse than Elton John or Madonna, with their grossly inflated ticket prices. This is just…*capitalism* in action, but without those pesky taxes. And I'm not going to stop you from whatever it is you'd prefer to be doing…whatever that is. Now that you're of age, you're free to do exactly as you wish. *No strings attached.*"

"That's exactly what I'm gonna do."

"Dear heart, every mother knows her son needs to find himself. But before you go"—she took his hands in hers—"I need to tell you something…something that will bring you back after you've had your little 'I'm finding myself' vacation."

Sebastian rolled his eyes.

She inhaled while steeling her posture. "I wanted to surprise you, but I've scheduled a meeting next Thursday with the prime minister of La Serena—that's that little island nation in the Caribbean I told you about. The prime minister is *strongly* considering making Evo-love the official religion of his country. Can you imagine what a huge step this is for us? La Serena will be the first country to discard Catholicism as its official religion in favor of Evo-love!"

"That," Sebastian told her, with an accusatory stare, "is something I'm sure you can handle on your own. After all, you're the ventriloquist, and I'm just the dummy." He pulled his hands from hers and began making his way toward the front door. "I'm getting out of here for a while, and I'm not sure when I'm coming back. So please give me some space, and don't come looking for me."

"What do you expect me to tell that prime minister, and the people at the *Today Show*?"

"Tell them"—Sebastian paused—"that like any other messiah, I've gone into the desert for forty days and nights." He picked up his overnight bag from the credenza in the foyer and hoisted the strap over his shoulder.

"If you're so concerned about your own safety," she asked to the back of his head, "then why don't you care about mine? *Aren't you afraid they'll do something to your own mother?*"

Sebastian wheeled around and slouched down so he was face-to-face with her. "If I'm remembering correctly, Mary lived into old age before being assumed bodily into heaven," he said. "Jesus, on the other hand, was crucified."

CHAPTER 4

When her ivory bedroom walls began glowing with dawn's light, Reed merely pulled the bedsheet over her head and turned her face back into her pillow. She had already made the decision to blow off her day's classes at Cal State Northridge, and there was nothing short of a fire or an earthquake that might expel her from the emotional safety of her bed.

She just didn't care anymore, and her heart sagged from the weight of its sorrow.

Then just after noon, she tumbled out of bed to use the restroom before returning to the lonely caress of her sheets. And finally, at just before two p.m.—and because she was thoroughly disgusted with herself—she got out of bed, ate two tablespoons of cottage cheese, and threw herself under a searing shower.

I hate him became her mantra as she rinsed the shampoo from her hair.

After dressing, she took her plastic laundry basket and began methodically collecting anything that held ties to Brandon: his toothbrush, gym clothes, jeans, motorcycle boots, pictures, the last birthday card he had given her—anything at all that stunk of his ownership or memory. Then she carried the loaded basket downstairs along with her own bulging kitchen trash bag, and she was about to toss everything in the apartment building's already brimming dumpster until she realized that knowing his

25

possessions were still under her roof would gnaw at her until the trash was collected two days from now.

Reed marched next door and threw the contents of the laundry basket into the neighboring building's dumpster, her face pinched with remembering as she watched Brandon's belongings and her mementos of their relationship settle in beside the greasy bags and coffee grounds and crumpled fast-food containers and buzzing flies. Then she un-cinched her own sack of kitchen trash and dumped the contents atop the hump of Brandon's clothing, watching with satisfaction as the hefty, rectangular glob of cold lasagna slid slowly down his leather boots.

She shuffled back up the sidewalk, fit her key into the security gate of her building, and trudged up the stairs to her unit. But once she opened her apartment door and looked in, the momentary bolstering of her spirits collapsed; she felt suddenly like an accident victim returning to an ill-fated intersection.

I need to get out of here. Ellie's place?

Reed grabbed her purse, keys, and BlackBerry from the kitchen counter and then hurried out the door and down the stairs to where her car was parked in the underground garage.

Then she suddenly remembered that Ellie was gone tonight— she was out somewhere for her mom's or dad's birthday. *Damn!*

She decided instead to spend the night at her parents' house in Ballena Beach, then to stop by and see Ellie tomorrow. They could talk and have lunch or just take a walk on the beach, and this might give her some badly needed perspective. And it might help her figure out where she had gone so wrong and what she could do to heal her grief.

And although she felt unsure about which direction her life was now headed, Reed knew one thing was for certain: *I will never, ever put myself in that situation again.*

Her footsteps echoed like slow, lonesome applause on the garage's concrete walls as she made her way across the subterranean parking structure toward her sky blue Camry.

CHAPTER 5

Wednesday, Late Morning

"The Bentley or the Cayenne, Mr. Black?"

Sebastian knew that absconding with Kitty's prized Bentley Continental would only antagonize her further, so he decided on his own more humble vehicle. "Yeah, the Cayenne."

"My pleasure, Mr. Black." The valet sprinted away.

Moments later his pewter Cayenne Turbo with the smoked windows rolled up. Sebastian slipped the young man a few bucks, hoisted himself into the driver's seat, and catapulted himself into the stream of afternoon traffic speeding west along Wilshire Boulevard toward the San Diego Freeway. The on-ramp curved into view. Traffic was moving unusually fast, so he gunned the turbocharged V-8 and elbowed his way into the approach lane.

Where should I go?

He needed to go someplace Kitty couldn't find him, where he might figure out what his next move should be without her manipulations and her unending demands. *San Francisco!* His friend Coby's family had just moved there, and he could disappear with him for a couple of days. He'd just follow the signs and keep heading north.

Once Sebastian had woven through the gauntlet of freeways dividing urban and suburban Los Angeles, the road began climb-

ing north toward the Tejon Pass. After the road peaked and plum-
meted down the northern face of the Tehachapi Mountains, the
vast farmlands of the San Joaquin Valley stretched before him to
where the mountains jutted skyward from the valley like prime-
val islands rising from a dried-up sea.

He spent the next few hours driving past lush vineyards,
corduroy-like strawberry fields, rows of laden orange trees, and
barren fields with telephone poles that shrank from the roadside
to the horizon like crosses awaiting martyrs.

Is one of those for me?

Eventually Sebastian saw that he needed to refill his fuel tank.
And since he'd skipped lunch and was hungry, he exited—upon
the recommendation of the Mary Poppins–like voice of his navigation system—the freeway at the next turnoff. The sign read:

Highway 46
James Dean Memorial Highway

And he wondered, *Who's James Dean?*

After traveling for a few miles on Highway 46, he saw a gas
station with a convenience store up ahead called Blackwell's
Corner. Sebastian wheeled the big vehicle into the gas station,
pulled up to the pump closest to the entrance, and shut off the
engine. After slicing his AmEx through the pump's card reader,
he pushed the nozzle into the tank, adjusted the flow handle, and
then headed across the parking lot, whistling, toward the barnlike
store's entrance; he was enjoying his solitude and figured he was
far enough out of Los Angeles to finally enjoy some anonymity.

But once inside, he discovered he was mistaken.

The fat lady in the dark blue smock behind the counter did
a double-take as he ducked through the door and made his way
toward the snack food aisles. And by the time Sebastian had made
his selections and was headed toward the counter, he saw a small

group of people—two fat ladies now, a teenage girl, and an old black man—huddled silently together, watching him approach.

"Forgot something," he announced to the wide-eyed group.

Sebastian made his way back to the toiletries section, snatched some black hair dye off the shelf, and dropped it into his handbasket. Then he approached the counter again, edged his credit card through the countertop machine, waited until he got his receipt from the clerk, and trotted out to his SUV.

As he slipped the gearshift into drive, he spotted, in his rearview mirror, the teenage girl standing just outside the building; she was holding the door open with one hand, while her other hand held up her cell phone to snap his picture.

Sebastian stomped the gas, and the big V-8 roared as the Cayenne's wheels kicked up some dust.

Moments later he was barreling toward the sun on Highway 46, tailgating an open semitrailer jammed with onions that shed their papery skins in the air, like a railway car filled with busted pillows.

The skins swirled past his windshield like unanswerable questions:

Why am I doing this?
Where am I going?
What am I going to do?
How did it come to this?

Then, as he often did, he remembered that day on the playground, when he was in the fifth grade.

He'd been feeling queasy since lunchtime, but he didn't know why. Maybe he was catching the flu, or maybe it was that awful cafeteria beef stew that oozed, like diarrhea, down his gloppy scoop of mashed potatoes. In any case, he'd opted to stay out of his usual lunchtime kickball game and sit on one of the benches next to the drinking fountains.

He'd just leaned against the stucco wall behind him when he heard their voices:

"Let's kick his ass before the bell rings, when we go line up."

"What about Mrs. Carpenter?"

"Yeah, she'll see us."

"I don't care. I hate that little fag."

Sebastian looked around for the voices, which he recognized as Anthony's and Josh's and Gabriel's, but he didn't see anyone.

He massaged his stomach through his T-shirt and focused on a tetherball tournament taking place near the volleyball courts.

"Anthony can get on the ground in back of him, and you'll push him over."

"No way! I wanna give him a dead leg, or punch him in the mouth."

"Yeah, Gabriel, you punch him, and we'll say he started it."

Sebastian, now startled, got up from his bench and looked around.

Then he spotted them: the boys were down by the cafeteria—much too far away for him to hear—but he could see the trio was heading this way.

As Sebastian got up from the bench, the boys started running faster across the blacktop toward him. And as they drew closer, their voices continued in his head, but now they were all jumbled: *"Used to be my friend…thinks he's better than…wanna see him cry pretty like a girl…hate him…Heather likes him…punch him hard like Dad…"*

Sebastian turned and began running. The three boys broke into a dead sprint after him.

Sebastian tore across the yard toward Mrs. Carpenter, and he'd almost reached her when the bell rang.

He doubled over heaving and then splattered the blacktop with his blended lunch.

The trio panted by him, laughing and pointing.

—

Sebastian looked over his steering wheel and saw the sun had just slipped behind the western mountains; he figured he should find a hotel for the night because his head hurt, and he no longer wanted to finish the long drive to San Francisco.

He pulled over to the road's shoulder to check his iPhone for lodgings up ahead. On the little glass screen, he saw there were a couple of motels in upcoming Salinas, but he wanted to cover more miles before quitting for the night; he also saw some big, luxurious places farther up the road in Big Sur, but the nicer hotels always had more guests and staff—and more people meant certain discovery. So he scrolled down to the very bottom of the list, where he spotted the final lodging in the Big Sur area: Inn of the First Wharf.

The bleak thumbnail picture—as well as the laughably low rates and scant customer reviews—enticed his curiosity, so he hollered the address into his navigation system.

Moments later, Mary recited her crisp instructions: "Continue on this motorway for sixty-three miles, then take the second exit on the right."

His hand found the cold glass bottle of milk in the cup holder. He picked it up, rolled its icy smoothness back and forth over his forehead, unscrewed the cap, and then downed three glugs of the white, foamy juice. *Ahhhh.*

Then Sebastian jammed his foot onto the accelerator, and the Cayenne launched off the dirt shoulder onto the twilit highway.

CHAPTER 6

Wednesday Evening

With Sebastian's energy bolstered by the apple and the milk, he continued on Highway 46 beyond Highway 101 to the Cabrillo Highway, which he took north past Salinas and then Cambria, before continuing through San Simeon. And just after night had completely darkened the countryside, Mary instructed him to take the next exit, simply labeled "Coastal Access."

The two-lane road rollercoastered down to the left, dug under the main highway, and then began edging along a cliff that over-looked the blackened sea. The road snaked and dipped and rose and fell until Sebastian finally spotted what he was looking for. Standing before the entrance to a driveway tunneled-over with trees was a post-mounted wooden shield with peeling paint that read, "Inn of the First Wharf."

The driveway was unpaved, and there was substantial water pooled in the long, deep ruts, so he toggled the low range switch on the Cayenne's transmission hump and began crawling along the muddy road.

The narrow drive bumped and twisted as it descended, with a steep bank of overgrown hillside to the right and a ravine to the left. At last the overgrown brush cleared just as the road lev-eled out, and Sebastian found himself rolling atop a wide slab of asphalt toward a warehouse-like building whose wood-shingled exterior shone silvery gray in the emerging moonlight.

Looks like a dump…but at least it'll be private.

Sebastian pulled up to the entrance of the inn beside an old red Buick LeSabre with a disintegrating white convertible top. He killed his engine, grabbed his overnight bag, and slammed the vehicle's door. And while standing in the moonlight scanning his surroundings, he noticed the silhouette of a trestle pier that crumbled amidst the waves just beyond the inn, while remnants of the structure still remained plumb and erect in the calmer waters farther from shore.

The inn's exterior was dark; there were no automatic security lights to signal his arrival or to assist his short walk to the door. But he could see lights burning inside through the curtained windows, as well as the flickering, amber glow of a fire.

Sebastian stepped up to the door and knocked.

A dog yipped somewhere inside, but no one appeared.

He tried the handle. It was locked.

He knocked again, harder.

Sebastian saw a light turn on behind the closed drapes and heard the dog's high-pitched, staccato yapping grow louder. The door opened, and he found himself looking into the bespectacled face of a short, elderly woman.

A frenzied Yorkie terrier orbited her dainty, slippered feet.

"Yes?"

"Yeah, uh, this is the hotel, right?" Sebastian half smiled. "I need a room."

"Of course." She opened the door wider and squinted at him analytically from behind her glasses. "Please, come in. I'm Libby Zorben."

"I'm Sebastian," he replied.

"I know exactly who you are," she said. "You're the boy from that church we loathe." She squinted at him again and then turned on her heel, Sebastian following behind her. "Visitors are always scant for us this time of year," she said over her shoulder, "and it's been terribly rainy, so you'll have your pick of rooms."

Moments later Sebastian was standing in what must have been a warehouse. The high, crescent-bowed ceiling was held aloft by redwood trusses, and the wide-planked oak floors were worn so smooth underfoot that the harder wood grain stood in swirling relief against the softer. The west end of the warehouse held a bank of high glass doors that framed the moonlit, tin-colored ocean. The remaining walls were covered in floor-to-ceiling shelves crammed with books, or were laid over with original artwork—of both classic and contemporary styles—dimly illuminated by halogen spots.

"Sebastian, this is Tess," Libby introduced. "Tessie, we have a guest."

Another woman with long gray hair, who was cradled in a sagging sofa next to a crackling fireplace, turned to him, put down the book she was reading, and appraised him over her silver-framed reading glasses. "Oh my," she said coolly, and then she patted the sofa cushion next to her. "Maxi, come."

The little Yorkie launched from the floor up onto the pillow next to Tess, then curled himself into a furry croissant.

"I need a room for the night," he told Tess.

"I see," Tess answered.

"Would you like some wine?" Libby asked him. "It's the perfect evening for this lovely Sea Smoke pinot noir we've been nursing, but if you prefer white I believe we still have some of that nice Talley Vineyards."

"And it's the Rincon Valley," Tess cut in, "*not* the Arroyo."

"I don't drink yet," Sebastian told the ladies.

"Shame," Tess replied.

"You look tired," Libby observed. "Are those your only belongings?"

Sebastian nodded. "Yeah."

"From whom are you fleeing?" Tess asked, and then she knocked back the last of her wine.

Sebastian pondered the question. "My mother, I guess."

"Isn't everyone?" Tess muttered. Then she scratched the belly of the dog next to her, and the creature flipped onto its side and began batting the air with its paws. "My dear, I think he'd like the Monette Room. Don't you?"

"Isn't it pronounced *Mo-nay*?" Sebastian asked.

"*Mo-net*, young man," Libby corrected. "We've named each suite after a late friend of ours; in this case it was the noted author Paul Monette."

"Oh." He thought for a moment. "I don't care what the room looks like, as long as it's close to the water; I want to hear the waves."

"Then he should take the Curcio Suite," Tess suggested, "because it's practically falling into the sea. But once you've settled in, why don't you come out and tell us why you're running away? Dr. Zorben is a psychotherapist. And she's quite good, if I do say."

"Yeah, no," answered Sebastian, "I really need some sleep."

"So your species actually requires rest?" Tess asked, her voice heavy with sarcasm.

"Leave the poor boy alone," Libby chastised, eyes twinkling.

Glances were exchanged.

"Very well then," said Tess. "I'll get him the key." With a groan, she lifted herself out of the sofa and then shuffled down a darkened corridor.

"Don't mind her," Libby told Sebastian after Tess had disappeared down the hallway, "she's a bit grumpy tonight. We've just had some news we weren't...*expecting*." She smiled thinly. "You should like the Curcio Suite; the view in the morning is unsurpassed, but I'm afraid you'll have to sleep with Maxi." She looked down at the dog panting up at her from the floor. "He's very fond of the new mattress we've just put on the bed."

Tess reappeared, dangling a key. "Here."

Sebastian took the key with one hand while reaching for his wallet with the other. "You need a credit card?"

"We'll get that from you in the morning," Tess replied. "The Curcio Suite is down the hall"—she pointed—"last door on the right." She began making her way across the room toward the sofa.

"Have you eaten?" Libby asked Sebastian.

"Actually, I'm starving."

Libby turned to Tess, just as she was poised over the sofa cushions, readying her collapse. "Dear, why don't you warm him a bowl of that wonderful ziti you made tonight? He can take it in his room."

Tess glared at Libby. "Of course," she answered dryly. "Why didn't I think of that?"

"But no meatballs or anything," Sebastian told her. "I'm a vegetarian."

"No meatballs," Tess muttered as she began crossing the living room toward the kitchen.

"We'll bring it to you in your quarters, so you can get all the rest you need," Libby told him, with a reassuring smile. "And then in the morning, we can all get to know one another better."

"Whatever," Sebastian mumbled as he picked up his bags.

CHAPTER 7

A McDonald's commercial interrupted the pointless reality show he'd been watching, so Chuck Niesen took a moment to examine the brimming ashtray on the coffee table in front of him, scanning for any castaways that might hold promise.

He flicked through the heap of tan-colored, burnt butts with his fingernail.

Nothing.

He picked one out anyway, sparked his lighter, and sucked down a hit that was barely sufficient to push the craving back for probably as long as it would take to stroll down to the corner market and buy another pack—which he should do right away; after all, it was getting dark, and in an hour or so the streets wouldn't be safe to walk alone.

Then he remembered how nice it had been in the old days when he used to splurge on cartons of the damn things…but now that he was trying to quit again, and the cartons had become so pricey—especially since his unemployment had run out, and his disability hadn't yet kicked in—he figured another single pack of Merits would do him just fine.

I should just quit once and for all and save myself the bucks.

Then he rationalized that having gotten himself sober had been difficult enough…and if he could keep *that* up—one day at a time, of course—he figured he was doing great.

So screw the smoking.

He patted his front pocket and, feeling a scant wad of wrinkled dollars there, threw his arms forward, leaned out of the couch, and stood.

"Hank?" he called out to the man in the kitchen. "I'm gonna run down to the store. You need anything?"

"I'm good," Hank answered as he continued unloading the dishwasher. "Hey, are you goin' to the meeting at seven or eight?"

"Probably the eight o'clock tonight, 'cause I wanna finish reading that article you gave me," Chuck answered. "I'll be back in ten or fifteen."

Chuck clomped down the steps of the old Craftsman to the front path, unlatched the chain-link gate, made a right, and began strolling down the uneven sidewalk.

This particular evening in Mid City was both hot and humid, even though it was already the end of September. And although the weather this week had still felt like the middle of July, he didn't mind because he knew that the first weeks of autumn in Los Angeles always felt like summer—with a bad hangover. And because the residents of his neighborhood were heat exhausted, and most were too poor to afford air-conditioning, everyone's windows were open, doors were wide, and a few clumps of folks sat motionless on their porches and steps just waiting for that relieving five-thirty sea breeze to kick up.

As Chuck walked, he waved to the few neighbors he knew: Mrs. Rodriguez and her slow daughter Mia, who'd pulled their TV out onto their veranda; old Joe Nash dutifully watering his tiny rectangle of green lawn and his huge blue hydrangea bush, even though each day he seemed more bent over and a little slower in his movements; and just rounding the corner was Benny

Jefferson and his new wife Angela, taking their pit bull Charlene out for her evening walk.

All in all it was a decent neighborhood, at least during the day; this was the main reason Chuck's probation officer had chosen this particular sober living house for him. And Chuck was grateful to the woman for doing so, because in addition to the house being in a relatively drug-free area, most of the home's residents were quiet, if not very friendly—with the exception of Hank, his very talkative roommate.

A few minutes later Chuck ducked through the doorway of High Class Liquors, where the silent man behind the counter, upon noticing Chuck, deftly selected a box of Merit Lights from the overhead rack and balanced it upright on the counter.

"Hey now, Mr. Kim," Chuck said to the black-haired man.

The man threw him a quick nod, his blank expression unchanging. "Is that all today, Mr. Chuck?"

Chuck contemplated getting a Snickers bar, but then he remembered how he needed to stretch out his cash. "Guess so."

Mr. Kim's cash register peeped, Chuck handed over the cash with one hand while snatching the smokes with the other, and Mr. Kim returned his change.

"Thanks," Chuck called out over his shoulder, on his way out the door.

For the sake of self-discipline, Chuck didn't open the cigarette pack until he was home. But once he'd jumped up the front steps, pulled open the front screen door, climbed the stairs to the room he shared with Hank, and sat down on the side of his bed, his fingers quickly found their treasure. *Ahhhh.*

Next he pulled the glossy *Vanity Fair* off his night table and returned to the article Hank had marked for him that highlighted a new spiritual movement that was spreading like crazy. Because

Hank knew Chuck had a phobia for traditional religions, he supposed this new movement might fill that "higher power" crevasse that had long been yawning in Chuck's twelve-step program.

Chuck sucked down a second drag and re-read the provocative title: "Has the End of the World Been Postponed?"

The article offered an objective, yet subtly titillating, retrospective on the birth and rise of a movement that had begun steamrolling through trendy social circles, as well as exclusive hot spots, notable blogs and podcasts, mainstream talk radio, and even television. This movement—laughably dubbed Evo-love—centered around a messianic figure named Sebastian Black, whom fans described as having certifiable telepathy, as well as the greenest eyes and hottest body this side of a Brazilian calendar shoot.

Yeah, who cares?

But as he progressed further into the article, he began to like what he was reading: the acceptance of all cultures and sexual orientations; working together toward a cleaner, greener world; acting with consideration toward all creatures; reincarnation and adaptive karma; evolution as a means of keeping in step with a similarly evolving God, and so on.

Then further in, the article expanded upon a recent murder/suicide involving family members who were briefly associated with Evo-love; the victims' relatives were allegedly readying a colossal lawsuit against Sebastian and his mother for using "carnival-style trickery and psychological coercion for monetary gain."

But the part of the article that almost made Chuck's heart stop was not the tales of this young man's telepathy or the string of women and men he'd allegedly bedded or his dubious claim to be the next species of man, but rather the dramatic black-and-white photo of the young man's mother—seated in a sleek white chair—over a caption that read: "Cool, Cool Kitty: The New Black?"

Her face strummed a chord deep inside him.

Chuck squinted more closely at the magazine page, but he couldn't place her. So he tramped down the stairs to the computer that everyone in the house shared—it was in the corner of the living room, so the house's resident sex addicts couldn't abuse their particular sobriety—and Googled "Kitty Black."

Page after page offered unflattering anecdotes and gossip and speculation about the woman, but there were few pictures of her to be found. So Chuck searched her name again under Google Images.

A nanosecond later, Chuck found himself staring at the older, but still lovely, face of that chick he'd met at a party so many years ago—only it wasn't Kitty back then, it was...*Katie*. Yeah, Katie. And they'd spent the evening doing shots of cinnamon schnapps that tasted like Lavoris mouthwash. He was really nervous, and he couldn't believe he actually had a chance with someone as pretty as she was. Then later, they'd smoked some Hawaiian from a bong, and the rest of the night was a giddy, buzzy blur. But no matter how messed up he'd been or how many years had flown by, he never forgot that moment when he and Katie had stumbled, giggling, into a vacant bedroom and locked the door.

Although the short time together had been blissful, he'd never bothered to look up Katie afterward; Chuck had a girlfriend, he didn't know Katie's last name, and he imagined that once she'd sobered up she would've wanted nothing to do with a tall, goofy, unemployed surfer.

And by the looks of the company she was keeping now, he'd assumed correctly.

So that's little Katie? He smiled at the photo. She's done pretty well for herself.

He snuffed out his cigarette in the ashtray and headed down-stairs—magazine in hand—to help Hank with dinner because it was their night to cook.

CHAPTER 8

Thursday Morning

Sebastian had hardly slept. His mind had been spinning like a hamster wheel with thoughts and worries and regrets all night. Then as the first birds of morning chirped—even before the nighttime sky began to brighten—he fell into a deep sleep. He dreamed he was piloting a noisy little motorcycle along a dirt road bordered by tall, leafy cornstalks…he swung up in front of a white, two-story farmhouse with a high, peaked roof and a wide, friendly porch…a sturdy old woman in a long dress and apron stepped out of the house waving at him. *Grandma!*

The room was filled with light.

Time to get up.

Cursing, Sebastian propped himself up on one elbow, yawned, and examined the features of the sun-dazzled room.

The "Curcio Suite" was really just a bedroom with generous windows overlooking the placid ocean, so from his bed he had the impression of waking up in a ship at sea. The walls were knotty pine, and the trim around the drapeless windows was painted buttery yellow. Atop the weathered plank floor lay an assortment of faded multicolor rag rugs, upon which Maxi—who'd been kicked off the bed the night before—was now coiled, looking like a sullen fur hat.

Sebastian, still drowsy and half-asleep, swung his legs out from the high bed. He stood, stretched, and then padded over to the bank of windows. As his bleary eyes made sense of the panorama before him—the rocky cliffs ringing the eastern end of the bay, the crumbling pier to the west, and the distant silver thread of horizon that divided sea and sky—his vision clouded, and he saw Libby and Tess in an office. A doctor's office.

They were holding hands, and their faces were pinched with stress. The doctor had just delivered some bad news: Libby's breast cancer had metastasized.

"Jesus," Sebastian whispered.

Maxi lifted his head, and his dog tags gave a faint jingle.

Sebastian blinked away the vision and made his way to the bathroom to start the shower.

—

He found the ladies seated by the fireplace, in the same positions they'd been in last night. "Do you have any coffee?" he asked.

Tess pointed, without looking up from her novel. "There's a fresh pot in the kitchen. Help yourself to muffins."

Sebastian vanished and then reappeared with a steaming mug in one hand and a blueberry muffin in the other. He scanned the room for the seat furthest from the ladies, made his way over to the slipcovered wing chair by the window, and sat.

Maxi followed him, stopped in front of Sebastian's chair, and began studying the floor in anticipation of crumbs.

"Did you sleep well?" Libby asked from across the room.

Sebastian shook his head. "Uh…nope," he replied, biting off a chunk of muffin. It was delicious, so he shoved more of the moist, sweet pastry into his mouth.

Tess put down her book and looked over at him. "Guilty conscience?" she asked sweetly.

"Tess," Libby warned.

"So who'd have ever thought," Tess continued, her voice musical, "that we'd have the *amazing* Sebastian Black sitting right here, in *our* humble inn." She sipped delicately from the oversized coffee mug in her hand, her inquisitive eyes never leaving Sebastian's face.

Sebastian waited until he'd swallowed the clump of muffin to respond. "Look, I know some people don't like what I do. I get it. OK?"

"Do you actually believe what you espouse?" Tess asked flatly.

He thought about answering her truthfully, but he thought better of it. "I don't want to get into that right now—actually, I just want to have breakfast and get on the road."

"Where are you headed?" Libby asked.

"Sausalito," he mumbled through crumbs.

"Are you *performing* there?" Tess asked before sipping more of her coffee.

He shook his head. "I got a friend in town."

"Is this friend of yours *also* genetically superior?" Tess asked.

"Tess," Libby warned again. "Isn't it a bit early?"

"You're right, dear, of course." Tess smiled. "It's just that my ignorance is showing. Maybe"—she stared at Sebastian—"maybe you could educate us about…now what's this name you've invented? Is it the *Holocaust Transition*?"

"Holo*cene*," Sebastian corrected. "And all of that information is online. So if you're really interested, you can *educate* yourself there."

"Oh!" Tess grinned broadly. "Our guest has a spine, just like other humans!"

He rolled his eyes while shoving the remaining muffin into his mouth. "I gotta go," Sebastian muttered, and then he gulped the dregs of his coffee.

"We disagree with your dogma," Libby told him gently, "because if you and your followers are truly the next species of man, then you're claiming genetic superiority—and that makes old-timers, and 'undesirables' like us, genetically *inferior*."

"It's more than a little quasi-Nazi," Tess added.

Sebastian swallowed his food, feeling his anger rise. "Like I said, I need to get goin'." He stood and crossed the room to where Tess was sitting. "Thanks *so much* for your allowing someone like me to stay here." He dug his wallet out of his pocket, slid out his platinum American Express, and handed it over.

"So that's it?" Tess asked while pinching the hard rectangle of plastic out of his fingers. "You're not going to enlighten us?"

"Look," he began, "I need a vacation from it all, just like anybody else. My work is the last thing I want to talk about right now. But I will tell you that some of the things you've heard about Evo-love are *absolutely* true. Not all of what we preach is based on lies."

"So you admit it!" Tess exclaimed. "Much of what you espouse *is* untrue."

"And...I'm going." Sebastian turned and headed toward where his bag lay on the floor.

Tess, wearing a smug expression, glanced at Libby.

Libby shot her a disapproving glare.

"Must you leave so soon?" Libby asked Sebastian.

"Yes," Tess cut in, "he must."

"I don't blame you," Sebastian told Tess as he picked up his bag, "for not believing in my work. Sometimes even I have a hard time believing it all myself."

"Indeed," responded Tess as she headed down the hallway toward the office. "You'll have your card back in a jiffy—providing the towels are accounted for."

Libby stood up to see him to the door. "If things don't work out for you in Sausalito, we'll be here," she told Sebastian, looking worried. "Really."

"Yeah, thanks," Sebastian mumbled while fishing his keys from his pocket.

Libby's hand shot out and grasped his forearm.

"What?" He flinched away, but Libby grasped him tighter, her blue eyes searching his. "I meant what I said," she told him. "You seem far too anxious and preoccupied for a young man your age; you're jumpy as a jackrabbit. I believe you're in crisis, and I'd like to help you." She released his forearm and gently squeezed his hand. "Just to talk."

"I've really gotta go." Sebastian flashed back to Libby and Tess in that office. "But thanks. Really."

—

Sometime later, Sebastian was curling north along Highway 1, with the glittering cobalt ocean to his left and the steep, ragged mountainsides to his right. He had the sunroof open and the transmission in Tiptronic mode and the windows down, to better listen to the throaty V-8 as he upshifted and downshifted while speeding through the curves. But because of the preponderance of slower vehicles—rental cars stuffed with tourists and lumbering motor homes piloted by dim-sighted retirees—he kept his high beams on, and he found that just a few moments of tailgating encouraged other drivers to drift toward the road's shoulder, thus enabling him to blast past them.

But as he approached the signs advertising Carmel-by-the-Sea, he realized he'd not even called Coby to let him know he was on his way.

He pulled into the next turnout, snatched his new iPhone from the center console, located Coby's number from his list of contacts, and hit the "dial" button; ignoring his mandated earpiece, he pressed the phone to the side of his head and listened.

The phone rang numerous times and then connected him with Coby's voicemail.

Sebastian waited.

"Hey, Coby, it's Sebastian. I'm comin' up to the city, so let me know if you're around, 'cause I need a place to crash for a couple of days. Call me back, brother, and let me know if it's OK. Yeah?"

He ended the call just as the blue Mustang convertible he'd passed a mile or so back sped past him, horn blaring.

The driver flipped him off.

Sebastian checked his mirrors and hit the gas. And just as he was coming up on the Mustang's bumper again, his phone rang.

He glanced at the screen: coby

He slowed slightly and answered the call. "Cobes?"

"Hey, Sebby, glad to hear from you, brother. What's up?"

"I needed a vacation and thought I'd see if you're around. Are y'up for it?"

"Oh man, I wish I'd known you were coming! I'm on my way to the airport, but I'll be back in a couple of days, on…Friday. You could come up then, and we could do some damage. Yeah?"

Sebastian hesitated. "Not a problem." He was careful to hide the disappointment in his voice—which wasn't difficult, as long as he continued parroting Coby's dudespeak. "Friday'll be cool. I'll just find a place to hang until then."

"What's going on? Some chick after you for child support?"

Sebastian managed a laugh. "I've got something going on at home and needed a break. I'll explain when I see you. But no worries. Then I'll see you Friday?"

"You know it. I've got just the girls—and even a few dudes—to hook you up with; I'll pass the word that you're coming up, and you'll have a hundred to choose from—or you can take 'em all."

"Hey man, *please* don't tell *anyone* I'm coming, OK? I'm hiding out. I'll tell you why when I see you. It's pretty serious."

"Got it, man. Your secret's safe."

"Thanks," Sebastian told him, feeling relieved. "Hey, where you going today?"

"It's my dad's birthday. He wants me to go out on his yacht with his new wife and her daughter, who looks smokin' hot from her online profile. I gotta fly down to Newport Beach, but it'll be worth it; I'm hopin' to have some good stories about my new 'sister' when I get back."

"Sounds cool. So I'll see you then? On Friday, like, in the afternoon?"

"I'm flying back in the morning, so I'll be home by the time you get there. Looking forward to it."

"Yeah, me too." Sebastian ended the call and then pulled onto the road's shoulder to devise an interim plan.

His phone rang. He wondered what Coby had forgotten to tell him.

He picked up the device and saw it was Kitty calling. He let her go to voicemail.

The Cayenne idled expectantly while Sebastian considered where to go next: he debated continuing his drive to San Francisco—but once there, he would probably need to hide in the hotel until he could meet Coby in Sausalito. Then Sebastian remembered the hair dye he'd bought at Blackwell's Corner: if he changed his appearance sufficiently, he could run around San Francisco like any other tourist.

He reached behind the seat, took the package of hair dye from the plastic bag, tore the box open, and skimmed the instructions.

The process looked simple enough, but he needed a sink and hot water.

I could go back to the inn...

But Tess had been such a bitch!

Then he remembered Libby's hand on his arm and the concerned look in her eyes: *I believe you're in crisis, and I'd like to help you. Just to talk.*

He checked his mirrors, pressed the accelerator, and wheeled the Cayenne into a tire-squealing U-turn.

CHAPTER 9

"All I can say is I feel so *stoo-pid*," Reed told Ellie from where she sat at the foot of Ellie's bed. "But I'm not saying any more than that because you'll bore me with one of your horrible lectures and I'll feel worse than I already do."

Ellie had been applying her eyeliner but stopped, holding the tiny pencil in midair as if threatening to jab it into her eyeball. "Have you eaten anything today?" she asked, glancing sideways at Reed through her vanity mirror.

"I had some cottage cheese."

"How much?"

"Not very much," Reed replied while fiddling with a ball of lint on Ellie's bedspread.

Ellie rolled her eyes and huffed. "I'm not saying another word until we get you some food." She held out her hand. "Come."

"I will. *I promise*. But let's talk first."

"Have you called your therapist? Does he know about the breakup?"

"Uh-uh." Reed shook her head. "I wanted to talk to you first. He reminds me too much of my grouchy father."

"Oh! I've got something here you can eat. OK?" Without waiting for an answer Ellie leapt across the room, grabbed her purse, dug out a Clif Bar, and handed it over. "They were giving away free samples at the gym. I hadn't seen one of these since third grade."

Reed looked at the bar suspiciously, tore open the wrapper, and bit off a big chunk. "See? I'm fine," she muttered, and then she crumpled the wrapper into a ball and launched it into a nearby wastebasket.

Ellie sat down beside her. "Now. Tell me everything that's happened."

Reed held up her finger in a "hold on" gesture while she chewed and then swallowed. "Do you remember Brandon's crazy sister Brianna?"

"Red hair, big boobs, Harley tattoo?"

Reed nodded. "She called me yesterday and told me he actually started seeing some woman who interviewed him at Google, and they've been hot and heavy ever since. And he's been trying to get up the nerve to break up with me for the past month but was afraid that if he did, I'd stop eating again." Reed's huge, dark eyes began to glisten, and she dropped the remaining half of the Clif Bar onto her lap. "He was staying with me *out of pity*, Ellie. Am I really that...*pathetic?*"

Ellie put an arm around her shoulder. "Well, in a way I guess it shows that he did care about you."

Reed folded herself into Ellie's embrace. "That doesn't make me feel better." She sighed heavily. "I'm just so tired of these relationships not working out. I mean, I did everything my therapist said I should: I was honest with him and talked about my feelings and compromised with him on him buying that dumb motorcycle, and just when I finally allowed my guard to drop, *BAM!* This happens." She picked up the Clif Bar, considered it, and put it down again. "Ellie, when will I finally meet some guy who's worth the effort? This is my last year of college, and if I can't meet a guy at school, then where will I? *Rehab?*"

"You've got to be more assertive, baby," Ellie said. "The right guy's out there just dying to find you, I can *feel* it. But you're always so shy! I've never met another black woman who's so…*bashful!*"

"Guess that's because I'm only *half* black," Reed replied wistfully. "Anyhow, it doesn't matter because I'm finished with men." Her gaze drifted toward the ceiling and then snapped back to catch Ellie's concerned stare. "Will you *please* tell me what's wrong with me? Bad breath? Fat ass?" Reed narrowed her eyes, leaning forward. "*Does my weave look cheap?*"

"Believe me, I'd tell you," Ellie replied dryly. "But what I want to know is how this is affecting you. Are you taking care of yourself?"

"Well, um…yesterday I didn't get out of bed until two in the afternoon—which could be construed as getting plenty of sleep. But…I've hardly eaten anything but a little nonfat cottage cheese since it happened."

Ellie glared at her. "Please don't tell me that—I mean, I'm *glad* you told me that, but it makes me worry; let's not forget what happened after you and Jeremy broke up."

"Lots of healthy women are a size zero," Reed stated defensively.

"Not when they're five-nine they aren't," Ellie countered.

"But who can eat when something like this happens? Just as I was stupid enough back then to make plans with Jeremy, Brandon and I had plans, you know? We were going to Santa Barbara this weekend and Vancouver after graduation, and I even bought tickets for us to go to some big, stupid motorcycle show that he wanted to go to. And if you can believe it, I even had it on my list to look into how much a wedding would cost at the Ballena Beach Yacht Club! But now the only plans I have are to refill my prescription of Prozac." She picked up the Clif Bar and bit into it again. "This is really stale."

"It's better that you broke up now," Ellie said, squeezing her hand. "Can you imagine if you'd gotten engaged and moved up there, and then something like this happened?" She grimaced. "Jilted fiancée is a thousand times worse than jilted girlfriend."

"I know, I know. Everything *always* turns out for the best." Reed rolled her eyes, sighing. "I just wish I had *something* to look forward to. Anyhow, here I am boring us both into comas, babbling about myself. Why don't you tell me what's going on with you?"

"There's nothing really new except—" A sudden grin brightened Ellie's face. "I know! Come with me to Coby's this weekend, up in San Francisco!"

Reed laughed. "That's so sweet of you to invite me. But you've been looking forward to seeing Coby for weeks, and I'm not gonna tag along like some dumpy sister who couldn't get a date."

Ellie shrugged. "Girl, it's only me and Coby. You said you needed something to look forward to, and I know that the second I'm in the same room with him I'll be needing time away from him…so we can go shopping and then have a clever lunch by the marina. And there's this one shop you'll love with the most amazing selection of perfect, vintage sandals…"

Reed's eyes brightened, and she fought a smile. "That does sound kind of nice—"

"And here's a little secret to tempt you," she said, leaning in close, "but you can't tell *anyone*. Coby swore me to absolute secrecy."

Reed blinked at her. "OK?"

"Coby's throwing a big party Friday night, and you'll *never* guess who the guest of honor is." She blinked expectantly.

"If it's Coby's party, then I'd say Coby's gonna be the guest of honor," Reed answered dully.

"*Sebastian Black* is going to be there! *Sebastian Black!*"

"That weird religious cult leader?"

"Yes, that gorgeous, *rich* weird religious cult leader. *And he's single!*"

"I read that he's *always* single. How does Coby know him?"

"Apparently, Coby hooked up with some girl during one of our many breakups, and Sebastian was dating her older sister. But please don't ask me for further details; I heard some nasty rumors about some scandalous switching around." Ellie wrinkled her nose.

"Ewww." Reed thought for a moment. "Isn't he younger than we are?"

"I think he's nineteen or twenty. So you'll be a junior cougar."

"Do you really think now's the time for me to be chasing after some skater boy who thinks he's God?"

"For that matter, I've never met a skater boy who *didn't* think he was God," Ellie quipped. "But what's more important is that now's the time for you to enjoy yourself and stop taking life so damn seriously. And who knows? You might actually have some fun for once."

Reed laughed sourly. "Imagine me. *Having fun.*"

"Besides," Ellie continued, "I need you to come along as my traveling therapist for those moments when I'm questioning my sanity for staying with Coby. Just think of the texts you won't need to reply to by being right there with me. What have you got to lose?"

"But I've got school," Reed argued.

"You're a senior in college now, dummy. No one cares if you skip a few days—and someone from your classes can e-mail you the missing notes. You've got, like, perfect attendance so far. Right?"

Reed paused. "Are you *sure* you wouldn't mind if I went with you?"

Ellie squealed, stamping her feet. "Can you be packed by tomorrow morning, say like eight o'clock? With scandalous dresses and fabulous shoes and your new huge Louis Vuitton bag?"

Reed shrugged. "God knows I've got nothing else to do tonight."

"We're gonna have the greatest time!" Ellie exclaimed. "I've got the best feeling about this!"

"But one thing, Ellie," Reed asked suspiciously, "if nobody's supposed to know that the party is for Sebastian Black, then why is Coby telling everyone he's going to be there?"

"That's simple," Ellie replied. "It's only going to be a surprise for Sebastian."

CHAPTER 10

Upon waking, Dyson's head hurt and his mouth was dry and his eyes burned.

Hangover.

Last night he had passed out on the couch—no pillow, no covers, even his shoes were still on. And apparently, he hadn't even stirred when Amber left for work this morning.

Amber. She must be really pissed.

He should check his e-mail for messages from her before submitting himself to prayer; if she was upset with him, he'd need to do some damage control. *Quickly.*

With his head throbbing Dyson opened his laptop, waited for the device to start, and tried to focus on the messages filling his inbox. Then, just after spotting Amber's transmission in the bold-font queue, a wave of nausea slugged him in the belly.

He barely made it to the bathroom in time.

After flushing the toilet, he rinsed out his mouth with sweet water from the sink's tap and staggered back to read her message:

Dy—

We'll talk about last night later. My source heard he's driving to Sausalito to a friend's house—huge party Friday night, and we might be able to get in because his buddy wants the place packed for the paparazzi. I even thought we could

pose as paparazzi, what do you think? He'll be distracted—
lots of hot guys and girls, plenty of opportunity for us.
Let's leave tomorrow morning. Let me know when you get this.
—Am

This was exactly what Amber had been waiting for: a chance to get close—again.

Dyson thought for a moment and then typed his reply:

Am—
I need to pray today, and I'm starting my fast. I fell to temptation.
Sorry I was so out of it last night. Seeing that Olivier guy got to me.
Let's definitely go north. I'll fill you in later.
Praise God!
—Dy

Dyson sent the e-mail. Then his thoughts drifted back to last night, when he'd stopped off at a liquor store on the way back from Olivier's chateau and bought himself a cheap bottle of vodka and two cans of Red Bull. Upon arriving home, he'd told Amber he was staying up late to do his prayer work and some Bibliomancy—which was true. The vodka loosened his imagination, and messages from God seemed to make more sense when he wasn't sober.

But as the night wore on, his Bibliomancy session—where he prayed for guidance and took a shot of vodka and stood his Bible on its spine and let the book fall open and pointed blindly to a "divinely inspired" passage—was not eliciting answers, so he kept performing the rite until he found himself drunk.

Need water…and ibuprofen.

He kicked off his shoes and padded across the living room to the kitchen, grabbed a Dr. Pepper from the fridge, shook two brown pills into his hand from the bottle in the cupboard, and swallowed them. Then he downed half the Dr. Pepper, went back to the couch to lie down, shut his eyes, and sighed.

I can't believe I was stupid enough to let Olivier break my sobriety. Why?

But Dyson knew exactly why he'd chugged that evil green liquid.

He'd been nervous. And intimidated.

And deep, *deep* down, he'd felt tempted. *Maddeningly tempted.*

Because Olivier was beautiful.

Runway model beautiful.

Pornographic website beautiful.

The languid splendor of his physique, those smoldering eyes, even the basso timbre of his voice electrified Dyson from his eyeballs down to his ankles.

No. He pushed his hand onto his flip-flopping stomach. *I've come through too much to feel this way again. Nineteen excruciating months of "reparative homosexual therapy" must have done me some good.*

He recalled his therapist's instructions for situations like these: *You must examine what it is about the man's physique or personality that you're attracted to, because this attraction is merely envy for parts of your own masculinity that are broken or missing.*

Dyson considered Olivier's athletic build.

I could go to the gym more.

He pictured Olivier's tawny complexion.

I could lay out in the sun.

He recalled Olivier's redolent musk.

I could buy some cologne.

He heard Olivier's echoing baritone.

I could…try to sound more manly.

He pictured the feline stride with which Olivier crossed a room, his wide shoulders rocking and his high, firm buttocks shifting from side to side.

Maybe it was time for that gay exorcism Amber's minister recommended.

Dyson recalled the man's advice to him after completing his first six months of unsuccessful therapy: "I believe that in your case, nothing short of a gay exorcism is in order."

"What's a gay exorcism?" Dyson reluctantly asked.

"Sometimes the homosexual demon is so deep within an individual that reparative therapy will not work. You'll need the demon to be cast out, which we do with prayers and physical manipulation. We…may need to punch you or slap you until the demon is exorcised."

"How'll we know when the demon leaves?"

"The individual vomits or soils himself upon the demon's exit. Then we rejoice."

—

Dyson reached for the Bible sitting atop the coffee table, opened it to the inside cover, and read the scripture he'd scribbled: *I Corinthians 10:13, "God is faithful, and will not suffer you to be tempted above that ye are able; but will with the temptation also make a way to escape, that ye may be able to bear it."* Dyson lowered his head and squeezed his eyes shut. *Lead us not into temptation, and deliver us from evil. Also, just STOP thinking about him.*

OK. So he could block out his attraction to Olivier; he'd grown well accustomed to ignoring his prurient urges, and he always had his mental chastity belt at the ready.

I've been through this before. I can conquer this. God help me, I can conquer this.

But what about the more important issue at hand, which was Olivier's mission to *prevent* Armageddon so more souls might be saved? He'd never heard of anything before now that seemed more contrary to popular Christian ideology—but it did kind of make sense. But regardless of the veracity of the man's motives, Dyson knew Olivier—like Amber—was wholly dedicated to making Sebastian pay for the lies he'd been spreading, and for the people he'd been cheating and misleading.

I should go talk to Olivier again.

———

This time Dyson pulled his car all the way down to the padlocked gates, parked, and began making his way toward the side entrance. But before he even reached the doorbell he heard the latch buzz, saw the front door open, and watched a barefoot Olivier—grinning broadly, wearing a tight white T-shirt and old, loose jeans—trot his way. "God told me I should expect you today!" he called out across the cobblestone courtyard. "What brings you here?"

Dyson pushed open the entrance door and walked through it toward Olivier. "Let's just say I had a hard night."

Olivier met him, shook his hand, and placed an arm around his shoulder. "I have been up since early this morning with business in Akhisar, so I could use the distraction. It is good to see you."

"Yeah," Dyson replied while thinking, *My God, he's even more beautiful in the light of day.* "You too."

Once inside the chateau, Dyson sat on the sofa while Olivier vanished beyond the dining room. Moments later he reappeared balancing two demitasse cups atop a delicate silver tray. "Turkish coffee," he told Dyson. "Most Americans do not care for it, but something tells me you have different tastes than most."

He held out the tray, and Dyson pinched the handle on the miniscule vessel, feeling for a moment like he was at some little girl's tea party. But when he saw how sophisticated the dainty cup looked in Olivier's large hand, his awkward feelings melted away.

"I hope I'm not bothering you," Dyson said.

Olivier chuckled warmly. "There is always time for God's work. Why are you here?"

"Well…I was thinking about what you said last night," Dyson began, "about us being two sides of the same coin." He sipped the scalding coffee. *Bleh.* "And I figured it doesn't really matter that we disagree on our motivations for wanting Sebastian punished and gone."

Olivier smiled while placing his demitasse cup on the table beside him. "As I said last night, you are an intelligent man. I prayed that God would open your eyes to the opportunity I offer you."

"I also prayed last night about it," Dyson replied. "And as long as you can guarantee anonymity for me and Amber, I'd like to move forward."

Olivier nodded. "This is good."

Dyson grinned. "So…when do we begin? What's the first step?"

Olivier looked at him, and Dyson saw the worry and concern in his eyes.

"What's wrong?" Dyson asked.

"I am…*afraid* we have a problem, my friend."

Dyson's stomach clenched. "What? What is it?"

"I saw something last night that I did not wish to bring up—that is, unless you returned to me." Olivier looked away. "My friend, I do not know how to tell you this."

"Tell me *what*?"

Olivier swallowed hard. "Do you remember when I abruptly asked you to leave last night after looking at my watch, that there was a phone call to Europe I needed to make?"

"Yeah?"

"I am sorry, but I lied to you. There was no phone call. And I do not want to alarm you now, but I am afraid there is...*a demon* inside you. I saw it last night. This demon is controlling a part of you. And it needs to be cast out."

Dyson's breathing quickened, and he felt woozy. "What do you mean?"

"My friend, I can only be honest here, and I hope you will forgive the question I need to ask."

Dyson stared at him, biting his lip.

Olivier leaned forward, hands clasped. "Have you ever," he whispered, "had the desire to lie with man the way you lie with woman?"

Dyson gulped, nodding.

"I knew this...I knew this because I saw *a demon* standing behind you last night. It appeared twice, and for only some moments—but his presence was unmistakable."

"What did it look like?" Dyson asked, wide-eyed.

"It was horrific—in the form of a naked youth with flesh charred black by hellfire, and this youth had obscene horns like twin male organs coming from his forehead. He danced behind you, smiling at me seductively—like Salome dancing for Herod, like a girl-whore dancing for her supper. And as he danced, he stroked both erect horns obscenely at me. He stroked them to give himself pleasure—I even heard him moan. Then as quickly as this demon appeared, he vanished." Olivier's eyes shifted nervously around the room as he spoke. "But I saw him twice. Of this there is no mistaking."

"What do I do?!" Dyson's heart pounded. "Can you help me?"

"You must subject yourself to what people in your country call the 'gay exorcism,'" he replied. "You need to have this demon cast out, and then we can begin to move forward together against Sebastian Black."

Dyson recalled Amber's minister. "I know someone who can do this exorcism for me! He's a minister, and he offered to do it before now. I just didn't think I really needed one."

Olivier studied him. "Have they...explained to you this process?"

"He told me he would pray over me and scream at the demon, and punch me in the stomach"—he jabbed his fists at the air—"to get the demon out. He said if you throw up or crap your pants, that's proof that the demon has run away."

Olivier threw back his head and laughed. "American beliefs! This technique only makes the demons hide deeper within you."

"Are you sure? Why?"

"In Turkey we are much more familiar with exorcisms; many Christians there are trained to perform them and are very successful. But in your country, your ministers often commit ineffectual practices because they are frightened of what they will see. They are, deep down, terrified of demons, so they intentionally do the wrong thing, although they tell themselves they are doing what is necessary."

"Once again," Dyson said, "you're losing me."

Olivier took a moment to consider the best way to explain himself. "My friend," he sighed, "if you wanted to rid your home of a rat that hides in your closet, would you bang things around and make noises and shout?"

Dyson paused. "I've never thought about it. But I guess that wouldn't work."

"And why not?"

"Because the rat would just hide until it was safe to come out."

"Exactly!" Olivier clapped his hands together. "So how might you be rid of him?"

"I'd...probably set a trap with some bait and wait until he shows up to kill him."

Olivier smiled. "And that is exactly what we will do. But you must come back another day; I have an appointment soon that will occupy me this entire afternoon."

"But tomorrow morning Amber and I are going up to San Francisco," Dyson told him. "Sebastian is supposed to be there at a party."

Olivier's eyes grew wide. "You are seeing Sebastian tomorrow? You will have access to him?"

"We're gonna try."

"Then we will perform your exorcism this evening after my meeting, as the sun is setting. In Turkey we recognize this as the most holy time of day." Olivier got up from his side of the sofa and sat back down next to Dyson. "Trust me, my friend, you will be home to your wife in time for dinner. And after dinner," he said, pulling Dyson close, whispering so intimately in his ear that Dyson's shoulders bloomed with goose bumps, "your Amber will be *very* pleased with the change within you."

CHAPTER 11

Thursday, Noon

Sebastian rolled to a stop in front of the inn, switched off the Cayenne's engine, and grabbed his iPhone along with the bag containing the boxed hair dye. Then he spotted a new message icon on his phone from Kitty.

A ball of dread began inflating inside him.

I guess I should probably listen to it.

He tapped the screen and waited for the message to cue up on speakerphone; he didn't want her voice—even a recording of it—anywhere near his head.

"By now, I would've thought you had changed your mind about running away. I'm very, very disappointed in you, Sebastian. Have you forgotten about your position in this world? Have you forgotten about your own mother? Hello? Hello? I can't believe you're throwing every one of your responsibilities on me! I'm being pressured with e-mails and voicemails and meetings and depositions, and I won't even mention the—"

Sebastian stabbed the "delete" button with his finger and tossed the iPhone into his glove box. Then he leaned back in the driver's seat and blew out a long sigh. "Christ," he muttered to the windshield.

—

"Of course you may," Libby graciously told Sebastian while opening the front door wider. "But are you sure you want to color your hair? It looks very handsome the way it is."

"I need to," Sebastian replied while stepping over the threshold with his plastic bag in hand. "I've got some religious freaks and paparazzi after me, so I can't afford to get recognized in San Francisco. And my buddy won't be back to Sausalito until the day after tomorrow, so I'm stuck. Would it be OK if I used the bathroom in the Curcio Suite?"

"You could always stay here until Friday," Libby kindly suggested. "But help yourself. You know where the room is."

Sebastian rounded the corner on his way to the suite and spotted Tess in the kitchen, slicing cucumbers atop an old, stout butcher's block.

Tess looked up while her fingers continued their deft work. "Well, well."

"He'd like to use the Curcio bathroom to dye his hair black, so as to roam San Francisco incognito," Libby explained. "Oh!" She turned to Sebastian. "Instead of making your hair look like a Halloween wig, Tess could cut it short for you." Libby threw Tess a challenging glare. "Couldn't you, dear?"

Tess continued slicing mechanically, though her eyes were trained upon Sebastian. "I suppose."

"Tess used to work in a barber shop," said Libby.

"Really?" Sebastian asked, eyebrows raised. "Where was that?"

"In Boston, I was one of the city's first and only female barbers," Tess stated proudly. "Then in the late 1960s, when everyone turned into hippies and stopped getting haircuts, the old cranks

I worked with forced me to abandon my chair. But cutting hair is something I've never forgotten how to do. I cut Libby's once a month. Or at least I did before—" She snapped her mouth shut.

Sebastian pretended not to know what she had stopped herself from saying. "Sure. Thanks. Where should I go?"

Tess threw a nod toward the deck. "I'll be out in a minute." She squinted at him. "And I suppose you'll be wanting some lunch afterward; your face bears that unmistakable look of a hungry boy. How does a sandwich and some salad sound?" She held up a hand. "Of course I remember you're vegetarian, but I'm guessing some turkey might agree with you."

Sebastian *was* famished, and a simple lunch sounded fantastic—especially if it tasted as good as the ziti he'd had last night. "That would be great if it's, um…not too much trouble."

Tess blinked at him, and her knife froze in mid-cut. After a moment, she resumed her slicing. "It's no trouble," she replied.

———

An hour or so later Sebastian looked around his chair. And though a persistent sea breeze had swept most of his shorn locks from the sides of the deck onto the sand, there was still enough evidence scattered about his feet to let him know his appearance had changed drastically.

"You know you're not a bad-looking boy," Tess noted while whisking his shoulders clean. "You really should rethink growing back that Jon Bon Jovi mop." She presented a handheld mirror to him, and he examined the results: now, instead of falling down over his forehead and ears to graze his shoulders, his blond hair stuck almost straight up in front as it swept toward the back of his head, and the sides were clipped neatly, exposing his slightly pointed, almost elfin ears.

Not too bad.

He felt footsteps quavering the wooden planks beneath his feet, so he dipped the mirror and saw Libby approaching.

"Tess, you haven't lost your touch," Libby sang. "And you," she said, addressing Sebastian, "you have Barrymore's profile!"

"I look like Drew Barrymore?" Sebastian asked, puzzled.

Libby and Tess chuckled.

"*John* Barrymore," Tess corrected, smiling. "Drew's ancestor."

"If you're finished," Libby began, "lunch is ready. And Tess, Ramon's arrived to begin work on that leak over the hallway. Could you please show him where the water was coming in?"

"Be there in a minute." Tess began collecting her scissors and combs.

"Thanks for the haircut," Sebastian told Tess. They began walking back toward the inn. "It looks good."

Tess brushed the last of some stray clippings off his shoulders with her hand. "You can repay me by cleaning up after lunch."

Sebastian carried his salad, sandwich, and glass of milk out onto the deck and sat at the café table facing the tranquil blue waters beyond the scrappy, ruined pier.

By this time, the sun had laddered-up considerably in the sky and was warming the back of his neck and shoulders even through his sweatshirt, while the onshore breeze caressed and cooled his face. And Sebastian began feeling relaxed for the first time since he could remember—until this very realization called to mind all the reasons why he *shouldn't* feel relaxed: those rabid e-mails, Kitty's demanding rants, little dead Luke and the imminent lawsuit, and that one girl he'd been meaning to call, but couldn't even remember her name.

Sebastian cracked his neck and sat up straighter. Then he bit into his sandwich, and his taste buds were delighted by the tangy mustard and creamy Swiss cheese and juicy tomato and moist, salted turkey.

He washed down the sandwich with some milk and sat forward in his chair to watch a swarm of gulls gliding in the air up to the left, then switched his attention to a fleet of cormorants bobbing obliviously—like black rubber ducks—in the waters to his right.

It's so pretty here. I wish I could actually enjoy it.

A high-pitched, pleading whine caught his ear, so he glanced down and discovered that Maxi had followed him outside and set to begging. Sebastian ignored him while stabbing into his salad for morsels of cubed turkey, carrots, croutons, or chunks of ripe, red tomato smeared with blue cheese dressing. Occasionally the tiny dog would patrol the deck under the wooden table sniffing for crumbs, and then he would sit up, eyes hopeful and imploring.

Worn down at last by the dog's hungry gaze, Sebastian pinched a chunk of meat between his fingers and lowered it toward the creature; Maxi gently snatched the morsel with his teeth, his stumped tail wagging so fast it became invisible.

Maxi gulped it down, and the two beings exchanged a smile.

After finishing his meal, Sebastian carried his plate back inside the inn, washed it in the sink, and placed it in the drying rack. Then, remembering Tess's request for him to clean up, he scoured the remaining pans, plates, and glasses, wiped down the counters, and folded the dishtowel over the faucet. Finally, he withdrew his wallet from his pocket, picked out a ten, and placed it atop the sturdy, well-worn butcher's block.

Tess, in the meantime, pretended she was not observing him from where she sat across the room, ostensibly immersed in her novel until the bill of currency appeared.

"You can keep that," she muttered, without looking up.

Sebastian pretended not to hear. Instead, he wiped his hands on his jeans and then ran a hand through his new haircut—startled by the strange feeling the gesture elicited—while scanning the expansive room. "What was this old place?"

"A warehouse for the coaling station," replied Tess while settling her book into her lap. "It was built during World War II to replenish coal and supplies for patrolling ships. In fact, that old wharf out there"—she wagged her finger toward the sea—"used to stretch almost a mile out into the water, so the smaller warships could belly up to it; of course the bigger ones would only take supplies in port."

"Why was it called the 'first wharf'? Are there others?"

"There used to be seven up and down the coast," Libby added while entering the room with Maxi tip-tapping behind her, "from San Diego north to Seattle. They were at even intervals between the big cities, but now there's only one other besides ours still standing—if you can say that mess out there still stands."

"How long've you been here?"

"We bought it back in '73," Tess answered, "just after Libby published her first book."

"You're a writer?"

"In a manner of speaking," replied Libby modestly. "More than that, I'm a therapist. My books are written to help people adjust to life's various rough points—and to induce slumber, some might say."

"So what brings *you* here?" Tess asked Sebastian while settling herself deeper into the sofa pillows.

Sebastian shrugged. "Just needed some time. By myself."

Tess and Libby glanced at each other.

"You mentioned your mother," Libby said. "Last night."

Sebastian looked over at her. "I'm trying not to think about her right now."

"Fair enough," agreed Tess. "And you're headed to Sausalito?"

"I've got a buddy with a house overlooking the marina."

"We love it there," Libby told him. "But Tess and I always stay at the Omni Hotel in town on California at Montgomery. The general manager is a dear friend of ours, and whenever possible, he puts us up in the Presidential Suite. Have you been to that part of the city before?"

"Sounds nice," he said flatly while studying the view beyond the wall of windows.

"You seem distracted," Libby told him. "You know, anything we talk about will be held in strictest confidence."

"Libby only looks docile," Tess began, "but as a therapist she's *quite* aggressive."

"How old are you?" asked Libby.

"I turned nineteen last February."

"You looked nearly forty with that old rock star hairdo," Tess remarked.

"Oh, Tess," Libby sighed.

"So you guys are lesbians, right?" Sebastian asked.

"Grammatically, there's so much wrong with that question, I don't know quite how to answer it," Tess muttered.

"Yes, we *ladies* are lesbians," Libby replied. "And you?"

"I'm not a lesbian." Sebastian grinned. "But I love girls."

"And where is your girlfriend today?" asked Libby.

"I don't, um, have anyone I'm seeing steadily right now."

"I'm guessing your mother doesn't approve of whom you bring home," Libby suggested. "At least not for extended relationships."

Sebastian looked at her. "How'd you know?"

She blinked behind her glasses at him. "Lucky guess."

"What Dr. Zorben means," Tess cut in, "is that you exhibit many of the telltale signs of a young man with a domineering, castrating mother."

Libby rolled her eyes. "Tess?"

"I guess you could say that," Sebastian replied. "She runs the show, that's for sure. She's my publicist and controls everything from my allowance, to what questions they can ask me on TV, to the special effects at my gatherings, to the investments we make…"

"And she does not consult your opinion on these matters?" Libby asked.

Sebastian shook his head. "Uh-uh."

"Hmmm." Tess peered over her eyeglasses at him. "So how can you have such a castrating mother and still be a Casanova? I should think you'd be a eunuch, or at least a mincing sissy."

"That's the oldest therapeutic fallacy in the world," noted Libby.

"What's a eunuch?" Sebastian asked.

Tess turned to Libby. "Of course, I'm being facetious; I'm just trying to goad him into coughing up some colorful details."

"You'd really like it if I spilled my guts, wouldn't you?" Sebastian asked.

"For Dr. Zorben," Tess explained, "seeing anyone in psychic distress and not attempting to help him would be like…a paramedic driving blithely past a head-on collision on a country road. You should be so lucky to have her help you."

Sebastian shifted from foot to foot. "I don't know if—"

"You could at least have a seat," Libby suggested while motioning to the big, old red corduroy wing chair across from her, "and tell us more about your ministry. We both feel badly about the way we judged you last night, so we promise to keep an open mind. Don't we?"

Tess's mouth made a grim line, and she nodded curtly. "Yup."

Sebastian sat down in the wing chair and crossed his legs. "Do you want the long or the short version?"

Tess smiled as she shook her long, gray hair from her face. "The day is young."

CHAPTER 12

Thursday Afternoon

"Well," Sebastian began, "we believe that the 'God gene' exists as a universal genetic blueprint inside every animal and plant, and this gene allows each organism to evolve." He alternated looking at each of the women as he talked, as if watching a tennis match or delivering a timeshare sales pitch. "We're the complete opposite of those religions that believe evolution goes against God. In fact, we believe that when a species evolves, it's moving closer to God, and along with God's plan."

"I remembered reading that about your religion somewhere before," said Tess, nodding at Libby, "and I wondered why other religions haven't made that corollary."

"Because most religions try their best to avoid logic," Libby answered, and then she returned her attention to Sebastian. "Please. Go on."

"We also believe that plants and animals evolve because God evolves, and there've been many Gods—not all at the same time, like the Greeks believed, but a succession of Gods, like a monarchy or dynasty. And as each one gets ready to die, another more evolved God is waiting to take its place. And we believe all creatures die because all Gods eventually die—and this is what the Bible means when it says all men are created in God's image. Mortality is, in fact, holy."

"They must have our American healthcare system in heaven," Tess muttered, nestling back in her chair. "Sorry to interrupt."

"We believe there was one God here on earth for the amoebas, then another God for the dinosaurs, then another for early man—*Australopithecus*, then *Homo habilis* and the rest. And now we're on the brink of losing the God who's ruled for the past three thousand years or so—the one who's been in power since the time of the Egyptian pharaohs; this same God's been with the world through the Roman Empire and the Declaration of Independence, but now he's on his way out, and that's why the world is in such a horrible way. It's like he's got Alzheimer's and has forgotten how to do his job."

Tess slapped her knee. "Now *that's* a good story. You should write novels!"

"Where did you come upon these beliefs?" Libby asked.

"My mother, Kitty. These things came to her in a series of visions."

"She's the veritable Oracle at Delphi!" Tess exclaimed. "And based upon these stories, she's anointed you as the harbinger of the next God's reign? A sort of Angel Gabriel to awaken the masses with your electronic Internet horn to the impending doomsday?"

"I guess you could say that," Sebastian replied.

"And what about this 'Holocene Transition' that we've heard so much about?" asked Libby.

"That's something scientists have been talking about for the last few decades. It's a mass extinction, where seventy percent of our species will die out. And it's this mass extinction that we believe signals the death of the old God and the arrival of the new."

"OK," Tess began, "so if I buy that—which doesn't sound any more far-fetched than a lot of what the Bible says—then what about this idea that you, and your followers, are somehow *genetically advanced*, and that you've somehow gotten a jump on everyone? What proof have you about that?"

"Well," Sebastian hesitated, "the old story, the true one, is that my mother didn't know who my father was. She was at her friend's birthday party when she got so stoned and drunk she passed out. So a month went by and she missed her period, and found out, of course, that she was pregnant. She tried to find out who she'd been talking to that night, but everyone was tanked— so we'll never know."

"Maybe it was an immaculate conception," Tess suggested sarcastically.

Libby shot her a look.

"Her parents," Sebastian continued, "wanted her to give me up for adoption, or to have an abortion, but she wouldn't. Then they threatened to force her, so she ran away."

"A courageous act," Libby commented. "Where did she go?"

"She met some people out in the desert, out in Twentynine Palms, who were living in an old vacation ranch named Deerhorn Lodge. She said at first the people were like a family to her, but after I was born she left them because they all started acting like I was everyone's kid instead of just hers."

"Sounds rather Manson-y, if you ask me," noted Tess.

"She had no place else to go, so when I was about a year old she took me back to live with her parents. But it wasn't long before they were all fighting again, so she moved us out. We got a little apartment in Van Nuys because one of her old high school teachers helped her get a job working at the nearby public library as an assistant. And she liked it there because she loved to read, and she could research anything she was interested in. Like, there was this old crazy guy who used to come in and check out these weird religious titles, so my mother used to take the books he'd returned and read them herself.

"But she discovered he wasn't interested in the writings about Jesus, or the beginning of the church, or the Old Testament; this man was reading about the second coming of Christ, the Parousia, and about the Christian eschatology and prophecy about the Apocalypse—the works of Nostradamus, James Stuart Russell, things like that. Kitty, my mother, was fascinated with this new information. And I guess it really affected her."

"How so?" asked Libby. "And how impressive that these names and terms roll off your tongue so easily."

"Well, this is the weirdest part: when I was about eleven, I began hearing voices."

"I hear Libby's *all* the time," Tess joked.

"What did these voices tell you?" asked Libby, expecting the usual manifestations of adult onset schizophrenia.

"At first I thought there wasn't any pattern to when I'd hear them. But a few years back, I figured out I could hear other people's thoughts when they were angry at me, or when they were, um…*attracted* to me, or when they'd had something really bad happen to them that they were stressed out about. But other than that, everything's usually quiet."

"Why do you suppose," Libby asked, "that you're only able to perceive these particular thoughts?"

"We're still not sure yet. But"—Sebastian hesitated—"we think it has to do with survival skills: protection from harm, procreation, and giving assistance to those in need. Kitty and I think these extended skills will be needed by New Man to repopulate the earth after the Holocene Transition, and to establish thriving communities."

"So right now, you could possibly read our minds?" Tess asked.

Sebastian turned to her, laughing. "If you were planning on murdering me, or if you found me...*sexy*, I'd probably get those messages right away—that is, unless you were purposely blocking your thoughts by concentrating on something else. But if something traumatic had happened to you and you were in psychic pain, I'd need to be in a sort of altered state to perceive your thoughts— like going into or coming out of a sleepy, meditative state."

"Can you also tell the future?" Libby asked warily.

He turned to her. "I've gotten premonitions before, but they're kind of fuzzy—not like what I see of the past. Those visions, called retrocognitions, can be really specific. But I'm not the only one who sees those. There are lots of psychics around, and they're not all fakes."

"And how do these messages manifest?" Tess asked.

"It depends. Sometimes I actually hear voices, like you'd hear someone talking on the phone in the next room. I also get pictures in my head, like a memory flash—only they aren't my memories, they're someone else's."

"How unusual!" Libby exclaimed.

He nodded. "So when I told my mother about this, it was right when she was reading about the Parousia, and miraculously the next day she had this amazing vision where a sacred being told her I was the second coming."

"Good Lord," said Tess.

"Based upon that alone?" Libby asked.

"Actually"—Sebastian hesitated—"what Tess mentioned earlier about an 'immaculate conception' was exactly what she changed her story to. In fact, she convinced herself that she couldn't remember who'd impregnated her because *God* was my father." He looked at Tess, smirking. "So you weren't far off."

"Is this Kitty woman *all there*?" Tess asked.

"No." Sebastian shook his head. "No, she's not."

"So I imagine that she convinced you, an impressionable youth, that this special talent of yours made you somehow super-human?"

"Yeah. Plus, since we were poor, she figured she could use my abilities to make money."

"The old carnival act," Tess suggested.

"Only it wasn't an act," Sebastian replied. "We started going to those little *Iglesia Pentecostal De Jesucristo* storefront churches in Van Nuys—*Pentecostal* means they believe in a direct rela-tionship with God—so there'd be a section of the service where I'd 'receive messages from the Holy Spirit' and try to help the ones that needed it—there are so many people in pain, by the way." He looked at the ladies, and they saw the sorrow in his eyes.

"It's been my business for forty years now," Libby agreed in a soft voice, "so I know."

"And you speak Spanish?" Tess asked.

"No, I don't. But my mother would translate—she's half Colombian."

"But you have blond hair and"—Libby squinted at him—"green eyes. But I suppose you could have olive skin."

"Where did the name 'Black' originate, then?" Tess asked.

"Her father, my grandfather, was a big Irishman."

"A stunning combination, like Raquel Welch," Tess noted, deep in thought. "You must have created quite a scene, being this tall, handsome youth who communicated with God and relayed those messages to the grieving masses." She pondered the scenario. "Cortes, in fact, back from the grave."

"You must have made a small fortune," Libby added.

"Oh yeah." Sebastian nodded. "Pretty soon our services were standing room only, so we kept needing to find bigger spaces for our gatherings. But it was tough because it never ended. Night after night there were people crying and standing and praying and worshipping me, like *I* was God. So Kitty took it to the next level: she hired a firm to make a slick website—which started bringing in a lot of money because we charged membership fees to belong to our church and to download my services as movies— and we began holding services at banquet halls. Then a year later, I was headlining at convention centers all over the bigger U.S. cities. We started making piles of money, tax free, so I dropped out of high school. Then after Kitty started working as my publicist and I started making rounds on the talk shows, everything got completely crazy, especially with the economy crashing; people were getting desperate and doing stupid things, so they needed to feel hopeful. They needed something to believe in."

"So on what basis did she begin *selling you*," Libby asked, "if you'll pardon the expression, as the 'second coming'? What else is there in addition to your alleged telepathy?"

Sebastian grimaced. "People have this idea that if you're good looking, you're somehow superior. And since I'm tall and, you know, built like this, and my face looks this way—and I'm not being full of myself—it was easy to convince people. Plus, if you look at the extensive prophecy for the Apocalypse, you can pretty easily twist what's written in the Bible to fit your dogma."

"Such as?" Tess asked.

Sebastian blinked at the ceiling: "Second Timothy chapter three, verses one through five," he announced. "But understand this: there will be terrifying times in the last days. People will be self-centered and lovers of money, proud, haughty, abusive, disobedient to their parents, ungrateful, irreligious, callous, brutal, hating what is good, traitors, reckless, conceited, lovers of pleasure rather than lovers of God, as they make a pretense of religion but deny its power."

"That pretty much sums up eight years of the Bush administration," Tess remarked.

"But people have been predicting the 'last days' for millennia," Libby added.

"Yeah, so getting people to believe it all has been pretty easy—so far."

Libby scrutinized his face. "How do you feel, being at the center of all this?"

"Sometimes I hate it." He shrugged. "But then, sometimes it feels great, especially with all the money—I mean, how many other nineteen-year-olds do you know who have two homes and drive a Cayenne Turbo? And I don't mean to brag, but my next car's gonna be an Aston Martin—a red one."

Libby's face pinched. "That sounds like far too many horsepower, even for a man twice your age, to handle responsibly. But I can understand how the money—and the possessions and power and fame that come with it—is enticing." She thought for a moment. "So then, what's the downside for you? After all, you *are* running away."

They all heard a distant knocking at the front door, so Tess got up to answer it.

Once again, Sebastian considered disclosing his list of stressors, but he decided against it. "It's like right now, guys my age are just thinking about what, or who, they want to be. But I don't have a choice. Kitty's decided my entire life for me."

Libby adjusted her glasses. "So it *feels* like you don't have a choice in the direction of your life."

"Yeah, it feels like that, 'cause I guess everyone really does have one. Plus, Kitty puts a lot of pressure on me to keep this whole thing going. She says we've only seen the beginning, and we could be bigger than the Catholic Church."

"I see." Libby nodded thoughtfully. "But…if you don't mind me asking, and please know that I hope you'll answer this question only if you feel absolutely comfortable doing so—do you actually *believe* you're a genuine messiah and the next species of man?"

Sebastian shifted in his chair; he'd felt she was getting ready to ask him this, and he'd hoped she wouldn't. But he also felt that in her condition, she was ready to hear the truth.

"Yeah," he said finally, his eyebrows lifting. "Yeah, I really do."

CHAPTER 13

Kitty had been occupied all afternoon, first with her decorator and then her attorney.

Neither had brought her peace.

Caitlyn de Palma, her interior designer, was a tall, anorexic blonde with an obvious nose job and a long list of celebrity clients. She had arrived at the penthouse after lunch with an array of swatches, wood finish samples, and laptop mock-ups of Kitty's apartment minus its midcentury furniture and expressionist art. Instead, her plans showcased a country English motif, replete with chintz settees and wing chairs, toile drapes and throw pillows, pastel Aubusson rugs, chandeliers, a mahogany Chippendale dining set, and Chinese Fu dogs.

"There's enough crystal here to choke a meth addict," Kitty told the woman after grimacing through her slide show. "And those marble tops on the tables make it look like Forest Lawn. By the way, I'm just old enough to know that you've hijacked this page directly from Mario Buatta's portfolio, circa 1992." She looked at her and smiled. "I hate it."

"But once we bring in the Warhols, it'll look fabulous!" Caitlyn had protested.

"Fabulous for Princess Diana," Kitty suggested. "Perhaps you should look her up?"

Caitlyn had gathered up her things and fled in a huff.

Only a moment after the door slammed, Kitty's cell phone rang on cue—as if she'd been performing in some high school stage play or a bad sitcom.

"Kitty, it's Larry."

"Tell me the bad news," she replied.

"Are you sitting down?"

She sauntered over to her favorite Barcelona chair—a picture of her sitting in this chair had appeared in *Vanity Fair*, and she'd been pleased with the way the white leather had set off her wasp-like waist and jet black hair—and sat. "I am now."

"These people are rabid," Larry told her, "and they're out for blood."

"But there was nothing malicious," Kitty assured, "nothing intentional, Larry. I tell you, that crazy man, Luke's father, did what he did all on his own." She fumbled inside her giant Louis Vuitton bag for her cigarettes, found them, shook one out and lit it, and then pulled the heat deep into her lungs. "So now I've got to pay for that man's insanity?" She exhaled the words in a polluted cloud. "Come on!"

"It doesn't matter what the truth is," Larry began, "because they've retained the same attorney who went up against Scientology—*and won*. They're claiming psychological coercion, or brainwashing, and they're seeking *a lot* in punitive damages."

"Dammit." Kitty blew out another drag. "How many millions? Two? Three?"

"I don't want to tell you."

"How much?"

"Twenty-five."

She coughed violently and glanced down at the cigarette burning between her French-tipped nails. "So what do we do?"

She threw the cigarette down onto the white terrazzo floor and ground it out with her pump.

"We need Sebastian down here for a deposition tomorrow—I need to talk to him, and then we're going to try and settle this for something reasonable."

"I should think so," Kitty said. "But Larry, I'm…having a little problem with my son at the moment."

"What sort of problem?"

"Let's just say he's on vacation right now." She lit another cigarette.

"Get him back here," Larry barked. "I'll even open the office for him early tomorrow."

"He's…" She thought for a moment. "He's…not speaking to me."

"Kitty? What the hell is going on?"

"This whole *thing* with Luke really rattled him, so he took off and is headed north—I'm guessing he's headed to San Francisco."

"Where is he now? Do you want me to call him?"

She hesitated. "I'm…not supposed to know where he is, and don't ask me how I do know; let's just say that when a mother is worried, she finds ways to keep an eye on her child." She sucked in more of her cigarette's burning redolence. "I'll send him a text, and that usually brings him around; I'll word it so he's got to find out what's going on."

"The sooner the better, Kitty," Larry said. "In the meantime, I won't be sleeping tonight."

"Neither will I, Larry. Neither will I."

CHAPTER 14

"Ramon tells me the section of the roof that's leaking is too big," Tess told Libby upon entering the room, "so he can't fix the leak today."

Libby turned to her. "But there's a huge storm on its way. Why can't he just patch it with that magical tar he always uses?"

"He says there's practically nothing left of the roof there anymore for the tar to stick to, so he needs to put down some new sections of roofing paper over the old," Tess explained. "Fortunately, he just happens to have a big roll of tar paper on his truck for another job, but it's too heavy for him to get out by himself."

"Didn't he bring along Jesus?"

Tess shook her head. "Jesus went back to Mexico for a few weeks. His mother's ill."

"That's too bad," Libby said. "And here we've more rain predicted for tonight."

Tess turned and glared at Sebastian. "It's also *too bad* we don't know any strong young men who could help him."

Sebastian chuckled. "I think I can handle it." He pushed himself up from the big, comfy wing chair. "Where is he?"

"Out by his truck, which is next to yours," Tess replied. "And please, don't hurt yourself."

Sebastian trotted out to the front of the house, where an elderly, mustachioed Mexican man wearing pressed slacks, a long-sleeve shirt, and a golfer's hat stood next to an old brown Toyota pickup. "Need some help?" he called out to him.

The man's face brightened upon Sebastian's approach. He extended his hand. "*Gracias*, young man. Ramon."

"Sebastian." He took Ramon's hand. It was warm and dry and thickly calloused. "Is that the roll? Where do you need it?"

Ramon pointed to the section of roof over the inn's bedrooms. "That black part where the paper's worn, where there should be gray covering it? That part's very bad. I could cover it with plastic, but it would blow off tonight with the storm."

Sebastian easily spotted the deteriorated section where the roof looked flaky and peeled off. "So how do you fix it?"

"Usually I tear off the whole roof and put on a new one because laying down a patch so big only makes more problems."

"So why don't they just get a whole new roof?"

Ramon laughed. "I've told these ladies for years they needed one, but they can't spend the money. And the roof beams are getting so rotten that if the termites in them stop holding hands, that roof's going to fall in. But"—he scratched behind his ear—"today, a big new patch is the only thing. We'll nail down the sheets in stripes going sideways and tar real good under and over the seams. We can be done in a few hours." Ramon clapped him on the shoulder.

Sebastian laughed nervously. "Hey, uh, I can help you get that roll out of the truck, but I can't help you install it. Sorry, man, but I got other stuff to do."

Ramon looked surprised. Then he nodded. "OK. If you can help me with getting the roll out, I'd thank you."

"Is it even safe for you to get up there? No offense, but you look kind of old."

"I'll be careful," Ramon told him while squinting up at the top of the building. "If I cut the paper in eight-foot sections, they should cover the leaks." He ambled over to his truck, and Sebastian followed. "Let's put the roll on the ground, and I can cut off what I need."

Sebastian helped the old man hoist the unexpectedly heavy roll from the bed of the Toyota, and then he assuaged his conscience by helping him measure, score, and cut the sections.

Half an hour later, Ramon looked at Sebastian. "Thank you for your help. But I'd sure thank you more if you could hold that ladder so I can carry these pieces up. That's the hard part, getting them up there with that old ladder. I'll pay you."

Sebastian looked down, and then up at the man. "You know, I really need to get going."

"How much do I owe you?" Ramon asked cheerfully, reaching for his wallet.

Sebastian shrugged. "Nothin', man. Good luck." He shook his hand and began walking back toward the front door. And he had almost made it inside when he glanced back and saw Ramon pulling himself shakily up the rungs, with the first of the roofing strips rolled into a tube over one shoulder.

Halfway up, Ramon's foot misjudged a rung and the ladder rattled and slid about a foot off center; his blazing, silent panic struck Sebastian where he stood like a speeding javelin:

Falling! Maggie!

"Hey, Ramon!" Sebastian began trotting toward him. "Why don't you let me get those pieces glued down for you?"

Smiling broadly, Ramon looked down at the approaching figure. "I'd thank you, very much!" He began descending the ladder, chattering. "If you'll nail this first piece down there"—he pointed—"we can put them on from bottom to top, with the top one folded over to the other side. It will look terrible," he laughed, "but it will keep the ladies dry." He gave Sebastian the once-over. "Your clothes will get ruined. I've got some boots and coveralls and gloves that might fit you; Jesus and you are about the same size."

"Sure."

Ramon trudged over to his rusting truck, opened the door, and dug out a pair of old yellow rubber boots from behind the seat, along with some folded and splattered painter's coveralls and gloves. He handed these to Sebastian.

Sebastian sat down on the tailgate and slipped them on. They were a bit large, but they'd do the trick.

Nearly four hours later, with the sky glooming and the temperature dropping, Sebastian lowered himself down the rungs of the ladder for the last time. He was exhausted, and parts of his body ached that had never hurt before: his hands and fingers were cramped from hammering and smearing tar, his thighs burned from going up and down the ladder, and his knees smarted even through his coveralls and jeans. But once on the ground he stood back and looked up, pleased with himself that the repairs to the gently sloping roof were secure, although—as Ramon had predicted—they did look terrible. The jagged black stripes delineated each of the new section's borders against the rest of the driftwood-hued roof like graffiti on a freeway overpass.

"You did a good job, *amigo*," Ramon told him as he began wiping off each tool. "I couldn't have done it without you."

Sebastian slipped off his coveralls. "I just hope it holds."

"Forty dollars is OK?" Ramon asked him after glancing at his ancient watch. "That's what I pay Jesus—ten dollars an hour." He withdrew his billfold from his back pocket and pinched out two crisp twenties.

Sebastian looked at the bills in Ramon's hand and realized this was the first money he'd ever earned that wasn't attached to Kitty. "That's great." He took the money and shoved it deep into his pocket.

Just then, the click and creak of the front door opening caused both men to turn around.

Tess and Libby approached, shoulder to shoulder.

"Oh my," Tess remarked, looking up. "My dear, Italian grandmother will be able to see that from heaven."

"It looks just fine," Libby reassured. "We're so relieved you were able to fix it in time."

Ramon put his hand on Sebastian's shoulder. "I couldn't have done it without my *amigo*'s help. I could use him again, next time Jesus is gone." He smiled at Sebastian, and Sebastian looked shyly away. "So now you don't have to worry tonight about water getting on the heads of your rich guests." He tossed his head toward the gleaming silver Cayenne with its blackened windows and sparkling chrome rims.

"Yeah, that's my car," Sebastian mumbled.

"But he's hoping for an Aston Martin," Tess said dryly. "A red one."

"Actually, that car belongs to my mom," Sebastian said after remembering he'd accepted money from the old man.

The ladies exchanged glances.

"Tess has just emancipated one of her famous tiramisus from the fridge," Libby announced, "so why don't you both come in and get washed up, and then join us?"

"I'll be right there," Sebastian replied, and he began making his way toward the Cayenne to retrieve his phone from the glove box.

Ramon followed Libby and Tess back inside the inn, while Sebastian unlocked the car's door, grabbed his phone, and trotted back to join the others.

"Where should I wash up?" Sebastian asked once inside.

"The Curcio Suite's still available," Libby told him, "so if you're in need of another night's stay, you're in luck."

Sebastian grinned at her. "Sure."

And as he made his way toward his room, with Maxi trotting dutifully behind him, he pulled the iPhone from his pocket and saw he had a text message waiting: call me asap - something happened with Luke - miss u - kitty.

Sebastian deleted the message.

CHAPTER 15

Amber was not expected home for another two hours, so Dyson left her a brief note telling of his meeting with Olivier and promising to be home in time for their usual dinner together.

He arrived at Olivier's chateau just as the sun was setting.

"What happens between us and God shall never leave this room," Olivier told Dyson.

Dyson nodded. "OK."

"As we agreed," Olivier continued, "we shall set a trap for the demon."

"How?" Dyson asked. He was shaking from the storm of fear and uncertainty gathering within him.

"Do you trust me?" Olivier asked. "*Completely?*"

Dyson did not trust him. But he wanted to. "Yeah. I do."

"Then you must stand before me." Olivier motioned for Dyson to approach him.

Dyson stepped closer, his eyes focused on the floor because he could not look into those intense black eyes—especially not now that Olivier knew his secret. But he stood in front of Olivier anyway and noticed that the top of his head only came up to Olivier's shoulders.

God, there's that feast of scents again: clean sweat, dark spices, soap and sweet musk…

"You must trust me," Olivier whispered.

"What should I do?"

In one movement Olivier peeled off his T-shirt and threw it on the floor. "Please, take my hands," he whispered.

Dyson reached out and found Olivier's hands. *So warm.* "Sh-should we pray?" he asked, staring directly into the arrow-like indentation of Olivier's suntanned cleavage.

Don't look at his nipples.

"Not yet," Olivier replied. "Remember, I will lure him out. Demons such as this are cowards, so he must feel safe."

Dyson was on the verge of tears, he was so conflicted. *Hands so warm, so soft.*

Olivier raised up Dyson's hands and placed them on his own chest.

Dyson felt the blazing, pliable granite of his pectorals, and his breath caught. "I can't do this," he croaked, knowing there was nothing more he wanted than to do this.

"Feel me," Olivier instructed. "Feel my body."

Dyson's hands began smoothing Olivier's naked torso: the sculpted armor of his chest; the stacked-apple ridges of his abs; the lyrical crease of his Adonis belt; the brawny width of his shoulders and the rigid swell of his biceps.

Dyson's body shook and his teeth chattered, although the room was warm. "D-do you see him yet?" he asked. "The demon?"

"Not yet," Olivier answered calmly. "You have not yet lured him out. He still feels scared. You must be more bold in your actions."

"You don't mean—"

Olivier's hands grasped Dyson's and directed them down to the ample swell of his crotch. "This is what that demon wants," he growled. "So this is what you must tempt him with."

95

Dyson's hand squeezed the hot lump through the worn jeans—and from the details evident to his fingertips, he ascertained that Olivier was not wearing anything beneath the denim. "No," he protested through a sudden burst of tears, although his hands continued to caress and knead. "I can't."

"I still do not see the demon," Olivier announced. "What did you do the last time you were with a man? Where did his seed violate your body and soul?"

Dyson mumbled something unintelligible.

"You must say it!" Olivier shouted. "Tell me!"

"My mouth!" Dyson shouted back. "I was in jail, and he violated my mouth!"

One strong hand clamped upon Dyson's shoulder and pushed him to his knees, while his other hand popped open the buttons of his jeans.

And as Dyson opened his mouth to protest, his tongue—as if in possession of its own sinful will—extended welcomingly, allowing Olivier to slide into the back of his throat.

"You must take in the essence of one who has been redeemed," Olivier told him as he began thrusting to and fro. "You must take me within, and it will chase out the demon's spirit that was left there before me."

Blissful tears spilled down Dyson's horrified expression as a strange narration met his ears: "*We beseech You to make powerless,*" Olivier recited in a slow, commanding monotone, "*banish, and drive out every diabolic power, presence, and machination; every evil influence, malefice, or evil eye and all evil actions aimed against your servant.*" Olivier gyrated faster. "*We beseech You to make powerless, banish, and drive out every diabolic power, presence, and machination; every evil influence, malefice, or evil eye and all evil actions aimed against your servant.*"

Dyson heard himself whimper as his lips stretched and his jaw yawned. "*We beseech You to make powerless, banish, and drive out every diabolic power, presence, and machination; every evil influence, malefice, or evil eye and all evil actions aimed against your servant...*"

And as Olivier's climax began he exclaimed, "Oh! OH! I see him! There he IS! The demon is RUNNING away! The... DEMON...is...cast out!"

But this all was too much for Dyson. As he jerked backward from Olivier and collapsed onto his elbows and knees, his back heaved and he sprayed the floor with vomit.

Once.

Twice.

Ashamed and supremely humiliated, Dyson sobbed hysterically.

Olivier buttoned himself up, slipped on his T-shirt, and bent down and placed a soothing hand on Dyson's back. "My brother, if I had told you ahead of time what was necessary to occur," he said in the kindest voice Dyson had ever heard, "you would have never allowed this to happen. I am so sorry for my body to join yours in this way, but it was the only way to save you. You are very brave. You are truly a soldier of God."

Dyson turned his head and saw the fathomless empathy in Olivier's eyes. "Is it really gone?" he whispered, his face streaked with tears and his mouth fouled with bile. "Has the demon really been cast out?"

Olivier stared into his eyes, into his soul. "Ask this of yourself."

Dyson quickly examined the spectrum of his desires and determined that he was, indeed, fully and completely disgusted by what had just happened between them.

He smiled up at Olivier, his face a filthy mask of relief. "It's gone!" he gasped. "I have no unnatural desires!" He giggled in spite of himself. "The demon is gone, my brother!"

"Let's get you cleaned up." Olivier extended his hand and pulled Dyson to his feet. "And afterward, we can talk about how you are going to deal with Sebastian Black."

CHAPTER 16

"Goodness! Look at that!" Libby pointed. "A deer out on the deck!"

Each at the table turned to look beyond the windows, and then they gazed in awe at the marvelous creature as it posed, like a life-sized plaster lawn statue, against the wooden railing. Then Maxi, upon also noticing it, flew at the plate glass, barking madly and causing the deer to leap into the air and bound away on steel-sprung legs.

"We usually don't see them this time of year," Tess noted, "unless they're fleeing a forest fire or hunters."

"It's the storm coming," Ramon suggested. "My wife and I always judge the weather by the movements of the deer. Up where we are, it's more reliable than the TV reports."

"How's Maggie doing?" Libby asked as she doled out the slices of tiramisu. "Has there been any improvement?"

"Not yet." Ramon took the plate from Libby. "But she's not getting worse—oh, this looks delicious, Tessita."

"What's wrong with her?" Sebastian asked.

"She has the Alzheimer's," Ramon replied. "She started about two years ago, with her forgetting the names of our kids; I should have known something was wrong then—especially when she called me Jesse, who was our youngest boy we lost in that horrible Iraq." He took his fork and edged off a piece of the dessert, but left it sitting on the tiny plate. "I didn't take her to the doctor until the day she got in her blue Saturn, but just sat in the driveway with the engine going. I kept hearing the garage door open and close and open and close, so I went out to see what was going on, and I saw Maggie trying to change the channels on the car's dashboard with the garage door clicker."

"Does she still live with you?" Sebastian asked.

"Yes, of course," Ramon replied. "She'll never go into one of those bad places, not while I'm still here."

"Is Mateo still taking care of her during the day?" Libby asked.

"Thank God yes," said Ramon, nodding. "Mateo got a job at a restaurant at night so he can be with Maggie when I'm working. He's a good boy and never complains about how bad his mother's thinking is, or what big messes she makes now. I'm a lucky man to have such good children." He smiled contentedly.

"There's very little luck involved in having responsible kids," Tess told him. "You have wonderful children because you and Maggie were wonderful parents—and it's terrific that you two have been so supportive of Mateo; so many parents cast aside their gay or lesbian children, emotionally or otherwise, upon learning the truth about them."

"My son is my son," Ramon stated proudly, "whether or not I understand him. He is a good boy, and I cannot imagine our lives without him." He dug his fork into the dessert and slid a large morsel of tiramisu into his mouth. "It just goes so fast," he said with his mouth full. "Seems like yesterday when the *ninos* were small, and now here we are—old." He laughed, and the ladies laughed with him.

Libby turned to Sebastian. "What does your religion have to say about diseases like Alzheimer's?"

Sebastian shrugged. "Just the body wearing down, like an old machine. There's no spiritual component to it."

"That's right, I'd forgotten," Tess added, "that death and disease are normal processes in your world."

"Like they aren't in ours?" Libby asked Tess pointedly.

"And what religion are you?" Ramon asked Sebastian.

"It's more"—Sebastian paused—"a philosophy than a religion."

"He believes that a new species of man has just arrived upon this earth," Tess added, "that signals the death of the old God and the arrival of the new."

"Sounds like science fiction and aliens," Ramon remarked blandly, then slurped some coffee from the mug in his hand. "I don't know why people need big churches to make them happy. I think happiness is good, hard work, having someone who loves you and you love them, caring for children and animals, and once in a while a night of romance—even if it's only in your head." He chuckled. "I also like a good glass of wine."

"Hear, hear," Tess agreed, clinking her coffee mug with Ramon's and then Libby's.

"But your wife is really sick," Sebastian countered, "and your son was killed in a war—and I hate to say this, but it looks like you've spent your life working really hard for not a whole lot, from the looks of your truck. I mean, don't you want nicer things? And don't you want to find out why bad things happen?"

"Young man," Ramon told him gently, "you cannot judge someone by what you see, like my old Toyota, because you cannot see in that truck's bed how much money we saved, or the property we own—or most importantly, the love I have for my family and friends. You see, I already have what I want, *from my God*. I'm a happy man, no question; I have years of happy memories to sweeten today's sadness, and I have good friends now to make more happy memories with." He smiled sweetly at Libby and Tess, and they mirrored his affectionate gaze. "You're too young to know that happiness does not come with a shiny truck"—he tossed his head toward where the Cayenne was parked outside— "or a big bank account, or a face people want to stare at."

Sebastian pretended to ignore the man's lecture while finishing his tiramisu in silence.

"Look, it's raining," Libby announced.

They all turned and saw that the wooden deck beyond the windows was dark and shiny, as if having just received a new coat of varnish, and the sea beyond the deck was churning now at a low boil.

"I better go," Ramon said as he scooted his chair back and then pushed himself up from the table. "Maggie might forget who I am, but she still likes sitting by the fire with me on a rainy day." He held out his hand to Sebastian. "Thank you, *amigo*, for your help up there. You helped me, and I won't forget it."

Sebastian stood to shake the man's hand. "I hope your wife gets better, and I'm sorry about your son."

Ramon clapped him on the back. "You make sure you don't put yourself in bad places, the way my Jesse did, because you never want to worry your mama like that." Ramon went first to Libby and then to Tess and gave them both pecks on their cheeks. "How do you ladies look younger each time I see you?" he asked. "You must be *las brujas!*"

"You old bull, still flirting with the ladies," Tess laughed. Then she took Ramon's hands and squeezed them. "Please take care of yourself, and give Maggie and Mateo our love."

"I will," Ramon replied over his shoulder while passing through the door. "And if that roof starts to leak, don't blame me," he shouted. "Blame the handsome boy!"

Then he was gone.

Sebastian began clearing the dishes from the table, but Tess stopped him. "You've earned your keep today," she said. "You go rest—tonight your room and board are on us, by the way—and I'll let you know when dinner's ready."

"Thanks. I mean it." Sebastian began making his way down the long hallway toward the Curcio Suite, with Maxi in tow. And when he opened the door, Maxi vaulted up onto the bed, but this time Sebastian didn't shoo him off. Instead, he sat on the edge of the bed next to the panting dog and kicked off his shoes.

Then he pulled his iPhone from his pocket and tapped his mother's number into the keypad.

CHAPTER 17

Kitty's text—along with a lingering feeling of dread—had been gnawing at Sebastian; the message "something happened with Luke" could mean anything, and his mind had been tossing around various possibilities until her words finally got the best of him. As a result he decided to break his vow to ignore her *just this once* so he might have some peace of mind.

The phone rang twice on the other end.

"Finally," her voice said.

"Hi, Kitty."

"I was so afraid you wouldn't call me," she lied, knowing good and well that her son could not ignore her for long.

"Yeah. So what's up?"

Maxi flipped onto his back, and Sebastian rubbed his protruding, tennis ball–shaped belly.

"Where are you?" she asked, knowing exactly where he was; she'd had a tracking device installed inside the iPhone before handing it over to him.

"That doesn't matter. But I'm somewhere safe."

"Are you at the desert house?" she asked coyly.

"Like I said, *it does not matter*. Why did you text me?"

She sighed heavily. "As we anticipated, Luke's relatives hired some huge law firm and they're suing us *for twenty-five million dollars,* so Larry needs you here first thing tomorrow morning for a deposition."

"Why?" he asked her, when what he meant was, *Why do you only need me when it has to do with money?*

"Because we're trying to settle this out of court."

"But we didn't do anything wrong, Kitty. Don't you think a judge and jury will see that?"

"Larry doesn't want to take that chance. These people hired some big firm that went up against Scientology and won. They're suing us on the grounds of psychological coercion."

"But we aren't Scientology," Sebastian snapped. "And we didn't coerce anyone."

"And that's why"—she took a heavy drag off her cigarette—"I need you here in the morning at Larry's."

"Kitty, I've gotta go."

"You can't *go,* Sebastian. You need to listen to me. *This...situation...could...ruin...us!*"

Sebastian was silent.

"So you'll be here tomorrow? Please?"

"No. I can't."

"You're turning your back on the *Today Show,*" Kitty told him, her words clipped and sharp. "You're turning your back on the island nation of La Serena. You're turning your back on Larry and your followers. But worst of all, you're turning your back on me."

"I'm sure you can handle it," he replied. Then he ended the call, switched off the device, and threw it into his overnight bag.

He fell backward onto the bed as her words tumbled in his head.

Then a vision overtook him from the time Kitty leased a ramshackle little Baptist church in Sunland-Tujunga and they were living in the adjoining rectory.

—

"Is this shirt OK?" Sebastian asked Kitty while extending his arms like a kid playing airplane, turning around slowly.

"Wear the new black one." She pointed into the open closet.

"Why?" he asked.

"It's more urbane," she replied.

He agreed, although he didn't know what "urbane" meant and knew he shouldn't ask.

"Are you ready for tonight?" Kitty asked, her voice both sweet and bland.

"I guess. It'll be the same as always, right?"

"The same as always. But this time, try not to forget why you're up there."

"I don't forget," Sebastian replied, honestly. "It's just that sometimes I start, um, getting nervous, and my mouth won't say the words I'm thinking of."

"Remember your breathing—and pretend there's no one listening to you or watching you, like we practiced." Kitty's mouth smiled, but her eyes did not. "OK?"

"Sure." He went over to the closet and pulled the crisp black shirt off its hanger, unbuttoned the white shirt he was wearing, and threw it onto the bed.

She stole a dispassionate glance at his bare torso. *God, but he's developing magnificently,* he heard her think.

He turned to her, and she looked away while he buttoned up the black shirt. "Is this better?"

"Much," she cooed. "And you should wear those new black boots." She pointed at the bottom of his closet. "They make you look taller."

"But I'm already taller than everyone else."

"Exactly," Kitty replied, with a sly smile. "So are you OK now? Because I need to go check on some things."

"I'm OK."

"I almost forgot: there's a girl who's dying to meet you afterward. Are you up for it?"

Sebastian shot her a half smile. "Yeah."

"I'll let her know." She turned on her heel, marched through the door, and disappeared.

Sebastian waited until the click of her footsteps faded before collapsing backward onto the bed, holding his head in his hands. *How long am I gonna have to keep doing this? I hate these shows!*

Then he remembered his conquests: Vanessa and Courtney and Erica, and that older woman with the blonde hair almost down to her waist...and Bernardo and Joey and that kid who cried afterward when Sebastian told him he had to leave. *Was his name Ryan?*

He smiled, feeling himself stir.

So it wasn't so bad after all. He'd have to get through tonight's sermon, which Kitty had written and he had memorized over this past week, and then he'd be done for another seven days. He picked up the paper and began practicing his speech, but realized he'd already memorized the lines perfectly. He folded the paper and slipped it into his pocket. Then after checking his reflection in the mirror one last time, he exited his bedroom and headed down the stairs.

Kitty was in the foyer, taking a hit off a joint.

Sebastian hated marijuana, as it scrambled his visions and left him feeling vulnerable. He held his breath as he brushed past her.

"Your belt," Kitty told him as he was halfway through the door.

Sebastian stopped and turned. "What?"

"You missed a loop."

He patted his waist, unbuckled his belt, pulled it halfway off, and then threaded it correctly before buckling it again. "Is there gonna be a big crowd tonight?"

Kitty nodded. "Bigger than ever. Are you nervous?"

Sebastian shrugged while making his way toward the door. "See you there."

"Right behind you," Kitty said. Then she rose from the chair, pushed a stick of Juicy Fruit into her mouth, and followed him out the door.

Sebastian welcomed the crowd and then proceeded with his sermon. He talked about God and forgiveness and love and the Holocene Transition, and then he launched into his readings: a teenage boy whose father had abandoned him and his mother; an elderly woman whose daughter was imprisoned for armed robbery; a man whose wife had run off with a younger man. And although he typically performed five to eight sessions during a gathering, on this night he found that with each reading he performed his energy was sapped considerably, so that the visions and the voices drifting his way were becoming more and more jumbled and indistinct.

Knowing he could not continue, Sebastian concluded the service early with an inarticulate rendition of Kitty's plea for more generous and selfless donations. "God's will is done here tonight!" he exclaimed, and the small crowd erupted into praise and clapping.

As the closing music swelled from the boom box in the corner of the chapel, Sebastian turned and exited the altar and saw that Kitty was waiting for him in the wings. Standing with her was a young lady, perhaps his same age or a bit older.

Kitty stepped forward. "You look tired," she whispered. "Are you still up to this?"

He glanced over at the young woman, sized her up, and nodded. "I'm OK."

Kitty held out her hand. "Sebastian, this is Amber. She's the one I was telling you about."

"Hello, Amber," he said.

"Hi, Mr. Black." Amber's eyes glinted with desire.

They shook hands.

"Call me Sebastian." Her warm skin sparked his lust. "Do you want to come with me?"

"Yes, please." Her red painted lips smiled, revealing imperfect teeth.

But the rest of her was pretty much perfect.

And as her fingers twined with his, he heard her thoughts: she was frightened, but her yearning for him was driving her; her father was ill, and her mother was almost never home; she'd been contemplating running away...

He squeezed her hand, and Amber squeezed his back.

"We're gonna go back to the rectory and talk," Sebastian told Kitty.

Kitty smiled. "Of course."

Sebastian led Amber down the rickety back stairs of the church, and then they crossed the parking lot to the rectory. Once inside, they made their way down the hall to a bedroom furnished with a sagging, gray loveseat and a queen bed draped with a pink crocheted coverlet.

Sebastian closed and locked the door and pulled Amber to the foot of the bed. "You are very special to me," he told her as they sat down. "But I need to know if you love me."

"I do love you," she whispered.

"Then are you ready?"

Instead of answering, her mouth moved toward his.

Her breath was sweet.

—

Reliving this encounter awakened his own lust, but Sebastian was too distressed by the clarity of his vision to respond to any yearning for sexual release; he knew from experience that this had been no fanciful recollection, and was most likely a warning.

Why is she out there thinking about me?

But he knew why…or at least he suspected it.

If it's true, that's something no one could forget.

He blinked at the ceiling, wondering: *How many girls have I used? How many guys? What would my life be like if I just gave up everything? Could I get along without Kitty? Would I be better off, or worse?*

Then he remembered what Ramon said, about happiness being based upon hard work and having someone to love.

But if Sebastian gave up his mission, what sort of work would he do?

Maybe Libby, or even Tess, could help him figure out what his next step might be.

He got up and walked across the room to look in the mirror atop the old cherrywood dresser. And as the rain drummed steadily onto the roof, he thought about the patch job he'd completed today, and he realized it was the first time in his life that he'd done an honest day's work with his hands.

He glanced up at tea-colored stains spiderwebbed across the dry ceiling and figured that he must have done a pretty decent job on that patch.

His eyes caught in the mirror, and he smiled at himself.

CHAPTER 18

Thursday Evening

"Hey, Hank, you know that article you gave me," Chuck asked, "about that new religion?"

Hank continued stewing the large pot of marinara on the stovetop. "What about it?"

"You know that pretty little lady in the article, that messiah kid's mom?"

"You mean Kitty Black?"

"Well, you'll never believe it, but I hooked up with her once."

Hank stopped stirring, looked at Chuck, and laughed. Then he went back to stirring.

"No really. I did." He held the magazine out to his pal, with the pages rolled back to the photo of Kitty sitting in her white chair. "Her name was 'Katie' back then, and we met at a party in the Valley. I couldn't believe she would, you know, even talk to me. And then later on, we got real messed up and found a room and, uh, got to know each other *real well.*"

"Are you serious?" Hank turned off the burner under the pot. "Are you *sure?*"

"I Googled her, so I'm sure. Hundred percent sure."

"How long ago?"

"Like"—he looked at the ceiling while thinking—"about twenty years ago."

Hank bit his lip, nodding. "So at one time in your life"—he held the magazine up to his face so he could examine the picture of Kitty more closely—"a chick like that was actually in your league, and you *still* let yourself go?" He gave a low whistle. "I'll bet I know what she'd say now if she saw you."

"You don't have be an ass about it," Chuck told him sourly. "I had all my hair back then, and I was in great shape because of all the surfing."

"So why didn't you go out with her after that party?" Hank asked. "If it was so great, then why was it only a one-night stand?"

"I had another girlfriend and we were trying, you know, to make it work."

"Well," Hank snickered, "you must not have been trying very hard. Hey, hand me that box of spaghetti."

Chuck handed over the box, and Hank dumped it into the big pot of steaming, bubbling water next to the marinara.

"How many are gonna be home tonight for dinner?" Chuck asked. "I'll set the table."

"Matt and LaBron went to that early meeting over at the church, but I think Jose and Alex will be here, for sure. You should—" He stopped suddenly and looked at Chuck, eyes wide. "You said about twenty years ago, right?"

"Yeah, about." Chuck began pulling fistfuls of flatware out of the drawer.

Hank picked up the magazine, started rifling through the pages, and then stopped. "Jesus tap-dancing Christ."

"Jesus, what?"

Hank held the magazine in the air while looking from the article to Chuck and back again. He started cackling.

"What the hell's so funny?" Chuck asked angrily.

"Do me a favor"—Hank laughed again—"and go get that old picture of you and your sister that's hanging on the wall over your dresser."

"Why?"

"Just do it." Hank smiled kindly. "OK? Can you just trust me on this?"

Chuck stood, looking puzzled.

"Trust me, man."

Chuck stomped out of the kitchen and returned moments later with the framed picture of him with his sister, taken at their grandfather's funeral many years back. "Yeah?" he asked Hank.

Hank stepped over to the old Formica breakfast table, where he smoothed the *Vanity Fair* open to the article about Sebastian. Then he placed the faded picture of Chuck and his sister just above the glossy, black-and-white shot of Sebastian at some swanky party in New York.

"And exactly what sort of protection did you and that chick use that night?" Hank asked playfully, pointing from one photo to the other and back.

Chuck's mouth moved, but no sounds came out.

"Oh, *that's right*," Hank said in a condescending tone. "You were probably too lit up to remember to use anything."

Chuck bent over to examine the side-by-side likenesses more closely. "No." He shook his head. "There's no freakin' way."

"Congratulations, Papa." Hank slapped Chuck on the back. "It's a boy."

CHAPTER 19

Since the vegetable stew was just beginning to steam under its lid on the stovetop and still wouldn't be ready for some time, Tess took a few moments to sequester herself in her office and check her e-mail.

After sorting through the plentiful spam and then answering the only message from an actual human—an old coworker named Frank who was planning a trip up their way—she decided to pick through the nuts and bolts of Sebastian's ministry.

She Googled "Sebastian Black."

Instantly, her screen filled with site after site referencing this handsome new "messiah"—gossip blogs and photo galleries and fan sites and a general plethora of e-garbage—but nothing from the actual Evo-love ministry.

Then finally, down near the bottom of the first Google page, she spotted his official website and clicked on it.

At once her computer screen went dark and some cheesy New Age music cued, so Tess clicked the "Skip Intro" prompt. That brought her to the main menu, so she selected the link for "Sebastian's Teachings" and began skimming though the table of contents until she found a page that caught her attention: "How the Concept of Sin Has Been Misconstrued."

She read through the text and then clicked onto the next page: "Obligations to Man, Animal, and Planet."

OK, Tess thought. *So far none of this is too far-fetched.*

She continued perusing the other sections of Sebastian's site just to see if she could dig up anything noteworthy.

And then she did.

"Libby?" Tess shouted from inside her office.

No answer came.

"Libby!"

Moments later, Tess heard the approach of Maxi's clicking toenails on the floor, like the enthusiastic gallop of Lilliputian hooves before Libby's slower moving carriage.

Libby's politely stern face appeared at the doorway. "You know I prefer it when you do not shout through the house for me."

Tess waved her hand dismissively. "I know, I know. But this is important." She shrugged and shook her head slightly while still reading the computer screen. "And I'm sorry."

"So what is it?"

"You should see this."

"*What?*" Libby asked sharply. "My feet hurt from standing here."

Tess focused upon the computer screen while scrolling through the text. "It's all blah, blah, karma…blah, blah, recycling…blah, blah, evolution until we get to this: '*Sebastian states that only through your generous tax deductible donations to his missions will the Era of New Man flourish upon planet earth. Won't you please help save mankind, as well as all of earth's living things, today?*'"

"Big surprise," Libby told her. "They are in it for the money."

"But my dear, why is it that people are so driven to believe in, and to be a part of, some group—even if it looks like a complete sham?"

Libby snorted. "The same reason why the Catholic Church became so powerful during the Middle Ages: coercion, guilt, and roiling fear of death."

"Speaking of roiling, do you think the stew's ready yet?"

"Are we done here?"

"I want you to see something," Tess replied. "I'm curious if you'll think what I thought."

"Only if I may sit down."

Tess got up from her chair, and Libby switched places with her.

"Now click on the pictures," Tess told her.

Libby leaned into the monitor while adjusting her glasses on her nose. "What pictures?"

"That galleries link on the side menu."

Libby clicked on the link and found herself inundated by images of Sebastian preaching. Sebastian serving food to the poor. Sebastian shaking the hand of President Obama. Sebastian guffawing with Bill Clinton. Sebastian shirtless, hammering two-by-fours at Habitat for Humanity. Sebastian in board shorts, swimming with dolphins. Sebastian in a stunning tuxedo at a *Vanity Fair* party. Sebastian in Africa, visiting an AIDS ward. Sebastian laughing with drag queens at a Human Rights Campaign fundraiser. Sebastian, drenched in sweat and grimacing, as he walked the Via Dolorosa in Israel.

Sebastian…Sebastian…Sebastian…

But what struck Libby about the gallery photos was the strapping, virile beauty the young man exuded—which, she quickly determined, was no accident. It was clear that each high-res frame was shot and cropped to advertise some anatomical detail sure to sate the prurient eye: a shirt flapping open to expose his sculpture-perfect torso, from protruding Adam's apple down to crisp Adonis belt; a cocked eyebrow over half-lidded turquoise eyes accentuated by a crooked grin; a T-shirt just tight enough to hug those heroic shoulders, triceps, and lats; a shot of his rear end that might have been used to sell millions of jeans, or a crotch bulge that was more than a little eye-catching…

"That woman's been pimping out her own son," Libby stated dryly.

"Exactly my thoughts," Tess whispered.

"He's been through a lot."

"Indeed," Tess agreed. "She makes Mama Rose look like Mother Teresa."

Libby peered over her reading glasses at Tess. "Makes me feel sad for the boy."

"And it makes me want to have a talk with Miss Kitty," Tess added darkly. "What should we do?"

"The only thing we can do," Libby told her while pushing herself up from the desk chair with a groan. "Be human."

CHAPTER 20

A sudden detonation of thunder popped Sebastian's eyes open.

His heart was racing, and his armpits were soggy—as was the pillow under his head.

Was that just a dream? What the hell just happened?

He blinked at the darkened ceiling, the vision vibrant against the plaster: His feet had been bound together with rope, as were his hands. And his entire body was held fast; he could feel the tree bark clawing into his back, and his shoulders burned in agony for the position in which he was hanging. He tried to push his body up on the stake to relieve some of the pressure on his arms, but his bare feet had nothing but splinters to use as leverage, so he kept slumping down.

A beautiful, copper-skinned young man with angry dark eyes bent down before him and touched a flaming torch to the hay and sticks and brambles piled—like a colossal bird's nest—about his feet.

The fire caught quickly.

Sebastian coughed, and his eyes stung. *I'll burn alive!*

Sebastian began struggling crazily against the bindings. He pulled and twisted and writhed and bent and swore as the flames roasted his feet, and the firelight flickered upon the pie-shaped, eyeless faces of the villagers ringing him.

"We beseech You to make powerless," the young executioner began chanting as he rubbed himself while gyrating provocatively, "banish, and drive out every diabolic power, presence, and machination; every evil influence, malefice, or evil eye and all evil actions aimed against your servant…" He pulled off his robe over his head, and the flames highlighted the tightly drawn muscles of his dancing, naked form. "We beseech You to make powerless, banish, and drive out every diabolic power, presence, and machination; every evil influence, malefice, or evil eye and all evil actions aimed against your servant…"

As the young man became more and more aroused, the flames grew. And as Sebastian's own robe caught fire, his futile dream screams were muffled behind sleep-sealed lips.

The vision faded as another thunder rumble drew him into consciousness.

Sebastian glanced furtively around the darkened room, momentarily forgetting where he was until spying the glowing yardstick of light visible along the base of the closed door.

He twisted the switch on the reading light next to the bed and grabbed his Rolex from the top of the nightstand. It was nearly seven.

Sebastian went into the bathroom and splashed some cold water onto his face, then ran a towel over his head. As he caught his reflection in the medicine cabinet mirror, he became alarmed at the sallow skin and anxious expression of the young man looking back at him.

This is wrecking me.

Quickly, he brushed his teeth and changed out of his sweaty T-shirt.

Some staccato panting caught his ear, so he followed the sound across the room and saw Maxi poised in front of the closed door with his head twisted back toward Sebastian, his tiny black eyes pleading.

"No worries, little guy." Sebastian crossed the room and reached for the doorknob. "Go find your mommies."

Once the door was opened, Maxi launched out of the room like a racehorse through the starting gate. Moments later, Sebastian caught up with him in the dining room, where the ladies were just sitting down to dinner.

"I'm glad that God's little alarm clock woke you," Tess told him. "We were just about to break down the door."

Sebastian pulled out a chair, sat, and rubbed his hands over his face.

Let it go. It was just a dream.

He looked from one lady to the other. "I haven't heard thunder like that since I was a kid," he said, feigning cheer.

"There's a cross-current out there"—Tess pointed at the sliding glass doors—"where the Alaskan air currents clash with the subtropical moisture coming up from Hawaii; it can make for some *very* dramatic storms. Some nights the rain comes down on our poor old roof like a hail of billiard balls."

"And how is the roof?" Sebastian asked. "Is the patchwork holding up?"

"So far, so good," Tess replied, with a grateful smile. "I think you've found yourself a new line of work."

"Now, whom did you say you'll be visiting in Sausalito?" Libby asked. Tess, meanwhile, began ladling servings of lumpy, steaming stew into bowls.

"My buddy Coby lives in an old church rectory up on the hill there," Sebastian said, opening his napkin onto his lap. "It's gated, it's got cameras, and it's really secure, so I don't have to worry about anyone spying on me." He blew on the steaming spoon in his hand and took a bite of stew: it was salty, creamy, and full of vegetables and chewy dumplings. *Mmmm.*

"So what's your plan?" Tess handed Sebastian the basket of sourdough bread. "Are you leaving your ministry altogether?"

"I never said I was thinking about *that*," he lied, taking the basket. "Why?"

"Because we're doubtful," Libby chimed in, "that someone who's just out for some rest and relaxation would be taking such a trip as this—*alone.*"

"Like I said before, I just wanted to start making my own decisions about where my life's going. Plus, I needed some space from my mother."

"Bullshit," Tess remarked coolly, then took a sip of her pinot noir.

He glared angrily at her, but the gaze returned to him was impassive. *Knowing.*

"People don't run away unless something bad happens," Libby told him in her best therapist's voice. "Usually there's an event that causes psychic pain, which results in an escape attempt."

"In other words," added Tess, "smart kids run away after Dad's beaten them up one too many times, and the not-so-smart ones think Dad's gonna change. And you look pretty smart to me."

Sebastian sighed loudly. "I've got this crazy Christian extremist group after me. They think I'm the new Satan, and they've been threatening me, so I'm trying to throw them off my track. That's it."

Tess nodded, her eyebrows raised. "That might explain some of it."

"But not all," Libby added. "Every time I've seen a client in physical danger, the last thing they'd do is leave the safety of their home environment—that is, unless the threat is coming from *within* the home."

"In my case," Sebastian told her flatly, "it isn't."

"I believe Libby's right, as usual," Tess agreed. "So what else is there that you're running from?"

Sebastian looked at each of the ladies and saw genuine concern reflected back at him. Could he trust them? *What the hell.* "Please don't tell anyone about this."

"Of course not," Tess and Libby both said in unison.

He looked from Libby to Tess and from Tess to Libby. "We didn't know his parents would react that way," he began. "If I'd known that, I never would've said what I did."

"Who?" Tess asked.

"What did you say?" asked Libby.

Sebastian paused, trying to figure out where to start. "Luke," he said at last. "He was this little bald ten-year-old kid with leukemia, but he looked like he was only six or seven. He'd had it for years, and his body hadn't grown out of how he looked when the disease hit him. And by the time his parents saw me, he was getting worse by the day…so they came to me for help."

"Don't tell me you did your best to 'heal' him," Tess interjected, "and his parents stopped treatment and he died."

"No," Sebastian shook his head emphatically. "I would've never done that. But I could see that his chances for recovery were nonexistent, so I told Luke and his parents that I could see how the New God was already waiting for him, and there would be great rejoicing in the next world upon Luke's release from this life. I also told him that his grandparents couldn't wait to see him, and they were very proud of how brave he'd been, and they missed him very much."

"What's so bad about that?" Tess asked.

Sebastian squinted hard, glancing up at the ceiling. "His parents were new to my ministry, and they assumed what I told them was the absolute truth…only this time I was kind of making it up, because more than anything I just felt really bad for them and wanted to make them feel better. But I guess I went too far when I picked up on Luke's mom's memories and described his 'Nonie and Papa,' right down to his grandfather's old black wool suit and his grandmother's favorite head scarf—it was orange, with yellow and red paisleys. I knew this because Luke's mom recalled these details from her own parents' funerals—her mental projections were amazingly clear, like no one else's I've ever come across."

"Uh-oh," Tess muttered.

"So what happened?" Libby asked, taking a sip of her wine.

"I...I can't even tell you," Sebastian said, looking down at his bowl of stew. "But please know that I was just trying to make that poor little kid feel better, and when I told them all what I did, you should've seen the look on Luke's face—on his parents' faces. They all looked so relieved, so damn happy, like I'd cured the cancer myself. They all started crying and bawling their eyes out. So how was I supposed to know they'd do what they did the next day?"

Tess started to say something, and Libby put her hand on her wrist.

"You don't have to tell us," Libby told Sebastian.

"Yes, he does," countered Tess.

"His father." Sebastian looked up at them, his eyes misting. "His father *killed* him. Shot him point-blank in the back with a shotgun. Then he turned the gun on his wife, then himself. All three of them were found in the back yard by the fence—he didn't want to mess up anything in the house, because..." He stopped.

"Because why?" Tess asked softly.

"Because he'd willed the house to my mother and me, as a 'thank you' for everything I'd done."

"Christ Almighty," Tess said under her breath, and then she knocked back more of her wine.

"Now I understand why you'd want to get out of this business," Libby told him. "That's a *terrible* burden for you to carry."

Sebastian hung his head and squeezed away tears. "How was I supposed to know he'd do that? I was just trying to help *those less fortunate*, like my ministry says we should."

"People do strange things when confronted with their own mortality," Tess told him. "And sometimes they do even stranger things when it's the mortality of someone they love."

"But Tess," Sebastian protested, "you'd never, *ever* do something like that to Libby—" He caught himself.

They saw the knowledge in his eyes.

"You can't possibly know," Tess whispered, eyes wide.

"I'm sorry." More tears spilled from Sebastian's eyes. "I can't filter the information I get. Sometimes it's like…like changing TV channels and running across a story on Darfur."

"Hopefully my *story,* or whatever you saw of it, isn't quite so dire," Libby snapped.

"And…it's not," he lied, sniffling. "I just don't want you thinking I was consciously reading or spying on your thoughts. I can't help it." He shook his head. "Really, I can't."

Glances jumped and crisscrossed around the table.

"It's all right." Tess patted his wrist. "We understand."

"What are your mother's feelings about that poor family?" asked Libby.

Sebastian wiped his nose with his napkin. "She said Luke was going to die anyway."

"Now *that's* a humanitarian!" Tess exclaimed, her face red. "I wouldn't be surprised if she sold the father the gun—at a profit!"

"Actually, Kitty was upset at first, too," Sebastian told her. "But it seemed like she got over it pretty fast. In fact, I talked to her this afternoon, and now she's only worried about the lawsuit

Luke's relatives have filed against us—and she's really pissed at me because I'm not coming home tomorrow for the deposition."

Tess skidded her chair abruptly away from the table. "I need to blow off some steam," she announced, standing up, "so I'm taking Maxi on his walk, and I don't care if there's a blasted hurricane forecasted." She gathered her empty bowl and her flatware. "If I'm not back in an hour, call the Coast Guard." She marched out of the dining room, with Maxi scampering happily behind.

The remaining pair poked at their meals absently.

"You'll forgive her for being so passionate," Libby murmured at last. "The subject of life-threatening illnesses is rather a sore spot for us these days."

"I can imagine. How're you dealing with all this?"

"What can I say?" Libby folded her napkin neatly beside her bowl. "Living with cancer is like always waiting for the other shoe to drop, but no one's told you that the guy upstairs only has one leg. I was supposed to be dead twelve years ago, so every day's been a gift...or at least a tightly wrapped box with something secret inside." She chuckled thoughtfully. "And because we've lost so many close friends over the years, our emotions are thick as shoe leather; I'm afraid that handling grief is something we're quite used to." She paused. "But most of all, I worry about how Tess will handle all this when I'm gone. We've been together thirty-three years, you know—so you're not the only one around here who can read minds." She took a deep breath, looking out beyond the darkened windows. "I've brought her breakfast in bed all those years, even when I was angry with her and didn't want to. Then each night I had a glass of wine waiting for her when she came home from work. I'd wait until I heard the garage door opening, and only then would I uncork the bottle." Libby turned to him. "Who's going to do those things for her when I'm gone?

I *know* her, and every time she has to put a single slice of bread in that damned toaster or dig the corkscrew out of the drawer, she's going to grieve. *Silently*. And the fact that I'm not going to be around, for the very first time, to help her through that grief is almost more than I can bear." Libby's eyes welled up, and she shook her head. "More than anything I don't want her to be alone, to be lonely. I'd be *terribly* disappointed if she didn't find someone else to share her life with." Libby drifted in thought for a few moments and then leveled an intense stare at Sebastian. "Could you?" she asked him at last, her voice nearly inaudible. "Would you? Please?"

Sebastian reflected the intensity of her stare back at her. "You want me to...?"

"You have already." Libby gave her petite shoulders a shrug. "What's a little more?"

"Are you sure you want this?"

Libby smiled.

"I'll try," he said, "but I can't promise you anything. It's one thing for me to be able to see the past, because what's happened has happened, but the future still has so many variables. Nothing's for sure."

Libby dipped her eyes, nodding. "I understand completely. But even I've had premonitions that've come true. Won't you please just try?"

The pain and longing in Libby's gaze touched him. "I'll try."

He tilted his head back and closed his eyes.

Sebastian pulled in a deep breath through his nostrils—held it—and then blew it out through his mouth. He repeated this over and over until his hands buzzed and he felt a sense of weightlessness. Then the sounds of the waves, and the rain drumming on the rooftop, and even Libby's breathing faded away...and he got a flash of Tess and another woman…a nobly-featured, thin woman with short, wavy gray hair. They were seated together in a sidewalk café…in a bustling city—New York. The pair was engaged in brisk conversation, and their happy smiles and glittering eyes told him they truly enjoyed each other's company.

Then he heard Tess mention to the woman the significance of the date.

"One year," Sebastian muttered—eyes still closed. "She'll be alone for exactly one year, and then they'll find each other."

Sebastian opened his eyes and looked at Libby, and he saw she had tears sparkling on her cheeks behind her glasses. "That's such a relief," she told him with a breaking voice as she dabbed at her face with a napkin. "And seeing as I'm Jewish, it's only proper that she waited until my matzevah was unveiled"—she chuckled ironically—"but not a day before."

"Matzevah?" he asked.

"My headstone. It's our custom to wait a year for its unveiling; it signals the official end of the mourning period."

"One year, and not a day before," Sebastian repeated, smiling back at her.

"How about some dessert?" Libby asked him, regaining her composure.

Sebastian pushed back his chair and stood. "I'll get it."

CHAPTER 21

Friday Morning

The brilliant post-storm sunrise pried open Sebastian's eyelids with the force of a bottle opener. He stretched his arms over his head and yawned, while Maxi—on the foot of the bed—also stretched his paws forward, with his elbow joints rigid and his legs momentarily quaking.

Sebastian got out of bed, slipped on his boxers, and stood at the window scanning the panorama. The booming waves from last night's storm had vanished, so now the inlet was placid as a mountain lake; sunlight glinted everywhere, as if each surface— wood, rock, leaf, and even the sand—had been freshly scrubbed, while overhead only a few wispy white clouds interrupted the expansive smoothness of the Crayola-blue sky.

After showering and dressing, Sebastian found the ladies outside under a pergola adjoining the beginning of what was left of the wharf; Libby was scribbling on a yellow legal pad, her legs propped up on one of the unused patio chairs and covered by a thick quilt, while Tess sat next to her engrossed in the same thick paperback she'd been reading since Sebastian's arrival, and which she now appeared close to finishing.

As he approached, they both lifted their eyes to him.

"Sleep well?" Tess asked.

"Yeah. There's something about the air here that's really restful. I haven't slept that good in a long time—and thank God no nightmares this time."

"You have nightmares?" Tess asked.

Libby turned to Tess. "How can he *not* have nightmares?" Then she patted the empty chair next to her. "Please, dear, have a seat. Coffee?"

"Sure." Sebastian sat, and Tess poured him a mug from a stout green thermos.

"We'll get our proper breakfasts going in a moment, unless you're starving now," said Tess.

"Actually, I'm not really hungry, and I need to get on the road soon." Sebastian looked over at the novel Tess had been reading and tried to make out the title. "What's that book about?"

"It's the poignant tale of a former Marine who's secretly in love with his ex-lover's grown son," she replied. "The author is an old friend."

"Was that the Monette guy?"

"Fortunately, this man's alive and well—otherwise we'd have to build another suite, to be named after him."

"Is the story any good?"

Tess put down the book and looked at Sebastian. "Well, let's just say that I more than like it a lot."

"I don't care for the way he draws his characters," said Libby. "They're always so maudlin."

"So it really is Friday already," Tess remarked. "We're sorry to see you go."

Sebastian sipped his coffee. "I'd like to stay here longer, too. But I think some time in the city will be good—especially if I don't get recognized, thanks to my new haircut."

"You could still go ahead and dye it black," Tess suggested, "but then people might mistake you for Elvis—instead of James Dean."

"Who *was* James Dean?" Sebastian asked. "I saw his name out on that highway I took to get here."

"He was an extremely talented, handsome young actor who died in a car crash on that highway back in the 1950s," Tess replied. "He was only twenty-five."

"Twenty-four," Libby corrected. "Oh, and before I forget, would you at least take a few cranberry muffins with you? Tess made them this morning, and I'm afraid they'll get stale before we can finish them."

"I'd like that." Sebastian smiled. "It'll remind me of being here."

Tess began refilling her own mug. "Well, we're not going anywhere, so if you need a place to rest on your way back, you know where to find us. That is, if you decide to head back this way."

"And speaking of," Libby interjected, "have you made any decisions yet about your mother and your ministry?"

"I *think* I'm getting closer. But I need to talk to an attorney—I mean, one that isn't paid for by Kitty. And I've got to make a decision about getting back to LA for that deposition."

"I'm certain you'll come to the right decision," said Tess. "And in the meantime, give us a call if there's anything on your mind; Libby's not bogged down with any bothersome clients at the moment, so aside from the book she's threatening to write, she's got plenty of time on her hands."

They momentarily glanced away from one another as Tess's words ricocheted.

"I'll remember that," Sebastian blithely replied.

"And speaking of time," Libby began, "there's one more question I've been meaning to ask you. Because each religion attempts to answer the big question of what happens to our spirits when we die, what does your philosophy, or at least your intuition, suggest?"

Sebastian hesitated and then took another sip from his coffee mug, as if divining an answer from the shot of caffeine. "Our official teaching, and you'll find this on my website, supports reincarnation—which is why caring for the planet right now means so much. But," he said softly, "whenever I've tried to actually go there in my meditations, I've run into a wall." He looked at Libby, then at Tess, then back at Libby again. "I'm not saying that reincarnation isn't what happens, because to me having past and future existences here makes sense—and there seems to be actual proof that reincarnation does exist. But what my intuition tells me is there's *something* after this, *something good*, but I can't tell you, at least right now, what it is."

He smiled apologetically at each of the ladies.

"I can live with that," Tess said at last.

"So can I," echoed Libby.

Tess got up from her chair. "I'll get you those muffins."

Sebastian and Libby watched Tess disappear inside the house.

"You've helped us so much," Libby told him. "And here I am the therapist. I wish there was something I could do for you."

Sebastian turned to her. "Actually…do you know anything about controlling your thoughts?"

"What do you mean?"

"Sometimes I get too much information, just like I saw you and Tess in that office," Sebastian replied. "I get thoughts…and sensations that really shake me sometimes—and I don't know what to do."

"Are these sensations"—Libby adjusted the quilt to better cover her legs—"anything you have control over? What I mean is, do you encourage them in any way?"

"I don't know where they come from," he replied, "and I can't predict when they'll hit me."

Libby sighed thoughtfully. "I don't know anything about telepathy, my dear. But I'm pretty familiar with the human psyche, and I can tell you what's gotten Tess and me through this whole cancer business."

"What?"

"Hope," Libby stated. "Hope and denial."

"Denial?"

"When there's no reasonable amount of hope to hold onto anymore, denial is still there as hope's dreary sister. And if you're facing anything like Tess and I have faced together, you construct a *wall* in your head—an impenetrable barrier between your consciousness and that which you fear most," Libby explained. "*Denial* is what we therapists work hardest to overcome, but sometimes, when all else fails, it's all one really needs to survive."

Sebastian considered her words. "I'm still not sure what you mean."

Libby sipped from her coffee cup and winced. "Cold," she said. Then she looked up at Sebastian. "I would imagine that when these unusual sensations come, if you try your best to concentrate on something else—*something nice*—you'll be just fine. Do you think you could try that?"

"Sure." Sebastian shrugged. "But is it really that easy?"

"It's never easy." Libby laughed while clinking her cup with is. "But it works."

CHAPTER 22

The autumn morning was brisk and clear, so Sebastian sped north from the inn at a jubilant pace—sunroof yawning and guzzling wind—with his iPod wailing and booming through the Cayenne's theater-worthy sound system.

He had never taken the coastal route up to San Francisco, so he was dazzled by the picturesque landscape. In some areas, the old shoelace of a road he was traveling knotted and squiggled as it tied together miles of steep, craggy foothills; then moments later, he'd be squinting through his windscreen at sunblazened knolls that slid gently off the road down into a tranquil, turquoise cove. At one point, he passed by a pasture that was home to a herd of lazy brown cows; later he drove through fog so heavy it cascaded upon the road like snowdrifts, obscuring his view around one curve, but vanishing just in time for the next.

Then after driving over the dizzying majesty of Bixby Bridge, Sebastian spotted a sign for a turnout. Because he felt hungry, he decided to pull off the road to eat one of Tess's muffins.

He wheeled the big vehicle over to the shoulder, set the brake, and shut off the motor. Then he grabbed the Ziploc bag of muffins and his bottled water, and after looking both ways, he trotted across the road to take in the seaside splendor.

On the steep hillsides beneath the road grew twisted pines that resembled giant broccoli stalks; below these the ocean splashed and tilted at the shore like a tremendous, hastily carried bowl of water. Emerald waves crashed onto jagged rocks, and mists steamed upward from the bases of the dark cliffs. The landscape was wild and windswept and ruggedly beautiful—yet peaceful. He began to relax...until his worries started tapping him on the shoulder again.

Then he remembered Libby's words: "You construct a wall in your head—an impenetrable barrier between your consciousness and that which you fear most...if you try your best to concentrate on something else—something nice—you'll be just fine."

Sebastian spotted a generous boulder that would make a nice perch, so he strolled over to it and sat. Then he cracked the cap on his water, pulled out a muffin from the plastic bag, and bit into the moist cake. The tart sweetness of the cranberries bloomed in his mouth.

If only every day could be like this.

And then he realized that each day could be.

Being here made him realize that his life and this road trip were one and the same: behind him were the years he'd already lived, like the highway he had just traveled, and there were miles of asphalt and decades still before him—but the slightest error might send him tumbling into oblivion.

But of which oblivion was he most frightened? Death? Loneliness? Failure? Poverty?

There was so much of his life that he truly enjoyed, and some of it he actually treasured. So why should he throw it all away and start over?

It wasn't just Luke—he knew that. Just as it wasn't the Christian militants.

It was Kitty and her insatiable nature.

"This penthouse isn't big enough," she'd announced to him one afternoon. "But there's one for sale three buildings down that has a library *and* its own elevator. You'd like that, wouldn't you?" Or: "I can't believe we still haven't heard from Larry King. He's going to retire soon, and if we don't get on that show now we never will." And finally: "Our stocks aren't performing nearly as well as I thought they would. God *damn* this fucking economy! We'll need to do twice as many shows per month if we want to reach the financial goals I set for us at the beginning of the year." And through it all, Sebastian had been a willing accomplice because he wanted to please her and wanted her to be happy.

But after Luke, something in him changed. *Snapped.*

The incident reminded Sebastian of the time he was with his school friend, David. They'd been taking turns practicing with David's BB gun in David's back yard. "I hit 'em all!" David exclaimed as the little pyramid of 7-Up cans tumbled onto the grass. "Here. See if you can hit that telephone pole." He handed the gun to Sebastian.

Sebastian held the gun up to his face, squeezed an eye shut, looked through the sight, and pulled the trigger. They both heard the BB strike the wood. "Ha! I did it!"

"That was too easy," David challenged. "I'll bet you can't hit that bird up there."

Sebastian looked up and spotted the snow white dove sitting peacefully on a telephone wire, but he did not want to hurt it. He put the gun up to his face again, but purposely aimed to the bird's side.

He fired and missed.

"I knew you couldn't hit it," David laughed. "Here. Let me try." He grabbed for the gun.

Instead of handing it over, Sebastian held it up, aimed, and fired again.

The thud of impact with the dove's body was sickening.

Shocked by the consequence of their actions, both boys watched in silence as the bird fluttered haphazardly down behind the fence into the neighbor's yard. Then Sebastian ran to that fence, his mind full of questions. Was it suffering? Had it died? Had a cat gotten it? Was it stunned for a bit, but then regained its senses and flew away? He also wondered, *Why did I just do that?*

He never got any answers. He only remembered the sound of the projectile hitting the poor creature, and how the echo of that sound in his head had nearly made him vomit—and could still, even to this day.

And this was exactly how Sebastian felt about Luke: instead of having the peaceful death that God and medicinal opiates could offer him, he'd died of bird shot mixed with gunpowder tearing through his flesh and bones and internal organs.

Because of me. And because I listened to Kitty.

Sebastian hung his head.

And he realized that this game his mother was playing wasn't just for money, it was for power—power that he did not want.

Yes, Sebastian truly believed he was the next coming of man.

But what did that really mean?

Did it mean he needed to go out and spread the messages Kitty allegedly received in meditation, in order to pad her already large fortune? Or did it mean he should spend his time screwing as many girls as possible to spread his "amazing DNA" throughout the population?

Guess I'll figure it out eventually.

Time to get going.

He stood and cast a last glance at the watery panorama: at the lumpy rocks, like giant biscuits floating in the bay, and at the sunlit kelp blades that sparkled, sequin-like, in the water.

At last ready to continue his journey, he left the remaining muffin pieces on a fallen tree as a gift for some wayward birds— and as penance for harming that innocent dove. Then he trotted back across the street and unlocked his car door.

Moments later, he was curling northward on the road thinking, *At least now I'll get some quiet time up at Coby's.*

CHAPTER 23

How can he do this to me?

Upon rising late in the morning—due to yet another night of sheet-tangling insomnia—Kitty had checked her laptop to ascertain Sebastian's location via his iPhone, and she'd discovered that instead of driving home he was traveling north from Big Sur and was even now heading past Santa Cruz into Santa Clara toward (she assumed) San Francisco. In addition, she found that he hadn't bothered to return either of her e-mails, just as he had ignored both the pleading voicemails and text messages she had sent last night before going to bed.

Clearly, he had no intention of showing up at Larry's offices today to sit for his deposition, and he had even less regard for dumping everything on her.

Shit!

She lit her first cigarette of the morning and called Larry. "He's not coming home today," she told him. "What should I do?"

"Do everything you can to get him down here," Larry replied, his words clipped and urgent. "By the way, I was up most of the night going over your website looking for psychologically coercive language."

"Did you find anything?"

"Of course! You need to be more careful about what you put out there, Kitty. I'm surprised this sort of thing hasn't happened before."

"Find me a church that doesn't push their members' crazy buttons"—she took a heavy drag off her cigarette—"and I'll show you a bankrupt cult."

"We'll talk about that later. You should know that their attorneys called a meeting for tomorrow afternoon at two. You'll need to be there, with or without your darling son."

"But Sebastian's the one who spent time with that poor sick child and his parents, Larry. I have no idea what he told them," she lied. "Isn't there some sort of confidentiality clause between priests and parishioners that you could build our defense on?"

Larry laughed. "I don't think now's the time to look to the Catholic Church for legal precedents. This looks really bad, Kitty. It looks like he's purposely avoiding the deposition because he's afraid to incriminate himself."

Kitty sighed. "I'll do what I can to get him here. And you can count on me to be there tomorrow for the depo. See you then."

She ended the call. *Is it too early for a martini?*

She badly needed a diversion to lift her spirits, so she logged into her credit card and PayPal accounts to check the receipts from the previous day's Internet traffic.

Looking at the numbers caused a smile to lift her scowl. Since that *Vanity Fair* article had been published, the numbers in her already ample bank accounts had been building steadily.

Next, Kitty checked her other e-mails to see what her assistant had forwarded her from Sebastian's social networking pages. She scanned through the usual pleas for help...and proposals from obsessed fans...and hateful scriptures from those militant

Christians…but she discovered nothing that required her immediate attention.

Good.

Kitty pulled on her robe and padded down the long hallway from her bedroom, by Sebastian's empty quarters, through the living room, and past the dining room to the kitchen for some coffee. She had just placed her creamy, steaming mug atop the oval Saarinen dining table, sat down, and lit another cigarette when a disturbing thought punched her in the gut: *What if he never comes back?*

A cold realization swept over her.

He's all I have. And he's left me. What should I do?

She began swiveling nervously in her white tulip chair, like a little girl on a diner's barstool; she sipped her coffee, smoked her cigarettes, swiveled, sipped, smoked…plotted.

Kitty considered what punishments other parents of teenagers might carry out to discourage such defiant behavior. Would they seize his car keys? Slash his curfew? Snatch his cell phone and cut off his allowance? Or would they send him off to some dreadful Mormon boot camp in the barren Utah desert?

Sebastian would only scoff at such punitive measures. In fact, he was so much like her in this regard that restrictions like these would only steel his intentions to abandon her forever.

She needed to lure him back with something he wanted, something lovely and extravagant. But with what might she tempt him that he could not refuse?

A trip to Tahiti or Ibiza, with some fashion models? *Hmmm.* Sebastian would most likely jump at the chance to spend some quality time with those Brazilian twins—a brother and sister— whom everyone had been gawking over at the prêt-à-porter show earlier this month during New York Fashion Week. And Magdaleno, the owner of that big agency in Manhattan, still owed her a huge favor…

But Sebastian needed to be close by, should Larry need him again.

Would moving from the penthouse bring him back? Recently she had suggested trading their condo for a neighboring model that was larger and had its own elevator.

But Sebastian had scoffed at the idea. "These high-rises feel like overpriced prisons," he told her. "Why can't we live in a real house, like real people? I want a yard and a dog, and I'm sick to death of the noise and the concrete and the traffic. I want to hear the ocean and lie in the grass, Kitty. I want to feel *human*."

But that would entail torturous hours with some hateful realtor. And then there'd be those pesky financial statements and cumbersome escrows and all that sorting and packing…

Now what was it he told me he wanted the other day?

Kitty squinted from the mental effort.

Of course!

She popped up from the tulip chair, trotted back into her bedroom, and began tapping away on her laptop.

After a few minutes, she found exactly what she was looking for.

Silver or black? Or how about red? Everyone likes red.

Kitty picked up her phone and called the number on her computer screen.

I can't wait to see the look on his face!

CHAPTER 24

Friday, Noon

Sebastian navigated the crisscrossing freeways leading into San Francisco like a native; the vague signage and unexpected lane changes were mitigated beautifully by "Mary Poppins" and her crisply enunciated instructions.

He had only been to San Francisco on a few occasions, but even the first time he visited, he felt as if he were coming home: the majestic skyline, the silver bay, that surreal orange bridge, and the quirky jumble of architectural styles delighted his eye. And he loved the tempo, the *spirit* of the city, and the way everyone just seemed more evolved than the people in LA because San Franciscans simply dressed better, ate better, and seemed better informed than their sloppy and self-absorbed southern counterparts.

He was glad he'd made the decision to drive up.

Sebastian skirted the center of the metropolis and continued on the 101 north toward Sausalito. Traffic was, of course, mostly bumper-to-bumper, so he kept his right foot light and his stereo loud.

Then, at just a few minutes after noon, he arrived at his quiet destination.

Sausalito had somehow retained its small-town atmosphere, in spite of its proximity to "the City" and its towering edifices, roller-coaster streets, and bustling wharf. This smaller town was composed instead of cheerful little houses planted along hills that rolled down to a sleepy marina, where modest yachts, jaunty sport-fishers, and sailboats with bare masts bobbed peacefully beside a row of stoic houseboats. The two locales reminded Sebastian of that famous statue of Athena he'd learned about in high school: whereas the metropolis of San Francisco was as imposing as the alabaster goddess of wisdom and war herself, Sausalito was tiny Nike, held aloft in Athena's stone hand.

Sebastian motored slowly—after stopping numerous times for street-crossing, zombie-like tourists—past the bustling cafés and T-shirt shops and slick art galleries, until he came upon the steep hill leading to Coby's. He turned up this street, followed it along the hill's twisting ridge, and then stopped in front of a rusty pair of tall, ornate gates that might have once guarded the entrance to a haunted cemetery.

He honked his horn and then flipped off the security camera aimed at his face.

Moments later, the gates began motoring open with a click and a low grind.

Sebastian drove into the center of the flagstone courtyard and stopped. Then he switched off the motor, grabbed his overnight bag from the back seat, and jumped out of the Cayenne. As he was strolling across the courtyard toward the old stone house, the immense wooden front door was thrown open.

"Sebby!" Coby yelled, jogging toward him.

"Hey!" Sebastian grinned at his old pal.

They embraced, with a drumbeat of back thumping.

"What happened to your hair?" Coby asked.

"Yeah, I can't afford to get recognized, but I still wanted to see the sights while I'm here."

Coby scrutinized him. "Not bad. But you should've just buzzed it off. The ladies love that bad boy look."

"I'm not looking for any ladies right now," Sebastian muttered.

"So you finally decided you're gay?" Coby laughed. "I knew once you had a taste of me you'd get turned off to girls." He grabbed at his crotch. "That was one crazy night with those sisters, huh?"

Sebastian laughed. "Sorry, dude, but it'd take more than even that very, *very* fun night to make me forget how much I love women. I'm just not in the market right now, man. *For anyone.* Like I said, I've got some serious shit going on."

"Believe me, I understand." Coby threw an arm around Sebastian's shoulder and began leading him toward the house. "I only got back a couple hours ago. We're about to eat lunch, so you can grab a bite with us—oh, and Ellie's here from LA. Do you remember her?"

Sebastian cracked a smile. "The bitchy blonde with the big mouth?"

"That's her, but she also brought her girlfriend. You'll dig Reed—she's hot as hell and newly single."

As he followed Coby into the home it took Sebastian a few moments for his eyes to adjust to the cave-like darkness. But within moments, he began to make out the details of his surroundings: the interior walls were built from quarry-cut granite, and the floor was overlaid with wide walnut planks, while timbers thick as telephone poles supported a castle-worthy ceiling. From the overhead beams hung twin opera house chandeliers whose crystals glittered opulently, while narrow leaded windows draped in burgundy velvet framed views of the sunny blue bay beyond. In bold contrast to this antique, baronial setting were the spare and modern furnishings: sleek black leather sofas, chairs, and chaises;

chrome-and-glass tables; thick, purple shag rugs; and gloomy, gilt-framed portraits of women and children with exaggerated, staring eyes and smiling—or were they grimacing?—mouths.

"Your dad's a freak," Sebastian said—his voice echoing—as he craned back his neck to take in the decor. "Why would he want to live in a place that looks like the castle of some queer vampire?"

"His new wife just redid it all. She's some big art dealer from New York who weighs about ten pounds and never smiles—she's even got a fake English accent. But it's cool, 'cause they're always traveling, so I get the house to myself."

"What about that new stepsister you told me about?" Sebastian asked. "Any good stories?"

He shook his head and shrugged. "Even though she looks like some chick out of *Playboy*, she's only sixteen—so I got those ideas out of my head real quick." He laughed. "Come on outside."

Sebastian blinked in the brilliant sunshine as they walked out onto the terrace.

"Ellie, say hi," Coby told the young lady with the long platinum hair, who was lounging upon a chaise and studying an Italian *Marie Claire* magazine through oversized sunglasses.

She pushed up her glasses onto her forehead and wrinkled her nose. "What happened to your hair?"

"Nice to see you again too." Sebastian bent down and pecked her on the cheek.

"People will still recognize you," she said, returning her attention to the magazine. "You should just dress in drag." She raised the frosty glass of iced tea to her lips and sipped. "Coby, sweets, will you please ask Reed to take my lunch order?"

"I think she already left," Coby replied.

"Actually, I just got back," sang a voice from inside the house.

Sebastian turned to watch a lithe, mocha-skinned beauty step daintily onto the terrace with three bulky white takeout bags in hand.

"Sebastian Black, may I please introduce Miss Reed Banks," Ellie muttered from behind her magazine.

They shook hands briefly while Reed looked at him, puzzled. "What happened to your hair?"

"I got it cut off," he told her, flashing his most chin-thrusting, charming grin. "I'm traveling incognito. What do you think?"

"It's nice, I guess." Reed turned to Coby. "Um, I just went ahead and picked us up some lunch because I know how grouchy that girl over there gets when the tranquilizer dart wears off." Turning to face Sebastian, she said, "I'm sorry, I didn't know there'd be more than three of us for lunch. We didn't know what time you'd get here."

"We'll just split whatever you brought, silly," Ellie droned. "It's not like you eat more than a few croutons a day, anyway."

Sebastian caught Reed's eye. "I'd be happy to eat whatever you can spare."

Reed looked away. "I'll start doing that…right, um, now." She turned and scampered back into the house.

"You'll have to excuse her," Ellie said to Sebastian, "but she's kind of bashful. Poor thing, she has terrible luck with guys."

"I think she's pretty," Sebastian said. "How old is she?"

"Same as me, twenty-three," Ellie replied. "Now, that shouldn't be a problem, right? I hear you're into older women—and guys… and Chihuahuas…"

"Unlike Coby, who's into sixteen-year-olds," Sebastian laughed.

Ellie threw down her magazine. "That better be a joke."

"So how long are you up here for?" Coby asked.

Sebastian shrugged. "A few days, if it's OK."

"You can stay in any of the bedrooms—even mine." Coby punched him playfully on the shoulder.

"No he can't," shot Ellie.

Sebastian had a thought: "Hey, tomorrow could you guys take me around to some cool neighborhoods? I'm thinking about—"

"My mother's broker," Ellie interrupted, "could show you some great properties."

Sebastian smiled at her. "That'd be great."

"So you're thinking of moving up here, brother?" Coby asked "Why?"

"I'm really overdue for some new surroundings." Sebastian turned to Ellie. "So you still live in Ballena Beach, right?"

"For the moment, yes," Ellie replied wistfully. "But ever since Coby moved here, I've been coming up to do my shopping and eating. I'm so *tired* of LA."

Reed suddenly reappeared carrying plates of food. "But not as *tired* as LA is of you."

"Oh pish," Ellie replied. "What kind of salad are we eating?"

"Cobb, no bacon, balsamic vinaigrette," Reed answered. "And we're all sharing Coby's turkey sub; I cut it into finger sandwiches."

"Thanks for going to the trouble." Sebastian tried smiling at Reed, but her eyes evaded his gaze.

"Hey, Seb! I forgot"—Coby hesitated—"to tell you we're having a few people over tonight."

"Like a few hundred," Ellie muttered.

Sebastian looked to Coby, then to the girls and back. "Are you serious, man? Didn't I mention that I was getting out of LA because I needed to hide out?"

"Told you so," Ellie sang.

"There won't be any press," Coby told him, knowing differently.

"But what about camera phones?" Reed asked. "Anyone can post pictures online from their phones."

Sebastian crossed his arms over his chest. "You didn't tell anyone else I'd be here, did you?"

Coby shrugged. "I planned the party before we talked," he lied. "Then I forgot to tell you about it when you called. Honestly, I didn't think it'd be a big deal—I mean, who has a bad time at a party?"

"The Donner family, for starters," Ellie mumbled into her iced tea.

Sebastian shoved his hands deep into his pockets. "I'll just hide out in the basement."

Coby squinted at Sebastian. "You're not in trouble with the police, are you?"

"I'll just deal," Sebastian stated. "No worries."

"We can hang out in the library," Coby suggested brightly. "Like…it'll be our private suite—VIPs only, velvet ropes and all."

"Oh no we won't," Ellie shot back. "I didn't buy that new Proenza Schouler dress so I could be hidden away like someone's crazy aunt."

"Whatever," Sebastian muttered. "Like I said, I'll just deal."

"Um, here's some salad," Reed said, holding out a plate for Sebastian.

Their eyes met.

"Thanks," he said, taking the plate from her—even though he'd more than lost his appetite.

CHAPTER 25

After lunch Sebastian put his things in one of Coby's spare bedrooms and then lay down to rest. But sleep was elusive, not only because of his swelling nausea, but also because of his obsessive thoughts: *Luke. Christian militants. Kitty. Deposition. My ministry. My future? Libby's cancer. Party tonight. Stupid Coby. Reed?*

God, I feel sick.

He stared at the ceiling, trying not to think. But his thoughts spun like a windmill in a storm. Then after some time his whirling mental blades began to slow as he recalled the last time he'd felt this ill.

It was the night a few months back when he'd met Luke and his parents.

He'd been feeling uneasy about appearing at this particular gathering, which was to be held inside a Veterans of Foreign Wars hall—a miniscule venue compared to where he'd been appearing—on the outskirts of Bakersfield. And he'd only agreed to lead this gathering because Kitty had insisted they make more outreaches to rural communities where the "simpler folks" were becoming more generous with their donations. In addition, Kitty had "dumbed down" Sebastian's usual sermon, and she wanted to see how this new, lighter material might resonate with people who "weren't as sophisticated."

But during the entire drive north from LA, as Kitty drove the Cayenne and Sebastian sat in the passenger seat memorizing his lines, he began feeling ill: equal parts headache and upset stomach. At first he'd thought it was because he was reading in a moving car, but after putting away the paper and opening the window and concentrating on the countryside rumbling by, relief still did not come.

Eventually they arrived at their destination, and the service began.

Sebastian stumbled through his lines, read from *The Book of Holocene*, ran through more of his monologue, and performed a few clairvoyant readings. As he was bringing the service to a close, he became aware of how dissatisfied the crowd was.

But he didn't really care. Something was wrong.

I need to get out of here.

"We'll talk about the service later," Kitty told Sebastian backstage as she followed him into their tiny dressing area. "But in the meantime, there's someone here to meet you. They drove hours to get here. It's a sad case; they're such nice people. And they *adore* you—especially the wife."

"God no, Kitty, not now," Sebastian complained as his nausea threatened to crest. "You know I hate meeting people after the gatherings. I'm gonna hurl, and my head is splitting, and we won't even be home for another two hours."

Kitty stood on tiptoe and reached up to palm his forehead. "No fever," she said. "Anyhow, that service was terrible, so now's your chance to make it up to these people. And when you see this kid, you'll be glad you took the time." Kitty glared at him. "Trust me."

Kitty led Sebastian to the door of his dressing room, where a grim-faced man and a tall blonde woman waited with a bald-headed child in a wheelchair.

"Sebastian, this is Steve and Dawn," Kitty said, smiling brightly. "And this young man is their brave son, Luke."

The psychic pain emanating from Dawn felt like a freight train's horn blast no one could hear—but Sebastian could feel the oscillating waves. So he steeled his posture and aimed a welcoming smile at each of the family members. "It's great meeting you," he said, shaking hands with each. "Let's talk."

If only he'd known.

And now he was having that very same malaise—his head ached like his brain was swelling against his skull, while his stomach felt as if he'd swallowed a butcher's knife.

It must be the party.

Someone's coming to the party.

But who?

And what're they going to do?

———

Kitty began scanning the remaining e-mails her assistant Courtney had forwarded to her. There was one from Larry, asking if Kitty had yet made any progress in luring Sebastian back home; one from Caitlyn DePalma, announcing she was officially terminating their business relationship but keeping her deposit; one from Prada about a sale; a very disturbing message from those Christian militants telling her they knew where Sebastian was holed up (she forwarded this to Agent Singer at the FBI); and finally one from Courtney herself, which was tagged, "You better read this."

She clicked on the message:

Hi Kitty, or Katie,

I don't know if you'll remember me, but we met about twenty years ago at a party in the Valley, at one of those big ranch houses down on Nordhoff Street. I'm pretty tall and had shaggy blond hair then (most of it's gone now, dammit), and I used to surf a lot. Anyhow, we got to know each other real well that night, and I never forgot you. Of course, I'm not hitting on you now, but I did have a question for you, and I know it's crazy, but here goes. Since I read that there is a mystery about who is Sebastian's father, I think it could of been me, because he looks a lot like I did back then and the age is about right.

Kitty gasped. "No no no no no no NO!"
She forced herself to continue reading:

I know this sounds crazy, and I hope you will excuse me if I insulted you. But I know you're that same girl, and I know what we did that night. Please let me know, because if he is, I'd really like to discuss it with you. I'm so sorry to hit you up with this. Your religion sounds amazing, by the way.
—Chuck Niesen

For years, the dread she felt about Chuck finding her and Sebastian grew with each event that thrust them into the public spotlight, but she'd assuaged her fears of discovery by altering her name. And she'd figured that after almost two decades, the chance of him discovering her and her son was slim to none.

But evidently not slim enough.

What am I gonna do? Ignore him? Deny it? Meet with the jerk and pay him off?

She jumped up from her desk and found her pack of cigarettes, lit one, burnt half of it away with three deep inhalations, and then sat back at her computer to tap a speedy reply:

Dear Mr. Niesen,

Thank you for your message. Unfortunately, I have no idea who you are or what you are talking about, and I suspect you have me confused with someone else. I wish you the very best in your quest to find this other woman, and I would encourage you to explore our website, which will introduce you to Sebastian's teachings. I would also suggest you pick up a copy of Sebastian's New York Times best seller, The Book of Holocene (available at Amazon.com), so you will be able to make an educated decision about joining our fold. Again, thank you for your interest!

Best,

Ms. Kitty Black

She sent the message, forwarded a copy of the e-mail to Courtney with explicit instructions to notify her immediately of any further messages from the man, and then sat back in her chair and groaned.

———

On the other side of town, Chuck Niesen received his disappointing reply from Kitty, which he immediately shared with Hank.

"Of course she's gonna say that," Hank told Chuck. "What did you expect? A tearful reunion at the train station?"

"So what do I do now?" Chuck asked, reaching for his nearly empty cigarette pack.

"Well, you know there's hope," Hank told him.

"How?"

"She signed it 'Ms.' instead of 'Mrs.'," Hank said, "and we all know that means she's in the market."

Chuck laughed. "Yeah, right. This chick's in *Vanity Fair*, so she's, you know, really in the market for a bald, broken-down meth addict like me."

Hank shrugged. "I've seen stranger things."

Chuck shook his head. "Anyhow, I'm not really interested in her as much as seeing if her son's my kid—and the only way I'll find that out is by meeting with her."

"Why with her?" Hank asked. "Why not with the kid?"

"What do you mean?"

"Find out where he is and go talk to him. Or better yet, find out what his e-mail is and arrange a meeting. That way you won't come off as some psycho stalker that's trying to get his old girl-friend back."

Chuck squinted at Hank. "Yeah, I could see that working. I mean, all I can do is try, right?" He shook his last two cigarettes out of its pack, offered one to Hank, and placed the other between his lips.

Hank slapped Chuck's shoulder as his other hand sparked his disposable lighter. "That's all you can do."

After dinner Chuck waited for his half-hour turn at the computer. When his time came he first scanned the old photo of himself on the combination scanner and copier, and then he made his slow fingers poke the keyboard while searching through the Evo-love website in search of some way to get his message directly to the young man.

With only a few minutes remaining on his computer time, he found a prompt with the message, "*Give Sebastian Black Your*

Nick Nolan

Feedback! Tell Him What You Think Needs to Be Changed in Our World!"

Chuck clicked on the prompt and began carefully composing his letter into the field:

Dear Sebastian Black,

I can imagine that you get lots of weird letters from weird people because of your work, and you probably don't answer them. I hope you will think about answering this one, even though it might be the weirdest one you ever got. But anyways, here goes.

I think very strongly that I might be your father. I met your mom at a party almost 20 years ago, and we spent the night together. We got pretty messed up, so I don't remember a whole lot about the night, but I'm very sure about one thing that happened that night between your mom and me. But aside from that, I think I'm your dad because of the way you look and how you look like me, or how I did look back then before I lost my hair like yours (blond). Plus your tall and so am I, and I'm still pretty lean like you are.

Anyhow, I know this sounds crazy but I'd really like to meet up with you and talk with you. I'm attaching a picture of myself so maybe you can see the resemblance, even though I look old for my age, which is 40. I should tell you that I look old because I had a problem with coke, then meth, and anything else I could get up my nose without sneezing it out. But I'm sober now and have been sixteen and a half months now, and live in a sober living house with some other guys. So I know I'm not at all the kind of guy you want for a father and I understand, but if you are my son then I think we should at least meet for once, you know?

I wrote to your mom tonight and she said she doesn't know me or remember me, but like I said she was pretty messed up that night and I don't blame her, we were doing shots of schnapps and other stuff and that's about all I can remember. Anyways, like I said I think we should at least meet once, if it's OK with you. You can email me back at this address.
Sincerely,
Chuck Niesen

Chuck had to trade an unopened cigarette pack to LeBron, whose turn at the computer he'd usurped because he needed to read over the message three, then four, then five times before sending it with the photo. But Chuck felt the loss of the cigarettes was worth the sacrifice because having a kid was something he'd never even allowed himself to dream about—and the thought that this young, good-looking, rich celebrity could be his own spawn made him lightheaded.

—

Moments later, across the city, Kitty opened her laptop with the hope of discovering that Sebastian had somehow regained his senses and was on his way home.

She scanned her inbox for a message from her son and almost broke into tears after discovering there was none. So she checked Sebastian's location once more and saw that he was still in Sausalito, exactly where those Christian maniacs said he was.

My world is collapsing!

But when she saw the new e-mail from Chuck, which had been promptly forwarded by Courtney to her current mailbox, her despair switched to fury.

Why doesn't he leave me alone? Am I going to need another restraining order? Who can I get to make this man disappear?

Kitty began reading the message Chuck had so carefully written to Sebastian, and she was about to delete it mid-paragraph when she spotted his reference to the photo.

She clicked on the attachment, and the twenty years between that night and this evening vanished...along with any doubt that Sebastian's father had finally come forward.

A dozen notions crowded her mind until one very clear impulse elbowed its way to the front: *This man needs to vanish. Forever.*

CHAPTER 26

Friday Evening

"How're you feeling?" Ellie asked Reed.

"Better, I guess."

"So…what do you think of him?"

Reed pretended to check her nails. "I've always loathed Coby."

"I'm not talking about Coby."

Reed glared at Ellie. "I know you're not talking about Coby."

Ellie narrowed her eyes at Reed. "Do you really *loathe* him?"

"Joking." Reed huffed and rolled her eyes. "Have you forgotten our conversation this afternoon when I told you Sebastian's too young, he's full of himself, and he's probably slept with more people than I have friends on Facebook? Talk about a horny teenager! I hope he's been safe."

"Missy," Ellie began, "I saw how you were around him: picking at your food, giggling at his nap-inducing story about Laura Bush, jumping up to get mustard for his sandwich. *You've got a thing for him.* And how many times in your life do you think you'll have another chance to get close to someone as rich and gorgeous as Sebastian?"

Reed smiled. "Look, I know you mean well. But I couldn't care less about him being rich; I wouldn't even care if he was some kind of royalty. Remember, I only date losers like Brandon—or at least I did until he dumped me—"

"Which is exactly why you need a diversion," Ellie interrupted. "I'm not saying marry this guy, but at least you could flirt with him. It's that old thing about falling off a horse."

Reed looked confused. "Flirting is as easy as falling off a horse?"

"*No*, you're thinking of falling off a log. If you fall off a horse, you're supposed to get right back on or you'll be too scared to ever ride one again."

"I'd rather fall off a log." Reed glared at her, and then her features softened. "I know what you're saying is probably true, but if I'm not going to fall into my *old habits*, I'll need to proceed slowly. Carefully. " She checked her reflection in the gilded pier mirror angled in the corner. "I hate what I'm wearing, by the way."

"Of course you should take things at your own pace," Ellie agreed. "I just think you should leave yourself open to possibilities—and what you're wearing is fine, though you do need some real shoes."

"What's wrong with these sandals?" Reed looked down while twisting and pointing her feet. "You made me buy them today!"

"He's super tall, so why wouldn't you wear heels?"

"I didn't bring any. Guess I keep forgetting it's not summer anymore."

"Wear mine." Ellie kicked off her black pumps, one after the other.

"They're probably a size too small," Reed protested.

"So you'll sit down a lot."

Reed picked up the shoes. "Ellie, why do you think Sebastian's so paranoid about being seen in public?"

"I think it's just that typical celebrity whining," Ellie began, with a dismissive wave of her hand. "You know, *Poor me, I just hate it when I don't get any privacy*, and then they can't stand it if they go somewhere and everyone's not gawking. Barf."

"Well, to me he looked really worried when Coby mentioned the party. And as some big religious figure, can you imagine the psychos who're after him? In that case, he'd *better* be telepathic." She turned to Ellie, a worried look on her face. "Do you think he can tell what I'm thinking about him?"

"You mean about him being *too young and self-absorbed*?"

"You know what I mean," Reed said sharply. "He *is* cute."

"I think if you want to know if he can read your mind, why don't you"—she paused—"try picturing the cocktail you want, imagining how it'll feel in your hand and how it'll taste, and then send him to the bar with instructions to bring you back *something nice*."

"He's underage," Reed laughed. "He'll probably bring me back a rum and Coke. Or a bong hit."

"Look—just be yourself and look incredibly hot, like you *always* do."

"Yeah, right." Reed reached down, slid Ellie's pumps on her feet, and stood up. "Ow. These'll never work."

"You'll get used to them," Ellie told her. "Now look," she said, pointing to the mirror. "Isn't that better?"

Reed turned to examine her reflection. "I…guess so. And you're right; the shoes aren't quite so torturous once you've got them on." She tugged on her hem and adjusted her hair. "So, what's going on with you and Coby?"

"Well," Ellie sighed, "you know I'll always love him. I just wish he wasn't so *dopey*. Half the time I know what stupid thing he's about to say before he even opens his mouth."

"If you love the guy," Reed began, "then why do you always talk about him like he's brain damaged?"

"*Because he does dumb things*, Reed. Did I tell you that two days ago, he swore me to secrecy about Sebastian coming here? And then I found out that ten minutes after calling me he texted a thousand different people, telling them Sebastian Black was coming to *his* party. He did that, even though Sebastian told him he was coming up here *specifically* to hide out."

"Why'd he tell everyone?"

"Because he wants to feel like a player," Ellie replied, "and having some big celebrity here does that for him. But now that I'm old enough to start thinking about life after college, I'm worried about spending my life with someone who's got such little common sense—not to mention that if I marry him, I'll cheat my kids out of half their potential IQ." Ellie glanced at her watch. "Things are probably starting. We should make our grand entrance." She stepped to the door and opened it a crack, listening.

A dim murmur and the clink of glasses drifted up from downstairs.

"It's still pretty quiet," Ellie said, "so we should wait another five or ten minutes, and then devastate everyone with our combined lusciousness."

Sebastian was just getting out of the shower when he heard a swell of hubbub and figured the first guests had arrived downstairs, so he toweled himself dry and pulled on his favorite worn-out jeans, his dark brown Cole Haan boots, and a tight black T-shirt.

Should I even go through with this?

He considered the uneasy queasiness he was still feeling.

Maybe it'll be OK.
Then he thought of Reed.
It'll be OK.

—

The party mushroomed quickly.

One moment Sebastian glanced around and saw Coby's guests scattered atop the black leather sofas, chairs, and chaises; then it seemed like only the next time he scanned the room it was standing room only.

With Sebastian Black as the star.

Some revelers avoided him completely while maintaining an empty moat around the chaise in the corner where he and Reed were seated, others shot him sidelong glances spiked with disdain or jealousy, a few of the girls and guys allowed their eyes to advertise their availability and interest, and cell phone cameras captured his likeness whenever their owners thought Sebastian was not paying attention.

Even Reed seemed taken with him. She listened to his stories and replied with thoughtful, sensitive responses; she giggled when offered an anecdote and gave astute commentaries on the few occasions when he'd asked for her opinion about something.

He found Reed exotic and exquisitely beautiful; her mixture of equatorial and European bloodlines gave her an unusually graceful, sophisticated air.

And her body looked to be lingerie-model perfect.

But after the better part of an hour Sebastian felt Reed's attention waning, so he ratcheted up the "celebrity" aspects of his life: he regaled her with stories of meeting the Clintons, working alongside Jimmy Carter during a housing fundraiser, selling out the Staples Center in just under seven hours, and how the island nation of La Serena was about to adopt Evo-love for their country's religion.

But to his puzzlement, the more Sebastian talked about himself, the less interested Reed became; whereas earlier in the evening he'd begun to get *that special feeling* from her, she now seemed bored.

This had never happened to him. *What the hell's going on?*

He did a quick inventory of his fail-safe seduction routine and determined he had omitted nothing.

It can't be me, it has to be her. Maybe she's a lesbian? No, Coby said she'd just gotten dumped by some dude who was cheating on her. That's it! So...maybe it'll do her some good to think someone like me is into her...

While Sebastian refocused on Reed, and the music thumped and the candles quivered and the laughter echoed like a mist rising above the sea of chattering voices, Sebastian's sixth sense—like an invisible military drone—searched the room, the rest of the house, and its surroundings.

The report came back:

Someone's coming.

Sebastian decided to ignore the warning...for the moment. "So what's your plan for after college?" he asked Reed.

Reed smiled warmly at him. "I'd really like to work with either autistic or Down syndrome kids," she said, "and I'm also considering physical therapy with children who've suffered traumatic brain injuries—but with that, there's a lot of school involved; I'd be looking at either a master's degree or a PhD, and those are really expensive." She beamed at him. "So what about you? Are you going to devote the rest of your life to your church?"

Sebastian cracked his neck and shifted in his seat. "Honestly, I really don't know. It seems like right now I'm at a fork in the road, and I'm…trying to avoid a head-on collision."

"Well, what do you *want* to do?"

He shrugged. "The funny thing is I've never really thought about it before now."

"Why not?"

"Mostly because my mother always pushed me to give this mission of ours everything, so there hasn't been time for me to think about what my other options could be. She didn't even let me finish high school, if you can believe it."

"She *made* you drop out?" Reed laughed. "That's a new one. Why don't you go back to school, or take your GED?"

"Because I never thought I'd need a diploma for the kind of work I do. In fact, at one time—" Sebastian's stomach suddenly spasmed as his synapses launched into panic mode.

They're here! He scanned the room wildly, like a mother who's just noticed her toddler's gone missing at a shopping mall.

"What's wrong?!" Reed's faraway voice asked.

The alarm sounded inside him again. He needed to investigate—or hide.

"Um, Reed?" He steadied himself and forced a smile, hoping she couldn't tell how rattled he felt. "Is there, uh, something you want from the bar?"

Reed leaned back against the chaise's slick leather. "I'd love something, but I'm not sure what I want," she answered coyly, picturing a long-stemmed, frosty glass of golden chardonnay. "Could you just see, you know, what looks good?"

"Sure." Sebastian gave her a smile and got up from the sofa. Then he made his way through the crowd as it parted for him, scanning warily from side to side—not knowing what he should be looking for—as he made his way toward the bar.

At last, he reached his destination.

"Two, um…" He looked to see what other guests were drinking. "Two of those things." He pointed.

"Two mojitos?" the goateed, bald guy behind the wet bar asked.

"Yeah. Thanks." Sebastian noticed how worn out the bartender looked, with his cranberry juice–stained white shirt and his loosened black bow tie. He felt for his wallet and drew out a five for a tip.

"Hey, you're that guy, right?" the man asked, using a blunted stick to mash the mint leaves into the bottoms of the glasses. "So what'm I thinking right now?"

Anger. Red hot anger. Glowing anger. Getting closer. "You're, uh, wishing you weren't here."

"Anyone could tell me *that*," replied the man as he filled the glasses with rum.

Sebastian dropped his tip into the jar, snatched the drinks, and went back to find Reed.

She was no longer sitting on the sofa.

His eyes searched the room, but he couldn't spot her.

Maybe she's outside?

He crossed the living room, a glass in each hand, while making his way back through the crowd to the terrace.

At last in the open air, Sebastian trotted across the expansive flagstone walkway toward the balustrade, placed the slightly spilled drinks atop the stone rail, and readied himself to release his stomach's contents into the space below the terrace. Then something told him to look over his shoulder, and that's when he spotted a man arm in arm with a sandy-haired woman poised on the other side of the library's leaded floor-to-ceiling windows; the man wore jeans and a black T-shirt, with a huge camera slung around his neck, while she wore a knee-length, form-fitting sleeveless red dress.

As Sebastian squinted at the pair the man looked him up and down, while the woman glared boldly at him and threw him an alluring smile.

A jolt of recognition slammed him. *It's her!*

Sebastian's purposefully nonchalant gaze scanned beyond the pair, and he turned, casually, to gaze at the moonlit bay below.

But in that act of turning away from the intruding couple, the flesh on his back raised, as if someone were breathing upon his neck.

CHAPTER 27

Friday Night

"Where did you go?" Sebastian asked Reed, in what should not have sounded like an accusatory tone, but did.

"To the bathroom upstairs. And then I had to find Ellie so I could change my shoes." Reed scrutinized his face. *"And what's wrong with you?"*

"I'm sorry, I didn't mean to—uh, it's a long story…but I shouldn't have said it that way." He scanned the crowd for the couple. "Hey, let's go upstairs. OK?"

"Sorry, but"—Reed took a step backward, laughing—"I'm *not* going up there with you. We just met today. Remember?"

"No, no, it's just that there's someone here who's really creeping me out," he explained, "like exactly what I didn't want to happen is happening right now. And I need to feel like I'm safe—as weird as that sounds."

Reed saw from his expression how rattled he was. "OK."

"Oh and"—Sebastian handed her one of the cocktails—"here's your drink."

She looked at the mojito with more than a little disappointment. "Thanks."

"Come on, OK?" Sebastian put his arm around her shoulder and began steering her through the crowd. As the pair threaded their way, he tried not to let the cell phones being raised in their direction bother him.

Reed looked over and caught Ellie's eye, where she stood leaning against the bar talking to a hot-looking guy.

Ellie raised a leering eyebrow at Reed and shimmied her shoulders.

Reed shot her a satisfied smile.

Sebastian led Reed up to the top of the stairs and down the hallway into the bedroom he was staying in. He opened the door for her and followed her inside.

Then he shut the door behind them and twisted the lock. Reed noticed and switched her trajectory away from the wider loveseat where she'd been headed to a comfy club chair in the corner. There she sat, and then she sipped the first of her cocktail and coughed—it was strong. "So what's going on?" she croaked before coughing some more.

Sebastian eased himself down into the loveseat opposite her. "I'm in trouble."

"Drug deal gone bad?" Reed asked cheerfully, taking another sip from her drink. "Gambling debt? Pregnant girlfriends? *All of the above?*"

"It's a long story. But the short version is there's a group of Christian militants that are after me."

"*Christian* militants?" Reed giggled. "Do they sell machine guns at their church bake sales?"

"Ever heard of someone blowing up an abortion clinic?"

"Oh." Reed wrinkled her nose. "I'd forgotten about that stuff. I didn't know it still happened."

"It hasn't in a while because they've moved on to other causes." He looked at her, eyes wide.

"Like you? Why?"

"They think I'm in league with Satan and my mother Kitty is the great harlot that's written about in Revelation. They also think the end of the world is coming, and they need to kill the false prophet and the Antichrist."

"Wow." Reed screwed up her face. "I'm a Christian, but I would never take my religion that far, and neither would anyone else I know. That's totally creepy."

"Tell me about it."

"So are you?" Reed asked innocently. "Satan, I mean? Because if you are, there's this girl who stole my last boyfriend, and I'd like for them both to be burning in hell right now."

Sebastian laughed. "The only thing I have in common with Satan is most of the letters in my first name. And my last name, 'Black,' doesn't help either since the devil is known in their circles as the dark angel."

"I would've never thought of that." Reed paused for a moment. "How do they think of these things?"

"It gets worse: if you drop just a couple letters in my first and last names and then rearrange what's left, you get the message '*Satan is back.*'"

"Now that *is* weird," Reed told him, looking alarmed.

"Totally an accident," Sebastian reassured. "Anyhow, if my name had some hidden meaning, then wouldn't *all* the letters have to spell out something? Who says they get to use only the letters they want to?"

Reed shrugged. "It's kind of like those people who find visions of the Virgin Mary in their granola or Jesus in a pancake." She smirked. "So who are these freaks? What do they want to do to you?"

"They've been threatening us for the last few weeks, saying if we don't stop what we're doing they'll wage a holy war on us."

"What exactly does that mean?"

"Biblically, it means they want to kill me."

"Oh." Reed's eyes bugged. "But what about"—she hesitated—"that stuff about you reading minds? Couldn't you tell if they were coming for you?"

"Yeah, Reed, I can hear someone's thoughts—but only sometimes. And that's what happened tonight."

"Do you mean someone's actually here? *Right now, in this house?*"

Sebastian nodded. "Tonight, when I was looking for you, I felt something and turned around and saw these two fake paparazzi people: this guy wearing a black T-shirt, with a big old camera hanging around his neck, and this woman wearing a red dress who was pretending to take notes. And the dude was eyeing me, like some child molester looking at kids on a playground."

"I spotted them the second they walked in!" Reed exclaimed. "Even I got a weird vibe from them." She crossed her arms. "Do you really think they'll follow through with their threats? *Do you think we're safe here?*"

"I don't want to find out."

"So, you've reported this to the police. Right?"

"The FBI started a file on them, but so far they've been really good about flying under the radar. Most of the e-mails have been coming from anonymous computers, so they're almost impossible to trace without really throwing some manpower behind the investigation. And with everything else that's going on in the Middle East and Central Europe and the drug wars in Mexico, the FBI isn't very concerned about what happens to me—that is, until they actually try something. But recently, these people—they're called God's Furious Angels, by the way—gave me a deadline to stop my ministry. And if I don't stop, they'll do to me what they did to Joan of Arc; according to them she was also a false prophet, and they supposedly killed her to prevent the Apocalypse from happening in the fourteen hundreds."

Reed shook her head, shrugging. "I don't get it."

"They're just crazy, Reed. That's the whole point."

"So was the couple you saw here tonight part of this group?"

"I don't think so—or at least I don't think the woman is." *Should I tell her about Amber?* "But I got the feeling that the guy she was with is one of them; there was something really, really dark about him. *Twisted.* And now they're both somewhere in this house, which means it's not safe—not for me, and probably not even for you." He stood and began pacing the room. "Coby's got to empty this place, or I've got to leave. *Now.*"

"But where'll you go?"

"Further north, probably. Or back to Big Sur, where I made friends with these two older ladies."

"Are you leaving tonight? Now?"

"Probably tomorrow morning. For now I guess I can have Coby and his buddies throw those freaks out of here."

"You *could* stay for another day," Reed suggested. "Coby's got great security here, and we could help keep you safe. And believe it or not, Ellie knows how to shoot a gun."

Sebastian looked at her. "I can't stay here, Reed. And what pisses me off is I told Coby I was coming up here to stay with him so I could get away from something, and he threw me under the bus just so he could feel important."

"You knew about that?"

"Let's just say I figured it out. He's not the most complex guy."

"I know!" Reed exclaimed—but she wasn't talking about Coby. "Down the hill in the marina, I saw a sign for boats for rent! You could stay in one of those, and I promise I won't tell anyone where you are. The marina is really pretty, and we could even take the boat out on the bay…that is, if you wanted to, and you could park it anywhere; Angel Island, Tiburon, and Belvedere are gorgeous, or you could even travel up further north to Mendocino."

Sebastian considered this idea: being adrift in the bay might allow him to concentrate on more pleasant things, such as Libby had suggested, and his actual location could remain a mystery.

"OK, Reed," he agreed as his eyes held hers. "Will you come by here tomorrow morning, and we can go down to the marina together?"

Reed nodded, smiling. "About ten?"

"Looking forward to it."

CHAPTER 28

Saturday Morning

The next morning Sebastian awoke to the ping of his iPhone across the room, alerting him to a text message. He blinked at the ceiling, stretched his arms, and yawned.

God, what now?

He threw off the bedcovers and began stumbling over to where he'd placed the device atop the dresser the night before. But a sudden flash overtook his vision...a flash like when he'd been standing that morning in the Curcio Suite and saw Tess and Libby in the doctor's office. Only now he saw a country road at dusk, a two-lane highway cutting straight through dry, rolling hills ringing a flat valley. There were two mangled cars—one crushed like a beer can on the side of the road up against a telephone pole, while the other, larger vehicle sat askew on the highway, its front end folded in upon itself. Another car screeched to a stop. A man and a woman got out and ran to help. A stunned man, rubbing his head, emerged from the disabled car still in the road. Someone shouted. Sebastian saw something on the ground—a young guy with dark hair. He'd been catapulted from the car and was badly injured. But the other man tangled inside the crumpled wreckage was near death. His head lolled backward—too far backward—as if cloud-gazing. Blood covered the left side of his blond head. An old-fashioned white station wagon with wood on the side screeched to a stop. Two men jumped from the car. The guy in the wreckage gasped one last time and was still.

Stunned by the vision, Sebastian lowered himself back down onto the side of the bed.

The accident scene faded slowly, like a puff of cigarette smoke in a closed room.

"What…the hell…was that?"

He rubbed his eyes and scratched his chest.

Once he was in possession of his bearings—and no longer bleary eyed—he crossed the room once more, picked up his iPhone, and read the e-mail from Kitty: "If you're not back in 24 I'm returning it."

He opened the attachment. The tiny glass screen glowed bright red, like nail polish. He adjusted the picture's size. And then he saw a winged silver emblem inscribed with two very famous, evocative names: ASTON MARTIN.

Sebastian's heart pounded. And in an instant, he saw himself behind the wheel of the gorgeous car: the voluptuous red hood stretched before him and the growl of the exhaust pipes behind; the wind washing his face; the way the car took turns as if its wheels were locked onto rollercoaster rails; his favorite Coldplay song trumpeting through the sound system.

He looked at the photo again trying to ascertain whether or not his new car already had chrome rims, while at the same time considering what time to tell Kitty he'd be home this coming afternoon. But as he began tapping his message to her, his sight blurred again and he saw several figures trying to extricate a ragdoll-limp body from the same crumpled roadside wreckage.

That debilitating carsick feeling hit Sebastian again: equal parts squeamish nausea and pounding headache. He grabbed onto the bed's footboard to steady himself.

Did I just see the future...or the past?

Whatever it was, he knew it wasn't good.

After some minutes of consideration, he picked up the iPhone: "I can't come home now. Thanks for the car. Take it back if you need 2. Sorry."

———

Back home, Kitty was smiling.

She had returned to her laptop just after her second cup of coffee, expecting to read Sebastian's thrilled reply to her early-morning e-mail. She was excited because she figured that even now he would be on his way home to claim his prize, which was, at that moment, sparkling downstairs beneath the fluorescent lights of the parking garage, being drooled upon by the valets.

With relief, she saw he had responded almost immediately to the photo she'd sent of herself sitting behind the wheel of the car.

She clicked on his message, but she needed to read his response twice before comprehending its meaning. "*WHAT?*" she yelled to the empty penthouse. "I bought that stupid car for *nothing?*" And then another realization hit her that hurt even more than parting with her beloved money: *He hates me. He can't stand to be anywhere near me.*

Kitty pushed down the sting she felt, read his reply one last time, and then checked the status of his location via the iPhone's tracking device.

He's staying put. That'll buy me some time to figure out what to do.

—

Much later that day, while sipping her second martini and mirth-lessly watching a rerun of *Everybody Loves Raymond*, an epiphany descended upon her, as if God himself had slapped her across the face.

CHAPTER 29

"I got a twenty-seven-foot Sea Ray," the salty old woman—whose name was Lilly—told Sebastian while squinting at him, as if trying to figure out where she knew him from. "That's available now, and a thirty-five-foot Carver that's coming in later this afternoon. The bigger boat's one helluva lot better on rough water, but it'll cost you about twice as much to rent and fuel." She tapped her pen on the counter. "Which one d'you think you want?"

Sebastian glanced at Reed, and then he looked back at the leather-faced woman. "The one you have now is OK. I don't know if I could handle something as big as that Carver. Does the smaller one have a cabin for sleeping?"

"Specs says the Sea Ray sleeps six," Lilly answered, "but more than four is pretty tight. How long you want it for?"

Sebastian looked at Reed again, but she would not meet his eyes. "How about two weeks?"

"That's gonna run you *a lot*," she told him, her heavy eyebrows furrowed, "but I can knock off a day or two as a bonus. Payment?"

Sebastian fished through the credit cards in his wallet and warily handed over his American Express, knowing his mother could have already cut off his access to the account.

She examined the name. "Oh," she muttered. "Thought you looked familiar, 'cept for the hair."

"Yeah, so I need you to keep this between us." Sebastian picked through his wallet again and handed over a pair of one-hundred-dollar bills. "OK?"

Lilly secreted the bills into her pants pocket. "Not a problem. Just fill this out." She handed him a clipboard holding a lengthy contract. "You know how to run the navigation equipment and the radio, right?"

"I grew up on the water," Sebastian fibbed. "We used to have a yacht moored down in Marina del Rey. But I know each boat's different, so it'd be great if you could go over the controls with me."

"Not a problem," she said again, swiping his card through the machine.

Moments later—to Sebastian's relief—the register ticked cheerfully as it stuck out a long tongue of white paper.

Kitty hasn't canceled the cards because she wants to know where I am...but I don't care.

———

Moments later Sebastian and Reed—bags of groceries in hand—began following the woman along the weather-beaten and bowed dock planks, past the harbor shop toward the end of the marina. On this short walk the trio passed luxurious cabin cruisers and jaunty schooners and whalers that looked ready for business, until they stopped at a forlorn-looking, dirty white boat with a faded and tattered blue canvas top.

"How *old* is that thing?" Sebastian asked.

"Same as you, about twenty years, give or take," Lilly answered, leaning her mailbox-like girth against one of the painted white railings. "But don't worry, she runs strong. We just had the motors rebuilt last season, and the bilge throws water out the side like a fire hydrant."

"It looks like it's gonna sink," Reed added.

"Oh," the woman continued, ignoring them, "and her tanks are full—both of gas and water—so make sure you return her the same."

As the trio walked around the boat and the woman pointed out its various features, Sebastian saw the craft had been christened *Lil's Bastard*. He pointed to the words. "I thought it was bad luck to give a boat a male name."

"Don't you know, a girl can be a bastard too," Lilly replied dryly. "Anyhow, this is San Francisco, so we don't pay much attention to what's a girl and what's a boy."

Using care, they all stepped aboard. Then after Lilly demonstrated the radio, the navigation equipment, the throttle levers, the bilge pumps, and the motor ventilator controls, the young pair helped her climb out of the boat, said goodbye, and then watched as she lumbered back down the dock toward her office.

"I'll put your stuff in the fridge," Reed told Sebastian, hefting a bulging plastic bag with one hand and steadying herself with her other on the bulwark as the boat began to rock.

"Could you leave out the pretzels?" Sebastian asked. Without waiting for a reply, he disappeared below to take a closer look at the boat's amenities: the head and shower were outlined with mold; the beds were cramped but had been made up with fresh linens; the tiny oval windows over the sleeping area were so grimy as to be opaque; and every surface seemed to be either scratched or scuffed.

But overall, the boat seemed solid.

"So where do you want to go?" Sebastian asked as he reappeared up on deck, flashing his best photo op smile: his face at a three-quarter angle, with emerald eyes glinting and white teeth aligned and bared.

Reed avoided his penetrating gaze. "I'm...not coming with you. I've got stuff to do today."

"But I thought you wanted to go out on the water."

"Stuff to do," Reed muttered. "Like I said."

"Oh come on," Sebastian pleaded, his voice sonorous and enticing.

Reed thought for a moment, measuring her ambivalence toward Sebastian against the celadon waters sparkling under the azure sky.

"I guess I could for a short drive," she said, glancing purpose-fully at her watch, "but I need to be back early this afternoon. Ellie and I are going shopping. For shoes."

"Great! So, what looks good out there?" He swept his arm toward the open bay. "How about Alcatraz? Maybe we can break into it!"

"That place gives me the creeps." Reed shuddered. "It looks like a bombed-out high school."

"Then where else?"

Reed looked at him thoughtfully as she dropped her purse onto the galley's table. "I think we should go out to Angel Island or Tiburon...or we could annoy those rich people over in Bel-vedere"—she wagged her finger at the waterfront bank of man-sions in the distance—"by having a picnic in this wreck next to their perfect docks." She opened one of the galley's cabinet doors and wrinkled her nose at the crumbs and wrappers and greasy shelves. "This all looks disgusting. How are you gonna live here for two weeks?"

Sebastian shrugged. "Stock up on Pop-Tarts, I guess. So, will you be my first mate?"

"What does that mean?"

"Mostly just making sure the boat doesn't sink."

She scanned the dilapidated vessel. "I don't think I'm up to the challenge."

"Neither am I." Sebastian laughed. "But I did happen to scope out some life jackets down below, so I think we'll be OK."

Sebastian lithely jumped from the boat onto the dock to untie the mooring ropes, then bounced back on deck and scampered up to the helm to start the first engine and then the second. Moments later, with the propellers foaming the water beneath the rumbling, smoke-belching stern, he backed them out of the slip, wheeled the boat into a sharp U-turn, and headed out of the channel toward the bay.

Since it was just after ten in the morning, the sun hung over the lumpy, crust-colored peak of Angel Island like a heat lamp over a giant apple pie, and the water was still flat enough that the boat sliced smoothly through the gentle waves.

"So what's it feel like to drive something like this?" Reed yelled over the rush of the wind and the rhythmic splash of the water against the hull.

"It kind of feels like driving a huge mattress," Sebastian answered with a laugh, throwing the wheel from side to side as the vessel hurtled forward. "See?"

Reed grasped a nearby handle. "You keep doing that and *you'll* see what I had for breakfast."

They motored fairly close to the buoys so they might appreciate the vivid coastline from the starboard side. From this distance, the brightly colored, tiny houses of Sausalito reminded Sebastian of a miniature town—complete with glued-down plastic trees—that one might find around a model train set, only these structures overlooked a diminutive marina lined with toy boats instead. Just beyond the hillside town, way off to the left, the tomato-red goal posts of the Golden Gate Bridge towered majestically over an oak-spotted hilltop one moment and then vanished inside a fog bank the next.

He pushed the throttles forward and leaned the boat into a graceful turn, and moments later they were in full sun, heading out into San Francisco Bay. "You know, I think this is the first time I've felt totally safe in a while."

"What do you mean? Oh, look out for all those little kayaks." She pointed.

Sebastian spotted the flotilla of petite, yellow watercraft—floating like giant sunflower petals atop the waves beyond—and snapped the steering wheel to the right. Then he looked calmly out past the bow, watching the water slide in under the boat. "I feel safe because no one can get me out here, and Kitty's not here screeching at me."

"Is it really like that all the time for you?"

"It seems like it lately."

"You know," Reed began, "you're too young to be so stressed out about your work; at your age, you should be working at someplace like Jamba Juice." She paused. "But if everything is so awful, then why don't you just walk away from it all? You're not anyone's slave."

"I don't want to walk away yet because a part of me actually believes there's going to be a mass extinction and a new world order."

"So…you *really* believe you're the next species of man?"

"I know it's hard to understand."

Reed pondered this. "So eventually you'll need to find the female, or male, version of yourself. Right? And how are you supposed to find someone like that?"

"Kitty says we'll eventually seek each other out; it's like having radar. Only"—his voice dropped a notch—"so far, mine hasn't worked."

"So is this ESP the only thing that sets you apart?" Reed pointed off to the side. "Look out for that sailboat."

"That's a lot of it." Sebastian corrected their trajectory to avoid a tilting schooner with pregnant sails up ahead. "But more than that, it's a knowledge I have inside me—like knowing you're alive—and it's something I don't have to think about."

"But so far, you haven't met anyone else like you."

"Not that I know of."

"And your mom, Kitty, is normal?"

Sebastian laughed. "I guess someone, somewhere might say she's normal."

"Then how did she have a child like you? Was your father superhuman?"

"To be honest, Kitty says she doesn't remember anything about him, but I'm guessing he was an amazing guy—like he was pretty close to being perfect."

"So this means you can procreate with just anyone, right? That since only one parent needs to be advanced, your wonderful DNA will get passed on?"

"Kitty says I should be looking for someone like me, just to be sure; it's like when you've got blond hair it doesn't guarantee that your kids will be blond, unless you marry another one. Kitty says that when *Homo erectus* emerged from *Homo habilis*, there was a genetic mutation on only one side, but somehow that same mutation was happening in other locations, and the new species found each other."

Sebastian cut back the throttles, and the boat began to slow. "Isn't it interesting, Reed, that each new species of man has been better looking and more perfect than the previous one?"

"OK," Reed agreed, trying to ignore her growing revulsion toward Sebastian, "but even if you're the latest model of man—and you are kind of good looking—that still doesn't make you perfect."

"Of course not," Sebastian said, dipping his eyes to glance at the ripe swell of her breasts. "That's your job—being perfect, I mean."

"Oh God—really? I'm not falling for that." Reed rolled her eyes. "You seem pretty arrogant, and I've been burned by guys like you before—and I've heard *way* too much about how many girls and boys you've run through for me to get involved with you."

"So, then…why are you here? And by the way, I get tested. Kitty makes me."

Reed looked out to a rusty red buoy as it drifted by. "I guess because you seemed nice last night, and I figured you might want some company after what happened with those weirdos. And because I was curious—I've never known someone who thinks of himself as 'non-*Homo sapiens*' before."

"You should just think of me like anyone else," Sebastian told her, feigning modesty.

Reed narrowed her eyes at him. "I'll try my best to do just that."

They continued north in the bay for some time, while Reed baited him with every question she could think of, and Sebastian soaked up the attention. Then as the hour drew close to noon, they headed toward the waters off Angel Island to eat lunch.

Sebastian piloted the boat northward, past a trio of patrician yachts, a ramshackle fishing boat, a pair of schooners, and a looming oil tanker that looked like a skyscraper on its side in the water. Eventually their destination drew close, so he cut back the engines and slowed the vessel to a rocking stop.

He scampered to the front of the boat and dropped the anchor over the side.

In the meantime, Reed distracted herself by assembling their lunches. She cleaned the flimsy little Formica dining table with hand sanitizer and water, assembled sandwiches from the groceries they'd brought, laid out napkins and condiments, and twisted open their bottled waters.

Moments later they were dining under the raggedy blue canvas top.

As the sea breeze feathered Sebastian's hair and the sun warmed his thighs even through his jeans, Sebastian devoured his sandwich. "Isn't this great?" he asked, mouth full.

Reed smiled mechanically back at him.

"When I get back to LA, if I ever go back, I think I'll buy a boat—a nicer one than this. You know: bigger, brand new, with a great stereo and entertainment system. Wouldn't that be cool?"

"Yes, it would be *cool*, but it sure doesn't sound like a good reason to stick with a job you hate." She bit into her sandwich.

They ate in silence a while longer. Finally Sebastian asked, "So what do you think I should do? Do you think I should go back or not?"

Reed chewed some more, swallowed her food, took a slow sip from her water bottle, and leveled her gaze at him. "Why did you ask me to come out here with you today?"

"What do you mean?"

"Just tell me. Why did you ask me to come here with you?"

"Because I wanted to get to know you better, and…I like you."

"You wanted to get to *know* me better?" she asked. "And when did you plan on doing that?"

Sebastian blinked stupidly at her. "Huh?"

Reed sighed, rolling her eyes. "You guys are all the same. Totally self-centered, totally self-absorbed. I mean, I know you're going through a lot right now, but has it occurred to you even *once* on this trip to ask me *one question* about myself?"

Sebastian held up his hands. "I—"

"No, it's all about *your* philosophy and *your* 'genetic superiority,' and on and on. But I don't mind listening, Sebastian, really I don't. It's just that once in a while, it would be nice to have a guy show some interest, you know? I mean, I may not be one of those 'perfect' people you can't find who might help you build your master race—but I'm here, I've had a pretty amazing life myself, and believe it or not, I've come up with some opinions about this world that I think are pretty interesting." She crossed her arms over her chest and looked out across the water.

"I'm sorry. I just—"

"But the thing that gets me," Reed continued, glaring at him, "is that if a guy doesn't ask me anything about myself, it goes beyond just bad manners, you know? What it really means is he just doesn't care about me, and that somehow I'm just not worth the effort of some polite questions, or of him even *pretending* for a second that I'm smart enough or funny enough to add to his never-ending monologue. And that makes me so angry!"

"I...can see that."

"*You* know that it feels good if someone expresses interest in your life. *Right?*"

Sebastian nodded. "Sure it does."

"So then why wouldn't a guy, especially one that can supposedly *read minds*, think that maybe girls, or at least *this* girl"—she thumbed her chest—"might like to be asked a question or two about herself? *Why?*"

"I have a feeling," Sebastian said quietly, "that this isn't just about me."

Reed glanced guiltily at him, sighing. "You're right. It's not. It's just that I broke up with my boyfriend a week ago, and I'm just feeling kind of…*upset* with myself for putting up with him for so long. But even still, you have to admit that you've been using up all the air out here."

"Yep, I have." He laughed. "So what happened with this guy?"

"I don't want to talk about it."

"Please," he said, lifting his eyebrows. "I want to know."

Reed squinted at the horizon and took a long drink from her water bottle. "There was someone else."

"What was her name?"

Reed looked at him. "Some woman named Lindsay. She's his new boss at Google."

"Oh." He laughed. "Everyone knows you can't trust a 'Lindsay.'"

"So what does your religion say about people who can't seem to find someone to love? Or is perpetual loneliness the unspoken, dirty secret about this coming extinction of yours?"

"Do you really want to know? Because now I'm kind of scared to say anything."

Reed looked at him, smiling. "I asked you, so now's your chance."

"We believe," he began, "that there's someone out there for everybody, but maybe you're not supposed to be with just one person in your life. I mean, look at how many marriages end in divorce and how much infidelity there is between married people—even those old, white Republican senators who're always screaming about *family values* cheat on their wives. It's like this whole monogamy thing goes against human nature."

"I disagree, *totally*," Reed stated. "I think monogamy is absolutely necessary to a relationship, whether you're bisexual, straight, or gay. And of course you're going to be tempted by other people, but that's like everything in this life. Every time I see a supersized bag of Nacho Doritos, or a vanilla milkshake and onion rings on the menu at Jack in the Box, don't you think I want to eat until I see spots? But I know if I do, I'll be a cow, so I stop myself from taking what I don't need. And that's the way I think it needs to be between men and women—or partners."

"That's interesting." He blinked at her. "I never thought of it that way."

"That's because you're a guy, and men get to eat whatever they want—at least until you hit thirty. Oh!" Reed suddenly looked at her watch. "You know, I think I'd better get going."

"I knew you were going to say that."

"Did you…read my mind?"

"I looked at my watch," Sebastian said, twisting his Rolex-cuffed wrist back and forth at her, "and it's already after two." He got up from the table, went over to the anchor chain, and pulled the big chunk of metal out of the water as easily as if it had been a wet box of cereal. "But I want to make this up to you," he said over his shoulder, "and to show you that I can actually be good company. OK?"

Reed shrugged. "Let me think about it."

"So maybe," he said as he walked past her, drying his hands on his jeans and stepping up to the helm to start the boat's engines, "I can take you out tonight, and we can have a real date? I promise I won't be as boring as I was today."

"Aren't you afraid of going ashore? I heard a dreadful rumor about there being Christians in Sausalito."

Sebastian laughed. "No one except you knows where I am, so as long as I don't go back to Coby's I'll be safe." Sebastian eased down the throttles, and the boat began gliding forward. "And I do get warnings if someone who's around has it out for me. That's what happened last night."

"So you're *sure* you'll be OK out here?"

"Sure I'm sure," he said, with a confident chuckle. "But since it'll be kind of hard for me to come pick you up in this thing for dinner tonight, could you maybe come back down to the marina, like around five?"

"I…think I could manage that."

"Then I'll take care of dinner, whether it's here on the boat, or we could go down to the marina district to one of those little candlelit restaurants. OK?"

"OK," she said, her eyes shining.

Sebastian returned her gaze, then pushed the throttles further forward, and they began slicing the wind and scissoring the waves between Angel Island and the distant banks of Sausalito.

CHAPTER 30

Saturday, Noon

"Wow, you haven't changed a bit," Chuck told Kitty. "At least that I can tell, from behind those big sunglasses."

Kitty looked around the teeming Denny's to see if anyone had recognized her, but all she saw were clusters of frumpy, dumpy people focused on their menus or digging into their piles of french fries, or haggard waitstaff run-walking from table to kitchen and back.

Disappointed, Kitty returned her attention to the tall man facing her in the booth just as their short, dark waiter delivered her glass of wine and Chuck's mug of black coffee.

"I'm still not sure I remember you," Kitty lied. "Or maybe you looked very different back then. What the hell happened?"

"Well," Chuck said and then took a careful sip from his steaming mug, "my hair fell out, so that makes a big difference, you know. But more than anything it was probably the meth; it really did a job on my skin after I started snorting it, and all of the sun and the smoking and the time in prison didn't help either." He laughed nervously. "But I brought a picture of me to remind you of what I looked like back then." With a shaking hand, he pinched a faded photograph from the belly pocket of his hoodie sweatshirt and handed it over.

Kitty slid her Chanel sunglasses up onto her forehead to examine once again the picture of the handsome young surfer, his shaggy blond hair grazing his shoulders.

How could someone who looked like that let himself age so badly? Good God, meth is as bad as they say.

At once, fractured images from that night came back to her.

"I'm still not sure I remember you." Kitty flipped her glasses back down onto her nose. "No specific recollection whatsoever." She handed back the photo and grimaced as she took the first swig of her cheap chardonnay.

Chuck was crestfallen, but he tried not to let it show. "Then why did you come here if you still don't believe me? I mean, why are you here?"

Kitty took another sip of her wine before speaking. "I'll be blunt, Mr. Niesen, because I only have a few minutes. Mostly, I came to find out what it is you want from me."

Chuck shrugged. "I'd just like to know if, you know, Sebastian's my son, and to get to know him. I think it's pretty normal for someone to wonder what kind of man their son turned into. That's all."

"And how do you propose to prove that he is actually your offspring?"

"I guess I'd just sit with him or take a walk together and see if we have a connection…see if it feels like we are, you know, related."

Kitty laughed. "So that's your plan?"

Chuck felt his anger rise. "You know I could ask for a DNA test, 'cause I hear those are pretty accurate now."

"And whom, exactly, might you ask? Sebastian is over eighteen, so he would need to consent to such a test—but he would never do so without my approval."

"Then forget I ever I mentioned it." Chuck sipped more of his coffee. "I just don't know what else to do. This is a totally weird situation in my life that I wasn't, you know, expecting." He looked down at the scratched, white coffee mug between his hands and began nervously rotating the ceramic vessel atop the table.

"Supposing"—Kitty pulled off her glasses—"I allowed you to meet with my son."

Chuck looked up. "Yeah?"

"If I did so, you'd have to follow some strict guidelines."

"Really?" Chuck scrutinized her face, his baggy, parsley-colored eyes bulging. "Like what? I would do just about anything you wanted me to."

Kitty threw back more of her wine and swallowed hard. "We have a bit of an issue here, Mr. Niesen, because there is a publicly accepted mystery surrounding Sebastian's paternity…and if you've looked in the mirror lately, you'll see that you hardly look like someone who might've spawned someone as magnificent and talented as the amazing Sebastian Black. So before continuing any conversation regarding this, I need you to sign this non-disclosure agreement"—she pulled a folded paper from her purse and handed it over along with a thick gold pen—"which states that under no circumstances will you go to the press or tell anyone else on this planet any word of our conversations, including any and all information regarding the possibility of you *actually* being Sebastian's father."

Chuck ignored the paper in Kitty's hand. "You know, I don't remember reading in that *Vanity Fair* article about who Sebastian's dad was. Is he supposed to be a superman or an alien or something?"

"Let's just say that I've been purposely vague in that regard," Kitty replied, dropping the paper onto the tabletop. "But my official stance is that he was a spiritual luminary with amazing physical attributes, which is why he was able to imbue my son with such extraordinary abilities."

"That's such a truckload of steaming crap," Chuck told her, laughing. "Sebastian looks just like I did at his age, right down to the color of his hair and his eyes. And how old he is, which I looked up on that Wikipedia, leads right back to that wonderful night with you and me, together."

"You are not my son's father," Kitty told him. "We need to get that clear."

"You're lying. I can tell."

"I'm being quite truthful," Kitty countered, grabbing her oversized Louis Vuitton handbag. "And if you do not sign that paper, I'm leaving."

"Hey now, don't leave," Chuck pleaded. "You came this far to meet with me, and I'm guessing you've got some kind of important reason for being here."

Kitty narrowed her eyes as she placed her handbag atop the table and unzipped it. "How much money do you want? Is that what not signing this paper is about?"

"Hey, I don't want your money," Chuck protested, even though the thought had crossed his mind. "It's just that after I was arrested, my public defender told me to never, ever sign anything without him being there."

"But everyone wants my money! My lawyers, my mortgage holders, my hairdressers, and everyone else I come into contact with, including the hobos on the street corner. So you'll please excuse me if I doubt your sincerity."

"You know, Katie," Chuck began, "if you'd just be honest about this, then maybe all it would take is me sittin' down and having a heart-to-heart with my boy…and then maybe I'd disappear—or maybe he wouldn't want anything to do with me, you know, which is just fine with me. But something tells me I shouldn't trust you, and I don't think that's what you came here to hear."

"First of all, my name is *Kitty*, Mr. Niesen, which is spelled K-I-T-T-Y." She shoved the paper toward him once again.

Chuck sat back in the rust-colored vinyl booth, contemplating the paper before him. It would be easy enough to sign the damn thing...except that big mouth Hank, back at the house, already knew what was going on—and God only knew how many people he'd told by now. But he could always go back and tell Hank he'd been wrong about the whole thing, at least until things got more straightened out. "You wouldn't be doing this thing with me and this paper unless you knew I was his father, huh?"

"My position on that matter is carved in stone," Kitty stated. "And what's important here is the role you will *and will not* play in our lives. For instance, since you've already stated you have no interest in our money, you will touch none of it, *not now, and not ever*. And you will also not entertain any silly notions of waltzing in and somehow 'completing' our family; you should know that this particular Mary and Jesus have done quite well without a Joseph."

Chuck furrowed his eyebrows. "Which reminds me, now that you brought it up, I always wondered whatever happened to Joseph."

"I'm sorry?" Kitty blinked at him.

"I mean, there he is all over the beginning of Jesus and Mary's life with the manger and Christmas and all, and then later on teaching Jesus how to be a great carpenter, but then what happened?" He looked expectantly at Kitty.

Kitty opened her mouth to reply, but she was interrupted suddenly by the screeching of a child in the next booth.

She waited for the mother to shush the creature.

"I don't follow you," she said. "And I don't see what this has to do with Sebastian."

"Joseph just drops out of sight," Chuck said, "and no one ever mentions him again. I mean, did he die or what? You know, he wasn't even at his boy's crucifixion with his wife."

Kitty stared at the man dispassionately, but inside, she was thinking that perhaps—all wackiness aside—he wasn't as stupid as he seemed. "I'm sure there's an explanation somewhere," she told him, her voice flat. "So...will you sign?"

"You know, something doesn't smell right here, *Kitty*," Chuck said. "Why do you want me to sign this thing? I mean, why wouldn't you just want me to, you know, go away?"

Kitty took two slugs of her wine, suddenly aware that she would have to insert some honesty into this transaction. "In case you hadn't noticed, I am very protective of my son. I'm worried about him right now. But I will not be telling you a thing until you sign this; that's what a 'nondisclosure agreement' is all about. This"—she tapped the paper three times with her French-tipped fingernail—"is your promise to keep your mouth shut."

Chuck sighed, opened the folded paper, and scanned the text. "Well, it doesn't seem like signing this would do anything bad," he said at last, taking the gold pen from her hand.

He scribbled his name, birth date, social security number, and address on the lines provided.

Done.

Kitty stifled a smile. "Now we can talk, Mr. Niesen," she began, her voice low, "so I'll tell you what's going on. Due to the stress my poor Sebastian is under, he has vanished, and although we are in contact by phone and by e-mail, he refuses to come home." She resisted the urge to put on her sunglasses again so he might appreciate the concern in her eyes. "I am simply hoping that if I alert him that someone has emerged who might be his father, it will be enough for him to return to me." Her mouth made a grim smile. "And that's the truth."

The big, bald man tossed the dregs of his coffee down his throat and eased his huge frame into the booth's seat back. "So actually, you need my help," he told her, his jade eyes shining.

"I don't *need* anything from you," Kitty replied. "But I could use your help."

"Then it'll be my pleasure to, you know, do what I can." And because Chuck needed a smoke, he began sliding himself out of the booth. "Is there anything else?"

Kitty shook her head and pushed her glasses back onto her face. "No," she said, grabbing her handbag. "But I'll be in touch."

"You do remember me, don't you?" Chuck asked. And as Kitty squared a look at him, he saw twin miniature images of his big head reflected in her glasses.

"What do you think?" She jingled her keys.

"That's what I thought," he said, digging his cigarettes and lighter from his sweatshirt pocket.

CHAPTER 31

"I still can't believe you did that last night." Dyson locked his hands onto his hips, glaring at his wife. "Why didn't you let me do it?"

Amber rolled her eyes. "Are we going to go through this again?"

"I just don't get it. Please. Make me understand, so I can try and explain this to Olivier. He's gonna be *pissed.*"

Amber pushed herself up from the sagging queen bed, tied her plaid bathrobe around herself, and began pacing the dimly lit motel room with its heavy drapes drawn shut against the sunlight. "Like I told you before, the whole plan was stupid—except for having us pose as paparazzi. You should thank me for stopping the whole dumb thing." She crossed the cramped room and grabbed her water bottle from atop the Formica-topped dresser.

"But Olivier and me planned it all out. We were *there,* Amber. *We were there.* And you wouldn't let me do it!"

"You didn't listen to me even before we left, when I told you it wouldn't work." She took a slug of water. "And with all the time you'd spent at Olivier's over the last two days, I would've thought you two could've come up with something better," she laughed, "than putting Visine in his drink."

"Eyedrops can kill someone, Amber. Like I told you, it causes lethal changes in blood pressure, it can stop someone from

197

breathing, and can even put them in a coma. I think it's pretty brilliant. The only other thing I could think of was rat poison, but Olivier said rat poison could be traced back to me—but lots of people buy Visine, so no one cares when you buy it. Olivier told me they even used Visine in one of those CSI shows, where a woman killed her husband with it."

"Now there's an idea." She narrowed her eyes at him. "I researched it too, Dyson, and it doesn't work every time. Do I have to remind you that we're only going to have one chance with him? *One chance!* But if we don't do it right, he's going to get himself some *real* security and we'll never get close to him again!"

"Why exactly do you want him dead so much?"

Amber flashed upon that night some two years back. She'd been delirious to have been given time with him after the gathering, and she'd felt like a cherished prize after she'd been made love to and had lain in his strong arms. But over the course of the next few days her glee had given way to disappointment, then to bitterness, and finally to self-loathing at allowing herself to be used and then cast aside by Sebastian.

Since then she had grown to hate him—especially after that ultimate sacrifice, that *unforgivable act* forced upon her by her parents; after all, it was *her* body, so it should have been *her* choice.

But then at the party last night, while stealing glances at his magnificent silhouette and noble features once again, she had wondered: *Will he acknowledge me? Or will he pretend like he doesn't know me? And even if he does reject me once more, should I tell him the truth?*

At one point, she used the excuse to find a bathroom to get closer to Sebastian and to see if he might find her as pleasing as he once did. But as she made her way toward him—with her shoulders squared and her chin poised and her mouth smiling in that alluring way she'd perfected, where her crooked teeth were covered by just enough of her full, painted lips—Sebastian's eyes had passed blandly over her face like a lighthouse beam scanning the barren coastline. Then later she'd seen him again: he was outside on the terrace with two drinks in hand, and he was looking around for that long-haired, dark-skinned girl. So when he turned around, she revealed herself boldly to him—but he'd only ignored her. *Again.* And that was when she made up her mind.

"God told me Sebastian must pay for how he tricks people and steals their souls," she said at last. "It's that simple."

Dyson shook his head, chuckling. "You've still got feelings for him."

Amber launched a high-pitched, incredulous laugh. "Oh, I've got feelings for Sebastian all right. *Very strong* feelings."

"Is that why you got all dressed up in that red dress of yours? That's a great way to not get noticed, by the way."

"It was a party," Amber snarled, her eyes afire. "A *nice* party."

Dyson smirked. "You're still in love with him, aren't you?"

"I am a soldier of God," she said. "I have no fear of Satan or any of his demons. But there are risks involved in killing someone as famous as Sebastian, and if we make a mistake, there'll be strong repercussions for both of us—or should I say *all three* of us?"

"You'd better keep your voice down," he told her warily, from where he sat at the end of the bed. "These walls have ears."

"I'm just waiting to see what his next move will be," Amber said, in a noticeably calmer voice. "This is like hunting. And you don't use a BB gun—*or eyedrops*—on a lion."

Dyson pushed himself up from the bed. "And how will you know what his next move is if you're not there to see where he goes?" He slowly stepped closer to her, his eyes challenging. "Or did fucking him make you telepathic as well?"

Amber raised her hand to slap him, and he flinched backward. "Do not forget that the husband is the head of the wife," Dyson told her, "even as Christ is the head of the church and the Savior of the body—Ephesians 5:24."

She put down her hand. "By the way, when am I going to meet this amazing Olivier?"

"When the time is right." Dyson's gaze drifted around the room. "Next week, probably."

She squinted at him. "You're not telling me something."

He went to the nightstand to retrieve his Bible. "My heart is with Jesus, and that's all that matters," he replied and began flipping through the well-worn pages.

"You spent Wednesday night, Thursday morning and Thursday night, and then Friday morning with him before we left."

Dyson flashed back to when he'd arrived on Olivier's doorstep at the crack of dawn yesterday morning, with the uneasy—yet heart-pounding—news that the cast-out demon had indeed returned.

"Like I told you, we were deep in prayer again," Dyson said to Amber. "*So help me God.*"

"If you go back to your old ways, you'll burn in deepest hell because God loathes sodomites—especially those who're adulterers."

"Olivier is totally committed to my salvation," Dyson replied. "But let's get back to Sebastian. If you think the Visine idea was so bad, then what do *you* plan to do? We don't even know if he's still at that house in Sausalito, or if he's moved on to somewhere else."

Amber considered his question. "I have faith that God will reveal His plan to us," she said. "Plus, we'll keep checking those tacky celebrity websites and the Christian message boards. No one escapes those." She downed the remainder of the water in her bottle. "But my guess is he's still somewhere up in Sausalito with that dark-skinned girl. And Sausalito is a very small town."

CHAPTER 32

Saturday Evening

Sebastian glanced at his watch.

It was after five, and there was no sign of Reed.

Worried, he began pacing the small deck of the boat, causing it to rock gently in its slip up against the dock. *They saw her with me the other night,* he thought as the hull splished gently from side to side. *How could I have left her alone? Why didn't I call Coby and Ellie to come down and get her when I dropped her off this afternoon?*

Once again his eyes scanned, through the diminishing light, the streets leading down to the marina from the overlooking hills. But the only people he could see were couples and families either headed toward the bayside restaurants for dinner, or meandering through the public parking lot toward their plain-as-toast rental cars.

He retrieved the iPhone from his pocket and looked to see if she had called, but there were no messages—not even from Kitty.

Where is she?

At last he spotted Reed rounding the corner of a building, wearing a turquoise strapless dress that squeezed her curves and swells enticingly. He watched her grow from doll-sized to human, clutching her purse in one hand and a sweater in her other, her long black hair fluttering like a veil behind her delicate, cocoa-hued shoulders. Her step was light—as if her body weighed almost nothing—and the swinging of her hips from side to side recalled a Hawaiian girl performing a drowsy hula.

God, she's fantastic.

She spotted him and tickled the air with her fingers in salute. And as he waved back, Sebastian felt not so much that familiar stirring below his belt, but an unfamiliar breathlessness in his chest.

He jumped over the bulwark of the boat and began the happy march to meet her halfway.

They met in front of a grand white yacht that looked too large to have squeezed into its narrow slip.

"I'm so glad you made it." He took her hand and leaned in to kiss her.

"Sorry I'm late," Reed said, offering her cheek. "Ellie wouldn't shut up about last night. I almost had to crawl out of the bathroom window to get here."

"It's OK. I just got a little worried."

"Speaking of that, have you run into any religious maniacs today?"

Sebastian put his hand around her shoulders, and they began their stroll back down the pier back toward *Lil's Bastard*. "I'm asking the questions tonight, not you."

"I'm glad you haven't forgotten already," Reed told him. "I'm impressed."

"Let's just say that I hate it when I'm wrong." They continued walking, their strides well matched. "Hey, I decided against going down to the marina district, if it's OK with you. It's because of the whole getting recognized thing, and I don't want it to ruin our night."

"So are we having turkey sandwiches again?"

Sebastian laughed. "Actually, I got some pasta from that deli where we got lunch from yesterday. Cheese tortellini with pesto, lots of parmesan, and I even bought some lemons."

"My favorite!" She turned to him, eyes narrowed. "How did you—?"

Sebastian grinned at her. "It's my favorite too. Hey, it looks like we've actually got something in common." They'd arrived at the boat, so Sebastian jumped over the bulwark and held out his hand to Reed. "Careful."

Reed took his hand and stepped delicately into the boat, but she still nearly fell over as their combined weight suddenly made the vessel tip.

Sebastian caught her forearms in a tight grasp and laughed.

"I'm usually not so clumsy. It's these stupid pumps Ellie made me buy today."

"Maybe you'd better sit"—he led her over to the white vinyl bench—"and I'll take us out into the bay. The night's coming, so if we anchor over by Angel Island again, we should have an incredible view of the city lights."

Reed agreed, so Sebastian untied the ropes, cranked the engines to life, and began carefully maneuvering the boat out from its slip into the channel. Moments later they were drawing steadily across the bay toward the distant island, as if being pulled there by a very long rope.

Reed scanned the panorama as it drifted by—the sea, the land, and the sky all surrendering their sunlit colors to the gray wash of evening. In the last few minutes she'd watched the topography of the approaching island change from whole wheat brown to lavender, while the sky overhead glowed Gatorade purple and the surrounding sea looked both metallic and dull, like the underside of aluminum foil.

But what enchanted Reed the most were the lights.

Oh, the lights!

Throughout the wide vista—the silhouetted hills and the turgid Coit Tower and the skyscrapers and islands and boats and streets—lights appeared…pins of light sparkling out from the darkness…more and more each moment, until the nightscape twinkled and glittered against the black humps of hilly coastline. And to their right loomed the mighty Golden Gate Bridge, with its tomato-red grandeur blazing against the darkness, its swooping cables rising and then dipping from tower to tower like the tracks of an amusement park rollercoaster.

"Look!" Reed told Sebastian, pointing.

Sebastian spun the wheel and cut the boat's engines. The boat drifted clockwise, and the colossal bridge filled the boat's windshield. Reed sighed as they settled into a gentle sway. "Have you ever seen anything more beautiful than that?"

Sebastian turned to her, wanting to say what was in his heart, but he was struck by an unexpected wave of self-consciousness. Then he regained his courage. "Yeah, I have," he said at last, reaching for her hand. "You."

"You're very polished for a teenager," she told him, dropping his hand. Then she backed away, staring at him. "I'm just curious…but has anyone, *anyone* ever told you no?" She settled herself back down onto the bench.

"Why is that such an issue with you?"

"Because I've read about your brief and numerous relationships, and I refuse to be another of your disposable groupies."

He leaned next to the helm, arms folded. "A lot in me has changed, Reed—and I'm not just saying that. I've been meeting people who are helping me reevaluate my life."

"Such as?"

Sebastian looked at her, his green eyes glinting and serious. "Such as you."

"And…how's that tortellini coming along?" She busied herself with buttoning up her sweater.

Sebastian stepped into the helm and started the engines. "You know, no one's ever put me in my place before like you did this afternoon."

Reed looked up at him. "Have you recovered yet?"

"I'm just surprised."

"Why?"

"Because when we met, you seemed so shy. But then you showed me how you have this fire inside you. I've never met anyone like you before." As he pushed the throttles forward to begin their trip back to Angel Island, Reed smiled at him in the darkness.

Moments later they were bobbing at anchor in the island's cove, amidst the few other boats that had moored there for the night.

Reed relaxed while Sebastian threw together their table settings, heated their dinners in the boat's microwave, lit a candle atop the tiny dining table, and twisted open a big green bottle of sparkling water.

At last, he placed their steaming dishes before them.

"Have you talked to your mother, to Kitty, today?" Reed asked while rearranging her tortellini with her fork. "By the way, this looks really good."

Sebastian studied his own bowl. "Nope."

"Sorry to bring it up." Reed stabbed her fork into the pasta, withdrew a morsel, and stared at it, as if she were trying to figure out what it was.

"Something wrong?" Sebastian asked.

Reed shook her head. "I just have some strange...habits. Don't pay any attention to me." Hurriedly, she ate the pasta. "It's been heated to absolute perfection," she said at last. "You're a culinary genius!"

"How long have you had...trouble with food?" Sebastian asked her.

Reed shot him an alarmed look. "Is it that obvious? Or did one of my dear friends tip you off?"

"Sometimes I pick up on other people's anxieties," he replied. "I can't help it."

"Then don't ever go to an Overeaters Anonymous meeting," Reed told him flatly. "Your head would explode."

Sebastian appraised her with gentle eyes. "You didn't answer my question—and if it's none of my business, I *totally* understand."

Reed put down her fork and looked directly at him. "My mama was diagnosed with colon cancer when I was twelve. We were—and still are—very, very close. But when my folks told me what was going on, I just stopped eating. I absolutely, completely lost my taste for food during the time she went through surgery and chemo and everything; I'd wake up every morning feeling like I had a stomach full of cement.

"So of course I started dropping weight; I lost twenty-five pounds in two months, just like she did—and all of a sudden everyone started telling me how great I looked. Then when she started recovering, I started eating again, and I put the weight back on too; I guess it was kind of like those guys who get fat when their wives get pregnant.

"But then, since I couldn't fit into any of my pretty new clothes, I discovered the joys of bulimia, which I won't get into here at the dinner table." She sighed heavily, absently twirling her fork in the air. "But I'm OK now. I just have to watch it. I know my demons very well, and I know what makes them start poking me with sticks. I—"

She stopped, looking at him with unnerving intensity for a long moment before appearing to decide something. She relaxed and gave a little shrug. "I need to do whatever it takes to take care of myself. And I think that's what you're picking up on when one minute it seems like I'm too shy and the next it's like I'm too sassy. I'm having a little battle inside my head, and I force myself to do things and to say things that I'm really not comfortable with, but I know I need to face. It's all part of my recovery. Does that make sense?"

Sebastian smiled. "It makes perfect sense." He poured them each a glass of fizzing water. "But I'm curious, since you and your boyfriend just broke up. Did that...um, make you stop eating again? Not that you look like it, I mean...you look very healthy. I mean you look *beautiful*. Um—"

"*I'm fine*," Reed interrupted. "And since I've got Ellie force-feeding me Clif Bars, I've been more than OK. Actually, even without Ellie's nagging, I'd be all right; my therapist has helped me figure out some good strategies." She ate more of her tortellini and smiled. "I guess I'm one of the lucky ones—some girls never get out off Anorexia Island."

Sebastian returned her smile. "I guess everyone's got some kind of heavy baggage, huh?"

"Does that freak you out about me?"

Sebastian laughed. "It takes a lot to freak me out. *A lot.*"

"So what about you?" Reed asked. "How do your demons torture you, as long as we're on the subject of baggage?"

"I guess my biggest problem is not knowing what the hell I'm supposed to do with my life. I like helping people, but I hate this whole church thing my mother's gotten us into."

"Well"—Reed took a sip of her water—"have you thought about where you want to be in, say, ten years? Sometimes I look at where I want to go and work backwards from there."

"I've never thought of that." He picked up his lemon wedge and squeezed its juice over his pasta. "So where do you want to be ten years from now?"

"I'd like…a meaningful career, some well-behaved kids, and a husband who's deliriously captivated by me. But I'd live in a tent on a prairie if it meant we could all be happy. I don't care about money."

"A week ago, I would've thought you were crazy for saying that," Sebastian told her. "But with everything that's happened lately, I'm starting to rethink *everything.*"

"Is there something else going on?"

Now it was Sebastian's turn to level his gaze at her for a moment. "We, uh…had a tragedy with some church members. A murder-suicide."

Reed put down her fork. "What *happened?*"

"I don't want to depress you." Sebastian drew his iPhone out of his pocket once again and checked it for messages; he'd been feeling the psychic itch of a premonition all day.

"My guess is you'd feel a lot more relaxed if you just shut that stupid thing off," Reed suggested, wagging her finger at the device.

"You're right. I promise not to check it again until after you're back at Coby's."

"Don't do it for me," Reed told him. "It's just that anyone can see how much you need to relax. I mean, here you are out in this beautiful bay, but you keep checking your phone as if you're waiting for an organ transplant. Are you expecting something *that* important?"

He slid the phone into his pocket. "No one knows where I am, so there's nothing I should be doing right now except enjoying your amazing company."

"You are so full of it," Reed laughed. "But even though your highly polished flirtation techniques are useless on me, I won't discourage you from trying."

"Like I said before"—Sebastian took her hand—"you're not like anyone I've ever met. You have this beautiful, quiet, sweet way about you that makes me feel peaceful. Like you're completely comfortable with who you are, so it makes me feel OK about who I am. And I'm not just saying that, Reed. I mean it. You feel as beautiful to me on the inside as you are to look at, like you've got...sunlight inside you."

Reed allowed the warmth of both his words and his skin to melt into her, and it stirred her. "Can you...tell what I'm thinking right now?"

"I'm more concerned with what's on my mind." He leaned across the table and kissed her lightly on the mouth. "Mmmm. Pesto."

Reed took a quick sip of her water. "Try again."

Sebastian got up, leaned over the table, and kissed her more fully.

Reed's lips parted for him. She felt her skin flush and her ankles tingle.

"Thank you," Sebastian told her after seating himself. "Tasting like Perrier is much more refreshing."

"Did I mention that you taste like parmesan?"

"I...like you," he blurted.

Reed leaned back and laughed. "I guess I'm starting to like you too."

"So, where do we go from here?"

"Dessert?"

"With...*us*."

Reed patted his hand. "How about if we take it a day at a time and see what happens. I'm supposed to go back to LA tomorrow, and if you wanted to, we could have dinner again there."

Sebastian glanced out across the bay and then brought his gaze back to Reed's. "I guess I'll have to go home eventually...but at least knowing we could see each other would give me something to look forward to."

They began working their way through their meals again.

"Can you tell me something?" Reed asked.

"Sure," Sebastian replied, mouth full.

"How much of what I'm thinking can you pick up on?"

Sebastian swallowed and put down his fork. "Just little bits—unless I'm waking up or in a meditative state. But that attraction vibe you probably heard about can hit me anytime."

"So what's it feel like when someone's interested in you?"

"Like you haven't been able to tell when someone thinks you're hot?" Sebastian laughed. "I just get a little clearer information, that's all."

"That's not fair," Reed said.

"But all's fair in love and war. Isn't that what old people say?" He began refilling Reed's water glass.

"I'll...tell you when I'm old."

Sebastian lowered the bottle onto the table and looked into Reed's eyes. "Are you saying we'll still know each other then?"

Reed felt her skin flush again. "I don't know what's happening here. I'm confused, because earlier today I thought you were the most arrogant, boring guy I'd ever spent a miserable date with, and now I feel—" She gave her head a shake and looked out toward the sparkling coastline. "If there's one thing I've learned, it's best to take things slow." She sighed heavily. "And I should tell you that I have trust issues."

He touched her hands. "I can handle that."

"Then I guess I can too. But why would you want to be with some normal human—and one who's recovering from an eating disorder, on top of it? I thought you were looking for Wonder Woman—or Superman."

"I know you're joking," Sebastian answered. "But can I be honest?"

"Please."

"Ever since I can remember, I've felt—probably because Kitty convinced me of it—that I was different from everyone else. Better than everyone, as horrible as that sounds. But now I'm starting to believe that I *belong* somewhere...and I really like the feeling."

"So how do I fit in with this new feeling of yours?"

"You...make me feel human. *Vulnerable.* And as much as that scares me, it's also exciting because...I've never felt this way before."

Reed stifled a giggle. "That is so cute," she said. But the hurt expression on his face made her regret her response. "I mean, sometimes you seem so mature, and then at other times I remember that you're still a teen—"

Sebastian's iPhone pinged, and his hand reflexively reached down for it, but stopped.

Their eyes met.

"Go ahead," Reed said. "You have my permission."

"Just let me just check this one e-mail, OK? I've been waiting for something important; I've had this weird, uneasy feeling all day."

Reed said nothing and began eating more of her tortellini while Sebastian pulled out his phone and launched his e-mail.

The message from Kitty was brief, but it felt like Sebastian had been waiting a lifetime for it:

A man claiming to be your father has come forward. I met with him. He sent me this e-mail to forward to you, but I'm not giving you his e-mail address until you come home. We're both waiting. –Kitty

CHAPTER 33

Sunday Morning

The next day Sebastian drove back to Los Angeles at a reckless pace: seldom did he allow the Cayenne to drop below ninety, and he frequently had the big silver SUV blasting past the almond orchards and vineyards and stockyards and cornfields of central California with the speedometer needle wagging into the triple digits.

And during this time, his mind spun even faster than the wheels beneath him.

His mental frenzy had begun the evening before, with those anticipatory premonitions that had almost unsettled his evening on *Lil's Bastard* with Reed; then after scanning that e-mail from Kitty with its message from Chuck, he'd decided not to enlighten Reed about what he'd just read—at least for the time being. Instead, he did his best to ignore this news, while doing his best to flatter and engage Reed and to make her feel like the only woman in the world.

And it worked. He watched Reed's posture and facial expressions melt from *en garde* to languid as the evening passed.

But throughout the night a cascade of questions about Chuck nagged at him. What did he look like? Was he employed? Did he share Sebastian's telepathic gift? Where had he been hiding all this time? Was he an asshole who'd abandoned a young pregnant girl, or had Kitty left him in the dark? Was he a kind and loving and successful man whom Sebastian might look up to? And was Chuck really his father, or was he another nutcase looking for some money and a lot of press...*or was this all just something Kitty had orchestrated to entice him home*?

Then at the end of the night with Reed—after intuiting that his stalkers were nowhere in the vicinity—Sebastian escorted her back up the hill to Coby's. Then after giving her his most tender kiss, he startled her by announcing his intention to leave for Los Angeles in the morning.

He also offered her a ride, but Reed had declined; he could see that she still didn't trust him. Instead she promised to touch base once she arrived home, and they could make a date then.

The next afternoon, after four zippy, harrowing hours on the road, Sebastian pulled into the underground parking of his high-rise, handed off his car to the valet, called the elevator to the garage, slipped his key into the slot for the penthouse, and rode skyward.

The sound of the elevator doors sliding open and Sebastian's footfalls on the terrazzo caught Kitty's ear. "So you got my message." She was sitting on the white leather sofa in the living area, a cigarette dangling in one hand while pecking the keys of her laptop with the other. She looked up and shot him that dead-eyed gaze of hers that said, *You will pay for all the grief you've just put me through.* "And what the hell happened to your hair?"

"What message?" Sebastian slipped the overnight bag from his shoulder and dropped it onto the floor. "I'm just out of clean socks."

Kitty giggled as she got up from the sofa. "I'm so glad to see you!" She went to him, stood on tiptoe, and pecked him on the cheek. "What've you been up to?"

"I went to see my old friend Coby, up in San Francisco."

"Wasn't it Sausalito?"

Sebastian glared at her. "How'd you know?"

"I joined the online group of those lovely people who hate us. Apparently, they've been charting your every move. I just set up another Gmail account under a pseudonym to find out what they were saying; they're not very smart, by the way. So, what's her name?"

"Don't know what you're talking about."

"Some pretty, dark-haired girl. Killer body. Mysterious ethnicity."

"Forget about it."

"Have you forgotten her name already?"

He started walking toward his quarters. "I'll be out in a minute, and then I want to know everything about Chuck. Plus, I'm starving, so if you could find me something to eat—you know, like a real mom would—I'd appreciate it."

After using the restroom he found her perched at the kitchen bar smoking another cigarette. "Hot Pocket. Chicken." She pointed to the whirring microwave. "See? I'm practically a soccer mom now."

"Aren't we vegetarian anymore?"

Kitty shrugged. "The maid bought some by mistake, and they're not half bad."

Sebastian stood by the microwave. "So what's going on with Luke's lawsuit?"

"It's still too early to tell. But Larry's found some encouraging precedents and legalese that he's confident will knock these jokers out of their money tree. But he still needs you to sit for that deposition ASAP; he's been stalling their lawyers for days now."

"I'll do it tomorrow."

The microwave beeped, so he withdrew the plate and its steaming, crusty log and placed it on the bar across from Kitty. He stared at the cigarette in her hand. "Do you mind?"

Kitty slid off the barstool and made her way over to the range top. She reached up and switched on the exhaust fan. "Better?"

Sebastian rolled his eyes and bit into his Hot Pocket. It burned the roof of his mouth. "So tell me about Chuck," he mumbled.

"I'd like to tell you that he's this highly accomplished scientist or neurosurgeon, or a Nobel Prize–winning philanthropist," Kitty replied, "but basically, he's a loser."

"Yeah, I kind of got that from his e-mail after I read it a few times—he doesn't come off as the brightest guy. So you met with him?"

"We went to Denny's."

"*You?*" Sebastian snickered.

"I didn't want to be recognized." She took a heavy drag off her cigarette, and as she blew it out the exhaust hood sucked it efficiently from the room.

"So is he my father?"

"You're the psychic. You tell me."

"Don't start."

"Let's get something straight," Kitty began. "Neither you nor I have anything, *anything* to benefit by recognizing this man as your father. He could do nothing but harm to our personal and spiritual and professional images."

"So you're telling me he is who he says he is." Sebastian bit off another chunk.

"I am remaining completely neutral on this issue because I fear you'll disclose to that man whatever I might tell you in hopes of forming some sort of silly bond with him."

"But he *is* my father."

"*No,*" Kitty stressed. "Chuck Niesen, if anything, was nothing more than a sperm donor. On the other hand, *I am your mother,* and I raised you—single-handedly, and against some very heavy odds." She threw her cigarette into the kitchen sink and made her way back across the kitchen toward him. "And despite our differences, yours and mine, I fought for you and guided you as best I could. And I hate even suggesting this to you, because you're too much like me and I know how this will probably set you off, but you owe me your loyalty, so I want you to promise me you'll treat this situation with utmost discretion until we can figure out how the hell to move forward."

"You smell like cigarettes."

Kitty backed away. "That haircut needs work."

"Did you send back the Aston Martin?"

"Have you heard *anything* I've told you?"

"I just think it's interesting," Sebastian began as his gaze drifted over to meet hers, "that you can tell me how much you guided me and fought for me and sacrificed and all"—he took the last bite of his snack, munched it, and swallowed it—"but I can't ever remember you telling me you loved me. So maybe… just *maybe* now with Chuck I'll have a parent who'll care for me instead of treating me like an employee."

Kitty's mouth opened to respond, but she stopped herself. Instead, she snatched her cigarette pack off the bar, shook one out, and lit it off the range top. "You yourself told me to send the car back to the dealer," she said, her words blowing out in vaporous syllables.

"Good, because I don't want it anymore."

"Too bad," Kitty said.

"Huh?"

"I went against my better judgment and kept it. Believe it or not, I was excited to see the look on your face when you sat in the damn thing."

CHAPTER 34

Monday Morning

Chuck had been sitting on the park bench overlooking Ocean Boulevard for over half an hour, waiting for Sebastian to arrive. And during this time, he amused himself by observing the parade ambling past: destitute homeless folks pushing junked-up shopping baskets; wealthy professionals jogging by with five-hundred-dollar running shoes on their feet; potbellied Russian immigrants jibber-jabbering and smoking cigarettes; and somber Guatemalan nannies pushing their months-old Caucasian charges in strollers that looked fit for a moon landing.

Only in Santa Monica.

And then he saw Sebastian. He was wearing a long black pea coat with the collar flipped up in protest to the chilling sea breeze, his tousled blond head was down, and his hands were jammed into the jacket's pockets. Chuck jumped up and went to meet him, and they came together beside a row of barren rose bushes.

"First of all, I don't expect for you to, you know, believe I'm your dad," Chuck told Sebastian after shaking hands. "I'm just glad you made the decision to come out and meet with me. I feel really, you know, honored."

"Hey, it's a beautiful day, and I wanted to get some air—but I've only got a few minutes before I need to be at our attorney's office."

"I won't take up much of your time," Chuck said.

"Like I said, I've got a few minutes. It's not a problem."

As they began strolling the old asphalt pathway that twisted between the shaggy eucalyptus trees shading Palisades Park, Sebastian tried to think of a way to break into a conversation. "So...how did your meeting go with Kitty? She told me you guys met at Denny's."

"You know," Chuck began, "your mother is still a very attractive woman, so I can see where you get some of your looks from. By the way, here's that picture of me from when I was your age or so." He took the photo from his jacket pocket and handed it over.

It only took a glance for Sebastian to see the remarkable resemblance. "That's pretty convincing," he said as an eruption of goose bumps feathered his spine. In fact, the similarity to the young surfer in the faded photograph so startled Sebastian that he failed to notice the man following behind at a measured distance.

"That's also what my buddy Hank said. He's the one who spotted how much I look like you—or I mean I used to look like you, kind of."

"It's OK, I get it. So tell me about yourself. What have you been doing for the last twenty years?"

"Kind of not a whole lot," Chuck replied. "Back when I knew your mom, I was a VW mechanic; since I was sixteen I had one of those old Karmann Ghias that looks kinda like an old bathtub Porsche, and I got pretty good at working on it, so I got myself a job as a mechanic. I was making pretty good money for a kid, more than any of my friends, so I blew all my cash on stupid stuff and got messed up with coke."

"I hear cocaine can be pretty addictive."

Chuck laughed, and the man following them began snapping pictures of the ambling pair. "Oh, that's nothing compared with the crystal meth I started doing after that. See, my work started dropping off after not too long because after a while there wasn't much of those VWs around to fix, you know, because they stopped importing them to the U.S. So I had a hard time making money and started snorting meth 'cause it was cheaper and easier to get to. Then when I couldn't find any other work, I started making the damn stuff in my kitchen with some other guys. Then I got arrested, did four years—which was the minimum sentence for manufacturing less than five hundred grams—and finally got myself sober."

"Wow." Sebastian glanced out at the sparkling blue ocean beyond the park and wondered why anyone would take such drastic measures to escape reality. "How long have you been sober now?"

"Not counting my time in prison, almost seventeen months," Chuck answered as they switched over to a cliffside path, "but you'd better believe it's something I fight myself over every day. After I got out of prison, I started thinking about how all this freedom would feel that much better with just a little meth, so the first thing I did was score some Pepsi—which we call it so it don't get confused with coke, which is, you know, coke; but then after I started sliding into it again and hanging out with those other bagwhores, I got the idea to call my PO, that's my probation officer, and get myself put in a program where I'd live in a sober house."

"So what kind of people live there?"

"Well, my friend Hank's an alcoholic—he's the one, like I told you, that spotted that picture of you and saw the resemblance. He got interested in your religion after reading that *Vanity Fair* article, because we're supposed to have a higher power as a part of our program, but since I was raised Catholic and that stuff never made any sense to me, there was no higher power I ever wanted to get involved with, you know. Well, like I said, Hank and me live in one of those sober-living houses—used to call 'em halfway houses—down in Mid-City LA. There are six of us, six guys, who help each other stay clean and sober. But then when my probation's up in two and a half years, I'm gonna go to Mexico, because they still got lots of those old VWs running around, and some of 'em aren't even that old because they still make 'em in Brazil, I think, and I figure I can get some steady work there and maybe even buy my own place. You know?"

"Sounds like a good plan," Sebastian told him cheerfully, although he was becoming bored and exasperated by the man's rambling. *Is this how Reed felt about me talking about myself?* He decided to change the subject. "So why did you want to meet with me?"

"Well, I guess it's because I never done anything that lasted, you know, never accomplished much in my life. And even some of the hardest inmates I knew at least had some kids they could see from time to time—you'd hear 'em talking after the weekend about whose kid came to visit, and it was like they were dads after some Little League game talking about which of their kids hit a home run. And I used to think about it because in jail you've got time to think about lots of things, thinking that if I had a kid, what I would've done different, like maybe even having a kid would've kept me off the stuff—given me something to keep myself straight for, and something to be proud of. So then when all this came up with you I just thought if, you know, if we hit it off, even just a little, we could, maybe, see if we could, you know, be friends." He glanced nervously at Sebastian and then looked away.

Sebastian smiled kindly at the man because even though it was clear that Chuck's mental abilities were frazzled, he seemed like a good, honest person. "I think I know what you mean. I always wondered what it would feel like to have a father."

Chuck's face brightened. "Now see? That's just what I'm talking about! I mean, don't get me wrong, I think your mom thinks I'm gonna somehow come in and mess up what you guys have going with your religion and your money and all, but I don't care about that. I'll be real happy to just disappear, you know, and just maybe see you…maybe a couple of times a year or so—just like all the other deadbeat dads out there." He laughed.

Sebastian laughed as well. "That would be cool."

"Hey, so tell me what it's like to have those abilities—like I heard you can actually read minds and stuff. Is that true?"

"Sometimes," Sebastian said in a low voice, and then he nodded at an exceptionally attractive blonde as she passed by with her leashed Australian shepherd.

The woman shot Sebastian a knowing smile.

"Like, can you tell when a chick like that is hot for you?" Chuck looked wide-eyed at Sebastian. "I mean, I shouldn't be asking you stuff like that, but it's like, the first thing that popped into my head, because I used to think I could feel when a girl liked me. I used to get a lot of weird things that would just pop into my head sometimes."

Sebastian stopped walking and stared briefly at Chuck. A moment later he resumed their stroll. "On occasion, I've been able to tell that," Sebastian replied coolly.

"And what other, if you don't mind me asking, messages can you get?"

"You know, Chuck, I think I'd rather not talk about it, if you don't mind."

"Oh yeah, now I'm sorry, guy, I should've known better than to ask you about that…it's just that I don't know what kinds of questions to ask someone like you. You know, it's like you and me are from two worlds that are completely different from each other." He thought for a moment as they strolled together, their footsteps scrunching atop the dirt path in unison: *left—right— left—right—left*. "So, I know: What can you tell me about yourself? Like what do you like to do?"

Sebastian pondered his question and decided there really wasn't anything he wanted to share about himself—at least not yet. "Why don't you tell me about the night you met my mother? I'll bet that's a good story."

Chuck gave a low whistle. "I don't remember a whole lot of that night, young man, because me and her got into the stuff early on, and then some of what happened I couldn't—and shouldn't— tell you. But what I can tell you, that I remember, is that the first minute I saw your mom—and she called herself 'Katie' back then—I thought she was the most beautiful girl I'd ever seen. I mean, not cheap and flashy like some girls, but she looked expensive, not like a hooker, of course, but like she had *real class*. And I could tell she wasn't trying to let me know she thought I was hot and all, like she was shy and all, but I just got this feeling that if I went over to her, she'd be cool with me. So, just for the hell of it, I smiled at her from across the room, and she gives me this look, like I knew she would. And then we start talkin', and then later this amazing thing happens with us, and here I am twenty years later walking along the beach with my son…the world-famous celebrity!" He slapped Sebastian on the back and grinned as he looked into his eyes. "Damn, but ain't life funny!"

"It sure is," Sebastian agreed, thinking it actually was. Then he remembered his appointment at Larry's and glanced at his Rolex. "Where did you park? I'll walk you back."

"I had to sell my old Karmann Ghia to, you know, pay for my fines and all," Chuck replied, "and I sure miss the old thing. It was restored to near perfect—silver with red leatherette and a black roof—and was the only thing I ever loved."

"Then how do you get around?"

"On the bus—but don't feel bad for me, 'cause it's been so long since I had my own car, so now riding the bus seems like the only way I ever got anywhere." He held out his hand to Sebastian. "So, I know you got to go and all, but…can we do this again sometime? I mean, you could even come over and meet Hank or something." He grinned.

"I'd like that," Sebastian said as he shook his hand.

And with that final mise-en-scène, the man taking pictures tucked his camera into his coat and began walking briskly toward his car.

CHAPTER 35

Monday Evening

The story broke sometime after six.

Sebastian had been speeding up the Pacific Coast Highway in his Cayenne, on his way to pick up Reed for dinner in Ballena Beach, when his cell phone rang.

He tapped his earpiece. "Hi, Kitty."

"Have you read what…saying about…and Chuck?" Kitty's hysterical voice cut in and out. "Why…you meet…public? What………thinking?"

"I can't hear you. The sunroof's open, my Bluetooth doesn't work, and my earpiece is dying."

Kitty repeated herself, this time at full shriek.

"What are you talking about?" Sebastian yelled back while wheeling his truck over to the highway's shoulder. "What's going on?" He rolled to a stop.

"Someone from one of those ridiculous Internet celebrity gossip sites posted pictures of you with Chuck in a park, with the caption, *Who's your daddy?* And now the Internet is blazing with conjecture. Someone's figured it out, Sebastian, and it's only a matter of time before they find him. I'm so angry at you I can't see straight! What the hell were you thinking?"

"Look, I didn't know anyone was taking pictures. I just went to meet with him, which is exactly what you called me down here to do—or did you forget already?"

"Don't give me that. I never expected in a *million years* that you would do something so senseless as to meet with him at a park—*in Santa Monica*, for God's sake."

"Kitty," he huffed, "where was I supposed to meet him? At our penthouse? There's no way you would've wanted him there. Even the doorman would've taken one look at him and figured out who he was."

"We need to figure out how…how we're going to *handle this,*" Kitty stammered. "It would be one thing if he were someone exceptional, but he's the most boring man in the world—except for his extensive police record, of course—and all it'll take is for him to open his mouth and start that stupid rambling and everyone will know I've—" She stopped.

"Will know you did what? That you made everything up?"

Kitty hesitated. "Certain details of my life have been *embellished,*" she said. "I think that under the circumstances, you might be able to understand how important it was for me to reinvent myself. But my belief in who you are is the absolute truth."

"I get it, Kitty. I understand a whole lot more than you think I do."

"So what're we going to do?"

"First, you've got to tell me the truth."

"About what?"

"Is Chuck my father? Yes or no."

She paused. "Yes. Chuck *is* your father."

Sebastian threw his head back against the headrest. "Thank you for that. *Finally.*"

"I was trying to protect you." She took a drag off her cigarette. "So now what do we do?"

"We'll make him go away—at least for now. I'll call Chuck and ask him if he has somewhere he can go, at least until things die down. And I'll make him understand how important it is for him to not talk to *anyone* about this."

"After you call him, will you let me know? My pacing is wearing out the travertine."

"Sure." He glanced at the dashboard clock and saw he was running late. "I'll give him a quick call right now."

"Please let me know what he says."

"I will."

He ended the call. Then he looked up Chuck's number and tapped it into his iPhone. It rang twice. "Hello?" a man's voice asked.

"Chuck? It's Sebastian."

"No, this is Hank. Oh! You're his son, right? I can't believe I'm actually talking to you!"

"Can I talk to Chuck, please?"

"He's kinda busy right now. His PO is here."

"Can you tell him I need to talk to him? It's urgent."

"Yeah, hold on."

Sebastian waited while a train of cars whizzed by in the adjoining lanes, swaying the Cayenne.

He heard the phone being handed over. "Yeah?"

"Chuck, it's Sebastian. Can you talk?"

"Hey, Son!"

"We've got a problem."

Chuck laughed. "I guess you heard."

"So did Kitty. She's going nuts."

"Yeah, she's the one who e-mailed me that link to that celebrity gossip site. I never in my life thought, you know, I'd be on *there*. Can you believe I'm a celebrity now?"

"Actually, that's just what we need to make sure doesn't happen. At least, not yet."

"Hey, tell her not to worry. No one actually knows who I am yet—except Hank and my PO. She's here, you know, talkin' to me about it."

"Why?"

"Because she saw the pictures too; I guess probation officers check those sites twenty times a day because so many celebrities are, you know, getting caught doing stupid stuff. So she came over wanting to make sure this thing doesn't put my program in jeopardy, and she also wants to make sure I don't go anywhere without letting her know. I need her approval, you know, to wipe my ass." He laughed.

"Actually, that's what I need to talk to you about—not about wiping your ass—I mean we need for you to disappear for a while, until this blows over."

"Where could I go? If I leave the state, the parole board'll throw me in jail."

"You wouldn't have to go far. We just need you to disappear." Sebastian thought for a moment. "Hey! I rented a boat up in Sausalito for two weeks and only used it two days; you could stay up there, and if I needed to I could rent it even longer."

"Are you kiddin'? You'd actually let me stay on a boat in Sausalito? Jesus, I'd pack me a suitcase right now if only I owned one."

"It's not a nice boat, Chuck, but it won't sink. And the motors are strong. Would that be OK with you?"

"But how, you know, would I get up there?"

"My car. We can go together. Tomorrow."

"Wouldn't someone see us?"

"My Porsche has tinted windows."

"You got a Porsche? I always wanted a Porsche." Chuck hesitated. "What the hell. But just let me clear it with my PO first."

"I'll wait," Sebastian told him.

Moments later, Chuck came back on the phone. "She says she needs an address, a phone number, and a contact person, but other than that, she understands what's going on and says I can go."

Sebastian sighed. "I'll give you a call first thing tomorrow, and when I pick you up, I'll have all the information for you to give to her."

"Thanks, young man. I can't believe how much my life is changing right now, thanks to you."

"Just hang in there, Chuck, and everything'll be all right. OK?"

"I can handle that."

Sebastian ended the call, checked his mirrors for approaching traffic, and jammed the accelerator to the floor.

———

Meanwhile, upstairs in the sober-living house, Hank was in the bathroom talking on his cell phone. The reporter from the tabloids had just returned his call. They were very close to an agreement.

And at a roadside Motel 6 in East Oakland—less than an hour's drive from Sausalito—Dyson received a very angry phone call from Olivier, wondering how in the world Sebastian managed to make it back to Los Angeles alive.

CHAPTER 36

Kitty scrolled down the now familiar message boards until she saw her son's name:

> We declare a holy war on Sebastian Black, because he says not to worship the Son of God, and makes himself an idol. The infidel is surely a demon of the dark angel. He gets messages from demons to trick his victims. With every lost sheep goes another soul who will never see the light of Heaven. Also Kitty Black is the Great Harlot as named in Revelation 17–18. Pray for guidance to accomplish His will. These are the End Times! Sebastian Black = Satan is Back!

These people are completely insane! Kitty thought as she read message after message responding to this inflammatory call to action, and the scriptures quoted to support their ridiculous claims. And as she began scrutinizing more of the posts, she noticed an especially angry tone to the messages written by "Reba M," who appeared to be the group's moderator; clearly this woman had an especially toxic grudge against both Sebastian and Kitty.

Suddenly, a batch of new entries began flooding in about the tall, mysterious bald man suspected to be Sebastian's father:

hoping4salvationn: Story says this man is named Chuck Niesen, and he is the infidel's father. hes got a police record, and has spent time in prison. Anyone know anything else?
lordspeaks2me: Just heard it too. Guys a junkie. Guess the infidel isn't so special with a drug criminal dad and a whore 4 a mom.

Kitty's eyelids narrowed at the computer screen; her heart hammered and her brain whirled with rage. *He told them! He defied me and told them!* Then a cooling mist of revenge extinguished her fury: *If Chuck wants to be famous, I'll make him famous.*

She created a new Gmail address and logged in under a fabricated identity—"Hilda," a shortened version of a name from one of her favorite childhood fairy tales.

Hilda: I just seen something about that man the infidels father. I have some info.

Moments later a reply came in:

Reba M: We are looking into this. Anyone with information is encouraged to share it. Who are you? What is your profile? Why are you just now coming to us?

Kitty thought for a moment, pondering what might be the most convincing reason for coming forward at this time.

Hilda: I am in LA and divorced with 9 kids am devout follower of our Lord and Savor Jesus Christ. I heard from a true source this man who just appeared now is the one who really controls the infidel and his mother, who I hear is a good, Christian woman under it all.

Reba M: Where did you get this information?

Hilda: My ex husband fell victim to this satanic church and he went to there meetings all the time and now works for them as a driver. He told me about him this man Chuck and drove him places. People closed to the infidel knowed this man for years but he stayed away secret till now, cuz he is planning on taking over the world religeons this coming year. He is evil more than the infidel. And he is the real liar. He took my husbands money and caused us a divorce so now I don't got no money for all my kids they got all my money the infidel and them

Reba M: Could you get more information about him? We need an address, if at all possible. You'd probably have to contact your ex-husband to do so, and that might be difficult for you, but we need this information to do the service of Our Lord. It sounds like this man needs to be stopped immediately.

Hilda: I could do it maybe tonight hes coming to see one of my kids birthday it is. I will ask him and see what he says about it all then will let U know. OK?

Reba M: Thank you for your assistance with this, Hilda! We praise His name for sending you to us today. This is truly a blessing! And in the meantime, anyone else out there with information about this new evil man, please do God's work and post that information here.

Kitty logged out, smirking.

Then she had an idea, so she went into her office, started the old desktop computer she hadn't touched in months, created an additional Gmail account, logged in under another screen name—Jacob—and posted a message corroborating Hilda's earlier posts. Then she trotted into Sebastian's quarters and, using his laptop, did the same again under the name "William G." Finally satisfied that she had manufactured an uproar, she lit a cigarette and sauntered over to the bar to mix herself a Bombay Sapphire martini.

She swallowed a sip, and the elixir both blazed and frosted her mouth and throat.

Ahhhh.

Then she picked up her cell phone and hit Sebastian's number. It rang twice.

"Kitty?"

"You should read all the Internet chatter about your father. Someone has spilled his trashcan full of beans. You'd better get him hidden away somewhere. *Quickly.*"

"I rented a boat up in Sausalito for a couple of weeks, and I figure that'll be a great place for him to stay until things blow over. We're going up tomorrow morning."

She sipped her martini again. "Why should you go all the way up there? Just loan him the Cayenne, and you can spend the rest of the day pretending you're James Bond, breaking in your brand new Aston Martin—come to think of it, do you think I could still have it outfitted with machine guns and an ejector seat?"

Sebastian laughed. "I *could* take the Cayenne over to Chuck's place in the morning and then have him drop me off at home on his way up there."

"That's a wonderful idea. And just so I know to look out for it on the Internet, does anyone besides you know the name of the boat?"

"Only Reed and me—she's the girl I've been dating. We're actually having dinner right now up in Ballena Beach."

"How nice. I can't wait to meet her. So what did you say the name of the boat is?"

"It's called *Lil's Bastard*."

"That's memorable—and fitting, if I may make an obtuse joke at your expense."

"But now that I've got a father, it's not so fitting, is it?"

"Touché. But isn't it bad luck to christen a boat after a male?"

"Can't girls can be bastards?"

"I suppose you're right." She fiddled with the twin green olives skewered on the glass toothpick. Should she eat them now or later? "Oh, and so you know, I bought Chuck a present—I got him one of those new iPhones like yours so he'll have e-mail and Internet at his fingertips to keep in touch with us should we need to reach him. I put the box on your bed in your quarters, so please don't forget to take it to him tomorrow. It's fully charged and activated, by the way."

"I'll make sure he gets it, Kitty. Anyhow, I gotta go. Our food just—"

"And I'll be sure," Kitty interrupted, "to keep you posted as to any new developments." She drew heavily on her cigarette. "So tomorrow evening, we've got a dinner meeting at Mastro's with Larry about Luke's case. Thanks to your convincing deposition this afternoon, Larry thinks we can start moving toward a reasonable settlement and wants to discuss it with us. And if all goes well, after the meeting we can take that beautiful new car of yours out for a spin; I had the valet take the cover off it and wash it just after you left, so now it's sitting downstairs under the fluorescent lights, shining like a huge red apple."

Reed glared across the table at Sebastian, with her food untouched and growing cold.

"Sounds great," Sebastian yammered, "but I gotta go now."

"Goodbye, darling."

Kitty went back to her computer, logged onto the site, and posted another message:

Hilda: I just learned from my ex husband the mans headed up with the infidel to some place called Saucealeeto near San Fracisco to live on a boat in the marina dock. But don't do nothing untill I contact you tomorrow as I need to confirm hes going there first I will be in touch first thing in the morning.

With clenched teeth Kitty slid the olives off the toothpick into her mouth, and while chewing contentedly she happy-danced over to the bar to make herself another cocktail. As she shook the shaker—the ice cubes and gin making their slick, samba rhythm inside the frosted chrome container—she smiled. With Chuck heading into the war zone as a decoy and her son safe at home, tomorrow was sure to be a banner day.

—

And at the very same moment, in that dreary Motel 6 in Oakland, a gloating Amber shut down her computer and—with Dyson passed out on the floor following another unsuccessful vodka-laced Bibliomancy session—scrolled through her husband's cell phone until she saw the number she sought.

She made the call.

"Dyson," said the deep, exotic voice. "Has the demon returned again?"

"Actually, this is Amber. *Dyson's wife.* What demon?"

"*Ammberrr,*" Olivier purred. "I am so happy to finally speak with you."

CHAPTER 37

Amber is smarter than I thought she would be, Olivier thought. *It was a delight devising such a plan with her. If they get out alive, it will be good to have them both as allies.*

Olivier made his way through the chateau's great room out to the limestone-tiled terrace, where he leaned against the balustrade—elbows locked, hip cocked, and knee bent. He tossed back his head and breathed deeply the tangy sea air, held it, and exhaled slowly. The scent of dried brush—sage and scrub oak and dead weeds—mixed with briny sea spray recalled those days as a youth when he'd been allowed to briefly leave the Guadalest monastery in Alicante and visit his family in their handsome, stone-walled home at the shore. There Olivier would take long walks on the sand with his beloved sister Aurore, talking and dreaming and trying to make sense out of life. Then all too soon he'd be back at the hilltop monastery, with his nose in his books and his fingers bleeding from his chores.

Olivier still hated that monastery, built during the Moorish occupation of Spain in the twelfth century. It was high in Spain's Costa Blanca mountains, which were rockier and higher than those surrounding most of Los Angeles. Its inaccessible location served its inhabitants well: the monks were especially brutal and lived without fear of retribution. There were even well-preserved dungeons at the monastery from the days of the Inquisition, and the accounts of punishments meted out within those cells was sufficient motivation for the boys and young men studying there to adhere to the most strident standards of behavior.

But sometimes the unexpected—and the inexplicable—happened.

Olivier began experiencing visions.

But not the sort of visions a devout Catholic boy should have.

He'd turned fourteen two weeks before, and it was high noon.

"Come play soccer with us, Olivier!" Federico had shouted from across the courtyard.

"I must study!" Olivier shouted back. "The test after lunch today in Latin—I have not yet memorized the Gospel of Mark, and the friar said he will beat me again if I fail!"

Federico waved and sprinted away, dancing a soccer ball between nimble feet.

The sun had been high, and the heat radiating off the cobblestones made Olivier drowsy; the olive tree under which he sat provided little protection from the pervasive, baking glare.

He hadn't even been aware that he'd fallen asleep until he awoke with a panicked start. His heart raced and his breathing quickened and he looked around the courtyard wide-eyed and disoriented. A moment later he'd felt the knife to his throat: it hesitated, then punctured and sawed through his flesh. And in that instant when his own hand flew up to clamp protectively around his unmolested throat, he'd heard the lamb's brief bleating echo out from the barnyard.

That evening he'd taken his place at the long wooden table with the other boys. But when his plate was served to him, instead of devouring his meal he became nauseous.

"Are you sick, young one?" the heirodeacon asked him after the other boys had cleaned their plates and scampered off for evening prayers.

Olivier shook his head. "No, brother. I just cannot eat this. I witnessed the lamb's slaughter."

"God made the animals to provide food to man. You do not appreciate what the Lord has given you? Have you become too proud?"

Olivier took a bite and spat it out.

The heirodeacon pulled him by his ear, all the way to the priory. And because the abbot had just finished his own meal and his belly was filled with greasy mutton and red wine, he was not in the mood to be disturbed.

Until he laid eyes upon Olivier.

Beautiful Olivier.

With his poetic, burgeoning musculature and fierce, dark eyes.

———

Later that night Olivier had returned—weeping and sickened—to his cot, long after the other boys had fallen asleep; the fact that the abbot had been gentle with him, and afterward had even begged his and God's forgiveness, was of little comfort.

But the next morning there was a surprise waiting for him after morning prayers. He'd been leaving the chapel when one of the stern-faced choirmonks pulled him aside.

"From the abbot," the choirmonk whispered, pressing a purple velvet box into Olivier's hand.

Olivier unceremoniously allowed it to fall to the floor. "I do not want anything from him."

The choirmonk slapped him and pushed him to his knees. His face was burning, and he fought back tears. Reluctantly he snatched the box from the floor, still kneeling. "Please tell the abbot thank you," Olivier growled to the man's feet.

The man turned and walked away, his heavy robe making dry, scratching sounds on the chapel's slate floor.

Once alone Olivier opened the box. In it was a rosary of fine white pearls with a delicate, lacelike cross carved from translucent ivory. In the center of the cross was a faceted stone the color of Christ's blood: a sparkling ruby.

It was the most beautiful rosary Olivier had ever seen.

Thus Olivier learned to garner favor from the abbot, and from the other monks and priors and even the heirodeacons; he quickly developed the uncanny ability to ascertain when one of them was hungry for him, eyes moony and minds racing with thoughts of forbidden pleasure.

Upon leaving the monastery at the age of eighteen, Olivier had grown to loathe the accursed place and all it represented. He'd also developed a keen hatred for the scriptures, which he knew by heart…though that same heart scoffed at the messages behind the words. But those cloistered years had not been for naught. He'd learned what a priceless asset he carried with him wherever he went: youth and charm and spellbinding beauty were his, and nearly everyone he met—male or female, young or old—fell under his trance-inducing gaze.

Then his travels took him to Ballena Beach, where he stayed with his great-uncle—a kind, scholarly gentleman who'd been widowed years ago. Olivier worked his magic on him, became the man's sole beneficiary, and then "accidentally" bumped into him at the top of the stairs.

The house and a modest trust was his a month later.

At about that same time, he began reading articles about Sebastian Black.

According to various sources, Sebastian hit puberty at an early age and matured quickly. He was taller and stronger than others of his generation; he was exceptionally handsome; and he was regarded as an extremely charismatic performer. He was also unapologetically sexual with, as one journalist described him, "a sex-drive befitting a satyr on Viagra."

But what rocked Olivier were the reports of his ESP: Sebastian Black experienced premonitions, retrocognitions, and emotion-specific telepathy.

Exactly the same phenomena Olivier experienced.

Upon learning about Sebastian, Olivier had excitedly phoned his sister and told her about him. "Aurore, *este hombre es como nosotros!*"

"What do you mean he is the same as us?" Aurore asked.

"He hears the thoughts of others and has visions of the future, and he is tall and beautiful like you. His new religion helps people in need. Perhaps he could help your Luke."

"Oh, dear brother." She sighed. "No one can help my Luke but God."

"But Aurore, this Sebastian knows about God—and not the God of those monks and abbots. You should go to him. Talk to him. He will be in Bakersfield next week; it is north of Los Angeles and will be a two-hour drive for you. I checked the directions already."

If only he had known.

Dawn. The morning star. *Aurore.* Americans could not pronounce the beautiful name their elegant French mother had given her.

After the tragedy, Olivier spent weeks devising a way to punish Sebastian and his mother. First he needed to scare the pair out of operation before they could trick any more vulnerable followers—hence the flurry of threatening, scripture-filled anonymous e-mails. Then he took nearly all that remained of his inherited trust and hired a legal firm that was certain to win a suit against Sebastian and Kitty.

But that was not enough.

Besides having their peace of mind and money stripped from them, Sebastian and Kitty Black needed to see, taste, and feel the fires of hell.

So Olivier decided to put to use all of that ridiculous, useless knowledge he'd amassed at the monastery. He remembered learning about that obscure anti-Armageddon cult, and he knew that if he could present himself as the latest generation of torchbearers and then convert even a couple of gullible believers, it would make his job easier.

And now the hunt for Sebastian Black was on.

Thanks to Dyson. And thanks to Amber.

"And I will give he that overcometh evil the morning star," Olivier muttered as he made his way back across the terrace toward the empty chalet.

CHAPTER 38

Tuesday Morning

At just after daybreak Sebastian, with the intent of throwing off any lurking paparazzi, picked up Chuck at the bus stop in front of Norm's Coffee Shop on La Cienega south of Melrose. At the same time Kitty—"Hilda"—was back at the penthouse posting a new message on the boards stating that both Chuck and Sebastian were indeed on their way north to "Saucealeeto" to hide out on a boat named "*Lil's Bastard*."

Kitty, of course, knew that it would only be Chuck on board that boat, since her son would be loaning him the Cayenne for his drive north and then meeting up with her later for their dinner with Larry.

But unbeknownst to Kitty, since Chuck owned no car he also hadn't renewed his driver's license since leaving prison.

Thus Sebastian discovered—just moments after Chuck climbed into his car—the need to drive his father to Sausalito himself...which was just fine, because he had no plans for the rest of the morning or afternoon, and he knew he could be back in time for dinner at Mastro's with Kitty and Larry.

—

After reading Hilda's message, Amber woke Dyson to begin treating his hangover; even though they were still in Oakland and only an hour or so from the marina, she knew it was going to take her husband some considerable time to shake his nausea and headache enough to make the drive with her through traffic and over the bridge to Sausalito.

—

At just before one in the afternoon, Chuck and Sebastian—after stops for sodas, gas, fast food, and bathroom visits—pulled into the Sausalito Marina.

Because Chuck had packed his plastic shopping bags lightly, getting settled in *Lil's Bastard* took no time. After that, Sebastian spent the better part of an hour explaining the boat's navigation system, radio, mechanics, and lights. Then finally, with the hour approaching two in the afternoon, Sebastian knew it was time to begin his long drive back home.

"I hate to ask you this," Chuck said, watching Sebastian gather his keys and sunglasses, "but would you mind helping me take this thing out on the water? I'd just like to, you know, watch you drive this thing around a bit to see how it's done, if that's OK."

Sebastian glanced at his watch and shot Chuck a grimace. "I should get going."

"Are you sure you don't want to stay the night and then go back tomorrow?" Chuck asked. "If I were you, I'd be real tired from all that driving, and I would sure hate to see you fall asleep or something on the way home."

Sebastian considered Chuck's suggestion. "I guess I *could* use some rest, but Kitty's gonna kill me if I miss the dinner meeting with our attorney tonight."

"Don't you think she'd, you know, rather know that you were safe?"

Sebastian laughed. "You don't know Kitty."

"What time you got to be there?"

Sebastian looked at his watch again. "I guess at about eight or so. You know, dinnertime."

"You probably ain't gonna make it anyhow," Chuck told him. "But if you got to go, I understand. I just wish you had a couple a minutes to show me how to use that new phone your mom got for me."

Sebastian smiled at him. "You just don't want me to leave, do you?"

Chuck laughed. "With that ESP of yours, you can see right through me now, huh?"

"Anyone could understand why you don't want to be out on this thing by yourself. You're doing Kitty and me a big favor by disappearing—so it's the least we could do to make sure you feel OK with it all."

"So you'll stay?"

"I've got to go first thing in the morning, but sure. I'll spend the night here with you; there's plenty of room for two."

"And you'll show me how to use that phone, right? I gotta call my PO and let her know where I am."

"No worries." Sebastian retrieved the box and unpacked the device. Then he showed Chuck how to turn on the iPhone, how to unlock it and surf the Internet, how to check his e-mail at home, and how to play with some of the apps, such as the weather channel and the news and even one to track his monthly expenses. He also impressed upon Chuck the importance of not getting the device wet.

"This sure is amazing! Now how did you become such an expert at working that?"

Sebastian was about to show Chuck his own iPhone when he realized he'd left his inside the glove box of the Cayenne. "Kitty also got me one of those, but I left mine in the car; I'm starting to think she has stock in Apple." Sebastian thought for a moment. "While you call your PO, I'll run up there and send her a text telling her I had to drive you up here and won't be home until tomorrow. Then we could go for a good run around the bay, and I can show you how this boat handles."

"Are you *sure* it's OK, you know, to miss that big meeting?"

Sebastian shrugged. "Why should I bust my ass getting back to LA just to talk about legal garbage?" Then he remembered the new red Aston Martin…but he quickly resigned himself to the situation at hand. "I mean, what's another day?"

"I'd love the chance for us to get to know each other better," Chuck told him. "We got twenty years to make up for—and I never driven a boat before, even though I spent my young years in the water."

"What do you mean, 'in the water'?"

"I surfed and was pretty good at it. Hey! How about if when we get back home, I could show you how to handle a surfboard?"

"I'd like that. Yeah!"

"So it's a plan." Chuck gave Sebastian's shoulder a friendly squeeze. "Now, let's both go and do whatever we need to, so we can get out on that bay." He scanned the wide expanse of sunny sky over their heads. "I never seen a prettier day!"

"Be back in ten." Sebastian hopped over the bulwark and began trotting up the dock toward where his car was parked in the marina's lot.

But as he loped past the moored sailboats and yachts and inflatables and fishing boats, his stomach suddenly squeezed in on itself and he felt dizzy.

He stopped, still as a stag caught in a hunter's crosshairs.

It's close.

He looked around.

Then the feeling drifted away, like the stench of sewage carried off on a breeze.

Maybe it was just a ghost of the panic he'd felt at Coby's party a few nights ago; after all, no one except Kitty knew that Sebastian and Chuck were here in Sausalito.

He shook off the feeling, aimed his key fob at the Cayenne, and unlocked the doors. Once inside, he composed a text to Kitty instead of calling her, so as not to risk another argument: Chuck didnt have a license so I had 2 drive him up to sf. 2 late 2 come home now. Sorry 2 miss meeting with larry. Fill me in later. B home tomorrow afternoon.—S

Sebastian sent the message, locked his vehicle, and began trotting down the dock toward *Lil's Bastard* with a happy smile on his face and the phone in his pocket.

"Did you tell her?" Chuck asked as soon as he was within earshot.

"Yep."

"What did she say?"

"I sent her a text because I don't *want* to know what she says," Sebastian laughed. And as he jumped over the bulwark, Reed's words to him from the other night echoed in his mind: *I mean, here you are out on the water in this beautiful bay, but you keep checking your phone as if you're waiting for an organ transplant. Are you expecting something that's that important?*

He took the phone out of his pocket, switched it off, and tossed it into the waterproof storage bin with his keys and wallet and Chuck's new iPhone.

Ten minutes later, Sebastian and his father were motoring at half-throttle through the waves of San Francisco Bay, chattering like old pals.

—

At the same time, Dyson and Amber were just completing their transaction with salty Lilly at the Sausalito Boat Rentals. They told her it was their first anniversary, and they had to almost max out their Discover card to afford the thirty-five-foot Carver for the night. Amber had asked if they had anything cheaper, but Lilly told them the only other cabin cruiser she had was already rented and had just gone out on the water.

Amber asked if this particular boat was named *Lil's Bastard* because a dear friend had suggested they rent it if it were still available.

Lilly assured Amber that it was the same boat.

Amber asked to see a photo of the craft so they would know it for next time.

Lilly pointed to a framed picture on the wall. "That's her when she was new," she said. "But now, that blue top is in need of replacement, and the hull could use a fresh gel coat. But since some rich kid just rented it for two weeks, now I'll have the dough to fix 'er up. Probably by the next time y'all come up, she'll look good as new."

Lilly led them out to the boat slip and then spent considerable time showing them how to get the large Carver underway.

Dyson was understandably nervous. And he was still nauseous.

Amber, on the other hand, was quite relaxed. She watched the woman studiously and took precise mental notes.

Then once the pair began motoring slowly out of the marina, with the woman waddling back to her dockside office, Amber turned to Dyson. "Cloak your thoughts," she instructed. "Starting now, you'll do that Christian crossword puzzle I gave you, and I'll be thinking of orphans and natural disasters. Agreed?"

"OK," Dyson replied, his head throbbing. "Orphans and crossword puzzles, until this is over with."

"And no praying," she told him. "He might pick up on that."

Dyson nodded. "We can pray later."

—

Back in Los Angeles, Kitty had just retrieved the text message from her son.

And as she read his words her vision constricted, as if she were suddenly looking at her computer screen through binoculars turned backward.

She steadied herself and hit Sebastian's number on her phone. She got his voicemail.

"Sebastian, you need to get out of there right away!" Kitty yelled. "I've just been reading the message boards, and someone knows where you are! You and Chuck are probably in great danger right now, and you've got to get out of there! Call me as soon as you get this, and let me know you're safe!"

Kitty ended the call, lit a cigarette, and began marching the length of the penthouse.

She needed to do something. *But what?*

Chuck's iPhone! She'd leave him a message too!

But after dialing the number, she heard the robotic notification that the recipient of her call had not yet set up a voicemail account.

Kitty raced to her computer and logged onto the message board:

Hilda: I just heard from my ex husband that that man who claims to be Sebastians father is right here in LA, not in Saucealeeto and he is having lunch with Sebastian at the Farmers Market right now, so where ever you are Reba M you need to find them there. My husband says he dropped them by there just minutes ago I'm sorry to been wrong but that's what he told me yesterday they had a change in plans today is all.

She sat staring at the screen for five minutes, then ten, then twenty, and then an hour without any word from Sebastian or even Chuck or Reba M.

What the hell should I do?

The police!

She would call the police and tell them that the people who were after Sebastian had been tipped off to his whereabouts, and she feared for his life. *That's it!*

Kitty picked up her phone and called information for the phone number of the San Francisco Police Department.

Then after relaying all she knew to the desk sergeant, Kitty had a thought. She went back to her computer to check the tracking devices installed in the iPhones and saw that while Chuck's indicated that he was out in the bay, her son's did not show up on the screen.

He turned it off!

She leaned back in her desk chair and grabbed her pack of cigarettes.

Please hear my thoughts, Sebastian. You are in danger, and you need to call me.

CHAPTER 39

Tuesday Afternoon

"So what was it like in prison?" Sebastian asked Chuck once they were out on the water.

Chuck looked away from his son at the helm and scanned the urban coastline. "It was pretty much just what you seen on TV. But the thing they can never get right in those prison shows is, you know, how scared you are always having to watch your back...and how damn lonely you get, or how frustrating it is to not be able to leave when you want to, or do the stuff you like to do. You dream about the simplest things like having your own bed to sleep in, or just being able to eat when you're hungry. But the saddest thing ever is when your birthday comes along...or Thanksgiving or Christmas. You have one hell of a time forgiving yourself for the stupidness that, you know, got you locked up there in the first place. That's why after I got out and started shoving anything I could get my hands on up my nose again, I knew I needed to get help or else I'd just wind up back there again."

Sebastian looked at his father. "That must've taken a lot of strength."

"The funny thing is that I could only do it—ask for help, I mean—when I was high, if you can believe it."

"What do you mean?"

"What I mean is that, you know, if I was high, I felt real good…and I had the balls to get stuff done. But I knew that when I came down, all I'd want is to get high again, and that would get me in deep trouble. So I got a meeting with my PO, and I didn't admit I was high, you know, otherwise she would've had to take me in. Instead, I told her I was worried about it and was getting cravings, so I asked her for a sober-living house and she hooked me up."

"What about that guy Hank? Was he in prison too?"

"No. Just jail, then rehab—three times. He had three DUIs, and it's a freakin' miracle he didn't kill anyone."

"So he's a good friend of yours?"

"He's a pal." Chuck nodded. "He'd do anything for me and me for him."

"That's great." Sebastian pulled back on the throttles, and the boat slowed. "I don't really have any good friends like that. Like, even though I told my buddy Coby to keep it a secret I was coming up to see him because I had some people coming after me, he told everyone I'd be at his party the other night and these freaks showed up who were the exact people I was running away from."

"You, running away? What's that about?"

"They think I'm some Antichrist, and I'm leading billions of souls into hell."

Chuck laughed. "People do the damndest things when it comes to their religion, don't they?"

"You've got no idea." Sebastian fiddled with the boat's controls. "Anyway, why don't I show you how to run this thing."

Chuck stepped up next to the helm, and Sebastian cut the engines back to an idle.

"Now here"—Sebastian pointed—"are the two throttles. You push these down to go forward, and you pull 'em back to slow down, or all the way back go backwards. The only time this gets tricky is when you're parking it, but if you baby the throttles and know there's a delayed response, you won't have any trouble."

"How so?" Chuck asked, looking unnerved.

"Like…with a car you can slam on the brakes, but not with a boat; the only way to stop this thing is to put the throttles into reverse—but you never want to shove it into reverse with full throttle because the back end will dig down into the water and you'll swamp the boat."

"Huh?"

"Never mind. Look, just do everything in slow motion and you won't be sorry."

"I think I get it."

"Now just push the throttles forward—slowly at first—and see what happens."

Chuck stood with his left hand grasping the steering wheel and his right hand resting on the throttles, and he eased the twin levers forward. At once, the engines went from burbling bass to a steady baritone, then rose up to a soothing alto as they climbed to a comfortable cruising speed. "Hey! This is bitchin'!"

"Slow down!" Sebastian yelled. The afternoon breeze had kicked up the waves, and the boat was starting to slam down atop the breakers.

Chuck trimmed back the throttles, and the hull settled back into a calmer rhythm of climbing and falling, as if the boat were hooked onto the children's roller coaster at an amusement park. "It's not really that hard to drive one of these," he told Sebastian, his expression proud and carefree.

"Just wait until we have to put her back into her slip at the marina," Sebastian laughed.

"So where should I take her?"

"Just make some big, wide circles in the bay. Get used to how she feels."

Ten minutes later, Sebastian was feeling hungry and bored. "Hey, Chuck. We haven't eaten since Bakersfield. Want to head back to the marina and get an early dinner?"

"Sounds good, Son. D'you want to take the helm?"

"That's OK. You could use the practice getting her back into the slip. I'll help you."

"Will do." Chuck began a slow, steady turn across the bay, heading north.

The low afternoon sun made the tips of the waves sparkle like so many camera flashes, and the sky had shed its midday silver glare for a deep, sapphire blue. The postcard-like tableaux soothed Sebastian; this and having a father—although he was, admittedly, strange—whom he could see and hear and touch and talk to completed him in some deep, inexplicable way. Then Sebastian's thoughts turned to Reed and how much he was looking forward to seeing her again. There was so much about her that excited and enticed him: her honesty, as well as her sassy, sarcastic ways; how even while challenging him, her eyes still held a warm and understanding expression; that she was equal parts shy and supremely confident. Even the way she picked and prodded her food was endearing. But most of all, he looked forward to how he felt when she was by his side—like his heart was filled with light that chased the blackest shadows from his soul.

Sebastian grinned happily at Chuck, and Chuck mirrored his delighted expression with an older, crinkled smile.

Then a bigger yacht swung into view. She was glossy white with a broad black stripe running along the top of her hull and a spacious-looking cabin underneath a flying bridge. She was running fast, and she defeated the waves beneath her with grace and ease.

The vessel seemed to be running toward them, but then turned way out to the left as she made a generous arc on her way past, cutting sideways through their wake.

Chuck waved to them, but the woman wearing sunglasses who was piloting the big craft ignored him from her perch atop the flying bridge, as did the man seated next to her who appeared to be reading a newspaper.

All this went unnoticed by Sebastian, who'd just spotted a pair of dolphins and was dreaming of Reed. It was Tuesday, so he figured she was already entrenched in the new college week. And since they had talked about having another date once he returned to Los Angeles, he considered where he might take her. He recalled a restaurant Kitty liked called Jeffrey's in Ballena Beach, and he pictured himself with Reed seated at a table tight against the windows and facing the sunset-colored waves, a single candle flickering against her lovely, laughing face.

When we get back to the marina, I'll give her a call.

Sebastian snapped out of his daydream and saw they were about halfway back to Sausalito. He scanned the western horizon and noticed that some dense afternoon fog had begun tumbling in; this worried him until he judged that *Lil's Bastard* would be safely tucked into her slip by the time the fogbank rolled this—

DANGER!!!

He looked around crazily and saw the same big white yacht banking into a fast U-turn behind them. Then the yacht's prow rose up as its speed increased, and huge white sprays flew out from her sides as the boat mashed flat the rolling gray waves. "Chuck!" he yelled, and Chuck turned to him with an oblivious grin on his face. "That boat's coming for us!" he shouted. "That big white boat's gonna ram us!"

Chuck's face became a mask of panic. "What do I do?"

"Go that way!" His arm shot out to the right. "Angel Island— we need to get closer to shore!"

Chuck eased *Lil's Bastard* into a starboard turn while pushing the throttles all the way forward, but the bigger, more powerful craft also changed its trajectory for a collision, and impact was only moments away.

Lil's Bastard's motors roared, and the boat began building speed; the hull slapped the waves so hard that Sebastian thought the fiberglass would split open. His head snapped forward with the force of hitting the waves, and he clutched the Formica table and then looked over his shoulder and saw the big yacht bearing down on them.

Sebastian braced himself on the bulwark. "That guy's gotta stop!"

CHAPTER 40

There was a crash—a frenzied, thunderous crash.

Sebastian realized he was flying through the air.

Then his head hit something hard—fiberglass?—and he splashed backward into the water.

Icy wetness enveloped him.

His arms and hands and legs and head flailed in slow motion.

He heard things cracking and groaning, grinding to a stop, sizzling as they landed in the water.

The sense of heat nearby told him to keep his eyes shut, but he shook his head and blinked the saltwater from his eyes and tried to scan the scene: *Everything's blurry...only water and fog—two boats, one's...on fire? Where's Chuck?*

He heard someone scream. *A woman.*

He gasped, and water mixed with motor fuel filled his mouth. He spit it out.

It's her!

Something pushed against him and dug into his pants leg; it was heavy and began dragging him under.

I'm sinking!

His lungs fought for air.

Which way is up?

He pulled at the water, but his arms cramped and stung, and he continued to sink.

Kicking furiously, he tried to free his leg but couldn't.

His lungs were bursting. *Need air!*

He fought his lungs' craving—fought it with every synapse in his brain.

Don't open your mouth, don't open your mouth!

Sinking, sinking, his head began to balloon.

I don't want to die like this!

He felt an arm—a groping hand.

The hand grasped him, yanked him upward.

His head broke the water.

Sebastian gasped and blacked out.

———

Chuck, his ears ringing, treaded water feverishly. He'd thrust his left arm under Sebastian's shoulders and was doing a good job of keeping him afloat while looking for something he might grab onto that would keep them both from going under.

Lil's Bastard was mortally wounded and lay burning on her side, and Chuck could see, as he watched her position in the water, that she would soon sink; however, the other vessel was just beginning to tip nose-down. She looked safe for the moment, and he briefly considered swimming toward her, but then he figured whoever had run them down would still be aboard, hell-bent on finishing the job.

A wave shifted the boat's stern toward him, and as it began lifting out of the sea for the water filling her bow, Chuck spotted the name on her backside: *Donald's Folly.*

He resumed scanning the scattered debris and spotted an ice chest bobbing ten or so yards away. *Yeah!*

Chuck began treading his way toward it, being careful to keep Sebastian's shoulders and head above water until he could grab the cooler.

The odors were terrible: his breath caught for the diesel fuel and gasoline and smoke that smelled of burning rubber and plastic.

Chuck had a terrifying thought: *What if the fuel catches fire?*

If that happened, they would most certainly be charred to death.

Then he heard the unmistakable sound of a big helicopter's rotors chopping the air.

Help is coming!

Chuck kicked his legs with all the force he could muster and began gathering the water toward him in broad sweeps with his one free arm.

He was almost to the cooler...

He grabbed the side handle and pushed the upper part of Sebastian's limp torso onto the rectangular plastic lid.

The immense sea rescue chopper's roar was deafening, like a 747 on takeoff—whirring turbines and spinning blades that produced a tornado-like down-force.

It descended closer, blowing the smoke from the burning hull away from them.

A spotlight sliced like a laser through the fog shrouding them.

Chuck released the handle of the cooler to wave.

A voice barked from a bullhorn, instructing him to hang on.

Lil's Bastard was now almost completely submerged, and *Donald's Folly* was sure to follow soon after—and they were drifting toward the wrecks!

We'll get pulled under!

Chuck fought panic as he tightened his grip on both Sebastian and the ice cooler.

He saw a wet-suited man descending on the helicopter's cable with a life vest, a C-collar, and a rescue harness in hand.

Chuck checked Sebastian's neck for a pulse and found it; the beat was fast and steady, though his head lolled sickeningly to the side.

God, don't let his neck be broken!

Some wagging lights to his right distracted Chuck.

Two rigid inflatable boats were drawing near, their spotlights scribbling crazily through the fog.

One of the rescue boats was nearly to them. He heard the engine cut.

Lil's Bastard vanished unceremoniously from the surface.

One down.

The man from the helicopter dangled—like an angel—beside Chuck, and then he dropped into the roiling water. "You OK?" he shouted over the wail of the chopper's turbines. He handed over the life vest to Chuck.

"My son!" Chuck yelled, eyes wide. "He's hurt!"

"Anyone else aboard?!"

"The other boat, there were at least two!" He flashed the "peace" sign. "They rammed us!"

"Got it!" The man fixed a C-collar around Sebastian's neck and deftly fitted the harness around his shoulders, chest, and crotch, while Chuck snapped himself into the life vest. Then after the rescuer signaled the helicopter's crew, a limp and dripping Sebastian—hugged tightly to the heroic rescuer's body—began ascending from the water up through the air, like a pair of huge, line-caught fish.

The divers from the inflatable reached down and—with loud groans—pulled Chuck's heavy frame up and into their craft.

Then while Chuck was being buckled and blanketed inside the tiny craft, a fireboat arrived to extinguish the flames now leaping from the stern of *Donald's Folly*, while a pair of divers climbed aboard to search the craft before it sank. And as the inflatable turned and began beating the waves as it sped toward shore, Chuck looked back at *Donald's Folly* and spotted a rescue cage being lowered from the sea chopper down toward the boat's smoking deck.

What demon did they find inside?

CHAPTER 41

Tuesday Night

Mateo glanced at his black plastic digital watch and grimaced. It was nearly midnight, which meant that after he finished his shift he wouldn't arrive home from Carmel to Big Sur until almost one a.m. And that meant he would get less than five hours of sleep before needing to help Papa get ready for his day and begin taking care of his mother.

At least he could squeeze in an hour's nap after lunch because even his mother's advancing Alzheimer's hadn't stolen her age-old habit of taking a siesta from one to two.

Mateo stepped up the pace of his sidework: wiping off A-1 Sauce bottles; repacking ramekins with sugar and Sweet'N Low packages; marrying ketchup bottles; and wrapping cutlery sets in those scratchy blue poly-cotton napkins for the breakfast shift tomorrow. Finally, at nearly a quarter past twelve, he was finished.

"Hey, Judie. You ready to go?"

She was tallying receipts at a nearby table. "I'm short nearly thirty bucks, so I've gotta figure out where it went. You go on without me. I know you've gotta get up early."

"I'll wait."

Judie's pencil froze in mid-scribble as she glanced at him. "Honey, I'm fine. But you look wiped out." She pointed to the door. "Just go, OK?"

Without replying, Mateo grabbed a washcloth and began wiping down the coffeemakers.

Judie sighed. "OK. I'll just figure it out tomorrow." She began collecting her receipts. "By the way, how's your mom doing these days? I keep forgetting to ask."

"Same as always," Mateo replied. "She meets me for the very first time every morning."

"Is your father still set against putting her in a home?"

"Yeah, and I can't blame him. Have you ever been in one of those places?"

Judie shuddered. "Just put me on an iceberg and push me out to sea."

"Me too. As long as I have my iPod and a picture of Cristiano Ronaldo, I'll be fine."

They laughed while Judie pushed herself up from the table and grabbed her purse from the cabinet beneath the cash register. "Things are really slow here lately, huh?"

"I know it." They began making their way toward the door, keys jingling. "I barely made fifty bucks tonight."

"I made almost ninety, but I worked a double. It hardly seems worth it sometimes."

"Tell me about it," Mateo said, switching off the lights.

Judie pushed open the front door. "Hey, what about that guy you told me about? Are you guys seeing each other this weekend?"

"Dominic is so great! He texted me probably ten times today." Mateo passed through the door, and Judie allowed it to drift closed behind them.

"Where are you guys going on your date?" She fitted her key into the lock.

"I'm working breakfast on Saturday, so we're doing a late lunch at Nepenthe, and then I wanted to show him Feiffer State Beach—you know, where that little road winds down to the big rocks and tide pools. I'm dying to see a nice sunset with him."

"I love that place." Judie rattled the door's handle to make certain it was locked. "That sounds so romantic."

"I just hope I don't get my heart broken," Mateo told her. "*Again.*"

"You just gotta go for it, Mattie. And if he's not the one, it's better you find out now."

The two trudged out to their respective cars in the corner of the parking lot: her old white Toyota 4-Runner, and the dark blue Saturn that had once belonged to Mateo's mother.

They started their cars, and he followed Judie out of the lot as they made their way up Ocean Avenue. Judie waved as she turned north, while Mateo headed south toward the main highway.

He glanced at his gas gauge.

Good thing that Chevron up ahead's still open.

Mateo turned into the driveway of the gas station and parked under the high metal canopy. Then he got out, pushed his debit card in and out of the pump register, tapped his PIN into the keypad, locked the nozzle into the Saturn's filler tube, and squeezed the handle.

As he was waiting, he heard the harmonious whir of knobby-treaded tires slowing behind him. A huge black pickup truck with a dented door pulled into the opposite filling bay. Then two big men jumped down from the vehicle, laughing.

Loudly. Boisterously. *Drunkenly.*

Mateo hunched slightly while focusing on his task, as if transferring gasoline into his vehicle required intense concentration. Then instead of filling his tank completely, he released the pump handle with just over nine bucks on the counter; at least this would get him out of the filling station with enough gas to reach Big Sur.

He returned the nozzle to the pump and ratcheted his gas cap back into place.

"Hey!" one of the men yelled to Mateo.

Mateo ignored him.

"Hey, you!" the other man yelled in falsetto. "Where can I get a pretty rainbow sticker like yours?"

Mateo went to the driver's door and got in, hit the door lock, and started the engine. *Asshole!* Moments later he was on the highway, heading south.

Some miles down the road he spotted some high-up headlights in his mirror, coming fast.

The truck came up behind him and started riding his bumper.

Mateo accelerated, but the truck stayed with him.

The truck flashed its high beams.

Mateo drifted over to the side to let them go by, but the truck did not pass.

He grabbed his cell phone although he knew there wasn't a signal along this stretch of highway; the cell service didn't resume until well past the other side of Bixby Bridge.

Keep calm. Keep calm and concentrate on the road.

He swung back into his lane and hit the gas.

At first the Saturn pulled away from the truck. But within a few moments the pickup was on his tail again—lights flashing, horn honking, riding his bumper.

Mateo's fear swelled. Highway 1 was treacherous even under normal driving conditions, and all it would take was one tap of his bumper for the car to spin off the road and over a cliff.

While doing his best to negotiate the turns, he fingered 911 into his phone.

Of course the call failed. *No service.*

There was nothing to do but run.

Mateo kicked the gas pedal to the floor and leaned into the first of the switchbacks. The Saturn's tires let loose a soprano's wail as he negotiated a sharp right that dipped and then climbed steeply; next he slowed a little as a left hairpin brought him down to a straightaway that bordered an abyss falling hundreds of feet onto jagged rocks.

Where are the other cars?

The truck fell behind on the turns, as he knew it would. But on the straightaways the big V-8 quickly gained on the Saturn's anemic four-cylinder, and those sinister headlights lit up his car's interior like it was daylight.

Please God, let someone see what's happening!

With the Bixby Bridge approaching, Mateo tried his cell phone once again, but his hands were shaking so much that he fumbled the device and it fell between the driver's seat and the transmission hump. He let off the gas a bit while reaching down, his left hand on the wheel and his right hand fishing between the metal tracks and the carpeting.

Where the fuck is it?!

The truck slammed his rear bumper.

Mateo's neck jerked to the side as the Saturn began spinning.

In an instant there was no forward or backward, and Mateo reflexively forced both feet down onto the brake pedal. He felt the car slide sideways before slamming into something—a wall of rock, thank God—just as his airbags deployed, and the cabin filled with smoke.

The truck sped away, its taillights glowing like demon's eyes as it rounded the bend.

Mateo's entire body shook from the adrenaline coursing through him, his breathing frantic. He sniffed the air. *Is that gas? I smell gas!*

He pushed open the door, jumped away from his car, and walked a safe distance from the wreckage. Then he turned and surveyed the car. Clearly, it wasn't drivable.

What am I gonna do?

Then, with relief, he saw the mountainside beyond brighten and dim with the approach of headlights. He positioned himself in the road and was ready to begin waving his arms when the approaching whir of mud tires turned his relief into panic.

The truck pulled to the side of the road and skidded to a stop, with the engine rumbling at an unsteady idle. The two men jumped down and began walking shoulder to shoulder toward him, one man stepping steadily while the other staggered.

Mateo looked over at his car, remembering the tire iron in the trunk. He jumped to the rear of the Saturn and shoved his key into the lock, but the collision had welded the trunk lid to the mangled side of the car, and the metal wouldn't budge.

"Hey, little dude, you weren't drinkin' and drivin' were you?"

Mateo started walking backward. "Leave me alone!"

"You should be nicer...when"—the drunk man belched—"someone asks you...a question."

Both men laughed while Mateo turned and ran, his feet barely making contact with the asphalt, his arms pistoning at his sides.

But the quicker footfalls behind him foretold his doom.

Hands shoved Mateo's shoulders. His feet lost their rhythm and he fell. And as the wind was knocked out of him, the road asphalt dug into his palms.

Mateo tried to yell, but his lungs wouldn't work.

Viselike hands grabbed his shirt and tossed him face-up.

Mateo's hands covered his face, but it didn't help.

The first punch shattered his jaw.

CHAPTER 42

Wednesday Morning

Voices talking…like at a crowded airport baggage claim.

Where am I?

Sebastian looked around the dimly lit room, but he saw only Chuck—wearing ill-fitting and faded blue hospital scrubs and slippers—dozing uncomfortably in a chair that looked too small for his gangly frame.

What happened?

The talking continued: some voices were loud, some soft, some panicked, and some without any emotion whatsoever. And they were so jumbled and garbled that he only was able to make out a word here and there:

Godwannatiredohhpleasehelptimewon'tbetterstaycan'ttreatme ntyesterdaysurgery…

He took a deep breath and focused his attention on Chuck, and as he did so, the voices went away, as if someone had finally turned off multiple televisions blaring on the other side of the wall. "Hey, Chuck. Chuck?"

Chuck's eyes startled open. "You awake?" He blinked exaggeratedly, and Sebastian noticed how bloodshot his eyes were. "How you feelin'?"

Sebastian took slow inventory of his body—wiggle, lift, stretch, shrug. "Tired. I feel really tired and...heavy."

"It's the painkillers. They wear off slow. How's your noggin?" Chuck knocked on his own head.

Sebastian grimaced. "Headache."

"What about your arms?"

"They hurt."

"Yeah, they're pretty bruised up. You must've braced yourself against the hull when the other boat hit us, you know, because they're both black and blue and swollen. And luckily, nothing was broken, but you did get some nasty cuts—especially on that left ankle." Chuck pointed to the bandaged heap at the foot of the bed. "It's pretty chewed up."

"What *other* boat?"

"You don't remember?"Chuck laughed. "I guess it's a good thing you got that concussion and passed out. We were out on the water, and some crazy chick in a cabin cruiser was playin' chicken with us—or trying to ram us on purpose."

Sebastian began recalling moments of what happened: he saw himself on deck of *Lil's Bastard* and remembered falling into the water. "Who saved us?"

"Coast Guard and the San Francisco Fire Department. Your mom called the police to tell 'em something like this was gonna go down. I guess she got a tip somewhere."

"What about the people on the other boat?"

"There's that chick I mentioned. The driver. She's up in the burn ward in pretty bad shape. And there was some guy with her on board, but they're still lookin' for him."

"What did the woman look like?" Sebastian asked, although he already knew the answer.

"Don't know what she looks like now," Chuck said, looking down, "but I'd say she was about your age. And she had on these big sunglasses."

Sebastian shifted in bed, trying to get more comfortable. "What's with the scrubs?"

"My clothes were soaked with diesel fuel." He held out his arms. "What do you think?"

Sebastian laughed. "You look like hell. What else is going on?"

"Well, there's been a lot of press—you know, reporters all over the place. But they're not lettin' anyone see you who's not family, which is, you know, just me right now." He laughed nervously. "Oh, and your mom's on her way up. Her flight from LAX left a couple hours ago, so she should be here any minute."

"Did you talk to her?"

"After we got to the hospital last night, I tried to tell her you were OK, but she's, you know, the hysterical type. She was really, *really* freaked out about this and was gonna drive up even though it was late. But the doctor told her you were OK and she should just fly up in the morning, so she's, you know, flying up. But I told you that already."

Sebastian nodded, and a pain—like a lit fuse—shot up the side of his neck. "Ow."

"What's wrong?"

"My neck's sore, too." Sebastian tried to massage his neck, but his arms smarted too much. "How long am I gonna be here?"

"Hey, man, we're both lucky to be alive, so, you know, just count your blessings and be patient."

"About how long've I been out?"

Chuck glanced at the clock above the bed. "Just over twelve hours."

"Has anyone heard from Reed?"

"You mean that real pretty girl with long black hair?" Chuck let loose a wolf whistle.

He smiled. "Yeah."

"She's downstairs. You know, *she* drove all night to get up here; last I saw she was sleeping in the waiting room. Oh! And before I forget, there's this other lady that's been trying to see you. Her name's Bessie or somethin', and she's been hassling everybody here. She's on one of the other floors taking care of someone else."

"Tess?"

"Yeah! That's it."

"God, I hope Libby's OK."

"Who's Libby?"

"Tess's partner. She's got breast cancer. Do you know what room they're in?"

Chuck pulled a slip of paper from his pocket. "She's in 211. The ICU."

"*The ICU?*" Sebastian thought for a moment. "That doesn't sound right. I was over at their place last week and Libby seemed OK."

Chuck shrugged and leaned over to hand him the paper. "Give her a call."

"Uh, my arms?"

"Sorry." Chuck reached over, picked up the phone, and pushed the numbers. "Hey, Tess? It's Chuck—you know, Sebastian's father. He's awake…sure hold on." He held the phone to his son's head.

"Tess, what's happening?" Sebastian asked.

"Are you OK? How do you feel?"

"I'm, uh, not really sure yet."

"We were so worried. You have no idea what we've been through."

"Why's Libby in the ICU? Is she OK?"

"Oh, it's not Libby this time. She's fine—at least for now. She just had another round of chemo and wasn't up for the drive, so she's home. It's Mateo. He's here in intensive care."

"Who's Mateo?"

"Ramon's son. Remember?"

It took Sebastian a moment to recall. "He's the one who takes care of his mom, right? The gay one?"

"That's him. He's—" Tess's voice caught as she fought back tears. "He's been beaten, savagely. And he's..."

"He's what, Tess?"

"The doctors are saying, but I will not believe it"—Tess's voice broke as she spoke—"that he's not going to recover. We, Ramon and Maggie and I, we need you down here. I've already spoken with the staff, and if you'll consent they'll wheel you down to see him. I know it's a lot to ask, but he's in terrible shape. Terrible. Are you up to doing this for us, Sebastian? Could you please?"

"But doing what for you? What can I do?"

"I don't know. I don't even know why I'm asking you to come down, but something is telling me you might be able to help—especially after what you told Libby about...about me. *In the future.*"

"Tess, it's OK." He exchanged worried looks with Chuck. "We'll call the nurse right now."

CHAPTER 43

Sebastian, tense with apprehension and doing his best to ignore the other patients' various whirlwinds of psychic anxiety, was pushed through the halls by a nurse—with Chuck in tow—and then taken down the elevator to the second floor.

They rounded a corner and Sebastian saw Tess sitting with a frail, elderly woman. They were holding hands, heads down.

"Tess!" Sebastian called out from his wheelchair.

Tess looked up. "Good lord," she said, getting up to greet them. Then she caught sight of Sebastian's bandaged foot. "I knew I shouldn't have forced you to come!"

"It looks worse than it is; actually, one foot still works." He tried a smile. "Is this Maggie?"

At the mention of her name, the tiny, dark-skinned woman smiled. "Hello," she said cheerfully, though her eyes were distant.

Sebastian looked at Tess. "Does she realize?"

"Thank God no," Tess replied. "For once, this damned disease is a blessing."

"What happened?"

"The police say Mateo was beaten by someone who made it look like he'd been injured in a routine accident. He was behind the wheel of his car and left for dead, then they air-lifted him from the accident site to San Jose, and on up to San Francisco because of some specialists they have here for head injuries." Tess leaned in, speaking softly. "But the doctors claim he's officially brain dead, so now it's only a matter of his father deciding when to say goodbye."

"Why would someone've beaten the kid up?" Chuck asked.

"They can't say," Tess said. "The bastards didn't even take his wallet, and his pockets still held tips from his shift at the restaurant. Their only guess—and they're probably right—is it was a hate crime, because of the rainbow sticker on his car."

"Is Ramon inside?" Sebastian asked.

"He's waiting for you. He's hoping you can do something. Anything."

"What does he think *I* can do? What did you tell him?"

"Libby shared your vision with him. You know, about me and some woman in New York."

"Libby told him about that?"

Tess nodded, smiling weakly. "She was quite touched by it. And so was Ramon."

"I'll do whatever I can. But please don't expect any miracles."

With Tess and Maggie following behind, Chuck helped the nurse maneuver the wheelchair down the crowded aisles of the ICU—past patients and visitors and doctors and orderlies—until they came upon Mateo's bed. Tess went behind the curtains and slid them open, while the nurse, with Chuck's help, pushed Sebastian's chair forward so the two were side by side, facing each other.

Sebastian saw that the young man's breathing was assisted by the ventilator at his side and his hands were heavily bandaged; only a small portion of his face was visible through the pristine white dressing covering his head, through which a thick plastic tube emerged. He glanced over at Mateo's bedside table and saw— next to a bouquet of red roses—a framed portrait of a handsome youth with kind eyes, laughing with his mother in happier times.

What monsters did this?

Ramon was sitting in a chair by his son's side. "*Mi amigo*," he told Sebastian once he was situated, "I am glad to see you are going to be all right. Forgive me for asking you this in your condition, but can you do something for us? I prayed my rosary until my fingers are numb, but there does not seem to be any help coming from the Holy Mother or from God."

"I'm...I'm not a healer, Ramon," Sebastian replied. "I can only—"

"They found him barely breathing behind the wheel of his car," Ramon interrupted. "His face was all blood, except for where his tears had washed down his cheeks." He reached over and smoothed his son's chest as it expanded and contracted robotically from the gasping ventilator.

Sebastian was suddenly distracted by Tess tugging on Maggie's elbow as she started to wander off. "Do you think Maggie should be here?"

"She was there to give him his first breath," Ramon answered, "so she should be here to witness his last." He bent over and spoke to Mateo. "*Mijo*, I would like you to meet our friend Sebastian. He is here to help."

"Hey, Mateo," Sebastian cheerfully announced to the unresponsive figure. His stomach was churning; he knew he was entirely out of his element, just as he'd been with Luke.

What can I do?

Sebastian closed his eyes and allowed his consciousness to drift, but the intense grief and anxiety emanating from Ramon conflicted with his concentration. "I hate to ask you this," he said to Ramon, "but could you please leave me alone with him for a few minutes? Like maybe ten?"

"He won't…*go* without us here, will he?" Ramon asked.

"I'll call for you if anything starts to happen."

"I know my wife would like some tea," Ramon replied. "Come, Margarita." He took her hand.

Tess and Chuck followed the couple out to the waiting area.

Sebastian turned to Mateo. "What can I do to help you?"

Predictably, there was no response.

"I don't have any idea what to do for you," Sebastian said softly. "You've been through something horrible, and all I can say is how sorry I feel for you."

Sebastian closed his eyes and began feeling his now familiar combination of queasiness and headache, but almost as soon as the feelings began, they dissipated. There was just too much going on in the ICU; the ethereal stress storms clashing around him made him feel like a broken radio simultaneously picking up all the wrong stations. He desperately needed something to concentrate on…something he could grasp both mentally and spiritually that might join him with Mateo.

He opened his eyes and began focusing on the framed picture of Mateo and Maggie atop the side table.

Nothing happened.

He concentrated harder.

Still nothing.

And as he was about to give up, he heard Libby's voice from across the ether: *When all else fails, be human.*

Sebastian reached out and placed his hand on Mateo's arm. And suddenly: *"You can't help me,"* a voiceless voice stated. *"Please just help my parents."*

"Mateo?" Sebastian whispered.

"Yeah."

"I was about to give up. The doctors said you're brain dead."

"I'm not sure how it works, but the essence of my spirit is here—kind of like how perfume is made from flowers, but the petals are nowhere inside those little bottles. You know?"

"I guess that makes sense."

"So how is it that you're the only one who can hear me?"

"I don't know," Sebastian replied. "It's just a gift I've had that I'm still figuring out how to use."

"Cool."

"So do you already know what's going to happen next?"

"I'm supposed to transition after my body dies, which should be pretty soon."

"Do you know where you're going?"

"It's not exactly a place, it's more of a feeling…I'm going to a feeling. I've been shown that it's like dreaming, where your consciousness leaves your senses and explores, and I've been seeing people I haven't seen in years, like my grandparents and this girl I was friends with in middle school who was hit by a car. We all know nothing bad can happen to us, and we're not really separate from each other anymore, we're together. But the important thing is that I'm not scared, and I want you to let my papa and my mom know I'm OK."

"Have you tried talking to them?"

"Yeah, but no one can hear me. It's like when you're in a pool and you're underwater and trying to yell at someone who's also underwater—you can hear yourself yelling, but they can't hear you, no matter how hard you scream."

"Who did this to you?"

"Two assholes—one was drunk—in a big black truck with snow tires and a dent in the driver's door. They were about my age or maybe older. But I didn't do anything to them, and they were laughing when they hit me, like showing off to each other how hard they could pound my face—and they did this just because I'm gay. I also heard them say that if they got caught they'd say I was coming on to them and it was self-defense. Like I'd ever look twice at any piece of shit like them."

"Is there anything I can do to help you?"

"Nothing. You can't do anything. And I'm getting used to the idea of going somewhere else—but what pisses me off is what I'll be missing."

"Like what?"

"Like...once when I was in San Francisco I was at this bar when I saw these old guys—one was in his sixties and was fat and bald, and this other guy was probably in his seventies or eighties. And I was thinking how nice it was for them to have a place where they could look at guys like me—you know, cute young guys—and I was all full of myself. Then they got up to leave, and I saw how the older guy was so thin he didn't weigh a hundred pounds, and he was wearing these new white shoes and these perfect beige pants with a matching jacket, like he'd gotten all dressed up just to come out to a gay bar.

"Then this is what hit me, is both the bald guy and the old guy stood at the corner, waiting for the light to change like any other old couple who'd been together forever, and I watched them cross the street, and they looked so vulnerable, but they were just happy to be together and to go home to see their dogs or cats and to have another night like they'd had for the last forty years. And I started imagining what they'd been through with the gay rights movement and Harvey Milk's assassination and AIDS and gay marriage, but all they cared about was getting back home and waking up together to some hot coffee. And I thought, that's what I want someday.

"But now I won't have any of that. I won't have those quiet moments, and I'll never find out if Dominic was that guy who's been out there waiting for me. We won't have that date on the beach this Saturday, and we won't ever get to choose our first apartment or which abandoned dog we want from the pound. And that makes me so fucking sad knowing he's out there—my special guy's out there—and we'll never know if it could've worked out because those assholes who killed me stole everything from us!"

"Will it help if I do everything I can to find them," Sebastian asked, "and to make them pay for what they did?"

"What's done is done—those guys have already ruined their karma from other stuff they've done like this. I've been shown that their lives won't be anything but complete misery. But I would like you to make sure they don't do this to someone else—I don't want anyone to go through what my papa is going through now. I don't know how he'll take care of my mom and still be able to work—and after that, who's gonna take care of him when he gets near the end? I was going to be the one to help him."

"I'll take care of it," Sebastian assured him. "But Mateo, what can I tell your dad that'll give him some peace? How will he know that I've spoken with you, and I'm not making up that you're in a safe place?"

"Tell him…tell him it's like with Rupert—I'm still wagging, but you just can't hear me anymore."

"What?" Sebastian asked. "I don't get it."

"He'll know what I'm talking about. Will you be sure to tell my parents that I love them a lot? Tell them I'll always love them, and I'll be watching over them—at least for a while. Oh, and your mom's on her way in, and your girlfriend's upstairs waiting for you. I've been told that your mom was the one who started this whole mess, by the way; it's all her fault. You should ask her about Hilda and see what she says. But I gotta go now because there's someone here to take me. Thanks for talking with me, big guy. And don't forget that you'll need to watch your back from now on—but then you already figured that out. See ya soon."

His last words echoed into oblivion, while the creak of the machinery and the voices of the people in the ICU gathered and swelled. Sebastian opened his eyes and saw that Ramon and Maggie and Tess and Chuck had made their way back to the bedside during his meditation.

Then he heard the heart monitor flat-line.

"*Mijo*," Ramon sobbed. "*Mijo, mijo, mijo.*"

Tess cried and Chuck wiped his eyes.

Even Maggie, in her diminished state, responded to the solemnity of the moment.

Sebastian looked up and saw that Mateo had indeed passed, and in spite of the mechanical insistence of the ventilator, there was no mistaking the empty shell of his body.

Sebastian took Ramon's dry, calloused hand. And as he did this, he was reminded of that day fixing the roof on Tess and Libby's inn, and how reluctant he'd been to help him.

A doctor appeared and placed a hand on Ramon's shoulder. "May I discontinue the ventilator?" she gently asked.

Ramon nodded. "His heart has stopped. My son is gone."

The doctor stepped over to a panel and pushed some buttons. The ventilator fell quiet.

"Time of death," she told the nurse, "is 9:42."

"I'm so sorry," Sebastian said to Ramon. "I'm so, so, *so* sorry."

Ramon squeezed his eyes so that tears glistened down his wrinkled, sunburned cheeks.

"We'll wait outside." Tess took Maggie's hand and began leading her away. "I'll let the police know what happened."

"I'll go with you," Chuck said to Tess.

And then it was just Sebastian and Ramon together.

"You do not know," Ramon began, in a low and breaking voice, "what my life will be like now that my beloved Mateo is gone. You do not know the murdering thoughts in my heart, or how I want to walk the streets until I find the devils that did this to my son. You do not know how I am ripped apart inside, as if God has taken...taken my heart out with an axe. And I wish to find these devils and throw them off cliffs or kill them with my truck or...or smash their heads with hammers to show them what this feels like! You do not know!"

"You're right to feel this way," Sebastian said. "And I hope that I never know what you're feeling right now. But I need to tell you that Mateo spoke to me before he died."

"He *spoke* to you?" Ramon looked horrified. "My boy talked and I was not here to hear him?"

Sebastian waved his hands. "No, no, no. I heard his thoughts. The two of us communicated, *with our minds.*"

"Like you did with Libby?"

Sebastian grimaced. "Kind of. Anyway, Mateo said that he's like Rupert now: *I'm still wagging, but you just can't hear me anymore.* Do you know what that means?"

"He told you about Rupert? About our dog?" Ramon's eyes shone. "Is this a trick?"

"No, I swear it isn't. Honestly, the message came from him just before he passed."

Ramon smiled. "God is good. God is good, God is good."

"So you understand what he was saying?"

"*Si*, I do," Ramon stated. "We have a beautiful black dog at home, and he is getting along in years like us all. And he had the most beautiful, proud tail—it was held high...like a parade whenever he walked. And I would come home from work every day, and Rupert would lay on the cool wood floor, and he would thump that tail like he was playing the happiest drum in the world."

"So what happened?" Sebastian asked.

"He, our Rupert, had something like cancer but not cancer on the tail, and it would not heal because of how happy he was banging it on the floor all the time, so the doctor had to take his tail off. It was so sad, but it was the only way to stop the infections. But that thumping…it was the music of our house; Rupert's tail signaled when a friend had arrived, just like his bark was telling us the enemy was at our door. Then afterward, whenever I came home from work I missed that thumping like I missed my own heartbeat, until I saw that he was still wagging his stump…he was still wagging it. He was as happy to see me as he ever was, and he was still showing me, only I could not hear it."

Sebastian felt his own tears rise. "So when Mateo said, 'I'm still wagging, but you can't hear me anymore,' he was saying that he'll always be close by?"

Ramon nodded while blowing his nose into an old blue handkerchief. "*Si, mi amigo,*" he said, fixing his bloodshot eyes on Sebastian. "My son, now he is with God and also with us. And my Maggie and I will see him soon."

"Excuse me, sir," the nurse announced to Sebastian, "but your mother's on her way in from the garage with a security escort, and there's a young woman waiting for you upstairs. We need space here in the ICU, so maybe we could take you back to your room?"

"Can you tell them we'll be up there in a few minutes?" Sebastian turned to Ramon. "Will you also come up and see me before you leave?"

"No." Ramon shook his head. "I need to find my wife, and we will say goodbye for now, because the night and day has worn on her especially—as it has on Tessita, but she will not admit it. I need to get the ladies home, and it is a long drive from here."

"Of course. Oh! Mateo also said that he loved you and Maggie very much."

Ramon smiled wistfully. "All that matters in life is how we care for each other." He peered deeply into Sebastian's eyes, laid a hand on his shoulder, and then carefully pulled the sheet covering Mateo's body up and over his bandaged head. "He would have liked to know you in this life."

"And I would've liked to know him," Sebastian replied.

"Please come and see us on your way home. I promise I will not make you get up on the roof, and we would like to have you stay for lunch."

Sebastian smiled. "I'd like that."

"*Adios*," Ramon said.

"*Adios.*"

And as he watched the bent man turn and shuffle out through the automatic doors, a quiet panic struck Sebastian as Mateo's final words resonated in his head:

"And don't forget that you'll need to watch your back from now on—but then you already figured that out. See ya soon."

CHAPTER 44

Wednesday Evening

Olivier switched off the news and threw the remote across the room.

It shattered against the far wall.

"Fuck!"

Instead of the boat collision appearing to have been the accident that Amber and he had planned—where Amber was supposed to wait until the fog actually rolled in and then pretend that her carelessness and excessive speed were due to panic and inexperience—various eyewitnesses had given the television reporter their accounts of how the pilot of the yacht had intentionally run down Sebastian Black's tiny cabin cruiser in clear weather; and though the fog had just begun to roll in, at that hour it had not yet hampered anyone's vision. The most damning testimonial had been relayed by some fat old woman named Lilly Strapman, the owner of the boat rental business that had rented the yacht to Amber. "After you been doin' what I do for as long as I done it," she'd told the news camera, "you get a sixth sense about some folks—and these folks that rented my Carver was weird. I could tell right off." She then explained how she'd grabbed her binoculars once the yacht left the marina and saw the entire incident, from wide-arcing circle to full-throttle T-bone. Lilly also confirmed that the man who'd rented the boat along with the woman was indeed aboard the yacht at the time of the collision; the reporter then concluded the news piece by informing viewers that the man's body had not yet been found, and a recovery effort was now underway.

Thus an attempted murder investigation had been launched by the San Francisco district attorney, and Amber's injuries—a concussion, smoke inhalation, and third-degree burns—were being treated in the county hospital's jail ward.

Could Amber implicate me? With any luck she won't survive.

Stupid bitch.

Olivier began formulating ideas about what to do about Amber.

And what to do about Sebastian Black.

———

Sebastian was rolled into his hospital room with Tess and Chuck in tow.

Upon seeing them, Reed launched herself from her chair and went to help the nurse get Sebastian into bed. "Are you OK?" she asked Sebastian. "How do you feel?"

"Better, now that you're here." Sebastian smiled at her as they maneuvered him into bed, being especially careful with his bandaged foot. "You must be exhausted from the drive. Did you at least get some sleep right now?"

"I couldn't sleep. And I couldn't believe it when I heard what happened," Reed said, eyes wide. "Do you think it was those same freaks from Coby's party?"

"I don't know yet," Sebastian lied. "I haven't even talked to the police yet." Their eyes lingered upon each other. "You know you really didn't have to come up here."

"How could I stay away?"

They exchanged smiles while watching the nurse get Sebastian's bed and monitors situated. In the meantime, Tess and Chuck stood about nervously.

Finally, the nurse finished his work and vanished.

"Reed," Sebastian said, "this is my dad Chuck and my friend Tess. She owns that cool little hotel in Big Sur I told you about."

"Actually, Reed and I met earlier," Tess said. "We all got to know each other this morning quite well while awaiting word on your condition and on Mateo." She turned to Chuck. "I'll bet these young folks would like some time alone, and I could certainly use some coffee for the drive back to Big Sur. There's no way I'll let Ramon take the wheel after what he's been through today."

Chuck grunted his agreement, and they shuffled out of the room.

"Aren't you missing school?" Sebastian asked.

"Doesn't matter," she said. "Did you go see Mateo? Tess was telling me about him. Is he going to be OK?"

"He died, Reed. And if I start talking about it, I'll bawl my eyes out."

"Oh no," she said, shaking her head. "Poor guy, and his poor father. From what Tess said, it's going to be so hard for him without his son. Will you tell me what happened later?"

Sebastian nodded. He had a knot in his throat and could not speak.

Reed saw the tears in Sebastian's eyes and moved closer to his bedside. "I'm sure you did whatever you could for them both."

She placed a gentle hand on his shoulder. "So…have they said anything about when you'll be out of here?"

"I haven't even talked to the doctors yet, but I'll probably know something soon."

The rhythmic clicking of high heels on linoleum caught their ears, and they both turned.

"Know something about what?" asked a soft, precise voice.

Kitty stood in the doorway with two security guards behind her. And as she entered, her eyes alighted on her son's bandaged foot and the monitors wired to his body. "My God, they almost killed you!" Finally, she looked at Reed. "Who are you?"

"Kitty, this is Reed," Sebastian replied. "The girl I told you about. Reed, this is Kitty."

Silence.

Finally, Reed extended a hand. "It's nice to finally meet you."

Kitty looked back at her son. "I suppose you'll want me to thank Chuck now."

"It's nice meeting you too," Reed muttered.

"Thank Chuck about what?" asked Sebastian.

"I was told he saved your life," Kitty said, folding herself down into a nearby chair. "He pulled you from the boat wreckage and kept you afloat until help arrived."

Sebastian squinted at her. "He didn't say anything about that to me."

"I heard he saved you too," Reed added, and then she turned to Kitty. "Do you know how that couple found out about Sebastian and Chuck being on that boat? No one knew they were up here except for me and Sebastian. *And you…*"

"The details are still coming in," Kitty said, "but I'll look into it. In the meantime, where's Chuck? I really need to thank him." She scanned Sebastian again, her eyes tearing up. "I don't…I don't *know* how I would've lived with myself if—" She dug out a tissue from her purse and dabbed at her eyes.

Sebastian suddenly recalled Mateo's words: *Your mom was the one who started this whole mess, by the way. You should ask her about Hilda.* He turned to Reed. "Hey, could you go find Chuck and Tess for me?" he asked. "I need to talk to Kitty. *Alone.*"

Reed pushed herself up from the chair. "Do you need anything from the cafeteria?"

"No," Sebastian replied, "but Kitty might be needing a doctor."

"I'm sorry?" Reed asked, shooting first Kitty and then Sebastian an inquisitive glance.

Kitty began studying the framed print of a springtime meadow nearby.

"Just about ten minutes," Sebastian told Reed. "OK?"

"Sure."

After Reed vanished out the door, Sebastian turned to Kitty. "Tell...me...about...*Hilda.*"

Kitty's face flushed pink. "Chuck told the press! He promised me he wouldn't. He even signed a nondisclosure agreement saying he would *keep this all a secret.* Then he wound up selling his story to those awful tabloids!"

"So you told those freaks where to find us, to get back at him?" Sebastian roared. "*What were you thinking?*"

"I didn't try to have him *killed,*" Kitty snarled. "If I'd put my mind to *that,* believe me, he wouldn't still be here. After he made the decision to ignore our agreement and publically come out as your father, I figured he needed to experience that hunted feeling we experience every day. But I had no idea these criminals would go so far!"

"He didn't tell the press, Kitty."

"And how would you know? Don't tell me you actually *believe* what he tells you."

Sebastian stared at her. "Just like I know you're guilty, I know he isn't."

Kitty focused on a stack of magazines on the table next to her. "If you *know* he didn't tell the tabloids, then you must know who did."

"Why don't you ask Chuck yourself when he gets here," Sebastian suggested, "which should be in about, oh, three minutes?"

"Don't tell him what I've done," Kitty begged. "*Please* don't tell him."

"I'm not going to tell him. *You are.*"

"You can't mean that."

"Kitty, what I've learned is that both our good and bad actions last forever. But the good we do doesn't require anything else because once you do something good, you're done. But our bad deeds need restitution, otherwise they keep hanging around until the debt is paid off."

"Thank you *so much* for the sermon," Kitty replied. "I'm glad to see that you're already getting back up to speed."

"Have you heard anything I've said?"

"All right. I'll let Chuck know how sorry I am for my part in all this—but Chuck started this by opening that big, *you know,* stupid mouth of his."

"Being sorry isn't conditional, Kitty. Either you did something wrong, or you didn't. So fix it!"

She narrowed her eyes at him. "You've no idea how much I love getting lectured by my teenage son."

"And you've got no idea how much I love lying here with a concussion and my foot chewed up, thanks to my middle-aged mother almost getting me murdered." Sebastian glared at her. "I'd be more careful if I were you."

"I'm always careful," Kitty replied as she grabbed her purse. "If you'll excuse me, I'm expected down at the police station. I'll call you later." She stood up and marched out the door.

Moments later, Reed returned with Chuck and Tess.

"Where'd Kitty go?" Reed asked.

"To the police station," Sebastian replied. "To turn herself in, I hope."

Tess walked in and dropped her empty coffee cup into the nearby wastebasket. "And I was *so* looking forward to meeting that woman."

Sebastian turned to Chuck. "She wanted me to tell you thanks for saving my life. Why didn't you tell me?"

Chuck shrugged. "It was really the fire department who did the work; they saved us both—and they saved that lady who's upstairs in the burn ward."

"Does anyone know her condition?" Reed asked.

"Even though she did this to me," Sebastian said, "I hope she'll be OK.

"She's pretty banged up," Chuck told them. "And I just saw on the news that they found that guy's body down by the Embarcadero—you know, the guy that was in the boat with her."

Sebastian flashed upon Amber with a man at Coby's party. "Did they identify him yet?"

"Some weird name like *Dacron*," Chuck replied. "But they did say he was that lady's husband."

Sebastian closed his eyes and sighed. *Amber injured, her husband dead, and me in the hospital. How did this all get so fucked up?*

"I heard that they're charging the pilot of the boat with manslaughter *and* attempted murder," Tess told them. "Plus, a good friend in the probation department told me they're looking for someone named 'Hilda,' because it appears that she was the one who set this whole mess in motion. They were only planning on charging this Hilda character with conspiracy, but now that the husband's body has been found and you've been so badly injured, I'd be surprised if they didn't charge her with attempted murder as well."

CHAPTER 45

Two days later Sebastian was released from the hospital. And because Chuck had taken the opportunity to renew his driver's license in San Francisco, he spent the better part of that day enjoying himself behind the wheel of the Cayenne while driving Sebastian south to Century City.

Then after Chuck dropped off both Sebastian and his SUV at the penthouse, he was chauffeured back to his sober-living residence by his housemate LeBron.

"You'll never guess what happened to Hank," LeBron told Chuck as they sped down Olympic Boulevard. "He bought a 2003 Pontiac Grand Prix, a nice red one with tinted windows. Then Tuesday morning it was his turn to make breakfast and we were all starving, so I went up to get him, but his room was all packed up, magazines and pillows and all. Now where do you think he got the money to buy that damn car?"

Actually, Chuck had a pretty good idea where the cash had come from.

—

On that same day, Dyson's remains arrived back in Los Angeles.

Initially, his friends had been disappointed by the discovery of his body the day after the accident because many thought that

Dyson—a fervent believer in the Rapture—had been assumed directly into heaven, and this was why no corpse had been found in or around the boat wreckage. And because of his heroic death these friends declared him a martyr and began planning an elaborate memorial service for the following week.

Unfortunately, Amber would be unable to attend.

Olivier, however, pledged to be there. Then he began composing an especially stirring eulogy, for he could think of nowhere better to find himself some raw, angry recruits than a funeral for someone as rabidly devoted to the word of God as Dyson had been.

—

During this same time, the investigation of Kitty and her participation in the boating disaster was snowballing. Her various IP addresses had betrayed her, and the messages from "Hilda" were incendiary—not only because of her obvious intent to put Chuck and Sebastian in harm's way, but also because of the intentional typos in Kitty's message board posts.

One particularly noteworthy Christian blogger wrote:

"With Kitty Black's calculated use of first grade grammar and wildly misspelled words, while posing as a destitute, abandoned mother of nine children, it is obvious that Ms. Black regards Christians as poverty-stricken backwoods yokels without any common sense or knowledge of birth control. Her intent to gain access to a group of devout Christians by portraying herself as a rambling, hostile, illiterate moron is tantamount to a KKK member thinking he can infiltrate an NAACP meeting by slapping on blackface and tap shoes."

Kitty's legal team was pushing for a plea deal, as their client had no criminal record and had dedicated her life to helping others. In addition, neither Chuck nor Sebastian was pressing charges. Probation and community service were anticipated, especially since Amber—not Kitty—had been piloting *Donald's Folly*.

And speaking of poor, disfigured Amber, she'd been charged with manslaughter because of Dyson's death, as well as conspiracy to inflict grievous bodily harm. Her upcoming conviction was expected, and rumor had it that she'd been placed on suicide watch.

This bothered Sebastian more than anyone knew.

He kept thinking back to that evening he'd spent with Amber after the gathering almost three years ago. And although he rationalized that he'd probably been too young to act responsibly back then, this mess was exactly what he'd been trying to warn Kitty about when he told her *our bad deeds need restitution, otherwise they just keep hanging around until the debt is paid.*

So Sebastian needed to find a way to repay his debt—regardless of what Amber had done to him. But he couldn't decide on exactly what to do. After all, there were complications…

In the meantime, the lawsuit brought by Luke's relatives was also progressing badly; the family had rejected two of Kitty's initial cash offers, and the negative press and legal entanglements from the San Francisco Bay incident only served to strengthen the family's assertion that Kitty used her criminal mind to coerce those at a psychological disadvantage—in Luke's case, a loving father and mother who were severely unbalanced by their son's serious (the lawyers omitted the word "terminal") illness—for monetary gain.

Meanwhile, Reed and Sebastian were becoming inseparable. Reed began spending an hour or so after her classes each day tending to Sebastian's needs for assistance and laughter. These cozy afternoons stretched into Friday night dinners, Saturday afternoons watching movies at the penthouse, and Sunday mornings people-watching along the Third Street Promenade—with Sebastian layered in cold-weather garb, his vintage tortoiseshell Tart-Arnell sunglasses firmly in place—or visiting Ellie up in Ballena Beach. And through it all, Reed kept her feelings about Sebastian at a simmer, being unwilling to wholly risk her heart again. But at least the hours together made their relationship stronger by the day, and she knew that the genuine affection she felt toward him was reciprocated.

Autumn crept toward winter. Twilight arrived a tad earlier upon each day's passing, and the formerly balmy afternoons became suffused with a Pacific fogbank that shrouded the penthouse in thick gray mist each evening.

Then Thanksgiving passed and Reed and Sebastian began planning a trip to Big Sur over the upcoming semester break because Tess had alerted Sebastian to Libby's recent downward slide. Sebastian ached to offer his support to the couple, and he wanted Reed to have the pleasure of getting to know both ladies—and Ramon and Maggie—while she still had the opportunity.

But what was becoming of his ministry? Kitty publically blamed Sebastian's cancellation of all Evo-love appearances on the injuries he'd suffered during the alleged murder attempt, and he was more than happy for this extended vacation. And at first all was well because the boat crash had garnered Sebastian considerable sympathy. But as the weeks became months and Sebastian shunned any further appearances or interviews—and even more unflattering press about Kitty emerged, while Chuck was further exposed as the bumbling ex-con he was—the usual river of donations dried to a mere creek.

"We've finally had an offer on the house in Rancho Mirage," Kitty told Sebastian one afternoon. "It's beyond laughable, and the goddamn realtor will make more money with her commission than we will, but at least I won't have to write those checks each month." She glared at him. "Would it kill you to finally make that appearance on the *Today Show*? Or does it thrill you that we're sprinting to the poor house?"

But Sebastian refused to help. And this made Kitty very, very nervous—especially since her legal fees were adding up, taxi meter–style, and she was the only one trying to stop their financial tailspin.

But where to begin?

Kitty began spending hours, burning cigarette in hand, brainstorming ways to repair her sullied name, knowing that if she could salvage her reputation there was a chance Evo-love might flourish again—that is, if she could only motivate her son.

She began with the well-worn, but accurate, adage: *There's no such thing as bad press.* And since Kitty knew that "*sin plus redemption plus forgiveness equals cash*" was the formula for profitable evangelism, she figured there was probably some way she might flip her impending trial into an opportunity for profit, in a similar manner to the other celebrities who'd been arrested for domestic battery, DUI, or even securities fraud, and then launched their signature lines of overpriced perfumes, useless gadgets, and spiffy housewares upon release from jail.

Thus Kitty decided first to broadcast *her* version of the events leading up to the assault on Chuck and Sebastian, then to express her profound regret for her actions, and finally to demonstrate her own brand of Godlike forgiveness.

And she knew just the poor soul who was in need of public absolution.

CHAPTER 46

December

Forgiveness...

With the Rancho Mirage home closing escrow, and because it was only a few days until Christmas, Kitty thought it fitting to post Amber's bail. She also paid for Dyson's outstanding funeral expenses, because shipping his body back to Los Angeles had been outrageously expensive. Next, she convinced Larry to find a decent attorney who could handle Amber's defense, even on Kitty's rapidly shrinking dime. Finally, she hired a therapist for Amber who specialized in treating survivors of religious cults.

But just after Amber's release on bond the therapist spoke with her over the phone, and then she contacted Kitty with her assessment that Amber was "totally unresponsive to the idea of therapy." The therapist graciously declined the opportunity to work with Amber, but she suggested that perhaps Kitty herself might benefit from some one-on-one time.

Kitty declined, resting assured that with the holiest day of the year looming, she had done everything in her power to make things right.

Then Kitty phoned Amber for a lunch date, suggesting they meet at the Ivy in Beverly Hills. "They are famous for their delicious chopped salad," Kitty mentioned in her voicemail, "and the weather this time of the year on the patio is absolutely perfect, with their outdoor heaters blazing away, of course." She pictured herself rolling up to the paparazzi-swarmed valet in her Bentley Continental with the now disfigured—but elegantly dressed, thanks to her—Amber, looking like the most gracious of gal-pals who was unafraid to be seen with the criminal who'd been hellbent on murdering her own son. Kitty would present herself as blithely magnanimous, and the bloggers would lift her into cyber-sainthood.

Almost immediately, Kitty received a response from Amber's attorney—instead of Amber—politely declining the invitation until after their respective trials were concluded.

In spite of this snub, Kitty was gleeful; she spent the remaining hours of that afternoon composing an essay entitled "To Forgive and Forget Is to Give and to Get," and then posted it on Sebastian's website, had it e-blasted from the public relations firm she'd hired, and had her publicist contact the *Today Show* to see about booking herself on it.

Her favorite passages from the essay were:

"When Sebastian's father tried to destroy my son's reputation by publically disclosing his own identity, my primal drive made me seek revenge, or 'forced retribution' instead of trying to understand his motivation. It was my mistake to provide sensitive information to those who sought to injure my son's father, and I freely admit that I am guilty of seeking a 'Neanderthal' means to punish this man..."

And:

"When we 'forgive' those who have wronged us, and then 'forget' what they've done, we are able to 'give' that person what he/she needs, and this results in our ability to 'get' what we needed all along, which is safety and security for those we love...To illustrate my belief in this philosophy, I reached out to the woman who (allegedly) attempted to murder both my son and his father. After posting her bail, hiring her an attorney, paying her husband's funeral expenses, and even finding her a therapist who specializes in religious cults, I invited her to lunch in Beverly Hills. Unfortunately she declined my invitation, but I'm sure that someday she will understand that we might even still be good friends..."

The next day, Christmas Eve, Kitty received a panicked phone call from Larry, advising her that the manifesto she'd e-blasted was an admission of guilt, as she could no longer claim prior ignorance of Amber's intent to physically harm Sebastian and Chuck. And she had barely finished this very, very tense conversation with Larry when another call came in from Amber's attorney.

"Kitty? You're not going to believe this."

She drew heavily on her cigarette. "I'd believe anything at this point."

"Are you sitting down?"

"Does it really matter?"

"My client, Amber, just killed herself. They found her body in her apartment, with four empty bottles of Visine and a large Jamba Juice cup on her night table. They also found a rambling, scripture-filled suicide note she left for the police, and although she had some colorful words to describe you, she didn't implicate you in anything."

Kitty made certain that she sounded shocked and horrified and deeply saddened, and she did her very best to camouflage the intense relief she felt.

Upon ending the call, Kitty tapped out another letter expressing the deepest of condolences to Amber's family and friends, and she e-mailed this to the PR firm for another e-blast.

The story hit the newswires and the Internet just before lunchtime.

This news devastated Sebastian—who was on his way north with Reed and Chuck to visit Libby and Tess—because he'd finally decided to apologize to Amber just as soon as he returned from their trip, and he wanted to let her know that he was now willing to do whatever was necessary to make things right.

But now he would never get the chance.

—

Two days later, Kitty received a letter in the mail. It was from Amber.

She read it dispassionately, shuffled her way over to the living room fireplace, and then set the letter ablaze with her cigarette lighter. Seeing as the morning fog had refused to burn off, she used the burning paper to ignite a cozy fire.

She stared blankly at the single flaming page as it curled into a blackened sheet of ash beneath the jumbled faux logs. Then she made her way to the bar and mixed herself a very large, very strong martini.

As she took her first sip, she thought, *I wish I'd known that before.*

This changes everything.

CHAPTER 47

Christmas Eve

It was almost noon, and Olivier was fiddling with his laptop when three e-mails alerting him to Amber's suicide came in.

He switched on his television and began surfing the news stations.

The story was on every channel, even those broadcasting from New York.

She did it. She really did it.

—

Nearly three months before—just days after the boating incident in September—he drove to San Francisco to visit Amber in the hospital. Once there, he convinced the nurses and the policewoman standing guard that he was Amber's minister and needed to provide some spiritual comfort to her.

With Bible in hand he emptied his pockets, and they waved a metal detecting wand around him and then allowed him, with an escort just outside the open door, into her hospital room.

Her condition shocked him.

The flaming boat wreck had burned a considerable part of her head, so she was propped up on the pillows with her face so concealed by the bandages that all he could see were her eyelids bulging from within the white gauze, and her mouth.

"Amber?" he whispered, caressing her handcuffed wrist. "Amber, it is Olivier. I was so sorry to learn of your injuries and of your husband's ultimate sacrifice for God. I came here as soon as I was able."

She opened one eye, peered at him, and then closed it. "You mean," she whispered, "you're sorry to hear that Sebastian's still alive. What do you want?"

"I am here with an important message from Our Lord," Olivier said as he backed carefully into the chair at her bedside and then eased himself down into it. "He has requested one final sacrifice on your part. I know it is very much for God to ask of you, but there is still something of immense importance that must be done."

"Are you crazy?" Amber slurred. "My husband is dead, I've just been barbecued, and I can't even move my hands with these handcuffs on—and by the way, that Hugo Boss cologne you're wearing is making me nauseous."

"But this trial, like all of God's trials, is only temporary," Olivier told her. "The Lord has shown me that you will recover and will be released from this hospital ”

"To go to jail," Amber mumbled.

"God's work knows no boundaries, no prison walls," Olivier continued, "for now we are on the cusp of the last days, and I've had a vision of a lamb with fleece as white as snow, lying on the golden altar of God. Scripture tells us that it is in the sacrifice of this lamb that the holy war begins between God and Satan. I have it *on good authority* that you, dear Amber, are chosen to be that lamb; your ultimate sacrifice will light the fuse of God's holy cannons to begin the Great War that all mankind has been waiting for."

303

They looked at each other, the silence thick between them.

"Dyson"—she coughed weakly—"told me you're from some old family that's trying to *prevent* Armageddon. So why do you want it to start now?"

"God has shown me that it is, at last, *the time*. This is exactly the year my family has been waiting two millennia for. And *you* are the one to begin it, my friend. *You* are the one who must make the ultimate sacrifice."

"Haven't I already sacrificed enough?" Sick with remorse, Amber thought of Dyson, and then she flashed upon her toddler son, wondering if he was happy.

Just as Olivier had intercepted a vision of this child upon his first conversation with Amber, when they had been planning the boat "accident," Olivier saw the little blond boy once again. "You already know what I am going to ask? God is great!"

"Why would you ask me such a thing?"

"But it is not I who asks, Sister. It is *your mission*."

"How do I know you're not just making this up?"

"God told me you might think this, so he revealed to me another vision. He showed me that your little boy is safe and happy and growing like a strong tree."

Amber's eyes opened wide. "You know about Eldon?"

"God is great," Olivier repeated.

"But not even Dyson knew about him! After my father forced me to give him up, I made myself believe he never existed." She began to cry. "Is he really OK? Do you know where he is?"

"I know *exactly* where he is," Olivier lied. "And I will make it my personal mission to see that his needs are taken care of. But God only enlightened me about your son to convince you of His need for your sacrifice. Are you ready to hear more?"

She sniffled. "I guess."

Olivier scooted himself forward onto the edge of his chair. "Your life has been designed by God so you could carry forth this holiest mission, much like Judas's life was written for him to carry forth *his* own mission. Must I remind you that you have no husband, and you have no children to raise? And you have been tragically scarred by this terrible turn of events." He scooted closer to her. "Even heathen Catholics consider Judas to be a saint for his role in our Savior's death and for his subsequent martyring of himself from that holy tree in Gethsemane. And I don't need to remind you that without Judas, there would have been no crucifixion, and without that crucifixion, all of mankind would still be doomed for all eternity." He sat back in his chair and grasped its arms, as if it were his throne. "And so it is that you, Sister Amber, will martyr yourself and set in motion the harkening of the last days. But unlike poor Judas, you will be celebrated into eternity for your faith in God, and not for your betrayal of Him."

Amber was silent as his words sunk in.

"Tell me more about your vision," she asked at last.

He was hoping she would request this, as he had been up earlier than usual this morning composing and rehearsing what he would say:

"During prayers last night I had a vision of two sheep," Olivier told her, as though telling her a bedtime story. "One lamb with fleece as white as snow, and the other a coal-black ram. The white lamb was playful…like an innocent child did she run through the flowering springtime meadow under a shining sun high in bluest sky. But then the black ram appeared; he began chasing the white lamb, flashing his red, glowing eyes and sharp fangs." He lowered his voice. "At first the white lamb tried to make friends, but the black lamb only wanted to steal the lamb's innocence and destroy her with his poisoned seed. This devil ram"—Olivier was whispering now—"mounted the horrified lamb, which caused the angels to weep. Then after the terrible deed was finished, God lifted up the lamb, knowing the innocent spawn growing inside her must be sent away." Olivier patted Amber's forearm. "Thus did God kiss the lamb and comfort her before sending her to be with His angels. And there was great gnashing of teeth by the evil ones upon the assumption of the white lamb into heaven; the black ram demanded possession of his spawn, but now would never know him. And so a great war ensued between the black ram with his bat-winged minions, and God with His scores of angels. Finally was the black ram defeated and sent to the pits of fiery hell, while the white lamb rests peacefully with her baby into all eternity...*at our Savior's feet.*"

Olivier watched as tears spilled from Amber's eyes onto her bandaged cheeks. "God is good, Sister Amber," he told her.

"Amen." Amber sniffled. "*God is good.*"

———

So here he was, nearly three months later—on Christmas Eve— spared the distraction of the possibility of Amber implicating him in her upcoming trial.

What a lovely Christmas present Kitty had given him by posting Amber's bail!

But now with both Dyson *and* Amber gone, it would be that much more difficult to carry forth his revenge for Luke's and Aurore's murders.

At least he was not completely alone.

Olivier had recruited three men at Dyson's funeral.

They'd been training together ever since.

CHAPTER 48

This year Tess knew she would have the trouble of decorating the inn for Christmas by herself. Libby just wasn't up for it. So the day before Christmas, Tess took her freshly sharpened axe out to the stand of redwoods and cedars she and Libby had planted some years back specifically for this purpose, selected a tree she thought might be the right size for in front of the plate-glass windows, and began hacking away at the base of the trunk.

Fifteen minutes later—and with a brand new crick burning up her backside—Tess was dragging the conifer through the woods toward the inn.

But she was so exhausted from the effort that she waited until the next morning before lifting the blasted tree into its base, and then she began decorating it with their vast collection of ornaments given to them by friends and guests over the years.

By noon she was down to her last box of crimson and emerald and golden glass bulbs when a noise caught her ear, and she turned to find Libby gazing up at the tree from her wheelchair.

"I never thought, as a Jewish girl, that I'd ever be sad to see my last Christmas tree," Libby said.

Tess ignored the comment and continued adjusting the balance and drape of the sparkling white mini-lights.

"It's a beauty, Tess," Libby tried once more. "You did an especially wonderful job. I'm sorry I couldn't help you."

Tess turned to Libby. "I didn't know you were awake," she said softly, her eyes glinting. "But I am glad to see you getting around so well in that blasted contraption."

"It's wonderful for saving wear and tear on my good shoes," Libby deadpanned.

"Are you hungry?"

"I can wait until they get here," Libby replied. "I haven't much of an appetite these days, as you well know."

"Speaking of appetites, I picked up some of that apple chutney you like." Tess groaned while bending over to pick up the wrinkled white plastic grocery bags that had held the mini-lights. "And the turkey's a bit smaller than we normally get, but oh"—she stopped and cocked her ear toward the entry and then quickly drew herself upright—"I think I hear them now." Just then, Maxi growled and leapt to his feet as Tess began scurrying double-time, gathering the boxes and the bags used for storing their holiday belongings. She had just succeeded in tossing everything into the nearby storage closet when the knocker on the front door clacked, and Maxi became a barking whirlwind.

As Tess went to answer the door, Libby straightened herself up in the wheelchair, adjusted her blouse, smoothed her hands over her forehead and cheeks, and tugged at her wig.

—

Hours later, with the inn's atmosphere heady with the aromas of crisping bird and baking pies and steaming vegetables and bubbling sauces, Sebastian and Reed and Tess and Chuck and Libby took their places around the old maple farmhouse table in the dining room, while Tess came and went from kitchen to dining room to kitchen and back with the fervor of a veteran truck stop waitress.

"May I please have the gravy, if it's not too much trouble?" Reed asked Libby.

"Of course, dear." Libby lifted the gravy boat from where it rested in front of her plate and passed it to Chuck, who handed it to Reed.

"Thank you," Reed said.

"You needn't be so formal," Libby told Reed.

"I think she's just a little afraid of you two," Sebastian interjected, "because I told her about how much you grilled me when I first came here."

"Oh, she has nothing to worry about," Tess assured as she appeared from the kitchen carrying a steaming bowl of risotto, "unless she's claiming to be the Virgin Mary, or the reincarnation of Natalie Wood, or some other such nonsense."

Sebastian laughed appreciatively.

Tess grinned at him. "How are the sweet potatoes?"

"They're great." Sebastian looked over at Libby. "Are you still feeling nauseous?"

"Thank you for asking, but let's talk about pleasant things," Libby replied, turning to Chuck. "Mr. Niesen, I'm so glad you could join us today. We've heard so many wonderful things about you."

"Now who's being so formal?" Chuck laughed. "Call me Chuck, and thanks for inviting me. I can't tell you the last time I had anything but, you know, spaghetti and meatballs for dinner." He grinned at everyone and then took a noisy sip from his coffee mug.

"Hey, how are Ramon and Maggie?" Sebastian asked, cutting into his turkey.

"Ramon finally seems to be recovering from Mateo's passing, now that those young criminals have been caught," Tess replied as she pulled out her chair and sat with a relieved grunt. "And I can't tell you how much he appreciated those amazing words of Mateo's you relayed to him in the hospital. They really gave him peace."

"Those words gave us all peace," Libby added, sending Sebastian a knowing look.

"What about Maggie?" Reed asked. "How is she doing?"

"Ironically, there seems to be a small improvement in her memory," Libby replied. "I don't know if it was the shock of losing Mateo—"

"Or divine intervention," Tess cut in.

Libby raised her eyebrows at Tess and turned back to Reed. "But Maggie has begun recalling some minor details from long ago. For instance, she suddenly remembered how Ramon would spend the night of each payday inside a bar in Tijuana, and she would have to send the eldest boy to drag him out; she even remembered convincing the foreman at his work to have his pay given to her instead of to him."

Sebastian laughed. "You'd never know he was ever like that, by looking at him now."

"The follies of youth," Libby noted. "We all did things we aren't proud of."

Tess and Libby exchanged knowing glances.

"Does she realize Mateo is gone?" Reed asked.

Tess looked at Reed. "Well now, that's the funniest thing. Ramon says he hears Maggie talking to him, calling him by name and having these one-sided conversations as she wanders around the house and yard. And before Sebastian came along with his visions, Ramon would've just thought his wife had completely lost it. But now, he refers to Mateo as their 'guardian angel,' and he keeps his room at home exactly as he left it...even with that huge poster of that gorgeous soccer player on the wall."

Reed smiled and then joined the rest of the table in a quiet moment of happy concentration on the feast. "Tess," Reed asked, finally setting down her fork, "what kind of work did you do before you and Libby came up here?"

"I was a probation officer for teenagers," Tess replied. "But after seeing so many of the gay and lesbian kids get beat up, I started my own group home agency." She twirled her wineglass before taking an airy sip of pinot noir. "Sometimes I find myself missing the business...the hustle and bustle, and helping those exasperating kids get their lives together. I'd consider starting something like that again, but that would mean having to move from the inn to someplace more centrally located."

"This place is so beautiful," Reed said, scanning the room. "I can't ever imagine wanting to leave it."

And Sebastian mentally agreed. With the placid, moonlit sea beyond the plate-glass windows, and the stone fireplace casting golden flickers against the slipcovered wing chairs and overstuffed sofas, the room begged its guests to linger, chat, read, and doze.

"We've had some wonderful moments here. Haven't we?" Tess gazed at Libby, and Libby returned her warm smile.

"Why did you pick Big Sur?" Sebastian asked. "This meal is amazing, by the way."

Tess smiled, and Libby dabbed at her mouth with the corner of her napkin. "I was lucky enough to get a job teaching group therapy courses at Esalen, which is a compound down the highway. Tess would drive up from LA and visit me on the weekends, and we both fell in love with the coastline and the redwoods— even the leftover hippie culture appealed to us." She took a quick sip of wine. "During this time I had an idea for a book written specifically for couples in same-sex relationships. So I wrote it, sold it, and Tess shuttered her group home and we moved up here to open this inn."

Sebastian felt the phone in his pocket vibrate. He pulled it out and saw it was Kitty calling. "I need to take this," he announced, scooting back his chair. "Sorry." He stepped quickly across the room toward the front door.

"Hi, Kitty," he said, stepping outside.

"We're settling with Luke's family," Kitty's flat voice announced. "You've left me to deal with this, on Christmas Eve no less, and so I have."

"OK."

"I've already signed the papers. It was almost twice as much as I thought it might be, but they were prepared to push forward with the civil suit—jury and everything."

"Like I said, it's OK, Kitty."

"But you haven't even asked me how much we've settled for."

"OK then. How much?"

She told him.

"That's a lot of money."

"It's all we have left. But Larry keeps telling me if we go to court, it could be more—and that's not counting the fortune I've already paid his team in legal fees for both this case and my upcoming criminal trial."

"And?" Sebastian asked.

"What I'm telling you is that I am now in the process of liquidating everything we have: the bonds, the stocks, our retirements, those meager profits from the house in Rancho Mirage, and even—if I have to—this penthouse. And it is all because of your refusal to resurrect your crumbling ministry."

"No. It's because you're getting the karmic retribution coming to you."

Kitty drew in a breath. "I want you to listen very carefully to my words: You have unbelievable gifts. You had, at one time, a thriving ministry. Now, because of your selfish refusal to work, your mother has been publicly humiliated and is about to be homeless. But there you are, hundreds of miles away from me and still in a unique position to help—while at the same time helping the world—and yet you still refuse to do so."

"What's your point?"

"You could come back home," Kitty said, "and we could design something together that would help the world and help us both, something that could raise money for clean water, and AIDS in Africa, and birth control in emerging nations, and wildlife refuges, and sustainable energy sources, and housing for the elderly, and so on, and so on. There is so much you could be doing right now, Sebastian, and...yet...you...do...*nothing!*"

"Kitty, I need to go," he told her. "Merry Christmas, by the way."

"What kind of man have I raised?!" she screeched.

Sebastian ended the call. As he made his way back toward the inn, he tried to push the echo of her voice from his head, but her words unsettled him. He knew she was right: he still had a name, his gifts, and his charisma. And he supposed he could actually revamp his ministry and focus on the projects that were close to his heart...but he'd only do it *his* way this time, even if it meant angering Kitty more than he already had.

But he still needed to think about it and talk it over with Reed.

She had a good perspective on things.

Smiling, Sebastian stepped up to the front door. As he pushed it open, an outburst of laughter met his ears.

He quickened his step to find out what he'd missed.

CHAPTER 49

"I don't think I'd ever get tired of Big Sur," Reed said as she gazed at the beach's nightscape. The moon cast a silver trail across the bay to the horizon and made luminous the sandy beach, while the jagged black silhouettes of the shoreline's Monterey pines appeared windswept, although the night was calm. "It's like every time I turn my head, there's a new postcard. Oh, look!" She pointed to a home perched atop a nearby hill, its windows glowing yellow against the cobalt nighttime sky. "Can you imagine watching the sunsets and sunrises from that house up there?"

"There is something magical here." Sebastian put his arm around Reed's shoulders and pulled her close. "You know, maybe when Tess is finally alone—and I hate even saying that—I could come up here to help out for a while. I was even thinking of working with Ramon because I know he could use the help, and there's a lot I could learn from that old man."

Reed turned to him, her expression serious. "How much time do you think Libby has?"

Sebastian shrugged. "It's hard to say. With cancer you just never know; then again, she's already survived a lot longer than anyone ever thought she would."

"I know the real reason you're thinking about coming up here to live. You want Tess to cook for you every day," Reed said, laughing. "That dinner was incredible. And I can't believe how much of it you ate!"

"I did eat too much, but the walking helps—hey, watch out." Sebastian gestured toward a large puddle in the sand, and they shifted course. "But I'm so torn up about what to do, Reed. Every time I think I'm coming closer to a decision, something makes me change my mind."

"Does any of this have to do with Kitty's phone call tonight?"

"Some of it does."

"Did she have more bad news?"

Sebastian slowed his pace. "I just don't trust her anymore. Not at all. But the part that's tearing me apart is the good work I still want to do, but I'd need her help."

"Like what?"

"Back when Kitty and I started this ministry, it wasn't so much about the money or the fame, but about helping people get through their grief. And even though I was only a kid, I knew I was making a difference. But then Kitty blew it all up into penthouses and Aston Martins and *Vanity Fair* interviews, which somehow got twisted into Luke's murder and boat crashes and Armageddon cults." He paused. "And now, after meeting you and Tess and Libby, and Ramon and Chuck and even Mateo, I'm convinced that love and being able to help people is all that matters."

"So if you could do anything in the world, what would that be?"

"I guess I'd want to fight the selfishness and the prejudice and the greed that makes people miserable, and to help people feel loved and safe."

"Sounds like you're competing for Miss Universe," Reed joked.

"I know it sounds stupid, but there's so much misery in this world that no one ever sees—especially not in America. Reed, have you ever seen the aftermath of a suicide bombing? Or pictures of an AIDS wards in Africa, or orphanages in Romania, or a mass grave in Darfur, or a public beheading…or even the inside of a nursing home or a slaughterhouse or a puppy mill?"

Reed looked away. "No. And I don't want to."

"But that's just it! You don't want to know about those things, *to see those things*, because it's fucking depressing, and we keep ourselves from seeing those horrors because once you do you can't get the pictures out of your head. And it scares me to think of going up against the forces that feed off that misery. It's overwhelming, Reed, it's *completely* overwhelming."

"Of course you can't change all those situations. But you could change *one* of them."

"But you don't know what it does to me, *inside*." Sebastian patted his chest. "That's one of the curses I live with. I can actually *feel* other people's pain. Did you know that tonight at dinner, I actually felt Libby's cancer."

"You did? How?"

"Not as much as she feels it, of course, but I actually *felt pain* when I passed the butter to her. And it took me a second to realize that what I felt in *my* body was actually the swollen lymph nodes in *her* arm and the scar tissue from her surgeries that was stretching as she reached for the dish." He looked into her eyes. "I guess before now, I'd been so self-absorbed that I'd never felt empathy. But now that I can, I'm also starting to feel the *misery* of others. Reed, can you imagine what would happen if I went back to Africa or the Middle East, or even to a nursing home? I'd go crazy!"

Reed thought for a moment. "Well then, there's only one thing you can do."

"Please, tell me."

"Raise money," she said. "That's one thing you're really good at, isn't it?"

"I guess."

"And maybe you could set up a new foundation and go on tour, raising money for these causes so other people—I mean, those who do have the stomach for it—could do what *they* do best without having to worry about the funds."

"Actually, that's pretty much what Kitty said in our conversation tonight."

Reed took his hand. "Which means she wouldn't fight you."

"As long as I threw a big chunk of the money her way."

"But how much you give her is all up to you now, isn't it? I think by now Kitty's realized who needs who."

"You're right. But if I went on some big tour, it wouldn't help out Tess or Libby, or Ramon. And I'd be away from *you*."

"Look, Sebastian, I'll be out of college this June, and maybe I could come up here to help out—you know, until you came back. That way, the inn could be your home base instead of that morgue-looking, cigarette-smelling penthouse."

"Do you really like Tess and Libby enough to do that for them?"

"Sure, they're wonderful. I was just nervous about meeting them."

"Why?" Sebastian tugged on her hand, and they stopped walking to face each other.

"Because they're important to you," Reed explained. "And you're important to me."

"I was hoping you'd say I was more than just important to you…"

Reed laughed. "Of course you're more than just important. You're my boyfriend."

Sebastian leaned in close. "Reed, I'm in love with you too," he said, "so you don't have to be scared about saying something or feeling something I'm not."

Reed lifted her eyes to his. "I do love you. But over the past few months I've been trying to convince myself that I wasn't, because I was scared. How seventh grade does that sound?"

"I've been scared too. Scared of a lot of things. But I've never felt scared about how I feel for you." Sebastian pulled her toward him and their lips touched.

Just then Reed felt as if a torch sparked within her. She felt— actually *felt* warmth inside her body that grew hotter as they kissed; she felt a fire radiating from his body into hers.

She broke her mouth from his. "What *is* that?"

"What's what?"

"That…*hot* feeling! I've never felt it before."

"Kind of like the seat heaters in my car?" He put his hand on her waist, just below her breasts. "Right here?"

"Yes."

"It's from me. But we can both feel it now because we're not afraid anymore."

"I don't get it."

"Here." He encircled her with his arms and held her tightly. *Love*, he thought. *Love*.

Reed lifted her mouth to his.

—

Once back inside the Curcio Suite, Sebastian gently lowered Reed onto the bed, their tongues dancing. Then his mouth broke from hers, and his lips inched softly from ear to nape to shoulder while his fingers unbuttoned her blouse. Once she was exposed, he pulled off his own shirt and lay atop her, allowing the heat from her silken skin to fully stoke his own flame. Her breath came more quickly as his tongue kissed the swell of her naked breasts, nibbling now and then at the hard tips. Reed gave a pleasured gasp, and her hand slid inside Sebastian's pants.

Sebastian unbuttoned his jeans, and her hand made contact with the hot shaft that was so much warmer than the rest of his body. He sighed. His hand reached up her skirt and found her panties; his fingertips detected dampness. At once Reed moaned—more loudly than she'd meant to—and Sebastian giggled. "Are you sure you're ready?"

Reed looked up at him, and their eyes met in the dimmed light. "Now that's a stupid question."

Sebastian helped her off with her clothes, and then after sliding off his jeans he stood before her, his nakedness shadowed and shining in the moonlight like an erotically carved statue. Then he crouched toward her and lowered himself.

At first Reed was concerned, knowing she was not quite ready for their union, especially after feeling the size of him; it had been months since she'd been with a man, and she'd never been with anyone as heroically built as Sebastian. But she was soon delighted to feel him kissing a trail down from her breasts, to her taut belly, and finally to the exquisite opening between her thighs.

A hot rush overtook her, and her back arched. But she wondered: would he continue pleasuring her, or would he perform just enough to be polite and then proceed with his own needs?

He answered her silent question with his own moans as his tongue buried deeper, then drew out to tease her over and over. And as she blissfully watched his rippled back and shoulders writhe and twist, it occurred to Reed that just as Sebastian had felt Libby's pain at dinner, at this moment perhaps he was also experiencing Reed's pleasure.

The thought nearly crested her. *OH!*

Sebastian suddenly pulled himself up from her. "I gotta stop," he said breathlessly, his huge green eyes shining like firelit emeralds in the darkness. "I gotta stop or I'm gonna cum."

Instead of replying Reed kissed him—the sharp taste of herself on his lips and tongue—while guiding him into herself. And as he slid slowly inside, she felt herself being more fully opened than she'd ever been, as if being entered by a divine phallus slicked with her own essence.

And just as his length had reached her limit, Sebastian began to withdraw. Then he pushed. And withdrew—over and over and over.

Then the strangest thing happened. Although Reed had been taking pleasure watching him, Sebastian's eyes thus far had been closed throughout much of their lovemaking. But the moment this thought formulated itself in her mind Sebastian's eyelids popped open, and a pure, dazzling expression of love passed from one to the other with the seeming magnitude of a starburst. At once Sebastian realized that he had never made love before this moment, while Reed realized that Sebastian and she had both been, in some inexplicable way, born for one another. "I love you," Sebastian told her. "I love you, I love you."

His thrusting quickened.

Her arms wrapped around his back and slid down to feel the hard crease between his buttocks, urging him further inside. She began losing herself to the pleasure this man, this superb beast was giving her. His breaths came faster, his mumblings less coherent and more childlike—or was it more...*feminine*? And she realized through the haze of her impending climax that she had somehow conquered this glorious creature and had made him vulnerable. *Innocent.* And completely hers. "I love you!" Reed whispered as steady waves began coursing through her. She clamped herself more tightly upon him, and as her orgasm began she felt...she felt? She felt that she was no longer only female! The pleasure in her body was a woman's, but the heated ecstasy in her mind was a man's—a man with a splendid, muscled body and a rigid cock! She bucked wildly at Sebastian and heard him whimper and moan, thus realizing that *he* was feeling...*he was feeling what only a woman can feel!*

In that euphoric moment, they became one.

CHAPTER 50

Early January

"The Staples Center is booked." Kitty blew out a plume of smoke and leveled her gaze at her son. "But the Forum is still available for that weekend."

"How many does it seat?" Sebastian asked.

"About seventeen thousand. And they've finally rehabbed those awful bathrooms."

"What about special effects?"

"Lighting, sound, and those guys who built the rising pedestal are all available and hungry for the work; thank God for this terrible economy." Kitty laughed.

Sebastian shot Kitty a worried glance. "What about security?"

"Arthur's company won't take the job because of what happened in San Francisco. He said it's too risky right now and to please call him in a year or so after things settle down."

Sebastian frowned. "So what do we do? We need security."

"The Forum's management suggested Secur-U-Best in Canoga Park. I spoke with them and they can do it, but they'll need to hire and train some extra guards because they usually only handle off-list performers and trade shows. They're also charging a bit more than Arthur does, but they've assured me you'll be safe. So what're you planning for the show?"

"I was counting on the same basic special effects, sound, and lighting because of the short time frame...but some of the actual service is new."

Kitty squinted at him. "And exactly how different will it be? We know what works. We know what brings in the cash."

"I'm going to shift everything away from the Holocene Transition," Sebastian replied. "And I thought if I started with Luke's family's murder-suicide and then talk about the boat crash and how it ultimately killed Amber and her husband, it'll be a good way to show how spiritually out of touch everyone is. Then I can go into our usual cheerful information about wars and famines and persecution."

"Lord, how depressing!" Kitty flicked a long ash into the nearby ashtray. "Remember, Sebastian, tearjerkers don't earn half the money that heartwarming films make. And do you really want to send people back to their already pathetic lives even more depressed? You'll have a dozen more Visine suicides on your hands the next morning." She ground out her cigarette. "You know we still have thousands and thousands of unsold books that are collecting dust instead of money for your causes. So I feel *very* strongly that you should read from *The Book of Holocene*, and then focus on your 'love is all that matters' philosophy and how this new mission will better cure the ills of the world. You'll go out on a high note. And people pay good money to feel happy."

———

Olivier was also making plans.

With the infusion of cash he'd received as a result of his settlement with Kitty, he'd hired a famous decorator—Caitlyn de Palma—and was in the process of having the chateau renovated.

He also bought himself a red Aston Martin convertible, just like Sebastian's, because Kitty would not sell him the one she owned. "I'll drive it off a cliff myself before I'd sell it to that prick," was the message that came to him from his lawyers.

Then just one week after receiving his lump sum, he read on Kitty's blog about Sebastian's upcoming gathering at the Forum; Olivier had correctly assumed that once the Black family's coffers were empty, Sebastian would get back to work.

Olivier did some investigation into security companies favored by the Forum, and he learned that a company called Secur-U-Best just happened to be hiring for an upcoming tour that would launch on the same date as Sebastian's opening show. He found the employment link on the company's website and completed the on-line job application; then he sent the link to the three men from Dyson's funeral who were now his faithful allies: Eddie and Juan and Andre.

God's Furious Angels was now officially open for business, even if what came to pass ultimately meant leaving behind his beautiful chateau and his snappy sports car.

After all, there was still that huge sum of cash just sitting in the bank, and he could always start over in Europe.

Olivier considered this for only a moment before reaching a conclusion:

It'll be worth it.

CHAPTER 51

February

After training each day at the Forum during the week before Sebastian's event, Olivier and his "Furious Angels"—Eddie, Juan, and Andre—met at a motel room in Hollywood to hone their plan; Olivier had chosen to rent this space by the hour to ensure his anonymity with the men, whom he knew better than to trust. He had even introduced himself to the trio under the pseudonym "Rico."

"There is a location at the very top of the stadium where the seats have not been sold," Olivier told the men, pointing to the schematic diagram he'd swiped from the Forum. "It has a clear sightline to the rising pedestal and has many places where Eddie can hide the gun he bought. There is also a fire exit to the left he can use."

"Why not just pick him off on the street?" Juan asked. "I read where he just bought a convertible sports car. We could pull up next to him at night, and it would just look like a robbery that went bad. Or road rage."

Olivier had already considered such a tactic, but had opted for more drama; he wanted Sebastian's death to be a loud and colorful historic event that he might fondly remember for the rest of his life. "Sebastian should be sent to hell while telling lies about

Christ's church. This will send a message to the other false prophets and their followers."

"So where's the gun, Eddie?" Juan asked excitedly.

"Right here." Eddie presented a large, expensive looking briefcase to the men. With a flourish, he placed it atop the motel's sagging queen size bed and clicked open its locks. Inside were sections of a rifle that assembled clarinet-style. "It's an Armalite AR-15 that I bought cheap off some broke meth head on Craigslist," Eddie bragged. "It's high powered like you can't believe, and with that military scope I could shoot both eyes out of a deer before it even hit the ground." He laughed. "But Rico, how will I know when to shoot it?"

"You'll shoot only when everyone is focused on him, and when you have a clear shot," Olivier replied. "But first you will move into position only after I tell you to."

Eddie looked at Olivier. "What're you gonna say into the radio?"

Olivier thought for a moment. "I will announce that some people are smoking marijuana in row K—K for *kill*."

"Do you think the gun case'll fit under the chairs?" Andre asked.

Olivier extended his arm along the perimeter of the case. "It will fit," he replied. "Today I measured the space with my hand."

"But we got to get it into the building somehow," Juan reminded, "and they check us every time we go in or out. How're we gonna get it in there?"

Each man looked from one to the other.

And since no one offered a reasonable answer, the four men prayed for a solution to present itself.

And the next day it did.

Around lunchtime on the day before the event a truck arrived to deliver boxes of *The Book of Holocene*, because Kitty had instructed the Forum's management that their roaming snack carriers should also perform double-duty as booksellers. And since time was growing short—it was only hours before show-time—the security guards were asked to help get the book boxes to various destinations throughout the Forum.

Olivier grabbed a dolly and stacked several boxes onto it.

Then he made a quick stop at Eddie's Chevy Cavalier, where the rest of the men made a show of taking a cigarette break while Eddie put the rifle case in one of the boxes, placed some books over the gun, folded over the top, and began rolling the dolly over to the elevator.

Minutes later, the weapon was stowed beneath the seats.

CHAPTER 52

Reed's phone rang. "Hello?"

"It's me," Ellie announced. "Did I catch you at a bad time?"

"Sebastian's coming over for dinner, and I'm kind of running late."

"Never mind. I'll let you go—"

"Actually, I need to know if you're coming to Sebastian's show tomorrow. I saved you a couple of great seats."

"Ooooh, I forgot that Coby's grandmother's seventy-fifth is on Saturday—his father's wife is throwing one of those big snobby parties where no one makes eye contact until they get drunk. Do you forgive me?"

"Of course. Listen, I gotta go, but we'll see each other after that. OK?"

"OK. And I'll be thinking of you guys this weekend. Tell your gorgeous boyfriend to break a leg, but not anything else. Love you."

"Love you too."

—

Reed heard a soft knock on her door and jumped to open it. "Did anyone follow you here?"

Sebastian walked in, shut the door behind himself, and kissed her on the cheek. "Nobody saw me. It worked out great having the clicker to your underground parking." He sniffed the air. "Lasagna?"

"I thought I'd tempt fate tonight." Reed laughed. "But you actually showed up, so the fates lost their bet." She watched him as he looked nervously around her apartment. "Is something bothering you?"

He looked at her, eyebrows furrowed. "Not at all. Why?"

"You look really anxious. Are you OK?"

"I'm…great. I just have a lot on my mind." From behind his back, Sebastian presented a bottle of champagne to her. "Kitty sends her regards."

Reed looked at the dusty bottle skeptically, noting the shield-shaped bronze label. "You mean she actually sent this? This stuff is *expensive*—not to mention you're still underage."

Sebastian chuckled. "I took it from her wine cooler. It's not Bombay Sapphire gin, so she won't miss it. Here, before it gets warm."

Reed took the champagne from him, opened the refrigerator door, and carefully placed the bottle on the top shelf. "What's the occasion?"

"I bought you something." He smiled sheepishly at her and then dug a tiny cardboard box out from his coat pocket. "It's not much, but there's a story behind it."

She held out her hand, and he gently placed the box in her palm. "Can I open it?"

"If you want to."

Reed pulled the lid off the box, fingered the cotton inside, and touched cold metal. *No!* She pulled the ring from the box, and the stone sparkled with miniscule rainbow flashes. "Oh, it's beautiful!"

Sebastian laughed. "It's not beautiful, Reed, but thanks for saying so." He dropped down slowly onto one knee. "And I'll get you a really beautiful ring if you'll spend the rest of your life with me." He looked up at her, his expression earnest and his green eyes shining.

Reed's heart pounded. "Are you asking me what I think you are?"

"Will you...marry me?"

Reed took a step back from him. "Oh, I...this is such a surprise."

Instantly, his gleeful smile dropped away. "*What do you mean?*"

She handed him back the box with the ring in it, and he secreted it inside his pocket. "Here." She held out her hand. "Get up so we can sit down. OK?" Sebastian got up from the floor, and Reed led him across the room toward the sofa. They sat down and she took his hand. "I'm so flattered, Sebastian. Really I am."

"I should leave now." Sebastian tried to pull his hand away, but Reed wouldn't let go. "And that fucking lasagna of yours is cursed."

"Baby, I'm not saying no. I love you, and I'd love to say yes, but I think it's just a little too soon." She tightened her grasp on his hand. "How about if we give it some more time before making a decision? Like even another six months?"

He looked at her, his eyes suddenly brimming and bloodshot. "But why not now?"

She sighed. "You know...I've been dreading the day when I felt like an older woman dating a younger man, and here it is. We've only been together for six months—and it's been wonderful, but I think we'd both benefit from getting to know each other better before committing to something like marriage. Do you understand?"

"No," he said, his voice cracking. "I don't understand."

Reed's heart swelled as she looked him. "We'll just keep going along like we have been. And before you know it, the time's going to pass and we'll both be *absolutely* sure about this."

Sebastian looked up at her. "You don't know what it's like for me, Reed. My religion talks all about love, but before now I've never really known what love felt like." A single tear dripped down his face, and he wiped it away with his hand. "I think Kitty loves me, and maybe Chuck's starting to too, and I've been with girls and guys who've wanted me and I wanted them, but before now—*before you*—love was a complete mystery…that is, until you helped me figure it out. And I don't want to lose that—I *can't* lose that. Because I don't know what I'd do if you ever went away…and the only way that won't happen is for us to"—his voice caught— "to get married. Because my heart aches when I think of losing you. It tears me apart inside. And tomorrow I'll be starting the tour and we won't see each other for a while." He dug the box out from his pocket again. "Seeing this ring on your finger will make me feel like…will let me *know* that you'll always be there for me."

Reed's heart ached for him, but her maturity told her she needed to be strong about this. "I'm not going anywhere," she told him. "And I'm telling you that we both need *more* time together, *not less*. OK?"

"Can you at least try the ring on?" he whispered. "I've been picturing it on your hand now for days."

"Let's see it again."

Sebastian opened the box, pinched out the metal band, and slipped it on her finger.

It was much too large. The stone slipped limply to the side. They both laughed.

"So tell me about my cardboard box ring," Reed giggled, sniffling. "You said there was a story."

"I bought it on eBay," Sebastian told her, wiping his eyes. "It cost me forty bucks."

"Am I really worth all that much?" Reed asked wistfully. "My last boyfriend only spent twenty dollars on the ring he got me. It's good to know that I'm coming up in the world."

Sebastian laughed. "Do you remember when I told you about fixing Tess and Libby's roof?"

"With Ramon?"

"He paid me forty dollars for helping him out, and I remember thinking it was the first time I'd ever made any money without Kitty being involved in it. So I kept those two twenties all this time until I found that ring last week on eBay for thirty-two dollars; but with tax and delivery it ate up all my reserves." He took her hand, and they both examined the sparkling band. "It's genuine sterling silver with a cubic zirconium rock."

"I'll get it sized tomorrow," Reed told him. "I absolutely love it, and don't you dare think of getting me anything else. I'll just tell people it's a promise ring. OK?"

He beamed at her. "A promise ring sounds good."

Reed's oven timer beeped. "Are you hungry, Mr. Black?"

He grinned at her and drew her into his arms. "For lasagna, or for Reed?"

"Tonight you can have plenty of both…"

"I'm starving." He leaned down and pressed his mouth to hers. They kissed deeply. "Will the lasagna burn if it has to wait another hour?" he whispered in her ear.

Reed's skin bloomed with goose bumps. She slipped her hands inside his T-shirt and ran her hands up and down the hard, velvet warmth of his muscled torso. "I think ovens come with an off switch these days," she told him, pinching his nipples playfully. "Why don't you go in the bedroom, and I'll be there in a minute."

His mouth found hers and they kissed again, this time so passionately that she felt the heat between her legs begin to simmer. "I think I like the idea of dessert before dinner," she murmured.

"Hurry." Sebastian gave her neck a quick nuzzle and then disappeared into her bedroom.

Smiling like a fool, Reed stomped around the kitchen turning off the oven and the range top burners and blowing out candles. Her heart was singing, and she couldn't ever remember feeling happier.

"Are you coming?" Sebastian's deep voice beckoned from within the darkness of her bedroom. "Because if you're not here soon, I will be." He laughed.

Reed tossed the dishtowel in her hand onto the countertop. *How did I ever get so lucky?*

CHAPTER 53

"I hate to say this, but I feel nervous." Sebastian wiped away the line of sweat from his upper lip. His anxious stare met Reed's in the dressing table mirror.

"I know why I feel nervous." She placed her hands reassuringly on his shoulders and began trying to squeeze out the knots. "But I can only imagine what it would be like to get up in front of that many people."

Sebastian cracked his neck. "It's not that. I could do performances like this in my sleep."

"Then what is it?"

"For one thing, I've never presented any material without Kitty's input—not that I don't appreciate all the help you gave me with it, Reed. I couldn't be doing this without you. But I'm still afraid people aren't going to like what I'm going to say. It's preachy…and it might go against what people have been taught to believe."

"Your speech is amazing, and it's going to resonate with people more than you know. I just wish Chuck could be here in time to watch you from the beginning; it's too bad he couldn't get out of leading that meeting earlier tonight." She looked at him and saw the concern still lingering in his eyes. "Is there something else you're not telling me?"

"I just"—Sebastian hesitated—"I guess I have this heavy feeling, and my stomach's upset. I started getting it during rehearsal this morning, right after the sound check."

"Are you just nervous about throwing away Kitty's script?"

"No. And I know she'll be furious when she hears me do my speech instead of hers, but I'm not scared of her. Not after everything that's happened."

"Well then…what did you eat for breakfast?"

"Bagel and cream cheese, same as always."

"Maybe it went bad," Reed suggested.

"It wasn't bad, Reed. *Something's not right.*"

They held each other's gaze while sharing the same thought. Then Reed continued rubbing his shoulders. "What can we do about it?"

"There's nothing I can do," Sebastian told her. "And I'm *not* running away. Maybe I'm just be picking up on them in the audience like I did at Coby's party, when they could've tried something and didn't. Besides, security's searched everyone and made sure they've gone through metal detectors, and I can't see someone doing much damage without a gun—or a bomb."

"But what if they crash a boat up onto the stage?" Reed deadpanned.

Sebastian grinned up at her. "You always know how to make me laugh."

"Is there anything else I can do?"

"Just stay here with me until it starts. And you'll be in the front row, right? I want to look down and see your beautiful face—and that huge rock on your finger." He laughed.

"I'll be there." Reed cradled his hands in hers. "I just hope the stage lights reflecting off my priceless diamond don't blind you."

Sebastian grinned at her, put his arm around her waist, and pulled her to him. Their mouths opened to each other, and Reed felt that amazing, giddy warmth bloom in her belly.

"How's your stomach now?" Reed whispered.

"Good, baby," Sebastian lied. "I feel really good now. How about you?"

Her eyelids dipped sensuously as she said a silent prayer. Then she opened her eyes and looked at Sebastian. "Never better."

———

From where Sebastian stood in the cellarage beneath the floor, he heard a muffled chant.

"S'bas-chun! S'bas-chun!"

He knew now that there was no turning back.

"S'bas-chun! S'bas-chun! S'bas-chun!"

The clapping and chanting became a muffled roar, and he felt the stadium floor above his head vibrate.

"S'bas-chun! S'bas-chun! S'bas-chun! S'bas-chun! S'bas-chun!"

Sebastian knew the drill by heart; this was the moment when the stage technicians did their trick with the spotlight that was supposed to symbolize life and death, where a pinpoint of white light spread slowly over the stage and then vanished just as gradually as it had appeared. The crowd always fell silent at this point, and their silence was when he could hear his heart beating out of his chest because he knew the moment he gave his signal, the tech next to him would throw the switch, the trapdoor above his head would open, and he would rise up through the floor.

"Dude," the man said. "You OK? You don't look so good."

Sebastian checked the straps and braces anchoring his legs to the turntable and smiled broadly at him. "I'm great."

But he wasn't. His nausea and headache had been building steadily all day, and he was certain that something was waiting for him up there.

"Just say when," the man told him.

Sebastian dropped his head and counted: *One...two...three... four...five...six...seven...eight...nine...* He drew in a deep breath, raised his head at the man, and nodded. "Now."

At once the trapdoor above him opened and a rush of cold air fell down like water upon his head. He was breathing like a marathon runner now as the pedestal pushed him up, up, up, up while his mind flashed with superhuman alacrity: *speech/security/Reed/ effects/Kitty/good/evil/life/death...*

In just a moment it would all begin.

His head cleared the floor, and at once his face was awash in dark, flowing air.

Then his torso was exposed. His skin prickled from the cold.

A shard of panic stabbed him.

We have great security, he reminded himself.

Everything was black and silent—as if the stadium was empty.

Then Sebastian, lit by a beacon that momentarily blinded him—this same light that he tried each time to prepare himself for, yet that always took him by surprise—stretched his arms wide and threw back his head and cried, "*Change...the world...with... me!*"

He heard his call—amplified to a godlike, superhuman volume—resonate and echo throughout stadium.

The response of the crowd was deafening, and their chorus of unity made his heart soar.

It's all going to be OK, he told himself. *It'll all be OK.*

"*S'bas-chun! S'bas-chun! S'bas-chun! S'bas-chun! S'bas-chun!*"

Wave after wave of gooseflesh washed over him and he grinned and fought back tears, so powerful was this crowd's outpouring of love.

"Together, we *will* change the world!" Sebastian sang to the crowd. "Together, we *will* help those who cannot help themselves!"

The turntable continued pushing him up higher, the crowd gasped and applauded, and Sebastian began gyrating atop his perch as some dance music cued. "You've come to alleviate misery!" he shouted. "You've come to spread happiness to each other and to love one another! *You've come because you dream of a better life for all creatures!*" The stadium lights pulsed and music blared and Sebastian saw people leap from their seats clapping, stomping, cheering, and crying.

Then the lights slowly dimmed and the music faded. People took their seats, and the pedestal sank halfway toward the floor and stopped. It was at this moment that Sebastian's eyes caught Reed's in the front row, and the love that passed between them flared and spread through each of their bodies.

"I *love you all* for being here with me," he said, looking directly at Reed. "I cannot thank you—" he started to say, but the crowd began to cheer again.

He held out his hands, and the crowd quieted.

"I cannot thank you enough for being here with me," he began. "The sacrifice you've made to be here tonight, that you bought tickets and drove the freeways and parked and walked and fed your kids before you left and everything you did to be here tonight touches my heart"—he grasped both hands onto his chest—"more than you'll ever know.

"But before I start boring you with what you came here tonight to hear"—the audience laughed appreciatively at this—"I want you to consider the questions I'm going to ask you. Consider these questions as if you'd never heard them before. Consider them, and then allow yourself to come up with your own answers. Are you ready?"

The crowd cheered, and Sebastian waited patiently for the audience to quiet again.

"Have you ever had to do something you were sure you couldn't do? Something so terrible and challenging and terrifying that you'd never even allowed yourself to think about how you would react if you had to do it? Maybe it was saying goodbye to a sick parent—or a child. Maybe it was learning that your lover had been unfaithful. Maybe it was putting a dog to sleep. Maybe it was saying goodbye to a best friend who was moving away. Maybe it was hearing from your doctor that the test results came back, and the news was bad. Whatever it was, I'd like you to have the courage to remember one of those moments that your heart would rather forget."

As Sebastian waited while their memories steeped, Kitty— sequestered in the control booth positioned to the side of the box seats—began shuffling through her script. And it only took her a moment to realize that he was stating his own words and had no intention whatsoever of following the message they had agreed upon.

That little bastard!

"Now hold onto that thought while I tell you where I've been."

A candlelit spotlight came up on him as he faced his audience. "I've been gone because I was miserable. I was getting death threats, and one of my followers whose child had cancer shot and killed his child, his wife, and himself because I let him believe that the afterlife was better than what his life was like today. I felt horrible and very guilty for unintentionally misleading him. And I was so upset by what happened that I ran away."

Danger.

A wave of nausea swept over him, but he did his best to ignore it. "On the trip I took, I met two women who've celebrated three decades as a couple. They've built a great life together in a world that doesn't always understand their kind of relationship, and they never let such ignorance stop them. Unfortunately, Libby's got cancer now, and she doesn't have much time. And her partner Tess is angry about it, as anyone would be. Both women spent a lot of their lives helping less fortunate people, and you'd hope there'd be a better reward than trying to beat cancer. But they still read books together and drink wine and love their dog and speak to each other with such respect and love. They showed me the importance of love. Love and courage.

"Next I met an old Mexican man with a strong accent and stronger hands, whose greatest joy was doing a hard day's work and going home to his elderly wife—a woman who's now got Alzheimer's. Ramon is the happiest man I've ever met. He works hard, he loves deeply, he cares for the weak, he finds things to laugh at, and he thanks God every day for his blessings—even when they're torn from him. Ramon, too, showed me the importance of love. Love and courage.

"And I met a beautiful young woman who'd been dumped by a guy who didn't deserve to have her in the first place. Does that sound familiar to anyone?"

The audience, who was listening raptly, burst into cheers and laughter. Sebastian himself laughed, although his unease was growing by the moment. When it was quiet again, he continued. "This amazing woman, although understandably reluctant to love again, saw something in me that no one has ever seen before. And after some convincing from me she allowed her heart to open and showed me how to open mine to her." Sebastian looked down at Reed and saw her eyes shining up at him. "She gave me love and showed me courage. Courage and love that I borrowed, in fact, when it came time for me to forgive a good friend who'd betrayed me.

"Then I met a man I've always wondered about. As you've learned by now, my father is a recovering drug addict who's been in jail. His poison was methamphetamine, a drug with a steel grip. He's had the courage now to stay clean and sober for two years, and it was his love for the child he never knew that made him overcome some pretty big obstacles to find me. But he believed in the power of love and knew how important our connection would be for both of us. He also saved my life after the boat crash in San Francisco Bay.

"Finally, I met Mateo—a young man filled with promise and love for his family. Mateo was beaten because he was gay, and then he was left for dead. And when he was found, still clinging to life, the only part of his face that wasn't covered in blood was where his tears had streaked down his cheeks. Mateo was the victim of hate and bullying. Hate and bullying that's encouraged by some religious leaders despite the fact that we are all equal before the eyes of God.

"Just like you've had terrible things happen to you, all the people I met have had to deal with something they thought they couldn't handle. Cancer. Loss of a spouse. Alzheimer's. Betrayal. Addiction. Murder. But they all made it through because of courage—and the love of people who cared for them."

You need to get down from here.

When the lasers start...if I can make it to when the lasers start...

"So I started thinking: what about the other people out there who're coping every day with things no one wants to cope with, but are choosing to because it's the right thing to do?"

Suddenly the television monitors ringed around the stage began flashing images of a tall, smiling man surrounded by grinning children and teenagers in wheelchairs. "Here's a man who donates medical equipment to disabled kids in the war-torn Middle East. All he wants to do is to alleviate the suffering of these kids who've been maimed and have lost arms and legs. He's not asking for your help, but he sure could use it."

The image on the monitors changed. "Here's a man in Alabama," Sebastian shouted, trying unsuccessfully to drown out the silent shouting within him, "who runs a soup kitchen for the homeless, and he needs suits and dresses and shoes donated to the people he works with so they can go on job interviews.

"Here's a loving and courageous teacher who uses discarded textbooks to teach English to illegal aliens in her garage so they might find better jobs. Her neighbors hate her, but she won't give up her work.

"Here's a loving, courageous doctor who donates her time to a free clinic in the poorest area of Chicago so there might be less teen pregnancies, and a woman in New Mexico who's working to end child labor in South Asia. Are any of them asking for your help? No, but they sure could use it.

"There was a time," Sebastian continued, "when I, the leader of a religious organization, convinced you to give me money so I could spread the message of Evo-love. I am now ashamed to admit it, but a lot of that money was spent on luxuries for myself and my mother. But tonight I am *not* asking for your money for myself; in fact, I'm begging you to give it to someone else."

The lights dimmed, and Sebastian's pedestal began rising and turning again. "From now on my foundation will focus on contributing almost every cent of each dollar we raise to these people. Why? Because although you can't feel another person's pain, it doesn't mean they're not suffering.

"And if you can't afford to give any money away, that's OK! It's just as important to listen to an old person tell a story, or to help a child learn to read, or to adopt a cat or a dog from a shelter. And do you know what'll happen if you do?"

"*What?*" the crowd answered in unison.

"*Do you know what will happen if you do?*" Sebastian shouted.

"*WHAT?!*" roared the crowd.

"*If we all do something together, we'll change this world!*"

Sebastian's rotating pedestal had almost reached its highest level again, and the crowd cheered mightily as the music boomed and the lights dimmed and green and purple and orange and blue laser beams sliced through the stadium's darkness.

Then a tiny, very bright flash way up in the highest seats caught his eye.

CHAPTER 54

Sebastian's chest felt like he'd been struck with a sledge hammer.

What?

The audience screamed.

Someone cut the music.

Then the scene before him drifted from real time into slow motion, and the wails of the audience faded to silence.

He saw Reed catapult herself from her seat, her eyes and mouth wide and her arms outstretched.

Technicians and guards stormed the stage below him.

The left side of his chest contracted in a viselike grip as his lung collapsed.

He felt the pedestal begin to sink toward the floor.

He looked down and saw blood.

That's my blood. They actually did it.

His arms and legs tingled, and his bones felt as though they were dissolving.

His vision began fading to white, static white all around except in the center…but he could still see Reed.

Drop the pedestal faster!

It hit the ground with a jolt, and he felt hands on him, pressing something into the wound.

That hurts!

He saw Reed's face.

She's scared.

His heart hammered.

She's trying not to cry.

There wasn't enough blood inside him to pump.

I love you. Sebastian mouthed the words to Reed.

His heart began to slow.

He felt very tired.

He forced his eyes open once more.

There was someone smiling at him next to Reed's anguished face.

Mateo?!

———

Olivier, Andre, and Juan, all positioned at different points in the stadium, leapt into action. Each began directing attention to the middle section of the Forum's seats directly opposite from where each knew Eddie was situated, while insisting to the other guards via radio that the shot had been fired from there. Eddie—after being knocked on his backside by the recoil from the single shot—was unnoticed as he slid the rifle under the seats, pulled off his gloves, and pushed them into his pockets. Then he lifted himself up off the floor and rushed about, helping to restore calm.

While some security guards and the onsite medics did their best to assist the stricken star, the stadium became a swarm of people running or standing around confused or craning their necks trying to see what Sebastian's condition was. Olivier saw some people crying and others hugging each other, even as an exodus formed and people settled into hoards that rumbled and swayed toward the exits.

The medical personnel who descended upon the stage did so with a decided purpose; they could see that Sebastian had been terribly wounded, and each second that passed was crucial. Upon her examination of the limp body, with its precise entry and gaping exit wounds, the chief clinician on staff knew his condition was grave.

"Get him out of here!" the doctor yelled to the other medics from her crouched position on the floor. "The gunman's still in the stadium, and we're all targets as long as he's here!"

Immediately the medics applied bandages and pressure to Sebastian's wounds, fixed a C-collar on his neck, turned him onto a backboard, and lifted him onto a gurney. Then they jogged him—like soldiers running a fallen comrade off the battlefield—into a waiting ambulance.

Once Reed had climbed into the back of the emergency vehicle and Sebastian had been strapped inside, the vehicle—with lights swirling and siren blaring and horn honking—jumped away from the curb and began pushing its way through the jammed-up parking lot.

The technicians knew, not only from Sebastian's vital signs, but also from the doctor's worried demeanor, that there was little hope for the gravely wounded man. But they also knew they could not give up on their patient, so they pushed fluids into him and monitored his vitals and bent over him with the defibrillator at the ready and helped to apply pressure to his wounds.

Then just blocks from the hospital, Sebastian flat-lined.

Reed screamed.

CHAPTER 55

Sebastian felt himself slowly falling…falling…falling as if in a descending elevator with no floor. But he didn't feel panic, or worry, or distress. He felt only curiosity.

He was curious about the warm, breezy air that carried him and pulled him downward by the head and shoulders. And he felt sleepy—but not tired sleepy. It was the kind of sleepiness you feel when you've just had a well-deserved afternoon nap. Energized, but relaxed.

"Isn't it like I told you?" a voice asked him.

"Is what like you told me?"

"Remember when I said that dying was like going to a feeling?"

"Mateo?" Sebastian seemed to open his eyes.

"Yeah. Are you doing OK?"

"Where am I?"

"You're in that in-between place, like when you first came to see me in the hospital."

"Oh." Sebastian allowed Mateo's words to sink in. "So I'm not dead?"

"Not yet."

"Will I die?"

"Everyone dies." Mateo laughed.

"I mean, now."

"They still aren't sure."

"Who isn't sure?" Sebastian asked.

"Your guides. They're still waiting for something to happen… or not to happen, I guess. You should just try to relax."

Sebastian allowed his spirit to drift and discovered what seemed to be an opening at the top of his head. This opening seemed to beckon his passing through it, so he began making his way out from it—like a snake shedding its crinkly skin.

"Dude, don't do that," Mateo warned. "You can't go back once you pass through it."

Sebastian stopped himself.

"Do you know what happened back there," Mateo asked, "and why you're here now?"

Sebastian saw himself on that high pedestal, looking down his robe at that scarlet bloodstain. "I think someone shot me. Do you know who?"

"You'll know everything soon enough, but there's something that needs to be decided first: How do you feel about not going back, or about going forward instead? Which one do you think you're ready for?"

"This feels so nice. How's it been for you?"

"It's great here, but I miss being with my mom and dad and my friends—but I didn't have a choice on whether to stay or to go. Those guys, you know…"

"Yeah, I remember. So before I decide, can you tell me what you do here?"

"Mostly, we learn about ourselves and what we did wrong or right on earth. Everything's out in the open—our lives are like pages and pages of a magazine that's been unstapled and spread out on the table. Then some people are reborn again in another body, while those who've learned what they need to can go back as guides who help others. It's kind of a cool system—there are options."

"So…what happens to the people who don't need to go back? Like the people who've already been guides and all?"

"They go to some other realm. But just like on earth when you don't know for sure what happens after death, we aren't shown where those people go either, other than they go to God."

"So what about God?" Sebastian asked.

"We all come from God. All living things, even plants and animals have some of God: flies, only a little, but dogs and dolphins and cows and elephants—and humans, we have a lot. I think of God like…like the sun that's always giving off warmth, and we're all created out of that warmth, which is life and love. Then most of us go back and rejoin with God, with that huge sun of love, when our souls are ready."

"Does anyone get to meet God before that?"

"Sure," Mateo laughed. "You already have."

"When?"

"Right now—that great feeling you have? That's God. God is what love feels like. It's this wonderful force that sweeps you up and holds you…it's also that joy you feel when you make someone feel good—like that time you told that old lady on the corner that her new haircut made her look pretty, and she gave you this smile like you'd just told her she'd won the lottery?"

"How'd you know about that?" Sebastian laughed.

"Certain things get around. But that joy you felt is to God what raindrops are to a big thunderhead cloud. Those raindrops wash and soothe and clean and nourish. And eventually, as you learned in school, all raindrops return to the sky."

"I don't get it."

"Sebastian, all people are really just raindrops who help others grow. Then when we die, we return to God—that big cloud in the sky."

"I thought you said God was like the sun."

"Think of life as sun and joy as rain. On earth, that's how God makes everything grow."

"I think I get it, Mateo. Thanks for explaining that."

"My pleasure."

"So," Sebastian hesitated, "how long can I think about going backward or forward?"

Mateo listened. "They're telling me it's…like, now or never."

Sebastian closed his eyes and allowed that sunny blanket of peace to wrap around him.

———

The ambulance wailed and bumped and rushed and swayed through the streets of Westchester on its way to Dr. Martin Luther King Jr. Medical Center, where the trauma team was standing by. Strapped helplessly into her seat in the back of the ambulance, Reed watched and prayed frantically while one of the medics prepped the defibrillators once again, and another attempted to perform chest compressions on Sebastian's leaking torso.

"He's lost too much blood!" the doctor yelled. "Get another pint in him, now!"

As the medic and the doctor did everything possible, there was nothing Reed could do but hope.

But then she remembered *that feeling*.

While the medical personnel grabbed this and administered that and the radio squawked and the engine gunned, Reed quietly unbuckled her seat belt.

Then, crouched over, she made her way to Sebastian's body and bent over him. The medic doing the chest compressions glanced at her, then went back to his work.

"I know you're still with me, Sebastian. I can feel you." She settled her hands on his stomach, the same way he'd placed his hands over hers on that beautiful moonlit beach. "I love you, and I can't stand you leaving me now, just when things are getting so wonderful." Tears began rolling off her cheeks onto his blood-soaked robe. "I wanted so badly to build a life with you: kids, a house, dogs, arguments and all. We were meant for each other, and if you leave now, I'll be like that guy who'll never sleep by Mateo's side, but for me it'll be worse because I *did* know you, and I fell in love with you. So every morning until my time comes," she sobbed, "I'll be in pain, because I never got to grow older with you, and I never got to tell you, *Yes, I'll marry you.* And I'll just miss you so much."

"We're almost there!" the driver shouted. "Tell him to hang on."

"Hang in there, my love," Reed whispered. "Please, hang in there for me. Hang in there for us."

—

"What's that?" Sebastian asked Mateo.

"What's what?"

"That feeling—it's still warm, but it feels heavy and sad."

"Oh, that," Mateo replied. "I remember that same sadness coming from my dad. You're feeling Reed's grief. She's already missing you."

"It makes me want to cry." And at once Sebastian ached to go back. He wanted this to end; it did not feel right anymore. "I need to go back," he said. "Is it too late?"

Mateo listened. "They're saying it's fifty-fifty. You need to do some work here."

At once Sebastian felt that opening in his head grow larger, and a great light began spinning around him, pulling at him like a whirlpool. And he saw Reed's tear-streaked face and felt the heat of her hands on his body, so he pushed against the vortex and filled his spirit with determination and love. Then he felt a vibration surrounding him, carrying him…a low drone that invaded every part of his being.

"Clear!" the doctor shouted.

The defibrillator sparked.

Sebastian felt the vortex pull away as dizziness overcame him. Dizziness and pain. Terrible pain.

"We've got a rhythm!" the doctor exclaimed as the heart monitor began beeping steadily.

Sebastian gasped into his oxygen mask.

CHAPTER 56

Kitty spent the night in the hospital, curled up in the chair by Sebastian's side in the trauma-neuro intensive care unit. But she didn't sleep; she alternated between sick from worry with her eyes open, to sick from worry with her eyes closed.

Sebastian had been in surgery for over four hours and went into recovery just before midnight, after the doctors did their best to repair the damage caused by the well-aimed bullet. Thanks to the revolving pedestal, the wicked projectile had missed his heart by millimeters and grazed his spinal cord on its way out; in addition, they did not yet know the extent of brain damage he might have suffered after his heart stopped. Thus, Kitty ran various horrifying scenarios through her head: paralyzed with brain damage; paralyzed with no brain damage; brain damage with no paralysis, and so on. The only scenario she couldn't quite allow herself to entertain was that of a full recovery, because she was too deeply guilt-ridden and terrified by Sebastian's suggestion of karmic retribution.

Reed had also stayed the night in the hospital, where a kindly nurse allowed her to use a vacant bed in the room next to Sebastian's. There she was able to sleep because an intuition had told her that Sebastian was in good hands and would recover. Then when the voices, shuffling, and rattling of the incoming shift woke her early the next morning, Reed rolled out of the high hospital bed and padded sock-footed over to the next room. There she saw Kitty curled into a wooden armchair, her feet tucked under herself and her arms hugging her ankles.

"Kitty?" Reed whispered. "Are you awake?"

Kitty slowly raised her head and peered at Reed through her bangs. "How could I sleep with that ventilator gasping and grinding all night?"

"How's he doing?"

"He's alive," Kitty answered. "Thank God."

"You look exhausted. Do you want a break?"

"I'm not leaving him." Kitty slowly extended each of her arms and legs, as if she'd been trapped inside a wooden box all night.

"What have they said about his condition?"

"Someone's been in every ten minutes to check his blood oxygen and blood pressure and chest tube and all. They tell me his vitals have stabilized, his lungs are holding air, and his urine's running cleaner now. But one of his ribs was terribly shattered, so they took forever looking for fragments, and they tell me that his recovery time could be anywhere from three to six months." Kitty's face screwed up as she fought tears. "He nearly died, Reed. The doctor said he flat-lined in the ambulance!"

"I was there when it happened."

"What did you do?"

"I told him I loved him, and I begged him not to leave me— and I prayed."

Tears streaked down Kitty's cheeks. "I'm so glad you were there."

"You would've done the same."

Kitty sighed, her misting eyes focused on Sebastian. "Love," she said. "Evo-love. All this stupid business about *love*…and here

I am in the business of selling love when I can't give it away or even buy it from my own son. Ha! I should've named our goddamn religion *Evil love*."

Kitty closed her eyes, breathed in, and then looked up at Reed. "I tried to give him the love he needed, but he never needed me. So I gave up." She wiped her eyes. "You should've seen him as a boy. He was always laughing, and he was talking in sentences before he was two. And such a beautiful child—as if he'd jumped out from some Renaissance painting of Mary with the baby Jesus. People used to stop me on the street, and they'd look at me and look at Sebastian and say how cute he was. Then I'd wait for the question I always knew was coming: they'd ask whose child he was—as if I was incapable of giving birth to such an *adorable* creature."

"But you're a lovely woman," Reed told her. "Why would people think that?"

"For one thing, he got his father's hair instead of this." Kitty grabbed a shock of her black locks. "But more than anything, it's Sebastian's magnetic quality. Even in preschool the teachers fawned over him and children fought to be his best friend. Then after he reached manhood it got worse—all the girls, and some of the boys, would become *obsessed* with him. It's like he became a drug for people, and they would do anything for his attention. But when parents asked him over for birthday parties and sleepovers, they'd meet me, and it was usually the same reaction: that good-looking blond kid is *so* delightful and *so* charming, but his mom's a bitch.

"A part of me felt jealous of him, like those unfortunate girls whose mothers are prettier than they are, but this was worse. Sebastian has always been loved, but the best reaction I could hope for was to be tolerated—especially by men."

A nurse suddenly appeared, so Kitty waited until the woman checked Sebastian's vital signs and IV bag, scribbled some notes in a binder, and exited before continuing.

"There's always been something about me that puts people off," Kitty said, catching Reed's gaze. "Do you know what it is?"

Reed's eyebrows lifted. "You really want to know?"

Kitty gave a curt nod. "Yes."

"For one thing, you're not very nice," Reed told her. "When you met me, you didn't make any effort to shake my hand or even to say *nice to meet you*. And from what Sebastian's told me, you're overbearing, and everything needs to be your way. It seems like you're obsessed with money, and you treat Sebastian like he's your employee instead of your son."

Kitty blinked at Reed. "Anything else?"

"I've never heard you say anything nice to anyone, and you never smile. And you know when you're telling someone a story and they make little 'uh-huh' and 'oh really' noises just to let you know they've heard you?"

Kitty raised her eyebrows.

"That's exactly what I'm talking about." Reed pointed at her. "Right now, you should have said yes, but you just looked at me. It's unnerving—and it's not the way polite people deal with each other."

"You're saying I'm impolite?"

"That's only one of your offensive traits. But more than anything, you come off as someone who's self-absorbed and better than everyone—and that's a *big* turnoff."

Kitty took a moment to consider Reed's words. "People are how they are," she said at last. "Just as Sebastian has a wonderful nature he couldn't change, even if he wanted to, my nature is what

I have. I am what I am. But it doesn't mean I'm a bad person or that I don't love my son."

Reed glared at her. "It also doesn't mean you have to go around having bad manners. At least you could change *that.*"

Without responding, Kitty got up from the chair, crossed the room to where Sebastian lay, and kissed his forehead. Then she turned to Reed. "When this is over, when he's safe and sound again, I'll think about what you've told me. In the meantime, I really don't care about anything else."

Reed stood and went to her. "I understand completely," she replied. "But I've been wanting to ask you something: why does Sebastian call you 'Kitty'?"

"Oh, *that*," she replied, laughing dryly. "I insisted he do it because if he stopped calling me 'Mom,' people would stop judging me, even if they understood I *was* his mother. His calling me 'Kitty' lets people think the distance between us was mutually agreed upon."

"So that distance…is it *still* agreed upon?"

Kitty looked longingly at the slumbering figure of her son. "We'll just have to see how he feels about it when he wakes up. Oh!" She turned to Reed. "And since we're talking about motherhood right now, there's something you should know—something I want you to tell him if anything happens to me between now and his waking up. Do you remember Amber?"

"How could I forget?"

"Sebastian may know nothing of this, and neither did I until just days after Amber's suicide, when I received a letter from her. She…bore him a son, and her fury toward him was a result of his rejecting her, especially since she felt he knew about their child."

Reed considered this for a moment. "But if Sebastian didn't know about the baby, how could she resent him for not doing anything about her pregnancy?"

"In the first place he never called her after their night together, and believe me when I tell you that I know what *that* rejection and regret feels like," Kitty explained. "Then by the time the child was born and given away, there was no point in her pursuing the matter further with him."

"I…still don't get it."

Kitty looked deeply into her eyes. "Amber knew the power of my son's clairvoyant abilities, as do you and I. She believed he must've known about the baby, that he must've intuited the child's existence. And she was probably right, poor woman."

CHAPTER 57

Chuck popped his head just inside the hospital room doorway.

Reed spotted him and waved. "Where've you *been?* Come in!"

"How's he doing?"

"He's stable," she replied. "When did you get here?"

"After ten last night, but I didn't want to bother anyone so I stayed downstairs in the waiting lobby." He rubbed his lower back. "Those sofas must've been picked out by someone with a mean sense of humor," he laughed.

"You slept all night down there?" Kitty asked.

Chuck shot her a kind smile. "Now, where else would I be? It's not like, you know, I ever got a chance to wait in the hospital for my son's birth, so this is kinda like my overdue turn."

—

Later that day Reed received a text from Ellie letting her know she and Coby were on their way down from Sausalito.

Then both Libby and Tess arrived from Big Sur.

"Ramon offered to have Libby stay with him and Maggie," Tess told them, grinning slyly, "but the stubborn old mare wouldn't hear of it."

"She wanted to board me like a dog at a kennel," Libby complained from her wheelchair, "but having seen the business end of too many hospitals, I wanted to make certain they were treating our boy right." She held out a yellow legal pad covered in scribbles. "I took notes the whole way down Highway 99, even though Tess was breaking the speed limit. I thought the convertible roof on that old Buick was going to blow off!" She handed the pad to Reed. "Now dear, these are some questions you should be asking the doctor."

Reed thanked Libby and handed the pad over to Kitty. "This is Kitty Black," she told Tess and Libby, "Sebastian's mother." Reed shot Kitty a challenging stare.

Kitty shook first Libby's and then Tess's hands. "Thank you for being here," she said. "Sebastian speaks very highly of you both. Have you met Chuck Niesen? He's Sebastian's…father."

"We're old friends," Tess replied.

Chuck bent down to kiss Libby's cheek. "It sure is nice to see you again. Sorry it had to be here. Are you feeling OK?"

Libby threw a glance at the prone figure in the bed. "Today I'm afraid that I'm feeling remarkably healthy."

—

Chuck had stepped outside for a cigarette and Tess had wheeled Libby to the cafeteria, so Kitty and Reed were alone with Sebastian when the doctor, a petite cardiothoracic surgeon named MacTavish, swept in and asked them to wait down the hall while she examined him.

Kitty and Reed shuffled their way to the cheerless waiting room, where they sat down and began flipping absently through the piles of well-worn magazines.

After the better part of a grueling hour, the doctor finally emerged from Sebastian's room.

Kitty and Reed leapt from their chairs to meet her. "How is he?" Kitty asked.

"It's not all good news and not all bad," Dr. MacTavish began. "He's experiencing some disorientation, which might also be a result of the medications. But I've also noted some loss in both his short-term memory and his ability to concentrate, so you might expect to see some mood swings, or even a change in his personality. Other than that, his motor functioning appears to be normal, so if you'll pardon the expression, he seems to have dodged the bullet quite well." She smiled and looked from Kitty to Reed.

"So it's good news?" Reed asked.

"I would say so," Dr. MacTavish replied. "Mostly."

"Where do we go from here?" Kitty asked.

"We'll set him up with rehabilitation," the doctor answered, "because the sooner we start rehab the better the patient recovers. But it depends on many factors—age, health, family history, attitude—and the quality of the therapy he receives." She pulled off her reading glasses. "I'll see that he gets the best physical and occupational therapists available, and we have a terrific speech therapist on staff, so I'll call him in for tomorrow. But you should take comfort in knowing that he's getting wonderful care, he's young, and he's very lucky."

"Can we see him?" Reed asked.

"The nurses are changing his dressings right now, so you should wait until they come out," Dr. MacTavish suggested, "which should be in about ten minutes. In the meantime, would you like to share the news with your friends and family?"

"We'll go find Chuck and the ladies," Reed told the doctor. "They're dying to hear."

—

Chuck jumped up. "How is he?"

"He's pretty much OK," Reed told him.

"But it's still too early to tell," Kitty added, "because the meds are probably adding to his confusion. But overall the news is very positive."

Libby and Tess squeezed hands, and Chuck clapped. "Praise God!" he yelled.

"Thank you, Jesus," Reed whispered.

"Praise the ambulance driver and the surgeons," Libby added.

While Kitty filled them in on the details of what Dr. MacTavish had told them, Reed excused herself to use the bathroom.

As she walked down the hallway, while hardly able to see where she was going for the tears of joy in her eyes, she said a prayer of thanks—to the ambulance driver, to the surgeons, to the hospital staff, and to God Almighty for sparing her man and her future. And she added a PS to that prayer, with the hope that Sebastian's little boy was safe, wherever he was.

Then, after finding the restroom and splashing her face with water, Reed returned to the relieved little group. "Do you think we can go back in yet?"

Kitty glanced at her watch. "It's been over ten minutes." She turned to Chuck and the ladies. "Come on up in a little bit; Reed and I need some time alone with him."

—

Dr. MacTavish was just leaving Sebastian's room as Reed and Kitty were making their way up the hallway. "He's awake now," she told them. "Just don't be surprised if he says something out of character, or if he seems belligerent or angry. He's been through a crisis, and he's in a lot of pain. And please don't stay longer than five minutes; more than anything right now he needs his rest."

"Absolutely," Kitty replied.

"Absolutely," Reed echoed.

They walked in.

Sebastian was sitting up in bed. The television was on and the ventilator was now silent, although his multiple IV machines ticked and creaked by his side.

Upon her approach, Reed saw Sebastian's emerald eyes flick her way, then hold her in his gaze. "Hi, baby," she said, her eyes filling with tears as she stepped over to him. She leaned over and kissed him gently on the cheek. "It's so good to see you."

The corners of his mouth inched up. "Hi, Reed," he whispered.

Kitty peered around Reed. "Sebastian?" Her voice broke as she said his name.

It took a moment for Sebastian to locate Kitty in the room, as if his vision was failing, or he was having trouble recognizing her.

Kitty felt a terrible panic rise within her.

No, no, no, no, no!

"Sebastian?" Kitty's voice was strong, although she was shaking.

Sebastian fixed his gaze on her. "Hi, Mom," he said at last.

CHAPTER 58

The months since that night at the Forum had been especially difficult for Sebastian and Reed and Kitty. His recovery from the bullet wound had been slow—complicated by a staph infection, a blood clot, and a shattered rib—so Reed postponed her final semester of college until autumn to care for him while Kitty completed her community service—helpfully brokered by Chuck—for her role in the boating incident.

Although Eddie, Juan, and Andre were in police custody awaiting trial, Interpol had lost track of Olivier after he vanished into Turkmenistan, allegedly with his horde of cash. But the determined agent who'd been assigned to the case was on the prowl, busily monitoring large real estate, automotive, or jewelry deals for any sign of the fugitive.

Now it was the week before Christmas, and since Reed had finally completed her college coursework, Jeremy Tyler—Reed's ex-boyfriend from their high school days—offered to let her use his chalet in the alpine forests of Lake Estrella. Thus Tess had driven down from Big Sur, and Reed and Sebastian had taken her with them up to the lake.

The morning after they arrived, a thunderstorm's canon fire and a deafening downpour had awakened them.

After showering and eating breakfast, Reed decided to make a pot of her favorite soup—tomato with blue cheese—from scratch while Sebastian returned an important phone call. She was chopping onion when she heard his footsteps approach. She looked up. "You're walking slower. Is the pain bothering you again?"

"A little." Sebastian grimaced slightly, holding a hand to his side. "It's probably just the change in weather and the high altitude. But I took some Motrin after breakfast, so I should be OK in a bit."

She shot him a worried glance. "Fever?"

He smiled, shaking his head. "Nope."

Reed began slicing her pile of tomatoes. "So what did the social worker say?"

Sebastian folded his arms over his chest. "She was very businesslike, but it was pretty clear to me that she thinks making any contact with Eldon's family is a bad idea."

"Why?"

"It would be too confusing for everyone, because up until now his only known parent was deceased," he said. "And I think I agree with her."

Reed stopped slicing and looked at him. "You *agree* with her? What about that business of being there to tell his parents not to worry when their son starts hearing voices?"

Sebastian sighed. "I know. We've been over this a hundred times. And I never realized it until now, but I was lucky that Kitty didn't medicate me—or worse—when my *strange voices* started—"

"At age ten or eleven, if I recall," Reed cut in. "Could you actually wait that long to get to know him?"

"Like you've told me, it's not about what I want—as much as I ache to know him—it's about what's best for him," he said. "But that doesn't solve my concern over not alerting his parents to what's probably coming. What if something happens to me before

I get a chance? We've got that European tour coming up this summer, and with that guy Olivier over there somewhere, I'm a pretty easy target."

"But you said your new security team's ready for just about anything."

"But *just about anything* could happen to me here too, Reed. Some stupid kid who's driving and texting at the same time could send me off to see Mateo and Libby—*tomorrow.*" He looked at her. "Why didn't I do something about Eldon when I had the chance?"

"Because you were young—and scared."

"That's no excuse." He tapped his fingers on the kitchen counter. "I wasn't young or scared when I saw Amber at Coby's party, and I knew she wanted to talk to me about him. And if she hadn't been with that freaky guy, I probably would've—but that's also a dumb excuse."

"Do you think things would've been different if you'd talked to her that night?"

"Sure. But I didn't. So now we're all paying the price."

"But you told me you think Eldon's happy where he is."

After a beat, Sebastian said, "You're right. Every time I've meditated about him I get this flash of a grinning little blond kid who feels loved. But is he safe? What if his identity gets exposed and the wrong people find out he's my son? That's another good reason why his parents need to know." He lifted his nose over the bubbling pot and inhaled. "I just wish I knew what to do. And that smells great, by the way."

"I think you already know what to do," Reed told him. "And thank you."

"What do you mean?"

"You've just given me some very convincing reasons to make contact with his family, and the sooner the better. You need to listen to yourself."

"I agree!" a distant voice called out from the other room. "And while I expound on my unsolicited opinion, you can sit and look at this spectacle!"

Reed followed Sebastian from the kitchen into the cavernous living room. There Tess sat in a club chair next to sliding doors that framed the deck and the lake; she had one book in her lap and another nearly-finished novel on the table next to her. Maxi was asleep at her feet. "You should call the boy's family and tell them what they need to know," she told Sebastian. "Then let them decide what role, if any, you should play in the boy's life. Morally it's *their* decision to make, not yours—regardless of what legal right you might have. So now stop driving yourself crazy and allow us all to enjoy the scenery." Tess pointed to the glass, her eyes sparkling.

Sebastian and Reed turned. It was snowing.

Reed grasped Sebastian's hand. "The last time I saw it snow, I was up here with Jeremy all those years ago."

Sebastian folded her into his arms. "During that disastrous trip you told me about? Where he and Coby got caught by Ellie?"

"I can laugh about it now." Reed half smiled. "I guess Jeremy's letting us all stay up here tells me how guilty he still feels about the way our relationship ended. It'll be fun when Ellie and Coby get here this weekend for New Year's; it's been long enough between visits that I'm actually looking forward to hearing them argue again."

Tess put down her book and peered over her glasses. "And it was so nice of you to invite this old lady to tag along. You have no idea how wonderful it'll be for me to spend Christmas with you two and then New Year's Eve with Ramon and his family. Thank you."

"You're not *old*," Reed said to her. "And you're very welcome."

"There was no way we were going to let you spend your first Christmas alone," Sebastian added. "We just wish Libby were here with us."

"I can't believe she's been gone almost a year," Tess said sadly. "And just the month after next her headstone will be unveiled." She looked out beyond the deck, pointing again toward the windows. "That little cedar out there by the boulders looks just like the Christmas tree I cut down last year at this same time. I was putting one up at the inn, and Libby rolled up behind me in her wheelchair and said, 'As a Jewish girl, I never thought I'd be sad to see my last Christmas tree.'

"I pretended not to hear her, of course, and kept laboring away. Then a few months later when she was going downhill so fast, I came across one of those old, tacky tinsel trees in our garage. So I dragged it out and assembled it across from her side of the bed. I told her, 'I'll bet you think this'll be your last Christmas tree too, but it won't.' Unfortunately it was, but that very tree is still standing in our bedroom. I've got it on a timer, and every night it goes on at five, just when she preferred to take dinner."

Tess slipped off her glasses and dabbed at her eyes with her sleeve cuff. "I don't know how I'd feel if I ever went by our room at night and saw it was dark." She smiled at them. "And it's funny, but sometimes I'll catch Maxi napping beneath that tree, looking like a furry present. It's like he's waiting for Libby to come back and scoop him up into her lap once more."

The trio was silent for a few moments while Tess relived her grief, Reed heard echoes of Libby's laughter from last Christmas, and Sebastian caught that mischievous glint in Libby's blue eyes once again. "Something tells me Libby's here with us right now," Sebastian suggested with a knowing smile as Maxi lifted his head—tags jingling. "Just like Mateo's somehow with Ramon and Maggie tonight."

"I know Libby's here with us too." Reed sat down on the arm of Tess's chair, threw her hand around Tess's shoulder, and pulled her close. "We just can't hear her wagging."

"Tess?" Sebastian asked gently. "Are you going to be OK?"

Tess looked at him, her expression pensive. "As sad as I feel, as lonely as I feel, and as empty as our house feels now without Libby rattling around in it, I know it's just grief I'm feeling."

"What do you mean, *just grief*?" Reed asked. "To me, grief is completely crippling."

Tess paused in thought as a wistful smile bloomed slowly across her face. "My dear, everything worth having in this life comes at a cost," she replied at last. "And *grief* is simply the price we silly humans pay for love. But even as grief-stricken as I feel some days for the loss of Libby—and our friends and even our dogs—when I weigh *all that love* against this grief, I still consider love to be one of life's great bargains."

AUTHOR'S NOTES AND ACKNOWLEDGMENTS

Snow White has almost too many permutations to count, and some of these versions are quite gruesome—even going so far as to include incest and torture. But the basic story remains: a beautiful youngster leaves home because of an evil queen mother and heads off into the wilderness where multiple dwarfs provide care and shelter and companionship. The evil queen learns of Snow White's location through her own magic mirror, and then the queen switches her identity and nearly succeeds in killing Snow White with a poisoned apple. The youngster somehow survives this murder attempt and returns to the kingdom to live "happily ever after" with her prince.

Sebastian Black, like Snow White, is also portrayed as a person gifted with youth and beauty; however, his "superiority" over others goes so far as to include the gift of clairvoyance. The "dwarfs" he meets are people who've been marginalized by society; their social stature is "shorter," if you will, than those who are exalted in mainstream advertising and the media. Reed (Bashful) is a passive young woman cast aside for another; Libby (Doc) is a terminally ill, elderly lesbian, while her partner Tess (Grumpy) is a retired social worker; Chuck (Sneezy) is a recovering coke/methamphetamine addict with a fried brain; Ramon

(Happy) is an old Mexican day laborer with a deteriorating wife; Coby (Dopey) lacks intelligence and common sense, and Mateo (Sleepy) is the comatose, young gay man whose tragic fate parallels the horrific murder of Matthew Sheppard. We also have a poisoned "apple" (an iPhone installed with a tracking device), and the mirror advising Kitty of her son's widespread adoration—and her own status as a controlling bitch—is the blogosphere.

Then there are some obvious changes:

Instead of the queen attempting to poison her own child, it's Dyson and Olivier who plot to poison Sebastian with Visine, which—from what I've read—has some chemical in it that's terribly toxic and even lethal if ingested, especially in combination with alcohol (please don't try this at home).

Then, having absolutely nothing to do with *Snow White*, I felt compelled to add the "gay exorcism" scene, because while writing of this book I came upon an article about the (largely Bible Belt) practice of gay men subjecting themselves to beatings and humiliation in order to drive the "gay demon" out of their bodies. (Vomiting and soiling themselves is supposed proof of the demon's departure!) After reading about this ridiculous and highly offensive act, I felt compelled to call attention to this abuse by making it even more ridiculous and offensive.

And now on to my inspiration for this story:

Way back in 1993 I began working for the Gay and Lesbian Adolescent Social Services (GLASS), a nonprofit residential treatment agency that provided social services to LGBT youth. GLASS was the brainchild of Terry DeCrescenzo, a licensed clinical social worker and former LAPD probation officer who—like Tess—refused to stand by and watch as countless LGBT youth were beaten up, thrown out of their family homes, and sent to live on the streets of Los Angeles as prostitutes and drug addicts. She

Nick Nolan

was further horrified by the way these kids were sometimes vic-
timized further in foster placement, so she mortgaged her house
and created her own licensed agency to provide a caring, supportive, and healthy environment for these disenfranchised and
at-risk and sometimes HIV-positive youth. GLASS—under Terry's supremely deft, iron-fisted direction—eventually grew to
encompass numerous licensed group homes, foster homes, tran-
sitional living apartments, family preservation programs, inde-
pendent living sites, and even a thrift shop/coffee shop that provided on-the-job training for teens. She sailed a watertight ship,
and her credo was, "We have to do our jobs better than everyone
because we are under far more scrutiny than anyone else."

During this time, Terry took notice of me—a young gay man
who'd been hired as a child care worker, the agency's entry-level
position. A short time later I was promoted to house manager and
then program director. And having been at that time estranged
from my own arch-conservative, homophobic, and Catholic parents, she became sort of a mother figure to me, just as she was
to the thousands of kids (and many LGBT employees) who were
lucky enough to find refuge under the roof of a "GLASS house."

Terry's partner for thirty years was the late Dr. Betty Ber-
zon, a social activist and psychologist who'd penned *Permanent
Partners, Positively Gay, The Intimacy Dance*, and *Setting Them
Straight*. Betty was tiny and Jewish and reserved, and she was
the perfect complement to Italian Terry's more outspoken East
Boston personality. As a couple they were the consummate yin
and yang, and they were a formidable and fearless team who spent
decades fighting for LGBT rights (Betty was one of the founders
of the Los Angeles Gay and Lesbian Community Services Center). Their friends were some of the most notable queer literati
and activists of our time, including U.S. Congressman Barney

Frank; gay conservative author-fundraiser Marvin Leibman; former *Advocate* editor-in-chief and writer Richard Rouilard; pioneering lesbian activist Barbara Greer; former state assembly-woman Jackie Goldberg; LGBT-supportive actress Judith Light; Betty DeGeneres; co-founder of the NGRA (National Gay Rights Advocates) Don Knutson; pioneers in the field of humanistic psychology Virginia Satir, Carl Rogers, Evelyn Hooker, and Abraham Maslow; author Paul Monette (my personal hero); authors Malcolm Boyd, Mark Thompson, and Katherine Forrest, to name but a few.

Eventually I moved my career in another direction, Betty succumbed to the cancer she'd so valiantly battled for decades, and GLASS—after thriving and surviving for twenty-five years—fell victim to the "Great Recession" of our time.

But Terry and I kept in touch, and one night at dinner I asked her permission to include, in my third novel, two characters based upon her and Betty that I hoped might honor their relationship.

I'm so glad she agreed.

And I pray that I did the pair justice.

Ironically, that hard-to-believe business in the story when Sebastian tells Libby about Tess meeting her partner a year to the day after Libby's death was true; Terry met her wonderful current partner, psychologist Carol Cushman—a New Yorker—on the first anniversary of Betty's passing, a date people of the Jewish faith mark as the official end to the mourning period.

Hmmmm.

Sadly, others who are no longer with us appear on these pages as well: Ramon is modeled after my partner's beloved, gentle, and hard-working father who passed away while I was writing this novel, and months later our treasured thirteen-year-old flat-coated retriever Rupert—who'd lost his grand, floor whapping tail years ago—was diagnosed with bone cancer while this book was in its final stages of editing. Making that decision to say goodbye to our ever-cheerful friend, companion, and protector was almost more than we could bear, especially so soon after Ramon's death.

So much sadness and grief—the price we pay for our comforting, edifying, unconditional love. I suppose that's why I made death a central theme in this book: the question of life after death has perplexed me for years.

So where do we go? Do human souls live on after the body dies? Do we float around, grinning ecstatically in heaven? Or are we reincarnated so that our souls can continue their hard-knocks education here on earth? Some of my own research and beliefs crept into the pages of this book—beliefs based upon the revolutionary work of Dr. Walter Semkiw (*Return of the Revolutionaries* and *Origin of the Soul*) and Ian Stevenson.

But what about Rupert? He had such a kind, patient, and *beautiful* soul—he was the Gandhi of dogs. I'm absolutely convinced that if dogs don't go to a better place, no one does.

But enough about that...

I will always be so very, very grateful to senior acquisitions editor Terry Goodman at AmazonEncore for seeing the promise this book held, and for having the vision to join me with my story editor, the brilliant David Downing, and my supremely knowledgeable copy editor Jessica Smith. Thanks to the fantastic author team at AmazonEncore: Jacque Ben-Zekry, Sarah Tomashek, and publicist Sarah Burningham. And thanks to literary agents Kevan Lyon and Taryn Fagerness for their guidance.

Big thanks also go out to my best friend Margo and our wonderful friends Art and Claudine for their endless support and love. Thanks also to my sisters Kathy and Jennifer, my aunt

Joanne, and to my mother (my parents and I have reconciled, by the way) for suffering through a much earlier version of this tale.

Thanks again to author Kathleen McGowan for her guidance and friendship. Your jump-starting my writing career has changed the course of my life.

But more than anyone, I thank my partner (and book cover designer) Jaime. Without you, I would be a shadow of the man I am today. I remember reading somewhere that true love brings out the best in people, and our love—and our nearly quarter century together—has been as rewarding as it has been synergistic. Thanks, Jay, for listening and encouraging and comforting me. Dreaming, planning, working, laughing, and crying by your side means the world to me. May we also find each other the next time around.

And thank you, dear reader, for taking a chance on my work.

Nick Nolan
March 2011

ABOUT THE AUTHOR

Budding novelist Nick Nolan wrote his first mystery in 5th grade and kept angst-ridden journals (featuring lots of sad poetry) during his teen years, but then had to surrender his dream of becoming a writer to fund college. While building a happy life with his partner Jaime, Nick earned two degrees, worked extensively with homeless youth, rescued dogs, restored two homes, traveled extensively through Mexico, and owned scores of unusual cars -- including a Dodge Challenger once used in the Mod Squad television series.

Nick originally self-published his modern fairy tales (and Book of the Year winners) *Strings Attached* and *Double Bound*, and after signing with AmazonEncore in 2009 began writing *Black as Snow*, based upon *Snow White*.

Today Nick, Jaime, and their two beloved retrievers divide their time between their home in the San Fernando Valley and a mountaintop cabin. Nick's fourth novel is currently under construction.